PRAISE FOR *WHEN ENEMIES OFFEND THEE*

"An unflinching look at sexual assault, Clementine Loftis' story is both timely and timeless. In the end, it isn't Clementine's quest for justice that saves her but the community she builds along the way. A hopeful tale of overcoming grief and trauma when you least expect it."

–Amy Meyerson, bestselling author of *The Bookshop of Yesterdays* and *The Imperfects*

"With evocative prose, complex characters, and an amazing sense of place, *When Enemies Offend Thee* is a first-rate thriller. And Sally Whitney is a writer to keep your eye on for years to come."

–Tom Bennitt, author of *Burning Under*

"Sally Whitney's novel, *When Enemies Offend Thee*, comfortably begins as the homecoming story of a widow returning to her roots and fulfilling her lifelong aspiration of opening her own antique shop—but her dream is brutally affronted by a relic from her past.

"The warm and inviting prose makes it easy to stand alongside Clementine every step of the way, even when she takes justice into her own hands in unexpected ways. 'You never know what you're capable of until something pushes you to the edge,' muses Clementine when even she realizes she may be taking a step too far.

"Whitney's characters and plot twists offer up more surprises than the most richly curated antique shop."

–Eric D. Goodman, author of *The Color of Jadeite, Setting the Family Free, Womb: a novel in utero,* and *Tracks: A Novel in Stories*

"*When Enemies Offend Thee* is a riveting tale of crime, retribution, and healing. Sally Whitney is to be congratulated for creating a protagonist rarely seen in contemporary fiction: a dynamic, sexy older woman."

–Patricia Schultheis, author of *St. Bart's Way* and *A Balanced Life*

"In her story of a woman in the aftermath of a brutal attack, Sally Whitney probes the uncertain line between the demand for justice and the hunger for retribution. The taut narrative keeps the pages turning in this exploration of what is gained or lost in one woman's struggle to rebalance the scales of her universe."

–Jennifer Bort Yacovissi, author of *Up the Hill to Home*

When ENEMIES OFFEND Thee

ISBN: 978-1-68313-211-0
Library of Congress Control Number: 2019951510

First Edition
Pen-L Publishing
Fayetteville, Arkansas
www.Pen-L.com
Printed and bound in the USA

Cover design by Eliza Whitney
Interior design by Kelsey Rice

When ENEMIES OFFEND Thee

SALLY WHITNEY

BOOKS BY SALLY WHITNEY

Surface and Shadow

When Enemies Offend Thee

To my sons, Nathan and Andrew

1

A rush of frigid air through the cluttered antique shop announced that the front door was suddenly ajar, even though the store wasn't scheduled to open for weeks. Clementine looked up from the box of oil paintings she was unpacking. Surely the door was locked, but maybe not. A thud on the wooden floor was unmistakably the sound of heavy boots. Clementine laid aside the painting she was holding and peered around a pair of bookshelves that were temporarily stranded in the middle of the floor. The shop was crammed with one- and two-drawer tables, wobbly ladder-back chairs, Victorian desks, miscellaneous lamps and mirrors, plus stacks of boxes yet to be unpacked. Since the space was only a little bigger than the average garage, displaying the antiques was going to be a challenge.

The thud sounded again as a man stepped from behind a large Empire bureau. Tall and heavyset, he reminded Clementine of an aging football player whose muscle had turned to flab. Thin hair combed away from his face made his forehead seem overly large. "Clementine?" he asked.

"That's me," she said, "but the shop's not open yet." A twinge of fear pricked her shoulders. She glanced quickly at the shop's back door before she curled her fingers around a bronze statue of a naked woman playing a harp. The chill of the metal in her hand made her feel silly. She wasn't in New York, for God's sake. This was Tanner, North Carolina, where most strangers weren't thieves or murderers. Feeling self-conscious, she slid her hand away from the statue. "Come back in a few weeks. We'll be open then."

"You don't recognize me, do you?" The man's lips sagged, accentuating the wrinkles in his chin.

Clementine studied his face for any clue of familiarity. Something about his eyes, maybe, but she wasn't sure. "I'm sorry," she said. "I don't." This had happened to her more than once since she moved back to Tanner. She hadn't lived here since she graduated from high school nearly forty years ago and hadn't been back at all since her parents died in the '90s.

"Gary Wiggins," the man said. "We were in the same class, but I'm not surprised you don't remember me." The frown spread to his eyes. "We never talked much."

"Wait a minute." Clementine focused on the name, since the face still didn't register. "We had homeroom together, didn't we? I remember Miss Perkins saying your name in roll call every morning."

"Yeah. Good old Miss Perkins. Dingy old crone." A smile flickered across his face, then disappeared. "I heard you were back in town. You planning on staying?"

"I am. I'm attempting to turn this mess you see around you into an antique shop."

Gary looked from the front of the shop to the back with no change in expression. "Amazing how many folks like this old stuff. We had a guy offer my aunt a thousand dollars for an old wardrobe one time, but she said it was a family heirloom and wouldn't let him have it. I'd a sold it in a heartbeat, if it'd been me." He reached for the naked lady statue. "But I might buy something like this. Where'd you get all this stuff anyway?"

"My husband and I bought some of it. Some of it I inherited, and some of it, like these paintings"—she pointed at the box at her feet—"I got at auctions in the past couple of weeks."

"Who'd you marry?" Gary's heavy eyelids rose above his dull green eyes. "Somebody from around here?"

Clementine sensed he might take offense that she hadn't found anybody local to marry, but she couldn't avoid answering. "No. You wouldn't know him. I met him in college. He was from Asheville, but he died a few years ago." Talking about Gordon still hurt, though not as badly as not talking about him like he never existed. Either way was painful.

"That's too bad," Gary said. "I'm divorced myself." He shoved his hands into the pockets of his coat, a blanket-lined canvas car coat with wrinkles and rough spots suggesting he wore it a lot. His eyelids drooped again as he licked his lips nervously.

"So have you lived here since high school, or did you get sucked back like me?" Clementine asked.

Gary's shoulders twitched. "I never left. I went to work at the mill after I graduated. Everything was fine until the mill got sold and they started laying people off. I hung on until about twelve years ago, but then I was dumped along with everybody else."

"Yeah, I heard about that. It was a real blow to the town, I know."

"Nothing's been the same since," Gary said. "I was a wreck for a while. That's when my wife left me. You remember Shelby Osborne? That's who I married, but, well, like I said, it didn't last. Lucky for me a few guys talked me into going to the community college. Otherwise I don't know what would've happened to me. I'm chef now at Johnny Johnson's restaurant. He needed somebody to help with the cooking after his wife died."

"I'm glad things turned out all right." Clementine didn't want to be rude, but she had a lot of work to do, and the personal turn his comments had taken made her uncomfortable. She hoisted a painting out of the box to hint that she was busy, but Gary didn't move. He stood with his hands in his pockets, and his dull eyes focused on her. Clementine set the painting on the table and reached for another one. Gary still didn't speak. "I'm glad you came by," Clementine said. "Stop in again when the shop opens."

Gary nodded but said nothing. His expression, which had been mostly passive since he arrived, grew more intense. "You been out to the drive-in since you've been back?" he finally asked.

The oddity of the question put Clementine more on edge as she tried to figure out what he meant. Tanner's only drive-in was a movie theater that had been closed for years. A victim of both the town's weakened economy and the tastes of the times, it stood abandoned on the outskirts of town with weeds growing through its cracked asphalt, and its posts, long ago relieved of their boxy speakers, standing in rows like beheaded soldiers still lined up for battle. "Why would I go out there?" she asked.

"Nostalgia, I guess. I go by it every day on my way to work. Sometimes at night I imagine I can still see lights flickering on the big screen. Elliott Gould, maybe, and Donald Sutherland dropping the shower tent wall on Hot Lips. Or Dennis Hopper and Peter Fonda on those motorcycles. We had some good times out there—and some not-so-good ones too." Gary ran his fingers through his brushed-back hair.

"I used to take a bunch of guys to the drive-in on Saturday nights," he said. "One Saturday I ran into you there. Remember?" Clementine shook her head.

"Well, I never forgot." A pink flush emerged across his cheekbones. He pulled his hands from his coat pockets and rubbed the side of his face. "Yeah, that night was a real hoot. The guys with me thought it'd be funny to kick me out of my own car and drive away, so that's what they did. Hilarious, huh? The best part was they held me down and stripped off my pants and shirt before they did it. So there I was in nothing but my boxers, looking for anybody I knew to let me in their car. And it was cold too. The end of October, just before the drive-in closed for the season."

Gary's face grew redder. His hands clenched and released. "I crept from car to car, trying to get a look at who was inside without being seen, but I couldn't find a soul I knew. Or at least that I could recognize in the dark. And then there was this green Plymouth with a bunch of girls in it, and one of them was you. Starting to sound familiar?" Clementine remembered the car. It was her mother's.

"I didn't want to talk to y'all 'cause I was so embarrassed about being in my underwear, but there was nobody else, and it was really cold. So I knocked on the window, and when you rolled it down, I asked you to let me in, just till the guys came back. But you wouldn't. I remember Emily Savage leaned across you and said y'all didn't talk to boys with no clothes on. And that little bitch Sheila Bowen, sitting in the back seat, said I must be some kind of weirdo running around half-naked. You could have let me in. It was your car. But you just sat there while the others giggled and locked the doors."

The incident began to form a hazy picture in Clementine's mind. The few times she'd taken her mother's car to the drive-in ran together in her memory, but looking at Gary's distressed face in the antique shop's shadowy light, she could hear the girls' laughter and see a younger version of that same face grimacing in the dark. Now she remembered more than just his name. He'd been the new kid for a while, coming to Tanner in about ninth grade. By the end of that year, he blended into the crowd, so there was no reason to notice him. He was just always around, in homeroom or passing in the halls—he and two other boys who hung out with him in his station wagon at lunch, playing the radio at ear-shattering volume. And one time in homeroom, he got up and walked out for no reason. She could still hear Miss Perkins calling after him in her croaky voice.

Clementine's heart beat faster. Why was he bringing the drive-in incident up now? She cleared her throat before she spoke. "I'm really sorry, Gary. I think I kind of remember a little about that night. I'm sure I didn't mean to hurt your feelings. I was just a kid and probably didn't know what to do."

Gary shrugged. "Well, welcome home, Clemmie. I'll probably see you around town." The old nickname crawled all over her. She'd told her friends in high school not to call her that. Gary turned to go, but before Clementine could say anything, he looked back. "You better get that lock on your door fixed. It's easy to jiggle loose."

"I will," Clementine mumbled as he clomped toward the front of the shop. When the door clicked shut behind him, she dropped into a rickety Shaker rocking chair and tried to slow her rapid breathing. The idea of somebody harboring resentment that long was creepy, even a little scary. She hoped throwing the incident in her face had gotten it out of his system. Was that the first thing he thought of when he heard she was back in town?

As soon as he was out of sight, she ran to check on that lock. The door was solid wood with a window in the top half, sturdy except for the piece of glass. The lock could easily be the original one—it worked with one of those old-fashioned skeleton-type keys. She hadn't worried too much about it because she figured any serious burglar would break the glass in the door, or there was always the huge display window that filled the entire front of the shop. She planned to get a burglar alarm, but she hadn't thought about keeping unwanted visitors from walking in. She'd have to get a deadbolt. Add that to the ever-increasing list of things she needed to buy. Getting this shop off the ground was going to take longer than she planned and probably cost a lot more money.

She knew when she came to Tanner she ought to get a job that assured her a steady income, but she wanted more than money. If she was ever going to fulfill her dream of owning an antique shop, she needed to do it now. For years, every time she went into an antique shop, she'd imagine what she would do with it if it were hers. She'd think about arranging the furniture and what she would say to customers about each piece. She loved antiques the way art aficionados love paintings. Antiques had stories to tell, and to spend her days with them would be heaven. She had no doubt that's what she would do when she moved back to Tanner.

And now was a good time for opening an antique shop in Tanner. The town council was trying to make the little town more of an arts center with a gallery, a legitimate stage, and venues for local artisans to sell their wares—anything to draw some revenue into the floundering economy. Clementine loved the idea of being part of an arts center, and her antique shop would fit right in. Or so she thought. Her landlord hadn't been too enthusiastic.

"We had one of those antique shops open up out on the highway a while back, and it didn't last six months," he said, right before he changed her lease to require the first month's and last two months' rent up front. Even his negativity didn't squelch her conviction.

The encounter with Gary, however, and her concerns about the lock dampened her enthusiasm for doing any more unpacking today. She kept looking at the door, wondering who was going to come in next. If she called the landlord, he'd take days—or maybe weeks—to get around to fixing the lock. She'd have to take care of it herself and hope she could squeeze a reimbursement out of him later. With a huff of determination, she got her coat and scarf from the back of the shop. She locked the door on her way out, figuring maybe the next person wouldn't think about jiggling it, and made her way down the windy street to the hardware store on the corner. The fact that this particular hardware store was still in business was a minor miracle, considering it was locally owned and had to compete with the Ace Hardware at the shopping center in the north part of town and the Walmart out on the highway. Clementine had been delighted to find the old store still here. She remembered shopping for nails and washers with her father when she was a child. The place had a distinctive metallic odor that announced it was a hardware store as soon as you walked in, just like a real antique shop smelled of varnish and mildew the way no other store did.

Unfortunately, the hardware store owner Clementine remembered had died, but Pete Ritchie, a former supervisor at the mill, had bought it and kept it alive. Notable mostly for his long, thin face, Pete was solemn but friendly, and since he didn't recognize her married name, he didn't put her through the "are you related" game that always popped up if she mentioned she used to live in Tanner. When she told him she needed a deadbolt lock for the empty storefront down the street, his eyes brightened and then dimmed when she said she'd be selling antiques.

"Why don't you sell something like those fancy little toiletries all the women like?" he said. "Bubble bath and moisturizers. Particularly the organic ones. We don't have nothing like that in Tanner, and women would buy that stuff. Believe me. My wife drives clear to Charlotte to get that kind of stuff. What's that place she likes? Something about crab apples."

Clementine sighed. Obviously he hoped she'd sell something he had more faith in to bring people downtown. But he sold her the lock and the screws she'd need, even offered to loan her a drill if she didn't have one. She didn't tell him she'd never put in a lock in her life.

Back inside her shop, Clementine called the only person she could think of who might know how to install a lock and would likely be willing to do it for her. She'd learned a funny thing about moving back to the town where she grew up. Her friends who still lived here had turned into different people with their own lives, just as she had. So to expect to pick up where she left off so many years ago was absurd. But even though she would likely not be close friends with these people again, many had reached out to her, asking her to join groups like the garden club and including her in dinner parties. She appreciated her old friends' efforts to make her feel welcome, especially when David Adams, a classmate she'd barely known, showed up for one of the dinners.

David and Clementine had been no more than acquaintances. They shared some math classes and were in band together, but that was all. When he walked into the dinner party, she was surprised she recognized him, especially since he was no longer the gangly boy she had known. She nearly choked on her chardonnay, amazed that such a skinny kid could turn into such an attractive man. He'd filled out beautifully, with strong shoulders and taut arms, not those of an athlete, but more likely of a man who battled stress. His deep-set eyes were sharp with wariness, and the collar-length blond hair she remembered was trimmed to just touch his ears. Instinctively, she ran her fingers through her own gray-streaked hair. What did she look like to him? She was a good fifteen pounds heavier, for sure.

"Clementine!" he exclaimed. "You haven't changed a bit." He took her hand, pulling her to a standing position so he could hug her. She deposited her wine on the table as she rose and returned the hug. With her nose pressed against his shoulder, she smelled dried apples and wood smoke.

Like so many Tanner residents, David was a former mill employee who'd had to find a new way to make a living since a conglomerate bought the cotton cloth manufacturing company that had been the largest employer in Tanner for decades. The dark factory with its empty parking lots was the first difference Clementine noticed in Tanner when she moved back. She remembered the red brick buildings with flags flying on the front lawn and the clack of looms churning away on the other side of the open windows in summer. Now the buildings stood silent, their façades marred with boarded-up windows. Their eerie specter seemed to stretch across the rest of the town.

David had moved his life forward by learning the insurance business and was now working in an office not far from the antique shop. David Adams, Property Casualty Agent, the sign in his window said, right beside the company's famous red ovals.

Since the dinner party, he and Clementine had grown to know each other well. His divorce years earlier meant they were free to pursue their relationship however they chose. During the many evenings they spent together, Clementine discovered they had a lot in common, not the least of which was the need for physical companionship. The truth was she hadn't had sex since Gordon died, and lurking in her mind was the fear that she didn't know how to be with another man. Or that she could never enjoy being with another man after her passion for Gordon. David must have sensed her apprehension because he was patient with her, and when he finally took her into his bedroom, she was not disappointed. His fingers on her thighs awakened sensations she hadn't felt since she was much younger. Maybe because David was an old classmate, being with him recalled the high school girl's thrill of forbidden sex. But her current self also felt the guilt of betraying Gordon. She knew Gordon would want her to be happy. Still, her feelings about her physical relationship with David remained a jumble.

Their friendship, though, was solid, and she was grateful he was in his office when she called about the lock.

"You had to pick the coldest day of the year to change a lock," he said good-naturedly when he arrived at the shop. "Couldn't it wait till we have one of those freaky winter days when it gets up to sixty-five degrees?" Clementine frowned at him.

"Sorry it took me so long to get here," he went on, "but I had to go home to get a drill and a couple of screwdrivers. You know, you oughta keep some tools around here. You never know when you might need 'em." He peeled off his gloves and examined the existing lock. "I'm just gonna bypass this relic entirely and put the new lock above it. Any objections?" Clementine shook her head. She'd perched on a tall tavern stool to watch the project.

David attached the lock's template to the door jamb and revved up the drill. Clementine felt a twinge of satisfaction as the whirring metal bore through the wood. For the past few hours, the shop had made her uncomfortable, its atmosphere hostile and sour. She wanted the old feeling back, the sense that this was the right place, even if it was too small and the only shop she could afford.

Her first impression of the space back in December had made her wince. Not what she'd had in mind by a long shot, it offered little room for all her antiques and had no opportunity for expansion since it was hemmed in by the CVS pharmacy on one side and Dunkin' Donuts on the other. These stores hadn't been in town very long, so they weren't going anywhere anytime soon. The only other possibility had been the old J.C. Penney location, which was big as a barn and impossible to heat. A lot of the buildings and stores that Clementine remembered from her childhood were gone, torn down and never replaced. So the little shop between the doughnuts and the drugs was her only choice. But in the weeks since she signed the lease, it had come to feel like home. The optimistic spirit of the other merchants and their determination to keep the Main Street retail district alive and prospering had inspired her to feel part of something bigger than herself and motivated her to work even harder than she already intended.

The drill made it almost all the way through one side of the door before David lined up the template and cut into the other side. A circle of wood toppled to the floor. David paused to look at Clementine. "You're taking this awful seriously," he said. "You worried about your antique door being violated?"

"Something like that," Clementine murmured. "Somebody jiggled the old lock open this morning and came in when I didn't expect them. It kind of spooked me."

David placed the drill on the floor and pushed the door shut. "Who came in?" he asked. "What were they doing here?"

"It's nothing to be afraid of," Clementine said. "It was just Gary Wiggins. I didn't recognize him, and I think it hurt his feelings. He brought up an old incident from high school that I hardly remember." She burrowed her cold hands into her pockets. Having the door open had lowered the temperature considerably, causing the old iron radiators to clank and hiss. "Do you see him much? He said he was working at Johnny Johnson's restaurant."

The wind whistled through as David opened the door again and started drilling into the door edge for the latch bolt. "Nope. Just at the restaurant occasionally. He's the chef. Doing pretty well, I think. Which is a good thing because he had some tough times when he was let go at the mill. Got his driver's license suspended for DUIs, I heard. And his marriage ended."

The plug of wood fell out of the door. David shoved in the bolt and marked where the latch plate would go. Then he took the bolt out again and started chiseling a space for the plate. "Shelby's still in town. That's his ex. They never had any children." Shelby had been in home ec class with Clementine. She had bright red hair.

"What about Johnny's wife? Gary said she died. What happened?"

"Yeah. He married a girl from Hickory. She did some of the cooking at the restaurant to help him out. Then about ten years ago she got breast cancer, the really advanced kind, and she only lived a year or so after she was diagnosed. Left Johnny with two teenage kids to take care of." David stuck the bolt back in the hole before he screwed the latch plate in place. With the bolt inside the door, he inserted the cylinder.

Clementine was suddenly sad. Thinking of Johnny's wife brought memories of Gordon, and she hated that Johnny had to go through the gut-wrenching pain of losing a spouse. She'd known him in high school, although not well. He'd been a year ahead of her, but he was popular with all the kids because his dad served free French fries at the restaurant after ballgames. In the years Johnny had been running the restaurant, he'd apparently enjoyed the food. The first time Clementine saw him when she returned to Tanner, she was surprised that he was several sizes larger than she remembered him. But his smile hadn't changed. He had the air of a man who was at peace with the world, despite the hard blows it had dealt him. She could imagine him offering a much-needed job to Gary.

"So you don't ever see Gary?" she asked David.

"I don't, but that doesn't mean he's some kind of hermit. We just don't run in the same circles."

Like high school, Clementine thought. She'd hardly noticed Gary, or David either, for that matter, because they traveled in different circles. Wondering how many people she'd missed knowing in her life because her circle almost never touched theirs, she watched David's husky hands twist the screwdriver to set the lock firmly in place. When the drill began to whir into the jamb, making a hole for the deadbolt, she resolved to try harder to get to know the people she saw every day, especially her customers. As a solitary shopkeeper, she'd be alone without them.

"I hope I have a lot of customers so I don't feel so alone," she said as David pressed the latch plate into the door jamb.

"For the time being," David said, "you're not alone. Look there." He pointed at a small gray mouse scurrying along the baseboard.

"Oh, Jesus," Clementine whispered. "Lousy locks and mice. What else?"

"Just get some traps," David said. "Pete over at the hardware store's gonna be your best friend. I can see that."

Picturing the dark expression on Pete's thin face when she mentioned she was opening an antique shop, Clementine wasn't so sure. "Maybe I should get a cat," she said as another mouse, or maybe it was the same one, darted around a corner cupboard. The cold air from the open door must have sent the creature looking for a warmer hiding place. The mouse sniffed at a few chairs before disappearing behind a row of bookshelves.

"How do you suppose Gary knew I was in here this morning?" Clementine asked. "He jiggled the lock loose and walked in like he knew exactly what he was doing. I doubt if he could see me from the street because I was behind all those bookcases." She pointed in the direction the mouse had gone.

David gave a final turn of the screwdriver, securing the latch plate against the jamb. "Somebody told him. Did you talk to anybody this morning?"

"No, I came straight here. And I've been working ever since."

"Well, it's a small town. Somebody saw you go in or Gary heard you were opening the store and figured you were here. You've been in town a few months, and you've told a lot of people about this antique shop. He could have heard it anywhere."

Clementine shrugged. She hadn't experienced the small-town grapevine in a while. "I still don't like somebody walking in," she said.

"You don't have to worry anymore. If you don't want anybody in here, this lock'll keep 'em out." David shut the door and turned the bolt. "Just remember to unlock it so customers can get in."

"Don't be a smart ass," Clementine said as she jiggled the knob. Its sturdiness pleased her.

David gathered up the tools along with the box and papers that came with the lock. "What are you going to call this place, anyway? Does it have a name?"

Clementine smiled. She'd been agonizing over the name for months. So much work and planning had gone into preparing for the shop, she felt like she was giving birth to another child. And the name she bestowed on this new creation was just as important as the names she'd given her children. David waited with an impatient expression. The expectant dad, she thought. She could tell him. "I'm going to call it 'Back in the Day.'" Now it was her turn to be expectant.

David's nose wrinkled as he stroked his chin. "Okay. But with an unusual name like Clementine, don't you think it would be good to include it in the name of the shop? Something like 'Clementine's Collectibles'? People would remember that."

Clementine frowned. She specifically did not want *Clementine* in the shop's name. She'd always hated her name. "If I'm going to put myself in the shop's name, I'd rather go with something more dignified, like "C. R. Loftis Antiques.""

"Just give it some more thought. How'd you come up with 'Back in the Day' anyway?"

"It's an expression my kids use. Not something I had ever heard until they started using it. I think it'll give the shop some pizzazz."

David nodded. "It's catchy. I'll say that for it. Whatever you decide on, you better start spreading it around." He looked at the paper and cardboard in his hands. "You got a trashcan?" Clementine pointed at an open box, and David tossed in the trash. "Go get some mousetraps. Then come back and set 'em up behind your locked door. I guarantee you won't have any more intruders." He gave her a quick hug and turned toward the door.

"Are you going back to the office now?" she asked.

David looked at his watch. "No. I don't have any more appointments today. I think I'll go down to the counseling center for a while."

Several years earlier, David and a few others had created a makeshift counseling service for the growing number of people in Tanner who were unemployed. Many of the people who lost their jobs when the mill closed didn't want to leave town. Some owned houses they didn't want to sell, and most had family in the area. So the hunt was on for other jobs. The problem was they didn't know where to look.

"We needed networking," David explained to Clementine on one of their first dates. So he had gathered a few doctors, lawyers, and merchants who not only sympathized with their friends and relatives who had been laid off but also saw the damage a lack of wages could inflict on their livelihoods. Together, the group set up the counseling center in a former beer joint next to the river that flowed just south of Main Street and tried to help their neighbors find jobs in Tanner or in the surrounding communities. For a short while, jobs had been available at the new superstores like Walmart and at other factories in surrounding communities, but then those dried up too, leaving pretty poor pickings.

"We had to tell the folks coming to us for help that they needed to learn how to do something else," David told Clementine. It had worked for him, and it could work for them. Some of the volunteer counselors had friends who worked at the community college, so they were able to set up interviews and get course catalogs with ease. This was David's favorite part of the service—getting people in their twenties and thirties to go to college, even though many of them never thought they'd want to or need to. Their parents and grandparents had always made a decent living at the mill, so they thought they should be able to do the same.

David's involvement with the center was one of the things that endeared him to Clementine. She knew he often took time away from his job to work there, a sacrifice few other men, maybe not even Gordon, would have made. She hugged him one more time before she let him leave the shop.

When he was gone, she bundled up for a second trip to the hardware store. The wind had picked up outside. It whooshed down the two-lane street, rattling metal signs that protruded above storefronts. A few canvas awnings that had been left unrolled bulged like pregnant women. From Clementine's shop

17

all the way down the block to the main intersection, not a soul was in sight. Empty cars waited patiently by the curbs. Images of mice and men like Gary swirled in Clementine's imagination. She didn't want to be this much alone.

2

With her new lock and mousetraps in place, Clementine threw herself into getting ready for the shop's grand opening. Timing was critical. She wanted to take advantage of Tanner's big push to draw a crowd—locals and tourists alike—into the Main Street area in the days leading up to Valentine's Day. Since the holiday was on a Monday, the town had the whole weekend to pull people in, sell them presents for their sweethearts, and convince them to splurge on romantic dinners in the local restaurants. In keeping with the arts center campaign, the community theater was offering a performance of *Hairspray* at the old Carolina Theater, which had been modestly renovated the year before, and the art gallery had somehow snagged an exhibit of prize-winning paintings from the University of North Carolina School of the Arts (on loan, of course).

With the unusually cold weather, business was booming at the ski slopes in western North Carolina, so Tanner civic leaders invested in a few small billboards along I-40 to try to lure skiers off the highway and into the town for "a holiday warm-up in a quaint Valentine village." They also sprang for small ads in the *Charlotte Observer*, the *Winston-Salem Journal*, and the *Statesville Record & Landmark*.

"Folks want to get out of the house in the winter, so we're gonna give 'em someplace to go," the town council chairman told Clementine when she stopped by his office to pick up flyers to distribute. "You better be ready, 'cause we won't have another extravaganza like this till summer." Clementine assured him she would be ready, even though she wasn't so sure.

Once she got the grime scraped off the fluorescent lights in the shop's ceiling, the faded walls screamed for a new coat of paint. She hadn't arranged the furniture yet nor filled any of the shelves, so it was easy to shove everything to the middle of the floor and haul out the paint buckets. David said he'd help her, but he had appointments stacked up on the days she needed to do it. The only other person she could ask for help was Erlene Duncan, but she felt a little awkward about asking.

Several months earlier, only a short time after Clementine moved back to Tanner, she was grabbing a quick lunch in the soda shop that had taken over the old drugstore site when she heard a familiar name mentioned at the table next to hers. "How's your mama, Erlene?" the server asked. "I haven't seen Miss Myrtle since she stopped coming in here to get her a dish of ice cream every day."

Clementine turned to look at the customer, a striking woman with skin the color of rich river soil and chin-length black hair. A spatter of dark freckles danced across her nose.

"Mama's fine," the woman said. "She just can't get around much since she broke her ankle last summer. Doctor says it's healed, but it's still weak as a noodle."

"Tell her I said hey," the server remarked as she carried the woman's dishes away.

Clementine studied the woman's features, softer but still familiar. Those freckles had surprised her the first time she saw them. Memories of her mother's kitchen with children chasing each other through fragrances of strawberry pies and coffee swirled in her brain. She smiled tentatively at the woman. "Aren't you Erlene Hubner?"

The woman's eyebrows rose. "Used to be. I'm Erlene Duncan now."

"My maiden name was Clementine Gardner. Do you remember me?"

Erlene observed Clementine's face until Clementine felt a blush creeping upward. "I do," Erlene said quietly. "My mother worked for yours when we were growing up. I came with her to your house a few times. You had a room full of dolls with dozens of dresses for each of them."

"Not that many," Clementine said, lowering her gaze. Realizing the dolls were Erlene's strongest memory about her made her squirm. "How've you been? I'm sorry to hear about your mother's ankle."

"We're both doing fine. Thank you for asking." Erlene's voice was soft, tentative. As a child, she'd clung to her mother's hand, causing Myrtle to shake her loose, telling her to "go play with Clemmie. Have some fun." A few years younger than Clementine, she'd been the joy of her mother's life. Whenever Myrtle took a break from ironing and cleaning for Clementine's mother, she'd tell Clementine all about what Erlene was doing at school and what good grades she got. Clementine asked her once why Erlene didn't go to Tanner Elementary like she did. A wistful smile curled Myrtle's lips. "Just a few more years," she said, "and maybe she will."

As it turned out, Erlene was in the fifth grade when she was allowed to enroll in the Tanner School System. Clementine, a confident seventh-grader then, watched her huddle with the other black girls in a corner of the playground. In high school, they rarely saw each other, but Clementine's mother kept up with Erlene through Myrtle and called Clementine a few years after she had her first job to tell her Erlene had earned a dental hygienist certificate at the county community college.

Looking at her now, Clementine recognized traces of Myrtle in the way Erlene held her head to one side. "I'd love to see your mother, if you think she'd want to see me," Clementine ventured.

Erlene hesitated before she replied. "I think that would be fine."

A few days later, Erlene took Clementine to see her mother. Pretty much house-bound because of her age and her ankle, Myrtle was grateful for the visit and delighted to see Clementine "all growed up. And such a proper lady." Clementine leaned over to hug the tiny woman, who she was sure must have shrunk, and it struck her what a reversal of roles had occurred since she had been the one reaching up to put her arms around Myrtle's waist.

In the early autumn weeks that followed her first visit with Myrtle, Clementine continued to stop by, bringing the old woman fresh fruit or flowers every Wednesday afternoon. To thank Clementine for her kindness, Erlene took her to lunch. They met at Johnny's Restaurant, which Erlene swore had the best food in town. After a few cautious attempts at conversation, Clementine happened to mention how different child-rearing was today compared with what it was like when her children were young.

"I am so glad I didn't have to deal with the Internet with my kids," she declared. "As long as I knew their friends and the places they hung out, I felt like I was keeping them safe, but the Internet's like a big dark cave with monsters you can't even imagine."

"You know that's the truth." Erlene nodded vigorously. "My granddaughter's only nine years old, but my daughter has to do all kinds of crazy things to her computer to keep that child from going to those monster sites. It's a struggle for me to organize my email. I don't know what I'd do if I had to worry about a kid on a computer." Her hearty laughter blended with Clementine's chuckle.

The topic of children opened up an abundance of shared experiences the women discovered. "Did you make your kids' Halloween costumes?" Erlene asked the second time they got together for lunch. The holiday was approaching, so jack-o-lanterns and stuffed witches were in all the stores.

"Me?" Clementine snorted. "I have a hard time threading a needle. But to be honest, I tried. One of mine wanted to be a black cat one year, so I bought a costume pattern and sewed up a black jumpsuit complete with a tail and ears. I drew whiskers on his face and sent him out to trick-or-treat with his sister. He was back, totally in tears, in less than an hour. Everybody thought he was a mouse." From costumes, their conversations moved to starting school, first dates, first cars, high school sports.

"We never missed a football game at Tanner High," Erlene said, "and we didn't even have a kid on the team. But it's what everybody in town does, especially if the Tanner team has a good year, like the time they won the state championship."

And then, as their lunch dates grew more frequent, they talked about the trials of grown-up children. Erlene and her husband, Alfred, had two children, one of whom took off to the far reaches of the country as soon as he was old enough, just like Clementine's kids had. "How often does your son get home to see y'all?" Clementine asked Erlene at lunch on a cloudy November day.

"Usually at Christmas and sometimes in the summer, if I can shame him into it," Erlene replied. "I know it's a long trip, all the way from Texas, but I miss him a lot. Thank goodness my daughter's still in town."

Clementine nodded. "I know all about that long-distance traveling. My son lives in Pennsylvania, and my daughter just started a new job in San Francisco. The world's supposedly gotten smaller, so nobody thinks a thing about taking a job three thousand miles away from family, but when it comes time to visit, three thousand miles is still a long way. Do you go see your son much?"

Erlene rolled her lips inward and shook her head. "Not much. It's awful expensive to fly, and Alfred's back bothers him if he sits in a car for too long. It takes us two full days of driving to get to Houston."

Husbands were also a frequent topic of conversation at their lunches. Alfred had been laid off from the mill, just like everybody else, and as Erlene put it, "laid around the house feeling sorry for himself," until he got up one day, went to the hospital—which had just added a new wing full of patient beds, so he figured they must need more staff—and got himself a job as a patient care assistant.

The hospital was Tanner's crown jewel. Founded in 1925 with an endowment from the family who owned the mill, it began as a small community hospital but had grown significantly, particularly in the years since the mill closed. It was as if the people who stayed behind when the exodus came realized a flourishing medical center could keep the town alive. By 2010, when Clementine arrived back in Tanner, it was the largest employer in town. She was shocked to see the sprawling complex that had swallowed up the little yellow brick hospital where she had her tonsils taken out.

She was grateful for its growth, however, and glad that Alfred found a job there. Her husband, Gordon, had been laid off from his engineering firm during the recession in 1982, so she knew what it was like to have a husband suddenly without work. It took eight months for him to find another job, and although he didn't exactly feel sorry for himself all that time, he was at loose ends, a stranger in his own skin, and that was every bit as bad.

A few days after David fixed the lock for Clementine, she met Erlene for lunch at a tearoom around the corner from the antique shop. Erlene had suggested going to Johnny's Restaurant, but Gary worked there, and Clementine had avoided that particular spot ever since Gary surprised her in the shop. Erlene told her she couldn't avoid him forever. She was letting him dictate what she could and couldn't do, which to Erlene's way of thinking was totally backward. The truth was Clementine hadn't been avoiding him, even though being around him made her uncomfortable. In fact, she'd seen him several times since the day in the shop. When she went to pick up her dry cleaning, he was there with his dirty shirts. They had said a few words to each other, commented on the weather, that sort of thing. And she had made a point of speaking to him when she saw him in line at the old Bank of Tanner, which was now Bank of America. She wasn't avoiding him. She just wasn't seeking him out.

Besides, she liked to eat at the tearoom. Lacy curtains and mismatched furniture gave it a cozy feeling, plus they served fabulous chicken salad with walnuts and dried cranberries. She knew Erlene liked it too. The first time they ate there, Erlene asked Clementine if she remembered the old Dairy Queen that used to be on the same site. "I loved their soft-dip ice cream," Erlene said. "I used to fantasize when I was little about sitting at one of the plastic tables inside and listening to the jukebox while I ate my ice cream cone, but we couldn't do that until I was much older. We had to buy from the service window."

Remarks like that were what made Clementine unsure about asking Erlene to help her paint the shop. Erlene might think she was putting them back in the roles of their mothers with Erlene cast as the help. As much as she enjoyed Erlene's company and respected her as an adult, the specter of their different childhoods still hovered over them. Always in the back of Clementine's mind was the fear that she would unintentionally offend Erlene. For two days, she worried about what to do and finally decided she was being silly. If Erlene didn't want to paint, she would say no.

Erlene said she'd be happy to help paint. She had Wednesdays off from the dentist's office, so she'd be there at eight o'clock sharp. She even had a few paintbrushes she could bring. Clementine was waiting when she arrived at the shop. The women spent the first hour covering the baseboards with masking tape and moving the bureaus that were too heavy for Clementine to move by herself. With each piece that was moved, Clementine braced herself for an escaping mouse, but none appeared. "I don't know why you're so scared of a little bitty mouse," Erlene scoffed.

"I'm not afraid. I just think they're nasty," Clementine said as she stirred the paint. She had chosen a deep gold color to give some life to the dingy beige walls. When she asked the landlord if it was okay to use that color, he said he didn't give a rat's ass what color she used as long as she didn't get any on the wooden floor, which struck her as funny, given the current stains on the floor and the mice in the baseboards. She'd bought the paint and rollers from Pete and rented a couple of stepladders from him too.

When he was ringing up her purchases, Pete had gazed at her solemnly. "It's good that you're cleaning that place up, even though I got a feeling you ain't gonna be there very long. It says in the Bible, 'Fill your surroundings with cleanliness and light, and your soul will be filled as well.'"

Clementine said she was glad he approved and thanked him for having one of the high school boys who worked there part time carry the ladders down to the shop.

"Have you ever heard that Bible verse?" she asked Erlene as they dragged the paint-covered rollers across the walls.

"Nope. And I've spent a lot of time in Sunday school and church. Have you ever been to a black church service?" Erlene turned on her ladder, holding on with one hand and pointing her roller at Clementine with the other.

"Never. It's true what they say about eleven o'clock on Sunday morning being the most segregated hour of the week."

"Well, let me tell you, if you go to a black service regularly, you will hear the entire Bible read, cover to cover, and more than once. Black preachers don't stop preaching just because it's noon, the way white preachers do. They don't stop till they're done." She chuckled and went back to painting. "I've heard every Bible verse there ever was, including all the 'begats.'"

Clementine jumped down from her ladder and stepped back as far as the crowded floor would let her to take in the effect of the gold color on the wall. She expected the rich hue to accentuate the mellow tones of the cherry, mahogany, and walnut furniture and to complement the colors in the paintings and prints she planned to hang. She was not disappointed. With a pleasant rush of satisfaction, she moved her ladder about three feet to the left. As she climbed to one of the higher steps, she stumbled, causing the bucket of paint in her hand to swing sharply against the wall. A crackling sound erupted, and a large chunk of plaster fell to the floor. "What the hell?" Clementine grabbed the paint bucket to steady it.

"Looks like the pipes must have leaked," Erlene observed. "Water'll do that to a wall. Eat at the plaster till it pulls away.

You should get it fixed and send the bill to your landlord. And while you're at it, charge him for the paint and add a little extra for the trouble this has caused you."

"I'd never overcharge him, and the hole's my fault anyway. I let the bucket hit the wall," Clementine said.

"He doesn't know that."

Clementine frowned.

"Okay. Just hang a picture in front of it." Erlene shrugged. "Unless, of course, it's still leaking, but there weren't any water stains on the wall."

Clementine kicked at the piece of plaster, a hunk the size of a hubcap and shaped like Brazil. "I just hope the rest of the walls don't start falling down. I don't have that many pictures."

"They won't fall down," Erlene said. "Have faith."

"Sometimes I think faith is all I have." Clementine stared at the hole in the wall. It angled inward like a moon crater with a spot of dark wood showing at the center.

Erlene climbed down her ladder. Posed with arms akimbo, her paint roller protruding from her right hand, she studied Clementine. "You know you're mighty brave to tackle this shop all by yourself. Especially with today's economy and in this town, where a lot of folks are struggling to make ends meet since the mill closed. I have to admit I don't know who your customers are gonna be, but you seem to know."

Clementine smiled. "I'll find them, or they'll find me. I will make this shop a success despite what everybody thinks. And I want it to be a success in this town."

"Why in this town?" Erlene's dark eyes flashed. "Why'd you come back here, anyhow?"

This was a question Clementine had asked herself many times. She could have stayed in New Jersey. She could have followed one of the kids. She could have gone to Florida or Arizona or any one of dozens of supposedly perfect retirement areas. For the first time since she married Gordon, she had a choice about where she would live. Until he died, she had always followed him and his career, finding substitute or full-time elementary-school teaching jobs wherever his new work took them. Not that she'd minded that role, but the new freedom was delicious, and she wanted to make the most of it. After spending her entire adult life with the crowds, noise, and complexity of metropolitan areas, the simplicity of a place like Tanner was enticing. "This is home," she said to Erlene. "It suits me."

Erlene nodded thoughtfully. "I guess. Do you reckon you also have some unfinished business here? You said it's important to make the shop a success in this town."

"Maybe. I don't know. I did well in school here, and folks seemed to expect a lot from me. I'm not sure I ever delivered." Clementine sighed. "But then running an antique shop is no big accomplishment, is it?" She looked around the shop. "It may not be any kind of accomplishment if I don't get my ass in gear. This place is a mess, it's only two weeks till the opening, and now I have a hole in the wall."

"Hang a picture," Erlene chanted as she climbed back up the ladder.

Clementine dabbed her paintbrush gently around the edges of the hole. She was trying to effect a crisp line next to the ceiling when someone knocked on the door. Surprised by the sound, she glanced at Erlene, who shook her head. "Probably David," Clementine said as she climbed down the ladder and walked around a couple of desks to see who was there.

The morning light slid under the covered entrance, but its angle left shadows across the person's face. Even in the dimness, Clementine recognized the man's height and shape. She didn't like that he had come here uninvited again. Pausing behind a tall mirror, she imagined him trying to shake the lock loose and finding that this time it held fast. He knocked again. At least she wasn't alone. Buoyed by Erlene's presence, she opened the door. "Hello, Gary," she said. "I'm sorry, but we're still not open." She tried to look pleasant, but not particularly welcoming.

Gary ran his gloved fingers through his hair. "I could see through the window that you're in there painting. I've got a couple of hours before I have to go to work. Can I give you a hand?" Soft footsteps sounded behind Clementine.

"Thanks for the offer, but I already have some help."

Gary turned his head to look beyond Clementine into the shop. The furrows between his eyebrows deepened. Clementine sensed Erlene standing behind her and turned so she could see her. "Do you know Erlene Duncan?" she asked. Gary shook his head. "Erlene, this is Gary Wiggins."

Erlene extended her hand. "I'm pleased to meet you," she said.

"Same here," Gary said, shaking her hand slowly. "You know, y'all have a lot to do in here." He dropped Erlene's hand, quickly shoving his own hand into his pocket. "Are you sure I can't help? I'm a whiz with a paintbrush." He pulled his hand from his pocket and waved his arm through the air as if he were brandishing a sword.

Clementine couldn't help smiling. "Thanks a lot, but we're fine."

"Well, what you could do if you want to get done in a hurry is hire a few Mexican guys. We have some working at the restaurant, and they all have a brother or a son or two who would jump at the chance to work. They're good workers." Gary scanned the shop, then focused back on Clementine. A big difference she had noticed about Tanner since her return was the large number of Hispanic people in town. David explained to her that people from Mexico, and later several Central

American countries, had come to North Carolina looking for work in the tobacco fields, but as tobacco production declined, they took jobs with restaurants, hotels, cleaning companies, lawn services, and other places that offered employment for unskilled laborers.

"Thanks for the suggestion, but we're fine. Really," Clementine said.

"Okay." Gary left the entryway and marched down the sidewalk without looking back.

Clementine made sure the door was securely locked. "Why does he keep coming around here?" she asked.

"Either he's awfully eager to buy some antiques or he wants to see you, and I don't think it's antiques. You better put a stop to this fast unless you're interested in him, and I don't think you are." Erlene's expression was stern like a schoolmarm.

"Lord, no. I'm not interested in him," Clementine said. "I hate to say it, but he kind of gives me the creeps. Like he's watching me."

"If he keeps it up, tell him you don't like it. Tell him he better back off."

"There has to be a gentler way to do it than that," Clementine said. "I don't want to hurt his feelings."

"Have David tell him. That'll make it pretty clear."

Clementine shook her head. She didn't want David fighting her battles for her. Gordon used to try to do that. In fact, he did it throughout their marriage. If she had a problem at work, he would tell her what she needed to do about it. She didn't want him telling her how to fix the problem—she just wanted him to listen. As for David, helping her install a lock was one thing, but she didn't want him interfering in her relationships with other people. Or her business matters. Or her finances. She might be timid, but she could handle it. "I'll take care of it," she said to Erlene.

They finished the first coat of paint around three o'clock. The shop looked better, even though the walls had sucked up that paint like they hadn't had a drink in years, which they most likely hadn't. It might even take three coats, but Clementine felt energized. The shop was going to happen. There was nothing else they could do until the walls dried, so Erlene went home. The second and third coats would go on faster. Humming an old Billy Joel tune, Clementine did a little work on the computer before she left for the day.

Outside, the sky was still light. The days were getting longer. A coworker of hers used to talk about "the dark season," the months when they left work after the sun went down. Today she looked for the setting sun in the gaps between the buildings lining the alley behind the shop. She felt like her personal dark season was starting to end. She smiled at the gleaming Mercedes van parked by the shop's back door. It had cost a bundle, but it was perfect for hauling furniture, and she trusted it not to break down on her at some farmhouse auction in the far reaches of the county.

The sight of her house as she pulled into the driveway was comforting as well. She'd spent a lot of time looking at properties around Tanner before she took the plunge into home buying. Because the mill's closing and the national recession had caused more people than usual to put their homes on the market, she'd had a large selection of houses to choose from—everything from early twentieth-century Victorians to recent colonials and split levels. She didn't want to take advantage of somebody else's misfortune, however, so she was delighted when she found a tidy brick bungalow with two bedrooms and a postage-stamp yard, which the realtor assured her was for sale because the owners were moving to Michigan. All the houses on the street were surrounded with mature trees and bushes, giving the area the settled, lived-in look of an older neighbor-hood. Many of her neighbors were families with young chil-dren, whose shouts and laughter brightened the afternoons and evenings. Traffic on the street was light, but then Tanner rarely had heavy traffic anywhere. She could drive almost anywhere she wanted to go in town in less than fifteen minutes. Life was easy here, and Clementine felt like she belonged.

After dropping her keys on the hall table and shedding her winter trappings, she went straight to the kitchen for a martini. Cocktails were no longer in fashion—everybody drank wine now—but in the privacy of her own home, she enjoyed an ex-tra dry gin martini, particularly after a day of climbing up and down a ladder and hauling buckets of paint around. Cradling the cone-shaped glass in her hand, she stretched out on her velvet fainting couch, a nineteenth-century relic she'd snapped up at an estate sale. Lying on the table next to it was the book she'd started reading the night before. The mail and dinner could wait—Henrietta Lacks was calling.

Much later in the evening, long after she finally ate a simple supper, she checked to see if she had any messages on the tele-phone. The blinking light showed there were two. The first one gave her a jolt: "This is Gary Wiggins. I don't have your work or cell phone number or I'd have called you at the shop. Too bad you didn't need any help painting. I was ready, willing, and able." His voice was smooth and earnest. Clementine almost felt bad about not letting him help. She should be nicer to him, but the idea of spending any time with him made her cringe. She was going to have to let him know their relationship would never get beyond the acquaintance level.

With the next message, she knew she had to speak to him sooner rather than later. "Clemmie, it's Gary again. I've decided I don't want to wait for you to call me. Let's have dinner to-morrow night. I'll pick you up at seven." Then he hung up. No call-back telephone number. No room for refusal. Clementine played the message again to be sure she didn't miss anything. His voice was more urgent than in the first message, a little harsher. She stared at the telephone and shook her head. The nerve of him! She found the number on the caller ID and was poised to call him when she decided she didn't want to talk to Gary that late at night. The darkness made everything worse. She'd handle it better in the morning. She checked the locks on all the windows and doors and went to bed.

3

Putting the second coat of gold paint on the walls in the shop proved harder than the first since Clementine kept turning to look at the door to make sure nobody was there. Alone all morning, she couldn't stop picturing Gary showing up again to confirm their date. Around noon she called the restaurant. A woman answered. She listened politely, and a few minutes later Gary's voice came over the phone. "This is Gary."

Clementine took a deep breath. She'd never been good at telling people things they didn't want to hear. At one of her teaching jobs, she'd had to reprimand an aide for mishandling a playground incident. She almost couldn't get the words out of her mouth, and she felt the same way now. "I got your message last night," she blurted. "Oh, this is Clementine. I got your message. Thank you for asking me, but I can't have dinner tonight."

A few seconds of silence. "How 'bout tomorrow night?"

She could tell from the despondent tone of his voice he knew what was coming. "I can't do it then either." She swallowed. "Fact is, Gary, I can't go out with you." No response from him. Even though she didn't have to, Clementine felt like she ought to give him an explanation. "See, I'm spending so many hours at the shop, and I don't think that's going to get any better after it opens," her fingers twisted the buttons on her sweater, "and I'm seeing somebody." Still no response. "But thanks for asking." She had nothing more to say. She was getting ready to hang up when Gary finally spoke.

"Okay. If that's the way you want it. You haven't changed at all, have you?" He hung up the phone before she could answer. A shudder ran across her shoulders. He sounded so angry. She couldn't imagine why a grown man would be that bitter about a simple rebuff. He acted as if she was out to get him and had been since high school. The irony was that she had never thought she was better than anybody or been out to get anybody. Truth be told, she often worried that she wasn't as smart or talented as everybody else. She'd like to do something nice for Gary, but that would probably make matters worse.

She put away the phone and took a deep breath. She had to stay focused on the shop. So much work needed to be done. The grand opening was less than two weeks away.

For most of those weeks, Clementine spent ten-hour days at the shop painting, cleaning, repairing (she learned to wield a hammer against protruding nails and to replace leaky washers in the bathroom), hanging paintings, arranging furniture, and setting up displays of jewelry, silver cutlery, and other little curios like thimbles and figurines. She didn't have any legitimate retail or marketing experience. Although she knew little about visual appeal, she knew what she liked to see when she walked into an antique shop, so she tried to copy that. Where she could, she squeezed furniture, lamps, and other items into small room-like clusters, but the close quarters of the space didn't allow for a lot of those arrangements. The jewelry case doubled as a counter separating the small office area from the showroom of the shop. With the help of a retro website, she downloaded Frank Sinatra, Glen Miller, and Rosemary Clooney recordings, which she planned to play on an iPod to create an atmosphere of nostalgia. David dug through the piles of paraphernalia in his basement and came up with several speakers, which he hooked up around the shop.

As opening day grew closer, Clementine's anxiety level was rising, exacerbated by her worries about Gary. At any minute, he could call her again or show up at the shop. A few times, she thought she saw him pass by on the sidewalk and stare into the window, but she wasn't sure. It could have been somebody else.

On the Friday before the Valentine's Village festivities, Clementine walked around the shop, taking careful stock of what she had to offer. The gold walls gave the impression of warmth she wanted, especially since she had covered any obvious crack repairs and holes with paintings, as Erlene suggested. The desks, chairs, tables, and bookcases were all dusted, polished, and arranged in groupings along the walls to show their best sides as much as possible. Lamps and accessories were gleaming, as was all the jewelry and silver in the cases. She had put a lot of thought into pricing items, leaving enough room to "do better" if customers asked her to and still make a reasonable profit.

Some of the items came from the collection she and Gordon had built in their thirty-two years of marriage. Seeing them with price tags made her sad. She could remember where and how they bought each of them. She took a deep breath and reaffirmed her decision to put pieces of their collection in the shop when she bought her small house in Tanner. She simply didn't have room for them. She comforted herself by remembering the antiques that remained at home, assuring herself that they were Gordon's and her favorites. When she left that night, she knew she was as ready as she'd ever be.

Saturday morning was bright and cold, a perfect day for a festival. The Tanner police had closed off Main Street to traffic from the east end near the old mill to the west end where the town's first residential area started. All of the stores had covered their windows with valentines, and the town council had hung a huge banner welcoming participants to the first Valentine's Village Extravaganza. The pink and red decorations may have been hokey, but they created a festive atmosphere, the test of which would be how much money was wrested from wallets in the next two days.

Merchants whose stores and restaurants weren't on Main Street set up booths and kiosks in the center of the street to advertise their wares and give directions to their locations. Clementine hoped they planned to rotate the people in those booths because the weather was too cold for anybody to stand outside very long. One of the restaurants equipped its booth with large stainless steel urns of hot coffee, offered free to anybody who stopped by, including other merchants.

The welcoming aroma of the coffee wafted around Clementine as she stood on the sidewalk outside the antique shop. *This is it*, she thought. *The moment I've been waiting for all my life, even if I didn't know it. This is mine and mine alone. I created this shop, and whether it flies or falls is up to me.* Despite the cold air, an inner glow engulfed her. The shabby old storefront was beautiful, its faded bricks the perfect backdrop for the tin sign she and David had hung outside the shop's front door on Friday. Suspended from a wrought-iron rod nailed to the building, the sign proclaimed Back in the Day in stylized Old English lettering.

David's initial ambivalence toward the name had worried her, but she didn't have time to worry long. She had to make a decision so she could advertise the shop's opening. In desperation, she presented all the choices to Erlene, whose main observation was that most people in Tanner and the surrounding areas weren't looking for the finest antiques and might be scared off by a name that sounded too presumptuous. "You gotta break 'em in gently," she said. "You might even have to teach 'em a little bit about what makes an old chair an antique, but they'll eat it up once you get 'em inside the door."

All things considered, Clementine went back to her original choice, and David found a painter to bring the sign to life. As she stood on the sidewalk, Clementine admired its carefully drawn lettering placed perfectly above the drawing of a pewter plate and goblet. Undoubtedly, it was the most attractive adornment on the familiar street. With a deep breath and a parting smile at the sign, she pushed the key into the door's lock. A quick shiver replaced the glow she'd felt a moment before. Like a reflex, she jiggled the lock to make sure it was secure. When all the metal held fast, she turned the key and went inside.

Customers began flowing into the shop as soon as it opened. Clementine found herself constantly replenishing the chocolate chip cookies and spiced tea she provided for the special occasion. She was almost grateful for the smallness of the space because people were forced to rub elbows with each other, creating more of a party atmosphere. Sales were steady, if not brisk. As she expected, the lamps, figurines, and small silver pieces were the most popular, but she also sold one painting and two small chairs, and one woman promised to bring her husband back to look at a chest of drawers. Clementine felt a niggling pang of regret when a customer bought the carnival-glass plates she inherited from her grandmother, but she reminded herself she never really liked them anyway.

When Erlene stopped in around one o'clock, she offered to run across the street to the soda shop and bring back a sandwich for Clementine's lunch, but Clementine had that covered—a month's supply of Yoplait fat-free yogurt in the bar-sized refrigerator she'd installed next to the bathroom.

"You having any trouble getting to all the customers?" Erlene asked with a wary eye on the parade of people regularly slamming the door and fanning out through the shop. Erlene had urged Clementine to hire a part-time helper, at least for opening weekend, but Clementine didn't want to spend the money till she saw how things went. "You'll make the money back by giving the good folks lots of attention and keeping the bad folks from slipping things in their pockets," Erlene had advised, but Clementine was sure she could handle it. Most shoppers didn't want to be bothered unless they had a specific question, and she didn't expect much shoplifting. The expensive silver and jewelry were locked in the display case. If somebody took an old piece of transferware china, either they needed it worse than she did or they didn't know how little it was worth. It wasn't exactly something you could fence.

"Everything's fine," Clementine told Erlene. "Nobody's begging for attention, and nothing seems to be missing."

Erlene frowned. She obviously still had her doubts. "If you want me to give you a hand later in the afternoon or come around at closing time to help you balance the receipts, gimme a call," she said. "I've seen about all I want to see of the festival. The bargains aren't good enough to write home about."

Clementine thanked her for offering her help for the umpteenth time and shooed her out of the shop. David had offered to help too, but Clementine didn't want either of them there. She had leaned on them heavily to get the shop ready for opening, and she didn't want to take advantage of them any more than she had to. But just as important, she had to prove she could run the shop by herself. Her son, Jackson, had told her she was taking on too much in opening her own shop. "Just find an antiques shop to work in," he said. "You'll have all the fun and none of the headaches."

Even her daughter, Elizabeth, whom she'd tried to raise as a feminist, opposed the idea. "We're worried about you, Mom," Elizabeth said. "You don't need that kind of hassle in your life now. Or the drain on your finances."

But they were both wrong. The shop was exactly what she needed. A creation of her own to focus her energy on. And now that it was up and running, she would manage it entirely by herself. As Clementine waved goodbye to Erlene through the heart-covered front window, she stared down the street and wondered what her fellow merchants were doing inside their stores for this first Valentine's Day affair. Maybe she wasn't doing enough with her decorations and refreshments. Not that she felt inadequate, but she'd love to steal some marketing ideas. Pete from the hardware store had already been by the antique shop twice, although she sensed he wasn't on a scouting mission. More likely, he wanted to make sure she was okay. After browsing around a bit the first time, he remarked about her improvements to the appearance of the place and left. The second time he stayed to eat some cookies. She overheard him tell a customer, "Blessed are those who make the most of the little they are given." Clementine smiled at his creativity and wondered if he ever quoted other books with such liberty as he did the Bible.

Halfway down the block, Clementine saw three middle-aged women carrying armloads of bundles walk out of the yarn and knitting shop that had moved into the old appliance store. When Lowe's and Walmart built stores close to Tanner, the local appliance dealer couldn't compete. He hung on for a few years before he had a going-out-of-business sale for his floor samples and went to work at Lowe's. The yarn shop had done well, however, and if their approach to Valentine's weekend was typical of their marketing, Clementine knew why. They had a pen filled with live angora bunnies in the middle of the shop. She'd heard so much about the bunnies that she ran by the shop on Friday to see them for herself. So many children and adults clustered around the pen that Clementine could barely see the bunnies. She walked out shaking her head. She couldn't do anything comparable to that unless she could bring back Abraham Lincoln to talk about her antiques.

A customer tapped on her arm and drew her attention back to activity inside the antique shop. "Do you have another one to match this?" the customer asked as she held up a porcelain vase. Her mouth drooped in disappointment when Clementine told her the vase was the only one in the shop. Nevertheless the customer handed it to Clementine to hold for her while she continued to look around.

After setting the vase behind the jewelry-case counter, Clementine strolled around the shop, straightening lampshades and knickknacks. She was down to her last dozen cookies and a few cups of tea. Fortunately, she had only a few hours to go. Fewer and fewer customers came into the shop. By five o'clock, Clementine was feeling the stress and exertion in her back. All the painting and repairing of the previous weeks should have toughened her muscles and built up her stamina, but this was different. Speaking to customers, answering questions, replenishing refreshments, trying to do just the right amount of haggling about prices, and constantly checking to keep the displays in good shape were a lot to keep up with. The spurts of adrenaline that had fired her earlier in the day were gone. She sank onto the tavern stool behind the counter and listlessly watched the final few customers browse among her wares. She wasn't sorry when the last one left, although remembering the day's parade of characters made her smile: the new bride trying to furnish her first apartment, the collector who was an expert on nineteenth-century furniture joinery, the elderly lady who wanted to bring in her mother's jewelry, and so many others. Clementine wondered what the next day would bring.

Foamy clouds covered the entire sky now, causing an early dusk. The street booths were all empty. As far as Clementine could see, no late shoppers walked along the sidewalks. Across the street, the woman from the yarn shop came out carrying a bunny and locked the door behind her. Apparently the other bunnies were spending the night at the store. Exhausted but pleased, Clementine lifted the day's receipts from the cash register. Although it was a small pile, some of the items sold were among her best. It had been a good opening day.

She called up the spreadsheet she created for tracking sales on her laptop. Smiling at the virgin column labeled "February 12, 2011," she typed in the first sale. When she finished recording the sales, she would call up the inventory file she had created, add the cost of the item to the spreadsheet, and deduct sales tax to calculate her profit. Someday, if the shop did as well as she hoped it would, she planned to buy software to take care of all these records and calculations for her, including overhead expenses, but for now she rather enjoyed doing it by hand. It gave her a sense of accomplishment. She was so wrapped up in the numbers, she barely noticed the darkness taking over outside or the streetlights coming on. Because Main Street was closed off through Sunday evening, no automobile headlights or tooting horns caught her attention. She worked steadily until the ache in her lower back became too much. With a nod of satisfaction, she shut down the computer, knowing she'd finish the next night. To be safe, she put the checks and large bills from the cash register into a bank bag to take home with her.

A quick sweep around the shop had everything straightened and ready for Sunday morning. When she lived in Tanner before, stores were forbidden to open on Sunday—blue laws, they were called. How times had changed. She checked David's lock on the front door to make sure it was securely fastened. Then she turned off most of the overhead fluorescent lights, leaving only a few scattered bulbs still glowing. After buttoning her thick wool coat, she grabbed her purse and the bank bag and went out the back door. She was just climbing into the van when she remembered the laptop. With a huff of annoyance, she turned back into the shop and scurried to grab the computer off the counter. When she turned to leave again, Gary stood in the doorway.

Clementine gasped. "What are you doing here?" she demanded. "Why aren't you at the restaurant?" The thought that he should be working to make the weekend a success like all the other Tanner merchants hit her first, even before the twinge of fear. The back of the shop was dark, sunk into shadows cast from the lights in the front. Gary was backlit by a streetlight in the alley behind the shop, but the glow disappeared when he let the door slam shut behind him.

"Equipment problems," he said. "Couldn't make Pete, or anybody else, understand what I needed to fix it, so I had to come get it myself." His voice was gruff with exasperation. "As if I could be away from the restaurant right now." He sucked in a loud, deep breath. "You're here awful late for somebody who doesn't need any help."

"I was just on my way out." Clementine tried not to sound flustered, although her heart began to race. "And obviously you need to get back to the restaurant. Why are you here?"

"To tell you I hope you had a good opening day. I saw you getting in your car and figured you were closing." His voice softened, but in the dim light and shadows, his expression was grim. "Did you have a good day?"

"Yes, I did. But I need to get going now."

"Going to celebrate, I suppose. Who you gonna celebrate with? Anybody but me, right?" The exasperation was back in his voice, ratcheted up a notch.

"Not anybody but you, Gary. Not anybody." The words were getting twisted in Clementine's brain. What was he talking about?

"So you'd rather not go out at all than go out with me?"

"No. No. That's not what I said." Heat rose in Clementine's head. She moved sideways, headed around him toward the door.

"Why not me? Why won't you celebrate with me?"

Clementine was close enough that his breath swept across her forehead. "Because I don't want to." In her agitation, the words flew out of her mouth before she could stop them. His face withered into a scowl. Clementine kept moving and was nearly past him when he grabbed her arm. She tried to shake loose, but his grip was like a tourniquet, and twisting only seemed to make it tighter.

"Let go of me!" she shouted as she tried to hit him with the computer she had clutched against her chest, but it was too heavy and fell clattering to her feet. Gary seized her free arm and began pulling her into the shop.

"Let go!" Clementine yelled again, this time kicking at his shins. "What the hell do you think you're doing?" He was pulling so hard she had to follow him or fall to her knees. Realizing she couldn't get away, she screamed, "Fire!" as loud as she could over and over until he released one arm, jerked her around so her back was to him, and clamped his sweaty hand over her mouth. Instinctively, she tried to bite the fleshy part of his palm, but he withdrew his hand just in time.

As she was starting to scream again, Gary whipped her back around and shoved her onto a camelback sofa. In seconds he was on top of her, straddling her thighs with his knees and pinning one arm beneath her. "Shut up," he hissed, "or I'll break your jaw."

Even though she was not a small woman, he had at least a hundred pounds on her. There was no way she could throw him off. Remembering a self-defense film she saw on the Internet, she tried to jab her fingers into his eye, but he caught her hand in mid-jab and pinned it against her chest.

Clementine strained to remember any self-defense technique she'd ever heard anyone mention. She recalled a story about a woman who talked a would-be rapist out of hurting her, but what did she say? Clementine cleared her quivering throat. "Don't do this, Gary," she said. "Let's have a drink and start this relationship off the way it should be started. I was wrong. You and I should get to know each other better. Let's take our time."

She tried to keep her voice soothing as she struggled to free the arm he had pinned behind her back. He still held her other hand so tightly she figured there was no hope of getting it loose. Even if she worked a hand free, she wasn't sure what she could do. The Gary she had known in high school hadn't seemed like the kind of person who would rape somebody, but then she obviously hadn't known him very well, and that didn't take into account what had happened to him in the past forty years.

"I told you to shut up," Gary said. "I'm in charge now." He leaned forward, putting more pressure on her thighs and back while he unbuttoned her coat and threw it open. The corduroy skirt she had chosen so carefully to wear on opening day was easily hoisted above her waist. Faced with the dilemma of her pantyhose, he pulled a pocketknife from his coat pocket and held it in his teeth while he released the blade. As he cut open her pantyhose, a sickening dread washed through her, telling her there was no way out of this. Still, she made a desperate effort to squirm out from under him. In a flash, he pressed the point of the knife under Clementine's chin. "Try that again and I'll slit your throat."

"No," Clementine sobbed as the pressure of the knife burned against her chin. Gary shoved a husky knee between her thighs. In the same instant, he dropped the knife onto her belly so he could unzip his pants. With a rough jab of his knee, he forced her legs farther apart. Clementine saw the bright metal of the knife loose against her skin and made one more attempt to free her hand. Gary swept the knife away from her reach. Forcing her hand down on the couch, he shifted his weight so he was squarely above her. His exposed penis found its mark. Again and again and again. Clementine's closed eyes couldn't keep the tears contained. Silently she prayed for it to be over soon. Mercifully, it was.

Gary finished with a shudder and a groan and flopped his heavy torso against her chest. His breath came in pants against her ear. Sensing his surrender, she tried again to throw him off her, but he immediately sat up and pointed the knife again at her throat. "I told you I'm in charge," he said, grazing her chin with the knife. For a terrifying second, she feared he was going to rape her again, or kill her, but he just sat there on her thighs, his pants still open, his face partially illuminated by the few fluorescent bulbs.

With one hand free now, Clementine hammered against his thigh, but he ignored her. Eventually he grabbed her wrist. "Stop it," he said. Then he climbed off her, still holding the knife as close to her neck as he could. "Don't you move until you hear my car drive away, or I'll come back, and we'll do this again." He was facing the lights now. She could see the grim expression on his face. It wasn't triumph or resentment or even hate. It was more like contempt. He quickly zipped his pants and went out the back door.

Clementine lay where he left her, her head spinning and her groin on fire. She had read so many newspaper articles and seen so many TV shows about rape that she should know what to do. Even though she never thought it would happen to her. Call the police. See a doctor. But knowing what to do and doing it were two different things. She had heard about rape victims who were obsessed with taking a long, hot shower or bath. She didn't feel that way, except that it might relieve some of the pain between her legs. She just wanted it all to go away. Act like it never happened. She could still see the disdain in his eyes and feel the weight of him pressing her into the sofa. With a rush of energy that came from God knows where, she sat up, then stood, gripping a floor lamp for support and balance. Her skirt, twisted around her midriff, fell to cover her legs. She swooned slightly, then sat down. In a few minutes, she would get up again.

4

The biscuit dropped from Erlene's hand when the phone rang. Usually she and Alfred didn't answer the phone during dinner, but Erlene felt a quiver when it rang this time, and she was a woman who paid attention to her quivers. When she saw Clementine's name on the caller ID, she grabbed the phone and blurted out, "What's wrong?"

Clementine's voice was low and raspy, but she managed to get out the gist of what had happened. "We're on our way," Erlene said. Then, to Alfred, who was munching on a pork chop, "Get your coat, old man. We're going downtown."

The shop was still dark when Erlene and Alfred arrived. Without the sun coming through the big front window, the temperature inside had dropped considerably. Clementine sat on a straight-back chair, her coat clasped around her. Erlene started to sit on the camelback sofa, but jumped up, pulling Alfred with her, when she saw Clementine's eyes widen. Noticing the lack of redness or swelling on Clementine's face, Erlene asked softly, "Did he harm you anywhere else? Is anything broken?"

"No." The word sounded thick, as if all the moisture had drained from Clementine's mouth.

"Then how . . . ," Alfred began, until Erlene glared at him.

"He had a knife," Clementine whispered as she pulled the coat tighter around her.

Erlene's breath caught in her chest. "You need to see a doctor, and we have to call the police."

"I told you it was Gary, didn't I?" Clementine lowered her head, looking up at Erlene and Alfred through her eyelashes.

Alfred turned to stare at his wife. She hadn't told him. "That son of a bitch," he mumbled.

Erlene put her hand on his arm while she spoke to Clementine. "The most important thing now is to get you to the hospital. Can you walk or should we call an ambulance?"

"Don't call any ambulance." Clementine rested her forehead in her hand. "Y'all take me to the emergency room, I guess. I know that's what I'm supposed to do." Her voice fell away at the end of the sentence, as if that were the last thing on earth she wanted to do.

"Alfred, go warm up the car before we get in," Erlene said. As he passed by her, she said, "Pull up as close to the door as you can," and added in a whisper, "Call the police." Alfred nodded. A few minutes later, he came back and told them the car was ready. Erlene took hold of Clementine's arm to help her stand, but Clementine knocked her hand away.

"I'm okay," she murmured. Pushing against the table beside her, she rose from the chair. In a single-file line with Alfred leading and Erlene following Clementine, the threesome went to the car. Erlene wanted to help Clementine get settled in the back seat, but she was afraid to touch her again. Clementine managed on her own, Erlene climbed in beside her, and Alfred drove away as a three-quarter moon broke through the clouds above Tanner.

After racing through the streets, ignoring traffic lights when he could, Alfred stopped the car in front of the hospital emergency entrance. "Stay here," he said to Erlene and Clementine. "I'll be right back." He waved to a couple of ambulance attendants standing at the edge of the driveway and pointed at his car. Then he disappeared inside the building. A few minutes later, he opened the car door. "I got it all set up. We're going down the hall past the waiting room straight to an exam room." Erlene said a quick prayer thanking God that Alfred worked at the hospital and knew the right people to talk to.

Carefully, Clementine climbed out of the car. She hadn't said a word on the drive over. Erlene figured she was in shock. Erlene herself felt a little stunned. She'd never known anybody who was raped at knifepoint. Sure, there were plenty of girls who'd had sex when they didn't want to. They got talked into it or they were drunk. This was different. The thought of what Clementine had gone through put a knot in her throat. She wondered what she would have done in her place. Maybe she'd have fought back more. She'd had to fight all her life for everything she'd managed to accomplish. There sure hadn't been any extra money in her family. Not even enough for community college, so she'd gone to school only when she could save enough from her job at the mill. It had taken her a long time, but she made it. And here she was taking care of Clementine, who seemed to have had everything handed to her. She followed Clementine into the hospital, ready to catch her if she stumbled or collapsed.

Hit with the bright lights snaking down the long corridor and bouncing off the pale walls, Clementine put her arm in front of her eyes. Erlene blinked, looking to see where Alfred was motioning for them to go. As Clementine entered the tiny room with only an exam table and a chair, she whispered to Erlene, "Y'all wait outside." Erlene started to object, but a nurse took her arm. "It's all right," she said. "I'll stay with her. She's probably more comfortable with just the doctor and me."

Alfred put his arm around Erlene's shoulders and guided her back to the waiting room. Standing near the door, dressed in police blues, Charles Yarboro and Vincent McQuarrie waited. When they saw Alfred, they nodded their heads toward the hall and followed Alfred and Erlene out of the waiting room.

"How's she doing?" Charles asked once they were in a secluded corner of the hall. Charles was one of only four black police officers in Tanner. He was nearly ten years younger than Erlene, but she knew him because his brother had been in her class in school. She was glad he was on duty that night.

"I think she's in shock," Erlene said in answer to his question. "She's not saying much, and she keeps staring at the floor."

"Is she beat up pretty bad?" Vincent asked. He was older than Charles, probably in his early fifties. Erlene had been at work the day he came to the dentist's office to investigate a robbery. Most of the pain medicine and anesthesia and some cash left in a drawer were missing, but they never caught the thief. "He's hocked the drugs in Charlotte and is probably halfway to Florida by now," Vincent had told them. "Or maybe he never left Tanner. Maybe he or she's still right here." Erlene remembered how he didn't look her in the eye the entire time he searched the office.

"Her face is okay," Erlene said, her voice gruffer than it needed to be. "He forced her with a knife."

Charles started writing in a small pad. "Did she tell you anything else?"

Erlene looked at Alfred, who nodded. "She said it was Gary Wiggins."

"Gary Wiggins?" Vincent's lip curled as his voice scaled upward. "That doesn't make any sense. Gary's worked his tail off to turn his life around since his wife left him. Got that good job at Johnny's and all. I can't see him doing something like this."

"She was quite definite that it was Gary." Erlene didn't like Vincent much, and she was liking him even less now.

Charles kept on writing. "If we're lucky, they'll find some DNA on her," he said. "And we'll check for fingerprints and trace evidence in the shop, although that's kind of pointless since so many people were in there all day." He closed the pad. "We're gonna sit in the waiting room until the doc says we can see her. Are y'all staying?"

"Aren't y'all going after Gary?" Alfred asked. "He's probably out there right now cooking up some alibi."

Vincent shook his head. "We can't question Gary until we talk to Clementine. What y'all tell us is just hearsay."

"Then why the hell'd you ask us what she told us?" Alfred snapped.

"It helps us know what to ask her," Charles said in a calm voice. "Are y'all staying or going?" he asked again.

"We're staying," Erlene said before she walked into the waiting room and planted herself in one of the plastic chairs.

Alfred dropped into the chair next to her. "We could go home now," he said. "Charles and McQuarrie will take care of her."

Erlene's head snapped around so her eyes stared straight into his. "Have you lost your mind? She called me when she was desperate. Me, Alfred. And I'm not going to desert her now."

"Yeah, she called you. Don't you find that a little peculiar? I mean, don't she have some friends she's closer to than you?" In the stuffy waiting room, sweat glistened on Alfred's bald head. More people had come into the ER as the evening wore on. "How come you even wanted to be friends with her?"

"It didn't have anything to do with wanting to. It just happened. You know I asked her to lunch because she went to see Mama and that made Mama so happy. I figured we'd have lunch and it'd be over. But it turned out we enjoyed each other's company, so we did it again."

"I just don't see why you'd want to be friends with her." Alfred pulled a large white handkerchief from his hip pocket and wiped his face and head.

"If you resent Clementine so much, how come you've been so eager to help her tonight?" Erlene spoke louder than she intended, causing two women sitting close to her to look in her direction. Nobody spoke for a few minutes. She'd had no idea Alfred disapproved of her friendship with Clementine. He'd never said anything before.

Then he spoke in a harsh whisper. "Because I can't stand to see no woman, white or black, hurt by some bastard of a man."

"Well, there you go," Erlene whispered back. "When she needed you, it didn't matter who she was. It doesn't matter to me who she is, either. As long as she's good to me, I'll be good to her."

Alfred said no more. He picked up an old copy of *The Tanner Observer* from the table next to him and noisily flipped it open across his lap.

Minutes crawled into hours before the nurse who had spoken to Erlene earlier finally came into the waiting room. "Y'all can see her now," she said. When Erlene, Alfred, and the policemen stood up, Vincent told Erlene and Alfred to wait. He and Charles needed to talk with Clementine alone. After another interminable time watching women ready to deliver babies, vomiting children, and adults with everything from sprained ankles to broken arms come and go through the waiting room, Erlene was relieved when Vincent and Charles came back and told her Clementine wanted to see her.

"Now will you go get Gary?" Alfred asked.

"We're gonna question him," Vincent said as he headed for the door.

"And we'll send somebody from the investigations unit over to the shop to look for evidence," Charles added. "I assume it's locked. We don't want to have to break in. Do y'all have a key?" Erlene nodded. She'd seen the key in the lock where Clementine must have left it when she went back for the computer. The last thing Erlene did before leaving the shop was lock the door and put the key in her pocket. She handed it to Charles now. "Thanks." Charles patted Erlene's arm before he followed Vincent out. Alfred settled into his chair with the newspaper he'd already read three times as Erlene hurried to find Clementine.

Back in the tiny exam room, the lights were off. Clementine, dressed in a hospital gown, was lying on a table under a blanket. She turned her head toward the door when Erlene walked in. No one else was in the room. In the light from the hall, Clementine's eyes were dull, framed with wrinkles accentuated by her pallor. Her damp, matted hair clung closely to her head. Her dry lips were the color of steel.

"Can you hand me those scrubs over there?" she asked softly. "I want to go home."

A set of green scrubs lay on top of Clementine's shoes on the room's lone chair. Erlene handed over the items. "Where are your clothes?" she asked.

"They kept them," Clementine whispered. "They're gonna test them for blood and semen. I don't care. They said I could wear the scrubs. I just want to go home."

Thinking about how cold it was outside, Erlene took off her socks and gave them to Clementine. She planned to share her coat, which was hanging in the waiting room, as well. While she was helping Clementine get dressed, Erlene noticed an array of red marks around her friend's upper arms. Her inner thighs were streaked with long raw scratches and blotched with spatters of pink. She wondered how many more injuries there were that she couldn't see.

"Wait here while I find the doctor and make sure it's all right for you to leave," Erlene said when Clementine was dressed. Clementine's lips tightened, and she gingerly folded her body into the chair where the scrubs had been.

Out in the hall, Erlene chased down a nurse, who said Clementine wasn't her patient, but she'd try to find out what her status was. Directing Erlene toward a metal chair, she took off down the hall. Erlene perched on the hard, cold seat and listened to the muffled sounds of crepe soles on the linoleum floor and urgent voices behind partially closed doors. Finally, another nurse carrying a stack of papers motioned for Erlene to follow her into Clementine's room. When the papers were all signed and the nurse was satisfied that proper protocol had been followed, she told Clementine again that the police would call with the lab results. She also pointed to one of the papers clutched in Clementine's hand, reminding her that it had phone numbers and information about rape counseling.

"She's coming home with us, and we'll make sure she gets some help," Erlene said, even though Clementine shook her head, her face twisted in a scowl.

Bundled in the back seat of Alfred's car with Erlene's coat and a blanket Alfred pulled out of the trunk, Clementine tried to get them to take her home, but Erlene wouldn't hear of it. The threesome crept into the couple's tidy cottage around midnight. Erlene made Clementine eat a little split-pea soup, which seemed to revive her a bit, but when she tried to get her to take a hot bath and go to bed, Clementine folded her arms and refused to move from the couch.

"Get me my phone," she said. "I have to call the police to make sure they arrested Gary." Erlene and Alfred both urged her to wait until morning before making any calls, but her face flushed and her nostrils flared. Nothing would do except for her to call the police station. As she pushed herself up from the couch, her face contorted in a flash of pain. She took a few careful steps toward her purse and cell phone on the kitchen table before Alfred picked up the home phone receiver.

"I'll call," he said. "You don't have any business stressing yourself any more." Usually a gentle man, Alfred seldom raised his voice, but at that moment he spoke with such authority even Erlene wouldn't have crossed him. With shoulders slumped, Clementine slunk back to the couch. Alfred lowered his voice when he spoke into the phone. Erlene couldn't catch everything he said, but he concluded with "Thank you anyway." Clementine waited, her face a mixture of eagerness, apprehension, and dread.

Alfred took his time replacing the receiver. "They wouldn't tell me anything. Said it was an open case and they can't discuss it."

"Let me call them." Clementine started to stand again.

"No. Not now." Erlene moved between her and her purse. "They won't tell you anything either. I promise we'll go down to the police station in the morning. I know you told 'em what happened, but we're gonna tell 'em again, and again if we have to. We'll tell 'em until they believe you." Clementine hunched over and put her head in her hands. Erlene started to rub her back but pulled her hand away when she remembered how Clementine had reacted when she touched her at the shop. "But now you're going to bed. You can take a bath if you want to or not, but you're going to bed."

Clementine looked up from her hands. The skin on her face sagged, giving her a haggard appearance. "Okay. For now. I do want to take a bath. I really, really want to take a bath." Erlene reached out her hand, and Clementine took it, allowing herself to be pulled from the couch. After her bath, Erlene gave her a clean flannel nightgown and soft cotton underpants to put on. She tucked her into the canopy bed that had once belonged to Erlene's daughter but was now only for company. Clementine slept off and on that night, only an hour or so at a time. Erlene curled up in the overstuffed chair beside the bed and dozed occasionally, trying to be awake whenever Clementine opened her eyes. Alfred went to bed, but Erlene heard him up a few hours later, pacing around the house. At three in the morning, the front door opened, and Erlene knew he'd gone outside for a cigarette. For once, she wouldn't fuss at him about smoking. They all needed whatever would get them through the night.

Around eight o'clock the next morning, Clementine sat up in bed and grabbed the clock radio on the table next to her. Erlene jerked her head out of the chair's deep cushion to see what Clementine was doing. "I have to get up," Clementine said. "I have to go to the police station. I have to open the shop."

"Slow down," Erlene said. "We'll go to the police station, but you sure as hell don't have to open the shop today. You need to take it easy for a while." Erlene had read about post-traumatic stress syndrome. She was pretty sure Clementine had been in shock the night before, and she didn't know what to expect today. Clementine needed to be where somebody could keep an eye on her.

"If I don't open the shop, the whole town will know something's wrong." Clementine threw off the covers and tried to stand up, but her knees buckled and she sat back on the bed. She took a deep breath before she continued talking. "And if they find out what happened, they'll either blame me or they'll feel sorry for me, and when they come into the shop, they'll think about me being assaulted there, and it'll make them feel uncomfortable, and they won't come back. And the shop will fail. I won't let Gary take that away from me." She was breathing heavily.

Erlene took hold of her hands. "No. You've got it all wrong. We'll tell people you're sick. Everybody gets sick."

"God help me, I am sick." Clementine's voice trembled and her eyes glistened. "Part of me feels like it's already dead." She lowered her head and rested her face in her hands. When she looked up again, she said, "But I can't close the shop the day after opening day. And not during Valentine's weekend."

With wobbly elbows, she pushed herself up from the bed, shaking loose from Erlene's grasp. "I have to go home and get some clothes and get down to the police station. Can you take me? Or can Alfred?"

Erlene saw the desperation in her friend's eyes. "I'll take you home and to the police station," she said, "but you can't open the shop." Anger flashed across Clementine's face. "You can't open the shop because the crime scene investigation unit's there this morning. And they have your keys."

"How did they get my keys?" Now the anger on Clementine's face mixed with incredulity.

"Charles asked for them last night, so I gave them to him. The sooner the investigators get there, the better."

Clementine looked stunned. "Oh, God. You don't think the police put that awful yellow tape around the shop, do you? Please tell me they wouldn't do that. If they did, the shop's ruined before it even got started."

Erlene had no idea what the police would do, but she wasn't about to let Clementine know. "Of course not. They just do that for murders. Don't you worry about that."

"Now we *have* to go to the shop," Clementine said. "I have spare keys. We'll get them at my house."

Erlene wanted to force Clementine to stay home, but Clementine was a grown woman and she was determined to go. Still, Erlene insisted that she eat breakfast first. "You need strength to do what all you want to do today," she declared and made her shovel in a few bites of the oatmeal Alfred had zapped in the microwave.

On the ride to her house, Clementine mapped out a plan. "After I get some clothes and the keys, we'll find out what's going on at the shop. Oh, lord, I hope we can open this morning. That's what I need you to do, Erlene. Can you please open the shop while I get my van and go to the police station? Please. I need you more than ever. Just let the folks look around, tell them I'll be there soon if they have questions, and take their money if they want to buy something. There's change and small bills in the cash register, and there's a bank bag lying around somewhere if Gary didn't take it."

"I don't know." Erlene stared at the road, not at all sure how any of this was going to play out. "I wanna help you, but you gotta take care of yourself, Clementine. You're in no shape to be driving around town alone. You probably shouldn't even be driving. You gotta be sore." Erlene let the last comment out without thinking. A flush of heat spread up her neck and face.

"I'm fine," Clementine said. "Just please do what I ask you to."

Erlene was getting irritated with Clementine's bullheadedness. If she wouldn't listen to Erlene, maybe she'd listen to somebody else. "You need to call your children and tell 'em what happened," Erlene said. "They deserve to know their mother's been hurt."

"I'll call them when I'm sure the police are going to arrest Gary. I don't want them worrying that it's going to happen again."

Neither one spoke for the rest of the ride. Erlene sat in Clementine's living room while Clementine went into her bedroom to change clothes.

When they arrived at the antique shop, two members of the crime scene investigation unit stood outside the back door. One talked on a cell phone, and the other loaded equipment into a police van. Clementine flung open the car door and rushed over to the one with the equipment. "What did you find?" Her voice was strained.

"This is police business, ma'am. You'll have to talk to the officer in charge."

"I'm Clementine Loftis. I'm the victim here, and this is my shop. Tell me what you found."

Erlene slid an arm around Clementine's shoulders to hold her still, since she looked like she was ready to punch the investigator. "We'll find out later," Erlene whispered. Then she turned to the investigator. "Are you finished here?"

"Yes, ma'am." He slammed the van door.

"You're not going to put up any of that yellow tape, are you?" Erlene asked.

"No, ma'am. We're done."

The other investigator ended his phone call, and both men started to get into the van.

"I want my keys," Clementine said, "the keys to my shop."

"They're police property, ma'am," the one who had been on the phone said. "You'll have to ask for them at the station."

"It's okay," Erlene crooned to Clementine as the men drove away. "You're going there anyway."

Clementine's van waited behind the shop just as she had left it. She patted the fender on her way to the back door. Before she could unlock the door, Erlene pushed ahead of her and insisted on going into the shop first. She didn't know how Clementine would react when she saw the scene again, particularly the sofa. Clementine, however, seemed to ignore everything as she searched for the bank bag, which eventually turned up in the corner next to the bathroom. Clementine checked to make sure the money was there, then handed the bag and the keys to Erlene.

"I'll be back as soon as I can," she said. "It's past time to open, so go ahead and do it." As Clementine drove away in the van, Erlene wondered what had happened to the papers with the information about rape counseling. If Clementine wouldn't call them, she would.

The Tanner police station stood two blocks north of Main Street in a dull-red brick building constructed in 1920. Offices for the station, the local division of the county health department, and the local registrar of deeds were on the first floor, topped with jail cells on the second. When Clementine was a child, she'd been terrified to walk into the building for her annual typhoid shot at the health department because sometimes she could hear yelling coming from the barred windows on the second floor. She remembered her small self, clad in shorts and a halter top, her sandaled feet planted against the concrete as her mother tried to drag her inside. The sidewalk was quiet today, with all the windows and doors closed up tight to keep out the cold. Still, the yelling echoed in Clementine's head.

She threw open the heavy door and walked in. It was the first time she'd set foot in the station. Although some of her teenage friends had been taken in for shoplifting, her parents would have disowned her if she'd been with them. No bigger than her kitchen, the entry space was separated from the open squad room behind it by a dark wooden counter topped with glass extending to the ceiling. A small hole covered by a piece of metal with slits for talking was located in the middle of the glass, directly above a scooped-out space in the counter for passing papers through, not unlike the ticket window at the movies. A burly policeman perched on a stool behind the slits, his shoulders hunched over a newspaper.

Clementine leaned toward the slits. "I'm here to see Charles Yarboro and Vincent McQuarrie."

The policeman turned his head toward the glass in a dream-like motion, his eyelids half-closed. "They went off duty at midnight, ma'am. Can somebody else help you?"

She hadn't expected that, but of course they didn't work all the time. She leaned against the counter, trying to decide whether to come back later. Her body ached and her mind felt foggy despite her determination to push through and get things done today. With a quick shake of her head, she said, "I suppose so. I'm Clementine Loftis, and I . . ." The policeman on the stool sat up straight before she could say anything else. The officer at the desk behind him looked away from the cell phone at his ear. "I'm Clementine Loftis," she said again. "I'll talk to the chief."

"Just a minute. I think he stopped by the office before church." The policeman slid his bulk off the stool and disappeared through a door near the back of the room. The other officer quickly ended his phone call and pretended to look at the papers on his desk, but every few seconds, he'd glance up at Clementine. Uncomfortable with his attention, she studied the wanted posters in the glass-enclosed bulletin boards along the wall. She was reading the small print to find out what the only woman pictured had done when a tall, slender man in a business suit came through the door beside the counter.

"Good morning, Mrs. Loftis," he said in a deep voice. "I'm Chief Arnold Tubbs. What can I do for you?" His eyes were steady, his mouth not smiling or frowning. There was no sign of caution or compassion.

"I want to ask what you've done about what happened to me last night," Clementine said. "I'm sure you had a report from Officers Yarboro and McQuarrie."

Chief Tubbs gazed over his shoulder at the policemen in the squad room. "Come with me," he said, leading Clementine through the door and the squad room to his office at the back. As she followed him, Clementine avoided looking at the other officers by fixing her eyes on the back of the chief's head. Within his buzz cut, the gray hairs radiated through the black ones from a central spot in the center, giving the illusion of a pinwheel. Looking at it made Clementine a little dizzy. She was glad when they went inside the dark office and he turned around to close the door. He gestured for her to sit in a vinyl-upholstered chair in front of his metal desk. Instead of sitting behind the desk, he sat in another vinyl chair next to her. "I'm really sorry about what happened," he said. "I guarantee you we'll do everything we can to catch whoever did it."

"I told you who did it," Clementine said. "It wasn't whoever. It was Gary Wiggins." The fluorescent lights in the office were turned off, so the only illumination came from two small windows behind the desk, a goose-necked desk lamp, and a floor lamp off to the side. It was hard to see the chief's face clearly, but she thought she saw a flicker of dismissal.

"You were in a god-awful situation, Mrs. Loftis," he said. "I can't imagine the fear and horror you went through. Plus, it was most likely dark. Didn't you tell Yarboro and McQuarrie that you'd closed the store for the night? So I'm sure you turned out the lights. In those circumstances, you could be mistaken about your attacker. I don't want to jump to any conclusions." His voice sounded factual, not condescending, but Clementine wanted to slap him anyway.

"I'm not mistaken," she said. "Not then, not now. It was Gary Wiggins. I know him, I saw him, I heard his voice. Why haven't you arrested him?"

Chief Tubbs tried to lay his hand on Clementine's arm, but she jerked away. "You have to understand I can't share all the details of our investigation with you. We've talked with Mr. Wiggins, and we may talk with him again, but that's all I can tell you. It's our job to presume innocence until we have reason to believe otherwise. And a rape accusation is a stigma that can stay with someone forever. You know how those things go. A man could be perfectly innocent, but people will always think of him as the guy who was accused of rape. There'll always be a shadow hanging over him. I'm not gonna do that."

Nausea began to crawl around Clementine's stomach. "What about me? What about my feelings and my reputation, not to mention my injuries? Do you want to see the bruises on my arms and the scrapes on my thighs, because I'll show you. I'll even show you—"

"No, no," the chief interrupted and leaned back in his chair. "I know you're hurt. I know somebody hurt you something awful. I'm just not convinced it was Mr. Wiggins."

"Why don't you believe me?" Clementine tried to keep the urgency out of her voice. She didn't want this impassive man to think she was getting hysterical.

"I need evidence. The investigation team is sending off some tests, including the swabs taken at the hospital. Maybe when they get the results back, I'll have more to go on. If we're lucky, the swabs will have the rapist's DNA. The shop was covered in fingerprints, so there's nothing usable there."

Clementine felt the heat rise in her cheeks. "So if you don't think it was Gary, who do you think it was?"

"We're trying to find anybody who was still downtown around that time," Chief Tubbs said. "They might have seen a man in the alley. It's all we've got to go on right now."

Placing her palms on the arms of her chair, Clementine pushed herself to her feet. She wasn't getting anywhere with this man. "Thanks for your time," she said.

"Before you go, let's set up a meeting for you with one of our victim's advocate volunteers." The chief was immediately standing.

"No need," Clementine said, "but I do need the keys to my antique shop. Your investigation unit has them. I assume they're through with them."

Tubbs nodded and made a quick phone call.

When Clementine left his office, a policeman met her in the squad room with her keys. She stared at him and any other officer who dared look at her as she marched out of the station. She didn't need a victim's advocate. She was damn well going to be her own advocate, no matter what it took

5

David learned about the rape around eleven o'clock on Saturday night. His day had already been a trying one. Congress had failed to act in time to extend the federal benefits program for displaced workers beyond February 13, which was the next day, and David had spent most of the afternoon at the counseling center fielding phone calls from worried men and women who knew about the deadline. The older ones depressed him the most. He couldn't imagine how bleak job prospects must look for a guy who's fifty-five years old and his only skill is running a loom. How could Congress have let the program run out? When he heard despondence creeping into his voice, he closed the center.

After a quick stop by Back in the Day to see how Clementine's opening day was going, he went home, had dinner, and was dozing in front of the TV when the phone rang that night. The noise startled him awake. Still drowsy, he fumbled for his cell phone. "Yeah?" he mumbled into the phone.

"David? It's Vince McQuarrie." It took David a few seconds to remember who Vince was. They'd both been in the Kiwanis Club a few years back, and David had sold Vince policies for his car and house. Maybe he'd been in a car accident. "I know it's late, but there's something you need to know." Vince's voice was hushed, almost a whisper. "Clementine Loftis was raped tonight."

David sat up. "Is she all right?"

"She was at the hospital when I talked to her. She looked okay to me. Nothing broken or bruised too bad. I've seen rape victims that looked a lot worse."

"How'd it happen?" David turned to his watch to see what time it was.

"I can't tell you no more. I'm at the station now, and we got more work to do. I know you two been seeing each other, and since she ain't got no family in town, I thought you oughta know."

"Is she still at the hospital?"

"I don't know. We been gone more'n an hour. I just now got a chance to call you. I gotta go. Check with the hospital." Vince ended the call.

David's brain swirled. Crimes like rape didn't happen in his world. He flipped his phone over to Internet access and found the hospital website. So many details. The phone number had to be buried there somewhere. At last he got in touch with the hospital answering service, but the woman said Clementine hadn't been admitted. He tried her home phone and her cell phone, but no answer. He couldn't think of anywhere else she would go. Maybe she was home but just wasn't answering her phone. Grabbing his leather jacket on the way out, he jumped into his Mini Cooper and tore out of the garage like Richard Petty breaking away in Darlington. Fifteen minutes later he was banging on the front door of Clementine's house loud enough to rouse dogs sleeping at the neighbors' houses on either side. But neither his banging nor the dogs' howling brought Clementine to the door. With only the shadowed beams from the streetlight for guidance, he went around the house to her bedroom windows and looked in. Inky darkness inside. He looked into the living room windows and the kitchen windows—more darkness. The neighbors' dogs had settled down, but a light came on in one of the houses. David hoped they wouldn't think he was a burglar or a peeping Tom. He quickly returned to the front of the house and rang the doorbell one last time. She wasn't there.

For the next ten minutes, he sat in his car, trying to figure out where Clementine might be. He wished to God she had called him. He could take care of her. He hated to cause a ruckus before he knew the details of what happened, but he had to find her. He called a few old friends he knew she had visited since she moved back to Tanner, even got one of them out of bed, but nobody had seen her since earlier at the shop. He didn't tell them why he was looking for her. Let them think it was some sort of romantic intrigue—he didn't care.

The only other person Clementine ever talked about was Erlene Duncan. She seemed like a long shot, but he didn't know where else to turn. He rushed back home and found the phone number in the Tanner directory. After two rings, Alfred answered. David told him quickly who he was and what he wanted, but Alfred told him not to come to their house.

"She's okay. I'm telling you. They gave her a good going over at the hospital and released her." Alfred's voice was a husky whisper. "She's got some bruises, Erlene said, and some scratches. She's scared and pissed off as hell"—David smiled for the first time since he heard the news at the thought of how angry Clementine must be—"but she's safe."

"I want to see her." David needed to make sure for himself that she was all right, and he was certain, even though she didn't call him, that she would want him there.

"I'd have to ask her what she wants, and she don't need to have to make any decisions tonight. She don't need anything else to upset her." Alfred breathed heavily. "She's in the bathroom now. Erlene made her take a hot bath. Then she's gonna put her to bed, and that's the best thing. If you want to see her, you come by tomorrow morning."

David was tempted to insist on going over there no matter what. Who were these people to take charge at a time like this? But upsetting them might upset Clementine, and he didn't want to do that. He rubbed his forehead. The image he'd been pushing out of his mind for the past hour was creeping in. "Who did it, Alfred?" he asked quietly. "Does she know?"

Alfred sucked in a loud breath. "She says it was Gary Wiggins."

David remembered when Gary walked into the antique shop before it opened. Clementine had been scared then, but that was a far cry from rape. And Gary was a respected member of the town. He came from several generations of mill workers and was already in his forties when he lost his job as a weave room supervisor. Even though he'd seemed too resentful at first to be helped, he'd become one of the counseling center's best success stories.

"I really need to talk to Clementine," David said.

"I told you. Come by in the morning. Let her get some rest tonight."

"All right." David couldn't keep the resentment out of his voice. "What's your address?" Alfred gave him the information. "Thanks," David mumbled and hung up the phone.

After a long night with very little sleep, David knocked on the front door of Alfred and Erlene's house. The narrow street, dotted with simple houses built in the 1950s to attract veterans flush with GI bill loans, was quiet—no one else stirred so early on Sunday morning. David knocked softly because he thought Clementine might still be asleep. Alfred, unshaven and droopy-eyed, opened the door. "I'm David Adams," David began.

"She ain't here," Alfred said. "She got up this morning still mad as hell and made Erlene take her to get some clothes and her car so she could go to the police station."

David could hardly believe what he was hearing. "You let her go to the police station?" His voice hammered the word *police*.

"We couldn't help it. It ain't like she's a kid and you can tell her what to do."

The idea of Clementine running around town so soon after being attacked was madness. David shook his head to clear his thoughts. "So is that where she is now?"

"I don't know. Let me call Erlene." Alfred left David standing at the door and went into another room. The sound of his muffled voice drifted through the stillness, and then he was back. "Erlene's waiting for her while she gets some clothes. Then she's gonna take her to get her car at the antique shop so she can go to the police station."

David was barreling down the road in minutes, headed for downtown Tanner. On the street in front of the police station, he searched for Clementine's car, but with no luck. He drove through the closest parking lots and still found nothing. "Hell," he said to himself as he maneuvered into a parking space on the street and ran into the station. The policeman behind the glass told him no one had been in the station that morning except himself and another officer sitting behind him at a desk. "And the chief just got here. Not like him to come in on Sunday morning." David banged his fist against the wooden counter in front of the glass. Before the officer could react, he was gone.

Since Alfred said Clementine's van was at the antique shop, he went there next. He didn't see the van in the alley behind the shop where it usually was, but he banged on the back door anyway. "Who's there?" Erlene's voice sounded from inside the shop.

When David identified himself, the door swung partially open, and he stepped across the threshold. Daylight streaming through the big front window brightened the front of the shop, but in the back, a single floor lamp shone over the jewelry counter. Erlene flicked several switches next to the door, and light flooded the shop. "Clementine's not here," she said. "She went to the police station."

"I was just there, and I couldn't find her."

"She left a few minutes ago. You must have just missed her. Probably passed her on the road, or maybe she went somewhere else she didn't tell me about." David turned to go. "If I were you," Erlene said quickly, "I'd sit down and wait. She'll be back before long. I don't know if there's anybody at the station for her to talk to this morning."

"Is she really all right?" David thought he might explode if he didn't get to Clementine soon.

"Physically, I'd say she is, but mentally, I don't know. She's running on adrenaline now, hell-bent on getting her attacker, but she's got to come down sometime. Then anything can happen." Erlene sat in a rocking chair a few feet in front of the jewelry counter. David walked toward the camelback sofa. "That's where it happened," Erlene said. David stopped. The images flooded his mind again. He wanted to tear the sofa apart.

"Is it true she said it was Gary Wiggins?"

Erlene nodded. "She swears that's who it was."

David winced. Now he could no longer question Gary's guilt. He looked at his watch and walked to the front of the shop where he could see Main Street. Lights were on in most of the stores. Vendors bundled in heavy coats and caps gathered at their booths, arranging the items they had taken inside for the night. A few early customers stopped to chat before they scurried inside the stores to get out of the cold. "Clementine's not going to work today, is she?" David called back to Erlene.

"Says she is." Erlene shook her head. David studied her as he returned to the back of the shop. This conversation marked the most words he'd ever exchanged with her. The only reason he knew who she was when she opened the door was he expected her to be there. Yet she apparently was Clementine's closest friend. He wondered how many more surprises were going to hit him today.

Although he wanted to sit down, he couldn't stay still that long. He rounded the camelback sofa, trying hard not to look at it, and walked to the front again. More lights were on in the stores, and more people milled around in the street. "I think I'll go down to the police station," he said.

"Suit yourself, but you might not find her. I know she'll be back here eventually. She told me to open the shop. She'd like it if you stayed and helped."

David made another turn around the shop. Erlene was right. Clementine would come back here or at least she would call. "Okay. What do you want me to do?"

"Greet the customers"—Erlene nodded at a few people coming through the front door—"while I see if I can find any cookies Clementine had left over from yesterday. Maybe there's even some tea."

A light stream of customers drifted in and out over the next hour. Nobody asked about Clementine, but David couldn't think about anything else. He envied Erlene's apparent serenity as she talked to customers or sat in the rocking chair.

When the back door finally opened, the sound shot through David like an arrow. He ignored a cluster of customers standing near him and ran to the back of the shop. Clementine stood inside the door, her face pale as the white collar rising above her wool cape. As David pulled her to him, a tremble shook her shoulders. He wanted to hold her close, to protect her from anybody who would harm her, but she quickly pulled away.

"I'm fine," she said softly, turning her head away from the customers. Erlene had nodded when she came in, but kept her place near the front of the shop.

"What can I do to help?" David whispered. "Anything. I'll do anything."

Clementine slid her arms out of the cape and hung it on the rack beside the door. "For now, act like nothing happened. I don't want to be the talk of Tanner."

"Did you go to the police station? What did they say?" David couldn't stand the idea of doing nothing. Somebody had to do something.

"I'll tell you later." Clementine looked toward the customers, her eyes fixed on the activity in the shop.

David wanted to scream. How could the world go on like normal? He couldn't stay there and act nice. But if she wanted it kept quiet, he could help her with that. Keeping a rape secret in Tanner would be no easy task. The police, the hospital staff, all had neighbors and friends they'd likely tell. One thing might help. "If you want to keep it quiet, you have to keep it out of the newspaper," he said. "They print everything on the police blotter, and some people read that stuff like it's a crime novel."

Clementine nodded. "You can do that for me. Find Quentin Harper and make sure he doesn't put it in the paper."

Quentin was editor of *The Tanner Observer*. He wouldn't be in the office on a Sunday morning, but David could find him at home or at church. Glad to have something concrete he could do to help Clementine, he kissed her on the cheek and left.

Outside in the cold air, he dialed Quentin's home phone number. "Stay there," David told him. "I have something important to talk with you about, and I'll be right there."

~

Quentin Harper wasn't the most amiable of men. After taking over the newspaper in 1995, he fired the only two reporters the paper had and replaced them with a single colleague he brought with him from Greensboro. Quentin was rumored to have said the new reporter could do more work in an afternoon than the first two did in an entire day. Like most people in town, David resented Quentin's ruthlessness, but he had to admit the newspaper articles were sharper and better researched than they'd ever been.

Quentin was waiting for him in his sparsely furnished living room. A brown leather sofa, a few tables, and a couple of chairs lined the mostly bare walls. Quentin invited David to sit on the sofa and offered him coffee. David took the seat but declined the coffee. He didn't want to drag the meeting out. "Last night," he began, "one of Tanner's merchants was raped in her own store."

"Yeah, I heard about it," Quentin said as he settled into an easy chair next to the sofa. "Clementine Loftis."

"How did you hear?" This was exactly what David didn't want to happen.

"Can't say. Newspaper sources, you know." Quentin sat in a straight-back chair, his spine rigid as the chair.

"Are you going to report it in the paper?"

"I should. It's news."

"But you don't have to. And you especially don't have to print her name. She'd like to have her privacy respected, and she sent me here to ask for that. She's been through enough."

Quentin's eyebrows crowded his eyes. "I also heard she accused a Tanner man of being the rapist, but there's been no arrest."

"So if there's no arrest, there's no news." David leaned forward to drive home his point.

"That's not exactly true. A crime is news with or without an arrest. I just can't name the accused unless he's been arrested."

"Then don't name anybody. Just let it go, Quentin. It'll do more harm than good. There must be plenty of other stuff to fill the newspaper. You don't need this."

"We don't just fill the newspaper. We're here to inform people. And maybe do the community some good. You know, most media people think that omitting names of rape victims from news stories perpetuates the stigma attached to the victims. That they have something to be ashamed of. We wouldn't omit the name of a robbery victim. Victims are guiltless." Quentin cleared his throat.

"Look," David said. "Clementine's just opened her store. She doesn't want customers staying away because they're embarrassed to look at her or standing around the shop staring at her like she's some kind of curiosity. That shop is her life right now. If you want to do some community good, help her protect it as well as herself."

"People are going to find out, whether it's in the paper or not."

"Yeah, but you don't have to help them." Heat rose in David's face.

Quentin folded his arms and pursed his lips. "Okay," he said. "I won't print anything until there's an arrest. But if there's an arrest, all bets are off."

It was a half victory at best, but David figured it was all he was going to get right now. "Thanks," he said and stood to leave. He walked toward the front door with Quentin following him. The cold air was like a splash of ice water on his hot face as the door shut behind him.

Back in the Mini, he drove toward the antique shop. At the last minute, just before he reached downtown, he made a right turn and sped north on one of Tanner's main thoroughfares. Maybe he wouldn't stop when he got there, but more likely he would. Johnny's Restaurant wouldn't open until noon when the church crowd came pouring in for lunch. But Gary would be there getting ready, David was sure. He drove past the neon sign twice before slipping into the parking lot. Only five or six cars were there, all parked in the back.

David tried the door, expecting it to be locked, but the knob turned easily. The dining room was empty except for a server filling salt and pepper shakers. When David was a child, the restaurant had looked more like a diner with a counter and stools facing a grill along one wall. When Johnny took it over from his dad, he ripped out the counter and grill, made himself chef, and upgraded the menu to include specialty items like salmon and crème brûlée. The people of Tanner loved it. In 2006, Johnny renovated the kitchen and built an addition to the dining room to accommodate twenty more tables. David looked across the expanse of gleaming tabletops. "We're not open yet. Come back at noon," the server said.

"I'm here to see Gary Wiggins. Could you ask him to come out here?"

The server disappeared into the kitchen. In a few seconds, Gary appeared, dressed in a striped shirt and sparkling white chef's coat. His navy-blue Dockers were boot cut to fit over his leather Wellingtons. "Well, don't you look all fresh and crisp?" David sneered. "You oughta see Clementine Loftis this morning. She doesn't look so good."

"What the hell are you talking about?" Gary's large forehead rolled into horizontal wrinkles. The server peeked around the kitchen door.

"You know what I'm talking about. You know what you did last night."

Gary turned his palms upward and shrugged in a gesture of innocence. "I was here late on account of we had problems with the main stove, and that backed us up. It was a busy night."

"Not so busy you couldn't stop by Clementine's antique shop." David's chest tightened. His arms tingled. Images of Gary and Clementine crowded into his brain again. He couldn't stand looking at Gary another minute. "You can lie to the police, you can lie to anybody you want to, but you can't fool me." Like a blast from a cannon, David's fist shot out toward Gary's chin. Gary turned instantly, catching the blow on his shoulder.

"What the hell?" Gary shoved David against the hostess desk. David regained his stance quickly, ready to take another swing, but Gary had maneuvered behind a table. "Get away from me, you crazy bastard. I wasn't anywhere near Clementine Loftis last night. I was here and I was at the hardware store. That's it. You can ask the police."

The loud voices and scuffling sounds had drawn the cooks and Johnny out of the kitchen. Johnny's necktie hung loosely around the open collar of his shirt, which revealed his massive neck. His surprised expression showed he wasn't used to seeing brawls in his restaurant and wasn't sure how to handle this one, but he raised his chin and looked directly at David.

"You need to leave," he said. "If you cause any more trouble, I'll call the police." His wide girth and bulging shoulders should have been intimidating, but David wasn't about to back down.

"You just do that," David said. He glared at Gary. "I'm not through with you." Wanting more than anything to take another swing and make sure this one hit its target, David stared at the man's jaw. Muscles twitched in his arm, ready to strike again. The twitch echoed at his temple. Aided by self-control he didn't know he had, he walked to the door. Next time he wouldn't miss.

6

After David left the antique shop to go see Quentin, Clementine stood inside the back door and surveyed the swarm of customers. Two women she remembered from high school sifted through a box of Victorian silverware, matching up place settings on a Queen Anne table. A group of older women sporting wool scarves with matching caps clustered around the jewelry case. Near the front door, a man extended a tape measure from the top of a walnut table to the floor while a woman stood next to him with an apprehensive expression. Some shoppers murmured "excuse me" as they squeezed by others. Clementine felt a trickle of pleasure at the sight. So many customers, and it was only the second day the shop had been open. She wanted to wallow in the experience, soak up the joy of a dream come true after so many months of planning, working, and worrying, but all she could think about was what had happened the night before.

An emptiness in her gut kept reminding her of what she had lost, even though she couldn't quite name it. Was it her innocence? Her trust? The part of her dream that said Tanner was the perfect place to carry out this chapter of her life? Or even worse, her belief that she could live without constantly being afraid. Whatever it was, it had taken up residence with the deep sense of loss that she'd lived with ever since Gordon died. His heart attack had been sudden and unexpected and left her stunned. What would he do if he were here now? She longed to talk with him, and the ache of his absence had grown worse since the rape.

For solace, she patted the small rose-quartz pendant that hung on the necklace beneath her blouse. Her daughter, Elizabeth, had brought it to her from California when Gordon died. "Wear it always, Mom," Elizabeth said. "It opens your heart and helps rebalance shock and trauma in the heart region."

Clementine had failed to wear it yesterday, but she made sure to put it on when she dressed that morning. At Elizabeth's suggestion, she also kept a small piece of amethyst in her purse. The power of the purple crystal lay in its ability to cleanse, protect, and calm. She liked knowing it was close by even though it had failed to protect her from Gary.

Tenderly, she moved her hand from the pendant across the denim jumper she was wearing. She had chosen it for its loose fit. Walking was uncomfortable, but she needed to move about. Suddenly someone was tugging at her hand.

"Com'ere," Erlene said. "We have a question for you about the reverse painting lamp."

Clementine struggled to refocus. She couldn't succumb to thinking about the attack or she'd be overwhelmed. All morning she'd been driven to get dressed, open the shop, go to the police station, and that had kept her mind straight. The moment's pause after David left had been a mistake. Pulling her mind away from the fear and loss that threatened to engulf her took all the strength she could muster. She followed Erlene.

A woman with a strip of fur covering her ears peeked under the lamp's large dome. As Clementine and Erlene approached, she jerked her head up and clipped the dome's underside. When the dome wobbled on its pin, Clementine shuddered. The dome gave the lamp its value, close to two thousand dollars. "What would you like to know about this lamp?" she asked as she steadied the dome.

"How old is it?" The woman ran her fingers up the lamp's dark bronze base.

"It was made around 1910," Clementine said. "It's art nouveau."

"Looks like a seascape to me," the woman said as she moved her fingers up to the painted scene.

Erlene patted Clementine on the back and slipped away. Clementine smiled, pleased that she didn't recoil from the touch. In her mind, she knew Erlene was only showing support and concern, but Clementine couldn't trust her body not to react. She wasn't completely in control. Fortunately, no one was staring at her. And there was no shortage of customers. Still, she couldn't help feeling they all knew and were just being polite. "Seascapes were popular in these types of lamps," she said. "And so were sunsets. With this lamp, you get both."

"It's not signed, is it?" The woman pushed her fur strip, which had fallen onto her forehead, back to the top of her head.

The question surprised Clementine. The woman didn't seem familiar enough with antiques to know that many of these lamps were signed by the artist. "No, it's not," she said.

The woman nodded thoughtfully. "Thanks for your help." Her voice trailed off as she moved away from the lamp. Clementine turned her attention to the man and woman who were still measuring the walnut table. Their attention to detail marked them as potential buyers, whom Clementine needed to approach. To reach them, she had to pass the camelback sofa. She wanted to avert her eyes, but her gaze was drawn like a sniper's laser beam. She was suddenly lightheaded. "Erlene," she said with a wobbly voice. "Help me slide this sofa out of the way. I think it's blocking some other pieces."

Erlene's eyes widened when she saw the problem. "Oh, honey," she whispered. "Let me take care of that," and she hurried to pull a few chairs away from the wall so the sofa could be moved behind them.

After much debate about space in their living room and numerous questions about the table's origin, the couple decided to buy it. The sale marked the most expensive item sold in the shop so far. Clementine took special joy in printing out the receipt, the horror of the sofa temporarily forgotten. The remaining hours of the morning saw sales of only small items—coasters, plates, Bakelite bracelets and boxes—but at least merchandise was moving. Clementine approached customers more than she normally would have. She knew antique buffs liked being left alone to browse, but talking with them kept her mind focused on the shop.

Around noon, David returned. His face creased with worry lines, he waited while Clementine finished her conversation with a customer. When she could get free, she cornered him at the back of the shop. "What did Quentin say?"

"Don't worry. He's not going to print anything." David's voice was edgy, and he seemed to be watching activity going on behind Clementine. "Don't you want to go home?" When Clementine shook her head, he said, "Then I'm staying."

"Good. I need you to do something for me. Take that sofa down to the basement. Please." Clementine pointed at the offending piece of furniture, her face still turned in another direction.

"Oh, my God. I should have done that when I was here before." David ran to the sofa and began tugging the arm. He moved the sofa a couple of feet before he went over and whispered to Erlene. Together they lifted the sofa and carried it down the stairs.

Clementine was relieved the activity caught no customers' attention. As David and Erlene worked, she said a silent prayer of gratitude for them. She didn't want to be a burden, but she needed them now. For her sanity, she tried to believe Gary wouldn't come back any time soon, but she couldn't be sure. "Thanks," she said softly and moved away as a small woman waved to get her attention.

She was explaining the significance of wear marks on a ban-ister-back chair when Charles Yarboro came into the shop. He wore a navy-blue overcoat, but the police hat showed he was in uniform, probably going back on duty soon. He walked directly to Clementine, causing the customer to shy away. When no one else came near, he said in a hushed voice, "I heard you were down at the station today, talking to Chief Tubbs." He took off his hat and brushed it against his sleeve. "Was he helpful?"

Clementine's hope that Charles had news about Gary van-ished. "Not much. He doesn't believe me." She tried to hide the despair in her voice, but couldn't.

"That's what I came to tell you. It's too soon." Charles turned his back to the shop, shielding their conversation. "We can't do anything till we get the DNA results back. Tubbs isn't going after any suspects until he has more evidence. They took fingernail scrapings, didn't they?"

"Sure, but there was nothing there. I didn't scratch him."

"Okay, but I know they took swabs. The chief is trying to get a warrant for the clothes Gary wore last night and for a DNA sample from him, but it doesn't look good. I shouldn't be telling you any of this, but I think you have a right to know."

A man with a short gray beard began examining the floor lamp behind Charles. Clementine put her hand on Charles's arm to signal him to be quiet. "We can't talk about this here."

She led Charles to the jewelry case in the back of the shop, which was free of perusers. Leaning across it, as if she were pointing out a specific piece to Charles, she murmured, "How long do I have to wait?"

Charles bent over the case. "Probably sixty to ninety days at least, depending on how backed up the lab is. We use one in Charlotte that moves things through pretty fast."

"I can't wait three months." Clementine's voice scaled out of its previous hush. When Charles glanced over his shoulder toward the front of the shop, Clementine realized her error and clapped her hand over her mouth.

Charles hunched closer over the counter. "The only time the lab will rush DNA results is for a murder case. I hate to say it, but rape is pretty low priority. Still, you're going to need DNA if Gary really did it. He has an alibi."

"What alibi? I told you he was at Pete's, which puts him just three stores down from my shop right before it happened. He was there. Did you talk to Pete?"

"We did. I called him last night and got him out of bed. He said Gary came to the store to get a thermostat to fix the stove. After he left, Pete saw him drive out of the alley without stopping. Said he was heading toward the restaurant."

"I don't care if Pete saw him drive away. He didn't watch him all the way to the restaurant, did he?"

"No, he didn't watch him all the way to the restaurant, but he knew exactly what time Gary left his store because he was pissed off. Excuse me. He was irritated with Gary for keeping him at work late." Charles cleared his throat. "Gary left the hardware store at five forty-seven. Pete said he looked at his watch when Gary walked out the door. Then he followed Gary out and saw him drive out of the alley as Pete was getting into his car. Johnny said Gary got back to the restaurant at six fifteen. He knew for sure because one of the servers asked to go home sick just as Gary walked in, so Johnny looked at the clock to see what time she left. Chief Tubbs says Gary couldn't have stopped off anywhere between Pete's and the restaurant."

Clementine sighed. "Do I need a lawyer?"

"Criminals need lawyers. You need evidence."

The front door banged shut, and one of Clementine's high school friends stood just inside. "Hey, Clementine," she called. Everyone looked in her direction. Clementine waved.

Charles replaced his hat on his neatly cropped hair. "I'll let you know as soon as we hear anything from the tests." He walked toward the door. Clementine wondered why Charles came to the shop. Before he showed up at the hospital, they'd never met, yet he was talking to her now like they were friends. She motioned to Erlene to come back to the jewelry case.

"Charles Yarboro seems to have quite an interest in my situation," she whispered when Erlene reached her. "He hardly knows me. Why does he care?"

A glimmer played in Erlene's eyes. "Because I asked him to. Charles is a good man. I know his family. They're kind people, always helping other folks, so I knew Charles would be sympathetic toward you. I just asked him to keep you in the loop of information as much as he could. A lot of those guys down at the station won't view you as kindly."

Clementine squeezed Erlene's hand. She wouldn't have expected her friend to act so boldly on her behalf. "Thank you, Erlene. Sometimes I think I don't deserve a friend like you." A sigh escaped her throat. "The news Charles brought wasn't good. He said it could take two to three months or more to get the DNA results back. Two to three months I have to wait for justice."

Erlene's expression showed the determination that characterized her face most of the time now. "We'll wait together," she said.

The next days passed in a jumble of customers, aches, and not being able to stop looking out the windows, wherever Clementine was. Erlene and David stayed with her all day Sunday, and David stayed with her Sunday night. After cooking spaghetti for dinner, he insisted they watch TV. When bedtime came, he asked for sheets and pillows to make up the couch, saying he wanted to be close to all the doors, just in case. Clementine knew he didn't have any romantic ideas—he just wanted to make her feel safe.

On Monday, Valentine's Day, he had to go work, and so did Erlene, but they both managed to stop by the shop several times during the day. As long as there were browsers in the shop, Clementine stayed calm, her attention focused on her beloved antiques and the pleasure of talking about the pieces, hoping someone would love them enough to take them home. A few lulls in the afternoon, however, left her alone. During those times, she checked the back door lock and stood near the front window watching people scurry from store to store and booth to booth. The hearty merchants with their outdoor sales areas had made it through the cold weekend and had obviously girded themselves to stick it out through the final day of the festival. The welcome banner sagged a bit after battling the wind for days, but its appearance was still cheery. Clementine watched it sway above the movement on the sidewalk below. Anybody who was close enough to notice her would think she was merely eager to greet any customers who came through her door. They wouldn't know she was standing there because she was afraid to be alone in the back of the shop.

At five o'clock, as the last shopper was leaving and Clementine stood by the front door ready to turn the bolt, Erlene rushed into the shop. "How you doing?" she asked quickly.

"I'm fine. Really. I'm closing now, and David's taking me to dinner. I appreciate your concern, honest I do, but you can go home and enjoy Valentine's Day with Alfred." Clementine recognized the curl in Erlene's lip. "I know you don't believe me. Why don't you stay until David gets here?"

Erlene settled herself on a Shaker bench. "And while I'm here, I've got something for you to do. You can't wait any longer." She slid her arms out of her blue wool coat. "Get your phone."

"What for?" Clementine had never heard Erlene sound so brusque.

"You're gonna call your kids and tell 'em what happened to you. Don't look at me like that. It's been two whole days. You can't wait any longer. They need to know, and you need to tell 'em. What if it was your mama? Wouldn't you want to know?"

"If my mother were raped, of course I'd want to know," Clementine said, her head bowed because she couldn't look Erlene in the face when she told her the next part. "And my children deserve to know about me, but I don't want them to know. I don't want their pity. I don't want them to think they have to take care of me." She stopped herself before she said more.

"For heaven's sake, woman." Erlene took Clementine's hand and gently pulled her to sit on the bench. "It's rape, not a punch in the eye. If you can't turn to family in bad times, what's the point in having a family? Now where's your damn phone?" Erlene rarely cursed. Her choice to do it now told Clementine she wasn't going to let this go until Clementine called the kids.

"In my purse. Behind the jewelry case."

Erlene retrieved the purse and pushed it into Clementine's lap. "Now call."

Clementine attempted to reach both her children, but only her son, Jackson, answered. With her eyes focused on a painting of autumn trees that always drew her in, she tried to avoid seeing the awful images as she described what happened as tersely as possible. But even the glorious colors of the painting couldn't stop the flashes in her mind—Gary's knee between her thighs, the knife pressing the soft tissue beneath her chin, the pain between her legs. She stopped talking and bent over with a wrenching cramp in her gut.

Jackson reacted exactly as she expected. "I'll be there as soon as I can get a flight. Is there anybody you can stay with? You shouldn't be home alone. I thought this was supposed to be a quiet little town. Don't they have any police there?" He raved on for a while before assuring her again he would be there as soon as possible and ending the call.

"No need to call Elizabeth again," Clementine said between deep breaths. "He'll spread the word, and I left her a message that I tried to reach her." She sat up and glared at Erlene. "Are you satisfied?"

Erlene nodded, her mouth clamped in a firm line. "You need them," she said. "You might not know it, but you do. Families have to stick together, so don't ever give yours a reason to break apart. If you do, the pain will dog you the rest of your life. I know that for a fact." She turned away from Clementine with a glint in her eye that might have been a tear.

Momentarily startled out of her own misery, Clementine wondered what family separation troubled Erlene so deeply. "I believe you," she said, "and I'm glad you're my friend."

The two women sat in silence until Clementine let out a short laugh. Erlene glanced at her sideways. "What's so funny? That's the first time you've sounded normal since Saturday."

Clementine pointed at a tiny gray mouse running between the legs of a table in the corner. "Can you imagine? A few weeks ago I thought mice and holes in the walls were the biggest problems I had. Wish I'd set a trap for Gary." She started to laugh again, but the laugh caught in her throat. Erlene silently patted her hand.

A few seconds later, David knocked on the front door. When neither woman moved, he waved and pulled his coat collar closer around his neck. "Reckon he's trying to tell us it's cold out there," Erlene said as she turned the lock and opened the door.

"I know I'm early." David smiled at Clementine. "I was afraid you were alone."

"No chance of that with both you guardian angels hovering over me." Clementine forced a smile. "Thanks for coming, Erlene. You can turn me over to David now."

"See you tomorrow." Erlene slipped out the door.

"Since we've got some extra time, let's go have drinks first. The restaurant has a great lounge." David walked toward the back of the store to get Clementine's coat.

The ride to Charlotte was difficult for Clementine. As she watched approaching headlights zip by and taillights glow ahead of them, the same disturbing images slipped before her eyes. She was glad when they reached the restaurant, a cozy space with white tablecloths and candles flickering in hurricane globes. She was especially glad she recognized nobody, so maybe she could relax. As she and David sipped martinis and soaked up heat from the fire in the colonial fireplace, he opened her hand and laid a large red envelope across it. Immediately, she remembered the valentine she selected for him the week before, the vintage valentine that was lying on the table in her bedroom. He must have recognized the look of regret on her face. "I didn't expect anything from you," he said. "It's just a card."

She ripped the envelope and stared at the simple heart design on the front of the card. Inside, the printed words read, "I'm so happy you came into my life," but David had added a caret in the middle of the sentence pointing to the word "back." The simple message unlocked the tears she had suppressed for days, and this time she couldn't stop them. "Excuse me," she said and started for the ladies' room, but David grabbed her arm. The pressure set off explosions in her brain. "Let go of me!" she yelled, jerking her arm away. Others in the restaurant stopped talking and stared.

David released her immediately. "I'm sorry. I'm so sorry." The words followed her into the ladies' room, where she darted into an empty stall. The tears that had felt like a waterfall froze in her ducts while her heart pounded against her chest. She had turned into a freak. Was the rest of her life going to be like this? When Gordon died, she'd been constantly afraid of what was going to happen next. It was all she could do to get up each day and push forward. Moving back to Tanner and opening the antique shop had been an important step for her. She believed that life could be good again. Until now.

She crumpled onto the toilet seat and leaned against the side of the stall. The door to the ladies' room opened and shut several times, toilets flushed, stall doors banged again and again before she was able to stand up.

Out in the foyer, David waited by the door. "I told them you were sick and asked for two entrées to go. They'll be ready soon." He ushered Clementine into a chair and stood in front of her until a waiter brought out two small boxes covered in aluminum foil. On the ride home, David made no attempts at conversation. Instead, he turned the radio to a golden oldies station. Clementine closed her eyes and imagined the music the first time she'd heard it, back when life was simple. They ate at Clementine's house in front of the TV before David made up the couch for himself again and told her to go to bed.

Early the next morning, a blaring telephone woke Clementine from the deepest sleep she'd had all night. The first several hours she'd lain in bed staring at the ceiling like she had every night since the attack. With her eyes still closed, she fumbled for the receiver next to her bed. The excited voice on the line sprang her to full consciousness. Her daughter, Elizabeth, spewed questions just as Jackson had, but she was more concerned about the rapist's coming back. "Don't stay alone anywhere," she said. "Get that man you're seeing to stay with you every minute until Jackson gets there. Do you want me to come too? You know I will if you need me."

Clementine assured her daughter she had hardly been alone at all since Saturday night. "I appreciate your concern, sweetheart. I know you love me, and I need that, but I don't need all of you to come here. Jackson is plenty." After promising to check in with Elizabeth the next day, Clementine hung up the phone and put on her robe.

David was waiting for her in the living room, fully dressed with a cup of coffee in his hand. "Just made," he said, pointing at the cup. "I'll get you some." He rose to go to the kitchen as the phone rang again.

"Good lord." Clementine followed David to the kitchen and grabbed the phone.

Jackson sounded calmer than he had the night before. "My flight gets to Charlotte at ten o'clock. I rented a car, and I'll drive straight to your house, which should put me there when?

About eleven thirty? Twelve? Is it an hour's drive or an hour and a half?"

"Somewhere in between," Clementine said. "Take your time. There's no rush." She sighed as she returned the receiver to the stand. "Now for a few minutes of peace."

David poured her a cup of coffee. "Since the shop's closed on Tuesdays and you're staying home, I canceled my morning appointments." He raised his hand when Clementine started to protest. "It's no big deal. I only had two, so I just rescheduled them. What would you like for breakfast, my darling Clementine?" Hearing the familiar old phrase made Clementine blush. "Oh my God." David said. "Is that pink tinge because you like to be called that or because you don't?"

Clementine pressed her cool palms against her cheeks, hoping to draw away the heat. "It used to embarrass me when I was a kid. You'd think I'd be over that by now, wouldn't you? But when you said it just then, I was right back on the playground surrounded by a bunch of boys singing at the top of their lungs. Third grade was a particularly bad year. Several of the boys learned the song just so they could torment me. I've never forgiven my father for giving me this name."

"Why'd he give it to you? Do you have an old relative named Clementine?"

"No! It's because of that wretched song. He heard Gene Autry or Roy Rogers or some other cowboy sing it, and he liked it. When I was born, my mother knew he was sorry I wasn't a boy, so she let him name me, and that's what he chose." She tried to smile. "Kind of morbid when you think about it. Naming your daughter after a woman in a song who drowns. Maybe he knew then that something awful was going to happen to me."

David pushed her coffee cup toward her. "Drink this and think about something more pleasant. You're alive, and we're going to make everything all right again. So, I repeat. What do you want for breakfast?"

Clementine had no appetite, but she agreed to oatmeal and cinnamon toast. When David gave her the food, she ate a few bites and then shoved it all away. Her stomach was so pinched she may as well have been wearing a corset.

Jackson arrived at about twelve thirty, just in time to meet David before the older man hurried off. Clementine studied her son, amazed as always by how grown up he looked, even if he hadn't taken time to shave. After discovering a container of tuna salad that Erlene must have left in the refrigerator, she offered him a sandwich for lunch. As he ate, he made her tell him the details of the attack again. How many times had she told it now? She'd told the doctors, the police, Erlene, David, Jackson, Elizabeth, and now Jackson again. Not to mention the dozens of times the scene had replayed in her mind. Jackson listened respectfully, his struggle to stay calm showing on his face. For the first time, Clementine got through the telling without a crack in her voice or a choke in her throat. But when she finished, she was so tired.

A muscle in Jackson's jaw tightened. He had always been a compassionate child. "Surely the police are going to arrest this man," he said. "They can't let him get away with it."

Clementine rested her chin in her hands. "I hope not. But we have to wait."

"Wait for what?"

"For DNA test results, and that'll take two or three months."

"Two or three months? So what do we do now?" Jackson's expression reminded Clementine of the way he'd looked when he lost his hamster the summer he was six. He hadn't known what to do then, either.

"We go on with our lives the best we can." Clementine took a bite of her untouched sandwich. She had to get strength from somewhere. "For me, that means working at Back in the Day." Jackson's puzzled expression reminded her she hadn't told him much about her shop. "If you'll drive, I'll give you a tour of the best antique shop in North Carolina. And then, let's drive out to one of the vineyards north of here. I've been meaning to talk to them about joint advertising, and today's as good a day as any. Maybe we can get something together for April, when the tourist traffic picks up at the vineyards and wineries."

With some reluctance, Jackson consented to be her chauffeur. "You really ought to rest, Mom," he said as she was putting on her coat. "Your body and your mind have been through a lot of trauma. Both need time to recuperate."

"Oh, my dear mister health magazine. I know you write tons of articles about how to be healthy, but I know what's best for me, and I can't lie around this house waiting for the police to do something. I have to keep moving until they actually do something or until I come up with another idea to prove what happened. If I don't, I'll go crazy." Clementine looped her arm through his. "Now take me out for a glass of wine on my day off."

The parking lot at Shimlock's Vineyards had more cars than Clementine expected. "Oh, shit," she whispered. "They must be having some sort of post-Valentine's celebration."

"Then let's go home." Jackson circled the rental car around a corner of the lot and headed for the exit.

"No. Let's at least go meet the manager."

The vineyards' rolling fields of dormant grapevines extending for acres in all directions were a more-than-welcome change of scenery. Clementine stood next to the rental car, surveyed the land leading to distant trees, and breathed in the fresh cold air.

Years ago, when Clementine was a child, all the fields near Tanner had been covered in tobacco plants, and most likely this one had been too. The area was a lush river valley, capable of growing almost anything. So it was no surprise that when the tobacco market dwindled, enterprising farmers found the soil and climate perfect for growing chardonnay, cabernet sauvignon, and other grapes that were used to produce fine California and French wines. Clementine loved the vineyards' sense of rebirth and had been to this particular one several times since she moved back to Tanner. While Jackson waited patiently on the other side of the car, she willed herself to soak up the energy pulsing around her. After a few minutes, she walked toward the modern building that had been constructed next to the original farmhouse to provide enough room for weddings and other big events.

As soon as Jackson opened the heavy wooden door, warm air and lively music tumbled out. Not exactly a party—just more people than usual for a Tuesday. The music came from a computer and a pair of large speakers, probably left over from Valentine's Day festivities the day before and waiting to be picked up by the rental company. Several of the tall tables, equipped with high stools, had two or three people standing or sitting around them.

Clementine asked a server if the manager was available. The girl approached one of the tables and spoke to an older man wearing a maroon knit shirt with the Shimlock's logo on it. He immediately left the table and approached them. "Hi, I'm Frank Jessop. How can I help you?" he said.

Clementine introduced herself and Jackson and explained she was the owner of Back in the Day. Since the name raised only a glimmer of recognition from the man, Clementine launched into a detailed description of the shop, being sure to emphasize the strong opening she'd had over the holiday weekend. "I have an idea for a combined promotion that could benefit both of us," she said, "at very minimal cost."

Frank's lined face brightened. "Let's go back to my office where we can talk without all the hubbub out here."

Clementine agreed, but Jackson shook his head. "You two go talk business. I'll stay out here, maybe sample some wine."

Thirty minutes later, Clementine joined her son at a table near the door. "How'd it go?" he asked.

"We made a tentative deal. He agreed to hand out my flyers to customers during April if I'll do the same with his brochures and, since he sells more wine than I sell antiques, I agreed to put one of his posters in my front window." She lifted the tiny sample cup of wine Jackson handed her and touched it to his cup. "Here's to a profitable campaign."

"Congratulations," Jackson said and swallowed his wine. "Shall we go?"

Clementine drank her wine and nodded. Jackson helped her slip into the coat she'd taken off in the manager's office. On the way out, she asked him what he thought of the place. "The wine was pretty good," he said. "And the surroundings are okay. The customers seemed to like it a lot." He stopped talking and looked away from her as if he were uncertain about what he wanted to say next.

Clementine waited for him to continue, but he said nothing as they walked to the car. "Jackson? What is it?" she asked after they were both seated on the front seat. Jackson held the keys in his hand, but he didn't start the engine. The cold began to seep through Clementine's coat, and she wished he would at least turn the heater on.

"I heard something while I was there," he said finally, still staring straight ahead. "I shouldn't tell you, but I think you'd want to know." Clementine had rarely seen him look so troubled. "A couple of women came in just as you were walking toward the back with that guy. I'd already gone over to the counter to order, so I guess they didn't know we were together, and of course they didn't recognize me." His large Adam's apple went up and down. "After they ordered, they came over to the table next to me. They probably thought the music covered up what they were saying, but I could hear them." He paused again. "They were talking about you, Mom. They saw you when they came in." His eyes were rimmed with sadness. "One of them said she had a hard time believing you were attacked in the middle of downtown Tanner. The other one said they shouldn't talk about you like that, but she agreed."

Clementine closed her mouth, which had inadvertently fallen open. The women's reaction didn't shock her as much as the fact that they knew about the rape when she had tried so hard to keep it secret. Jackson grasped the steering wheel. "I shouldn't have said anything, but I couldn't help it. I told them they had no idea what they were talking about, so they should keep their mouths shut. They finished their wine pretty quickly and left. I'm sorry, Mom."

"I want to know how they found out," Clementine said. "I was afraid this would happen. People will either doubt me or feel sorry for me, and I don't want either one." She looked at her watch. Three thirty. Was the *Observer* out yet? She got her copy home delivered on Tuesday afternoons, but what time did it show up on news racks in the stores? If Quentin Harper had written about the rape after all, she'd . . . well, she wasn't sure what she'd do, but first she had to find out. "Take me to Walgreens," she said. It was the closest store she could think of with a news rack.

Jackson offered to go in and look for the newspaper when they reached the store, but Clementine didn't trust him to look thoroughly enough. She found the *Observer* on the rack and rushed back to the idling car to search it. "It's clean," she said, tossing the newspaper into the back seat. "Bless Quentin's little pointed head. He came through for me—this time, at least. So the rumors are spreading by mouth. There's not much I can do about that." She slumped down on the car seat. She dreaded facing anybody, even customers in the shop, because now she'd worry that they knew, and she'd try to read every word, every gesture, for disbelief or pity.

"People were bound to find out eventually, Mom," Jackson said. "There'll probably be a trial when they catch the guy, and that'll have to be in the newspapers." His boyish face grew stern. "Don't pay any attention to what people say. Most of them are idiots, anyway. You know what happened, and it doesn't matter what they think."

"It matters if the antique shop is going to make it," Clementine said. "If the local people don't like me, they won't shop in my store. I've seen it happen before. There was a jewelry store here when I was growing up. My mother wouldn't set foot in that store, and she didn't want me to register my wedding china there because she said none of her friends would shop there either. All because the woman who owned it had an affair with a married man. Or so everyone thought."

"So you'll cater to the out-of-town folks," Jackson said. "That's the point of working with the wineries, isn't it? So the tourists who stop there will come over to Tanner and visit your shop."

Clementine shrugged. "The best thing that could happen is to get this over with quickly so maybe people will forget it. And the best way to do that is to get Gary Wiggins in jail."

Jackson slipped the car into reverse and backed out of the parking space. The sternness in his face had changed to concern.

7

Back in the Day was scheduled to reopen on Thursday. Clementine's plan from the beginning had been to open the shop Thursday through Sunday, take Monday as her day off (maybe), and spend Tuesdays and Wednesdays at auctions and estate sales to replenish her stock. In spite of Jackson's continuing protests that she needed to rest, she made him take her to a small estate sale in Hickory on Wednesday by pleading that she wanted to get out of town for a while. The sale turned out to include mostly junk. As often happens, the family had cherry-picked the good stuff before setting up the sale.

On Thursday, she went back to the shop with Jackson tagging along. She told him she would be fine, but he wouldn't hear of her going alone. Secretly, she was glad he was there. The sofa was out of sight, but jarring memories of what happened on it still flashed through her mind if she let down her guard for even a minute. Having Jackson to talk with filled the empty spaces between customers. He insisted on going again on Friday, Saturday, and Sunday.

On Monday, she began encouraging him to go home. He had a job to get back to and she didn't want to jeopardize that.

At supper that night, she said gently, "Jackson, sweetheart, I can't tell you how much I appreciate having you here this week. I needed you, and you came. But I can handle it on my own now. I have to. And you need to go back to your job so you don't lose it. There's not much else you can do for me, and I'm afraid that's worse for you than me."

Jackson's expression showed confusion and concern. "I don't think I should leave."

Clementine reached across the table and took his hand. "One of the worst pains a mother can suffer is to see her child hurting and not be able to do anything about it. Although it's not exactly the same in the other direction, I think you must be feeling some of that now. As much as you want to, you can't help me. Having you come down here has made me feel loved, and I needed that, but now you need to take care of your own life. And don't let Elizabeth give you any flak for not staying longer. I'll tell her this is what I wanted. I need to stand on my own."

Jackson stayed Tuesday, but on Wednesday he did what she asked. When he pulled out of the driveway, Clementine walked to the velvet fainting couch in the living room and sat on its edge. The house was silent. Not even a clock ticked. For the first time since the rape, she was truly alone. Carefully, she slid her robe and nightgown up her legs. The blue bruises inside her thighs were tinged with green and yellow, symbols of what she had endured. She waited for the waves of desolation to pass over her, the feelings of loss, and the gnawing fear that was her constant companion. She traced the bruises with her finger-tip, expecting to break down in floods of tears, but only a few drops escaped her eyes. Inside her, a hard core was sprouting. After she was dressed, she would go to the hospital to show doctors the bruises that hadn't yet formed the night they took photographs. She should have done that when the bruises first appeared. This battle was just beginning.

~

Although David and Erlene stopped by the antique shop as much as they could, there were still times when Clementine was in the shop by herself. She coped by obsessively cleaning and rearranging the antiques. And on her days off, she cleaned and rearranged her house. Time seemed to stand still as she waited for DNA results.

The first Saturday in March marked the three-week anniversary of the opening of Back in the Day. It should have been a day for celebrating. The antique shop had done well in its first weeks. Clementine had sold a few big items and lots of small ones. Total revenue was above what she had budgeted. But she couldn't celebrate. Although she managed to maintain her resolve and get through other days at the shop, Saturdays were the worst. Each Saturday brought a deluge of memories about how happy she'd been with no idea of what was awaiting her only hours away. As the clock on the wall behind the jewelry case chimed each hour, she remembered what she was doing at that time on that Saturday and thought, *In only five more hours, in only four more hours, in only three more hours, my world was going to come crashing down.*

March weather stayed cold and damp. Shoppers entering Back in the Day were happy to loosen their woolen scarves and remove their gloves. Then they tended to linger in the warmth of the shop. On a windy Friday, Clementine was wrapping a Rookwood vase she had just sold a visitor from out of town, while a young woman with a tiny baby strapped to her chest looked at cocktail rings in the jewelry case, and an older woman with a cane pushed keys on a Blickensderfer typewriter.

Clementine had managed to make it through the morning in a fairly calm state of mind. She kept the back door locked and kept her attention focused on the customers. When there were no customers, she still gravitated to the front of the store, but the pricklies in her spine were less active than they'd been before. She didn't want to let Gary win. If he had attacked her to crush her self-respect or her self-esteem, or just to make a mess of her new life, she had to make sure none of those things happened. She had to make a success of this antique shop.

With a smile of appreciation, she handed over the vase and remembered to include one of the business cards she'd had printed for the shop. She was proud of the cards. Just seeing her name in Old English lettering shining out at her from the tiny piece of cardboard made her happy. And the small photograph of the sign above the shop's door was perfect. Still smiling, she looked around to see if the customers needed her help. Just then, the young woman's baby began to whimper, causing Clementine to instinctively move toward her. If the baby was getting restless, the woman wouldn't be there long. As she walked away from the cash register, the heavy front door opened and shut. *The sound of the vase buyer leaving,* Clementine thought, although she was looking at the woman with the baby and not at the door. "Would you like me to take some of the rings out of the case so you can see them better?" she asked.

The woman twisted her mouth as though she were undecided. In the silence of the gesture, a footfall sounded from the front of the store. "No, thank you," the woman said, but Clementine was no longer looking at her. Her attention had been drawn to the footfall. The noise was familiar.

Just inside the door, wearing the same canvas car coat he'd had on every time Clementine had seen him, including the night of the rape, Gary Wiggins was watching her. He wasn't moving. He was just standing there, staring. The old woman with a cane and the young woman with a baby wouldn't be much help if Gary came after her again. But daylight streamed through the front window. Surely he wouldn't try anything in the middle of the day with other people in the shop. She returned his stare, determined to show she was not afraid. "If you change your mind, I'm happy to open the case," she said, conscious that the woman with the baby was still next to her.

The baby's whimpering escalated to crying, causing the woman to turn away from the case to jostle him and sway. "Thanks, but I can't stay. It's almost feeding time." Whispering to the baby, she moved up the aisle to the door and closed it behind her. Gary still stood a few feet from the entrance. Was he waiting for Clementine to approach him, or was he waiting for the woman with the cane to leave? Clementine's stomach clenched. She had to stay in control. She raised her chin as she walked toward the front of the shop. The woman with the cane kept clicking the keys of the typewriter. Gary didn't move.

"Get out of my shop," Clementine said quietly when she was close enough for Gary to hear. "Get out of my shop, or I'll call the police."

"And tell them what?" Gary's voice was loud and rough. Clementine turned a worried glance toward the woman with the cane. "She can't hear me," Gary said. "That's Ona Jones. She's deafer'n a doorpost. And don't worry. I'll leave soon, after I tell you what I came to say."

"Get out now," Clementine said. Her trembling fingers brushed the rose-quartz pendant beneath her blouse.

Gary took his hands from his pockets and pointed a finger at Clementine's face. "Listen to me, and listen good. Stop telling people I'm a rapist. I never touched you. You're just out to get me. So shut up about it, you hear? I'm warning you." He rolled the pointed finger into a fist and shoved his hands back into his pockets. "Shut up or I'll sue you for slander."

Clementine's throat tightened, and she fought back tears burning her eyes. "You know it's true. It's true, and I won't stop saying it. I don't care how much you threaten me. Just wait till the DNA results come back. Then you'll get what you deserve." The tears were streaming now, and she brushed at them with her fingers. "Get out."

"Don't forget what I said." Gary brushed past her and left the shop, almost walking into Pete on the sidewalk.

Pete spoke to Gary, who only nodded in reply. Then he turned into the antique shop and stopped cold, his long face pinched even more when he saw Clementine. "You poor thing, what's going on?"

Clementine wiped her hands on her skirt as she drew in a few deep breaths. "Nothing, Pete. I just thought of something sad. That's all." She sniffled as discreetly as she could. "Now, what can I do for you?"

"You know, it says in the Bible, 'Tears wash misery from the mind, just as water washes dirt from the body.' It's good to cry every now and then." Pete tapped his fingers against the wicker table beside him. "But that looks like the kind of tears caused by more than a bad memory." His face twisted, suggesting he had no idea what to say next. Clementine almost smiled through her tears, his discomfort was so visible and so pitiful.

"Thanks, Pete. I'm fine. Are you interested in looking at some antiques?" She studied his face, trying to determine if his uneasiness was caused by more than her crying. Probably he knew about the rape. The police had questioned him about what he saw that night.

Pete cleared his throat. "Uh, no. I just came to see how you're getting along and if you need to borrow any more tools.

I meant to stop by earlier, but with the festival and all, I've been pretty busy."

"How sweet of you. I'm doing fine." The worry on Pete's face compelled Clementine to reassure him. "Really. I know it's only been a few weeks, but sales have been good."

Pete nodded. "I hope that keeps up. Remember I'm just down the street if you need anything." Clementine expected him to head for the door, but he remained still. His sagging eyes seemed to soak her in. "You know," he said, "The Bible also says, 'Rise up with might when enemies offend thee. From the depths of retribution spring resolution and respect.'"

Before Clementine could reply, he slid out through the door, leaving her alone with Ona Jones, who was still playing with the typewriter. His parting words clung to Clementine. What was he talking about? Maybe he was concerned because Gary was in the shop. Or maybe he was encouraging her to fight for the success of her business. He'd told her the first time they met he didn't think an antiques business could make it on Main Street. She squashed the urge to run after him to ask what he meant. She needed to find out if Ona heard anything that Gary said.

"Hey, Mrs. Jones." Clementine approached the old woman. "That's an interesting typewriter, isn't it? It's a Blickensderfer 6, the first aluminum typewriter. Blickensderfer was known for making the first portable typewriters." Clementine's voice was louder than normal, but Ona didn't look up. Clementine tapped her on the shoulder. Ona turned to smile at her.

"Hello, dear. You have such a lovely shop. My grandmother had some of these things. My, my. You look as though you've been crying. Would you like a handkerchief?" Ona reached into her purse and retrieved a slightly crumpled handkerchief.

Clementine shook her head. "No, thank you. Can you tell me, though, if you heard what the man I was talking with earlier said to me?" Ona's face still had an expression of offering, so Clementine shook her head again. Ona tucked the handkerchief back into her purse and wandered off toward the front of the store. If she couldn't hear Clementine from two feet in front of her, she could never have heard Gary from the front of the store.

Clementine made her way to the tiny bathroom in the back to wash away the tear stains on her cheeks. A few splashes of cold water followed by a few pats with paper towels, their roughness scratching against her skin. "You have to tell somebody," she said to her reflection in the little mirror above the sink. Her first instinct was to call Chief Tubbs, but she couldn't prove what Gary said to her, so what was the point?

"Erlene," she said, but just then a crash sounded out in the shop. Clementine rushed from the bathroom, expecting to see Ona surrounded with shards of glass from a lamp or a vase, but the old woman was no longer there. Nothing in the shop moved. Clementine checked the back door to make sure it was still locked. Then she moved cautiously up the left aisle. In the middle of the store, she found the problem. A bowl of glass marbles lay on its side on the floor with the marbles scattering in all directions. Clementine retrieved the bowl, which was surprisingly still in one piece, and gathered up the marbles. If Ona was gone, how did the bowl fall? Maybe a customer left it too near the edge, and the vibrations of footsteps and closing doors eventually walked it off. Maybe Ona knocked it off and then fled before Clementine could come out of the bathroom. Maybe the shop had another mouse. Clementine knew there was a logical explanation for the crash, but after the matter with Gary, she was still spooked. She shouldn't make such a personal phone call now because a customer might come into the shop at any minute, but she couldn't help herself. She went to the telephone and called Erlene.

Erlene was at work, but she had a break between patients and could spare a little time to talk. Clementine gave her the details about Gary's visit and pointed out why she didn't want to call Chief Tubbs about it. "So what do I do now?" she asked. The knot was rising in her throat again.

"You have to tell the police," Erlene said. "Let me call Charles and see if he can come by the shop after you close. He'll know what you should do."

Clementine hesitated. A woman in red leather boots looked like she was turning into the shop, but she passed on by. "Thanks, Erlene. I didn't think things could get any worse. I'm glad Jackson left already. I don't want to have to tell him about it."

"Let's stay focused on Gary," Erlene said. "I'll call Charles. But as for Jackson, will you get it through your head that's what sons and daughters do for their mothers? They support them when they need it."

"I guess, but I hate that he's had to deal with all this nastiness. I know he believes me completely, but it has to rattle him to see his mother first get attacked and then be the subject of so much suspicion and doubt."

"He's a grown man, Clementine. He can handle it. Look, I gotta go," Erlene said. "Next patient just arrived. I'll call Charles when I get a chance. Why don't you see if David can come over to the shop? You shouldn't be there by yourself."

"I'll wait for Charles. Thanks again for your help." Clementine hung up the phone.

Charles got to the shop long before closing time. Clementine was showing a young girl's 1880 cross-stitch sampler to a middle-aged couple when he came in. Seeing she was busy, he leafed through a few of the old books that filled the lower shelves of one of the display cases. A woman in a floor-length black coat looked at him with curiosity but went back to examining a blue-willow tea set. Charles never took his eyes off the books. At last the couple thanked Clementine for her help and moved on down the aisle.

Clementine sped over to Charles and tapped him on the shoulder. "Thanks for coming. I don't know how to handle what Gary did this afternoon." She repeated Gary's words even though Erlene had given Charles the gist of them. "See what he's doing? He's threatening me with a lawsuit when he's the criminal. How can he do that?" Despite her anxiety, she managed to keep her voice to a whisper. The couple and the woman in the long coat still wandered around the shop.

Charles kept the book open and his voice low. "He can do it because nobody's proved he's a criminal. So going around saying he is could be grounds for a lawsuit. I doubt any judge would hear the case right now, because Gary's still involved in the investigation, but if he's proved innocent or never brought to trial, he could bring suit later."

"So he can just threaten me like that? Doesn't it make him look guilty? Like he's afraid that if I keep insisting he did it, the police will find the evidence?"

Charles shook his head. "Nope. If anything, it makes him look innocent. He's worried about his reputation."

"Nobody seems to care about my reputation. What am I supposed to do about that?"

"Be patient. Let us do our job." Charles pointed to his shield. "It's still an open case. If Gary keeps on harassing you, we may be able to do something, but not now." The front door slammed as the couple who had been looking at the sampler left. The lady in the long coat followed them. Charles put the book back on the shelf. "If you think of any other detail about the incident, let me know. We will get to the bottom of this." He shook Clementine's hand. Clementine knew Erlene had all the trust in the world in Charles, but she wasn't so sure she did.

8

In the days since Jackson left, David had encouraged Clementine to have dinner at his house as often as possible. He worried that she wasn't eating when she was home alone. She looked thinner to him. He also thought coming to his house was a good change of scenery for her, and she liked his dog, a female mutt he'd rescued from the local shelter. David enjoyed watching Clementine stroke the dog. Contact with another living creature must be good for her. He didn't know how she'd been relating to other people since the attack, but she'd kept her distance from him. He'd tried to put his arm around her a few times, but she always stiffened at his touch. He expected her to welcome reassuring hugs, but whenever he tried, she backed away. The most she would do was hold his hand for a few minutes.

He wished he knew Erlene well enough to ask her what she thought about Clementine's state of mind. In his opinion, Clementine was putting up a brave front, but he questioned her true feelings. When they were together, she was there, but not really there. Because she rarely mentioned the rape anymore, he never mentioned it to her. Their conversations centered on the antique shop, his insurance business, and his work at the counseling center. As much as he could without upsetting Clementine, he tried to find out if business was still good at Back in the Day. He worried, as Clementine did, that word of the assault would keep customers away. So far, she said traffic was pretty good, but David had no way of knowing if it would have been better, had she not been raped.

They were discussing business when Clementine first mentioned the idea of holding evening gatherings at the antique shop. The calendar was well into March, but the weather was still so cold that David had built a fire in the small fireplace in his living room. He and Clementine had finished dinner and were relaxing on his leather couch with the dog curled up between them. Furnishings in David's house were sparse—his wife had taken the pieces they owned jointly when they divorced—but at least now he had furniture he liked. He slumped in the soft leather, his feet extended toward the warmth of the fire. "I don't know about you being down at the shop at night," he said.

"Oh, David." Clementine frowned. "I can't be afraid to go to my own store after dark. And there'd be a lot of people there. I can wait until late spring, after we go on Daylight Savings Time, maybe, when it stays light longer. But I think it would be a good way to get more people into the shop and educate them about antiques. I could have a speaker and serve refreshments."

David was glad to see her enthusiasm. Maybe her mental health was better than he thought. "Who would you get to speak at these meetings?"

"I can start with the interior design instructors at the community college."

David laughed. "That's a coincidence. I'm getting ready to do some work with the community college myself. The mayor asked me to talk with the dean about offering trade courses at satellite locations in Tanner. Could be a help for some of our unemployed folks."

Clementine's forehead wrinkled. "How's the counseling service going? I've been so wrapped up in my own problems I've ignored yours." Her hand that had been rubbing the dog grew still.

"Things are a little better. Turns out the people who were getting the federal benefits didn't lose them completely like we thought they did. They're still getting some placement services and a little salary gap money." The return of the benefits had been the brightest spot in David's life in the past weeks. He couldn't stand to see the despair on the workers' faces, particularly the older ones who knew their chances of landing a new job were slim. In a few cases, he'd given them loans with his own money, loans he knew would never be paid back. But he would do anything he could to alleviate their sense of being the butt of some cosmic joke. Even some of the young ones had given up. Overall, mental health in Tanner was on shaky ground.

"The benefits may be only temporary," he said to Clementine. "You never know with the government. But at least they're something."

Before Clementine could reply, the doorbell jangled. The dog jumped to her feet, sounding a staccato series of barks. "That's odd," David said. "I'm not expecting anybody else tonight." He pulled back one of the heavy cotton drapes and stared out the living room window. Vincent McQuarrie waited on the small porch, his police-officer hat pulled low on his forehead.

David dropped the drape and opened the door. "Is Mrs. Loftis here?" McQuarrie asked.

"Just a minute." David closed the door partway. "It's Vince McQuarrie," he said to Clementine in a hushed tone.

Clementine's eyes brightened. "Maybe they arrested that bastard. Let him in."

David pulled back the door. "Come on in. She's here."

McQuarrie removed his hat as he crossed the threshold. "Sorry to bother y'all tonight." His eyes immediately found Clementine. "Good evening, Mrs. Loftis." He fingered the edge of his hat, causing it to rotate in a jerky motion. "I wish this could've waited till morning, but we have a possible suspect in your case, and we can't hold him overnight, so we need your help now."

As McQuarrie talked, David moved closer to Clementine. Her face was calm, but the tip of her tongue brushed her lower lip. "Need her help with what?" David asked.

McQuarrie cleared his throat. "Well, we've been working hard on your case. We've questioned every merchant on Main Street and all the people who had booths and kiosks set up that night, and anybody those people remembered being in their stores or on the street after five o'clock."

Color faded from Clementine's face. David knew what she was thinking. If the police talked to that many people about the rape, then everybody knew. They may as well have put a banner ad in the newspaper. "What exactly did you say to these people?" David wanted to get the question out before Clementine was forced to ask it.

McQuarrie rotated his hat faster. "Nothing that would let them know exactly what we were investigating. No. Nothing like that. We asked them if they saw anything out of the ordinary that night. Especially *anybody* out of the ordinary. That's how we found out about this guy. We finally got to talk to Marcie Davis. She runs a yoga studio a few doors down from the antique shop, but we hadn't been able to talk to her because she was out of town." He swallowed. "When she got back, she told us she remembered seeing this fellow in the alley behind Main

Street as she was getting into her car to go home that Saturday. She said the man was sitting on the ground next to the trash cans behind Dunkin' Donuts. She recognized him because she'd hired him to paint the walls in her studio last fall."

"Who is he?" David asked. "And what does he have to do with Clementine?"

"I can't tell you his name." McQuarrie held his hat still.

David started to object, but Clementine spoke first. "This is ridiculous. I told you and Chief Tubbs who raped me. It was Gary Wiggins. I know it was him, and there's no point in dragging up other suspects. Just do your job and arrest Gary." The color had returned to her cheeks, giving her face a forceful glow.

"I know this is inconvenient," McQuarrie said, "but if you'll just come down to the station with me, we've arranged to put this man in a lineup. Maybe if you see him, it'll bring back some memories."

"That you think I've repressed. Is that it?" Clementine exhaled loudly. "Oh, good lord. Spare us your playacting. Tell Chief Tubbs that the mayor and the city council may buy this charade of investigating the rape, but I don't."

"If you'll just come with me. It won't take long. There's evidence that suggests this man had no reason to be in that alley. He got off work two hours earlier and should have been long gone by then. Just please, Mrs. Loftis, come with me."

"No, she's not going down to the police station at this hour." David walked toward the door so he could send Vincent on his way.

Clementine, her lips tightly pressed together, had been observing this exchange. "Wait a minute," she said. "If I go down to the station and look at this poor man and tell you he's not the man who raped me, will you promise not to drag up any more innocent suspects? Will you spend your time finding evidence to arrest Gary instead?"

McQuarrie frowned. "You know I can't make promises like that. We're trying to help you here. Please. Can we go?"

David looked to Clementine to see what she wanted to do. "I guess you're just doing your job," she said to McQuarrie. "Let's get our coats, David. The sooner we get down there, the sooner this man and the others can go home." David went to the kitchen for water to put out the fire.

Huddled in the front seats of David's Mini Cooper, David and Clementine followed the police car. The residential streets were quiet with almost no traffic. Even the police station was silent. Nobody sat at the front desk, and no officers were hunched over desks in the squad room. McQuarrie led David and Clementine up the back stairs to an interrogation room across from a row of empty cells. "Slow night?" David couldn't resist asking.

McQuarrie gave him a look that said he wouldn't deign to answer that question. Instead, he pointed at a window that revealed five Hispanic men sitting in metal folding chairs in another interrogation room next door. They all wore jeans or work pants with open-collared shirts or sweatshirts. A few wore zippered windbreakers.

One of them David recognized as Francisco Coutino, a man he'd helped get a job at Dunkin' Donuts. David remembered Francisco distinctly because the wiry little man had paced around outside the counseling center for two Saturdays before David went out and told him to come in. When asked why he didn't come in the first time, Francisco said he was afraid the center was only for white people and wouldn't want Mexicans bothering them. He'd been working with a construction crew, but work had gotten slack, and the boss laid him off. A friend of his told him he'd find a better job if he got help from the center, but he wasn't sure. Francisco had working papers, but he still didn't trust everybody.

Like others in the interrogation room, Francisco stared into space, but his stooped shoulders showed a tenseness the others didn't have. David feared he was the one the police were after. McQuarrie rapped on the window, and a policeman David didn't recognize motioned for the men to stand. At his direction, they each took a numbered sheet of cardboard from him and formed a line in front of the window.

Francisco looked older than David remembered. Probably because of the dark shadows under his eyes and deep grooves around his mouth. "How long did McQuarrie say they'd been holding this man?" he asked Clementine, who was studying all the men with a passive expression.

"He didn't say. He just mumbled something about how they couldn't keep him here overnight." Her voice sounded tired, causing David to bristle anew at her having to come down here for nothing. And now he was worried about Francisco.

McQuarrie closed the door. "Don't say anything right away," he told Clementine. "Just focus on their faces. They can't see you, so you can take as long as you like."

Clementine turned her static eyes toward the policeman. "I could stare at them all night, but they still wouldn't look like Gary Wiggins, so none of them is the man who raped me. Can I go now?"

"Are you sure you don't see the rapist?" McQuarrie sounded exasperated.

"Yes, I'm sure."

David sensed the steel rising in Clementine, but he couldn't take his eyes off Francisco. "I know one of these men. Francisco Coutino. Can I speak to him?" he asked.

"No. That's against procedure. He's a suspect in this case."

"Not anymore, he's not. Clementine just told you he didn't do it. So let me speak to him."

McQuarrie shifted his weight from one foot to the other. "Okay. But just for a few minutes." He went into the other room and spoke to Francisco, who lingered behind as the others left. Then he waved at David to join them. The little man's face crumpled when he saw David.

"I didn't do nothing, Mr. Adams," he said. "I don't know what they're talking about."

"What did they tell you, Francisco?" David asked.

"They kept talking about the woman who owns the antique shop. They said she was attacked. I never been in the antique shop. I don't know any woman in the antique shop. But they kept saying I do." Francisco hung his head.

"I'm sorry this happened to you, but it's over now. They have to let you go home." David tried to make his voice as reassuring as he could and to keep anger out of it. "Let me take him home," he said to McQuarrie.

"No. I'll get an officer to do that. You take care of Mrs. Loftis." McQuarrie led Francisco out of the room and handed him off to a policeman waiting at the top of the stairs.

When David returned to Clementine, she was buttoning her coat, which she'd let fall open in the heat of the station. "Let's go," she said.

David was still worried about Francisco. "You're going to take him home now, aren't you? You're not going to question him anymore." He searched McQuarrie's face for signs of deceit.

"If Mrs. Loftis says it's not him, we have no reason to hold him. Thank you for coming down." McQuarrie led them back down the stairs and to the front door. David looked around the squad room for Francisco, but nobody was there.

On the drive home, Clementine rested her head against the back of the seat. "If the police are basing their investigation on who saw who in the alley that night," she said, "I want to talk to Pete. He saw Gary in the alley, but that's become Gary's alibi instead of evidence. I want to know exactly what Pete saw him do and exactly what Gary said to Pete that night. The police are missing something."

David could see her point, but he doubted there was much more to be learned from Pete. "Maybe he'll remember something he forgot to tell the police," he said, "but I wouldn't count on it."

The next day was Wednesday. If Clementine was lucky, the hardware store would have few customers on a Wednesday afternoon. The only person strolling the aisles when Clementine arrived at the store was an elderly man wearing a baseball cap and a denim jacket. Pete stood behind the worn counter at the front of the store, cracking rolls of coins and emptying them into the cash register. Intent on the coins, he didn't notice Clementine until she stood in front of him and spoke.

"Mercy me, Miz Loftis," Pete exclaimed. "You put the fear of God in me. I didn't know you were here. What'cha need today? A flashlight, maybe? I got a special on 'em."

Clementine assured him she didn't need a flashlight. "I want to talk to you about the night I was attacked. You know about that, don't you?"

Pete's face blanched. "I... I'm so sorry that happened to you, Miz Loftis. I guess I should have told you so sooner."

"No, it's okay, Pete. I understand." Clementine leaned across the counter and lowered her voice. "But I need to ask you about Gary Wiggins coming into your store that night."

Fear flashed across Pete's long face. "There's nothing to tell. He came and got a thermometer and then he left."

"How was he acting? Jittery? Angry?" There had to be some clue in Gary's behavior as to what he was going to do next. Pete was Clementine's only witness. He had to have seen something.

Pete shook his head. "He was just acting like Gary. He wanted a particular kind of thermometer for one of the stoves at Johnny's and insisted on looking at all my oven thermometers. Seemed like it took him a long time, and I was wanting to leave, but he finally found what he wanted. He paid for it, and he left."

"Did he say anything about me or about my shop?"

"No. Look, I said I'm really sorry this happened, and I am, but I don't want to talk about it anymore. I told the police everything that happened in my store that night. And that's all I know. The Bible says, 'Let truth guide thy way, and thy path shall be smooth.' I told the truth, but you're making my path mighty rocky."

"I'm sorry, Pete. Just one more question. The police said you told them you saw Gary drive out of the alley. Are you sure you saw him actually leave the alley and turn onto Mountain Street or did you only see him pull out of the parking place behind the hardware store?" Clementine was losing him, but this was the most crucial point.

Pete's narrow face hardened. "What I told the police is what I saw. I got in my car, and I saw Gary drive away. Now, I need to go check some things in the back of the store." He turned to walk out from behind the counter.

"Was your car facing Mountain Street or Elliott Street?"

"I don't know. Ask the police."

"Don't you remember?"

Pete walked away without answering. As he disappeared behind a tall row of shelves, Clementine watched a huge chunk of hope drift away with him. Pete obviously wasn't going to let himself be pressured. She'd have to figure out another way.

After the incident with Francisco, Clementine heard less from the police. The next time Charles stopped by Back in the Day, she told him Pete seemed uncertain about which way his car was facing in the alley the night of the rape, but Charles acted more concerned about her talking to Pete than about what Pete had said. "You're sticking your neck out there pretty far," he warned, "when you know Gary's itching to sue you for slander."

"I didn't say anything about Gary being the rapist. I just asked Pete how Gary was acting. And then I tried to get him to tell me more details about what he saw in the alley."

"You're asking for trouble is what you're doing. Leave it alone, Mrs. Loftis, before you make it worse than it already is."

"So what are the police doing?" Clementine had asked this question so many times and gotten so many unsatisfactory answers that now she felt like she was yelling into a void.

"Looking for new leads. But I have to tell you, there's not much out there. I wish I had better news. The DNA results should be back soon, though. That could make a big difference."

After that conversation, Charles quit coming around. Clementine went through her daily routine and tried to keep her attention focused on the antique shop, but keeping her attention focused on anything was difficult. Her thoughts were often elusive, scattering from her mind as quickly as they came. Sometimes she found herself forgetting what she'd done only a few hours or days before. At one point she was convinced an eighteenth-century pewter plate had been stolen because she couldn't find it anywhere. When it finally turned up among some silver pieces waiting to be polished, she remembered she'd put the plate there because she wanted to photograph it with the silver to post on her website.

She mentioned her frustration about the plate to Jackson during one of his frequent phone calls, hoping he'd make light of it and ease her concern about her memory, but he seemed more interested in the security of the shop.

"You do have insurance and a burglar alarm, don't you?" he asked.

"Of course I do," Clementine replied, annoyed that he would think otherwise.

"I'm just asking because you really could get robbed. We've been having some robberies at work. Nothing major. But a lot of small things like flower vases and fancy bookends have disappeared. And a backpack that somebody made the mistake of leaving there overnight. If it could happen to us, it could happen to you."

"I won't get robbed. Who do they think stole your stuff?"

"Probably the cleaning crew, although our head of maintenance grilled them all pretty hard, and nobody broke."

"I'm safe then. I don't have a cleaning crew, except for me."

"Just be careful, Mom. I worry about you. You don't need anything else bad to happen to you. Are you managing okay?'

"I'm fine," Clementine lied. She'd told him about the forgetfulness, but she couldn't tell him about the sleepless nights and ongoing fears. He was worried enough already. Those feelings she shared only with David and Erlene.

When the bruises on her thighs healed, she told Erlene, "You can't see the pain anymore, and I'm not allowed to talk about the rapist to anybody except my closest friends. Hell, I probably shouldn't even talk about Gary to you. It's like it never happened. I feel like this town's closed up around me, and I'm supposed to pretend nothing happened, and yet they're all free to think whatever they want to about me."

Erlene, who had stopped by the antique shop after work, squeezed Clementine's hand. "Nobody's thinking anything about you. Trust me, this story's old news now. There's fresh gossip for folks who like that sort of thing, and most people either never heard about it or they respect your privacy and have moved on. Nobody in this town wants to hurt you."

"I still feel trapped," Clementine said. "I can't talk about it, nobody's doing anything about it, and Gary's going his merry way, probably bucking for a raise at the restaurant, and everybody thinks he's a prince. Look how he pulled himself up after losing his job and his wife. Started a whole new career. What a guy."

Erlene's face softened, compassion written in every crease, but she said nothing.

9

Around the middle of April, as warm air signaled it had come to stay, Chief Tubbs called Clementine to say he'd received the DNA results. He offered to come to the shop, but she didn't want him anywhere near Back in the Day, so she agreed to come to the station after work. Waiting all afternoon nearly drove her crazy, but he wouldn't tell her the results on the phone, and she wouldn't leave the shop. She wanted to give Chief Tubbs her undivided attention.

When she arrived at the station, the same heavyset policeman she'd seen before sat on the stool behind the counter. This time he unlocked the counter door and let her through immediately. She strode directly to the chief's office and stood inside the open door. The space was even darker than it had been the last time she was there. The thinning light outside barely found its way through the windows behind the desk. Chief Tubbs sat in one of the vinyl chairs and invited her to sit in the other. He held a few sheets of paper in his lap.

"There's not much to report," he said when she'd settled in the chair, "but I wanted to tell you in person, because I knew you'd be disappointed."

Clementine's spine stiffened.

Chief Tubbs grasped the papers in both hands as if their concrete presence gave more weight to what he was about to say. "The lab tested all of the samples, and the only DNA they found was yours." He blinked twice, and his mouth stayed in a straight line.

Clementine reached for the papers. After holding on for a second, the chief let her have them. They showed a series of small boxes containing columns of numbers and photos of columns of bands. None of it meant anything to her, but she could see that the photos inside each box matched other photos. "This can't be right," she said. "He must have left something."

A tinge of pink crept into the chief's cheeks. "Did he wear a condom? That might explain—"

Before he could finish his thought, Clementine interrupted. "No. He didn't wear a condom. He had one hand holding the knife and the other one holding me down. He'd have had to put it on with his teeth, and I know he didn't do that."

"But there's no other explanation. Unless he didn't reach . . ." The chief pursed his lips. "The important fact is there's no other DNA. Without that, we have no lead and no evidence. I already told you there were way too many fingerprints on everything in the shop to do us any good."

"Okay." Clementine's mind was reeling. "So there wasn't any semen. But wasn't there something else? A hair or some blood? Skin cells?"

Tubbs shook his head. "Everything the investigators found on your clothes was yours. Maybe they missed something, but I don't think so. We couldn't get a warrant for Mr. Wiggins's clothes, but it wouldn't have mattered anyway. By the time we got it, he could have washed everything or even disposed of it."

Clementine tossed the papers into his lap. "It doesn't matter. I told you who did it."

"Without a witness or evidence, we can't prove it. I'm sorry." He squared his shoulders as he straightened the papers in his lap.

"Now what?" Clementine leaned toward the chief. "What will you do next?"

"Hope for a tip. Maybe one of the merchants will remember something new, or somebody else who was downtown that night."

Clementine sighed. "Can't you make Gary confess, so this will all be over?"

Chief Tubbs's eyes widened. "Mrs. Loftis, I know you're under a lot of stress, but this isn't a TV show. We don't force people to confess so we can wrap everything up in the last five minutes. We investigate crimes, and that takes time."

"I don't have time. I want Gary punished, and I want him punished before I'm old and gray. And before gossip makes me the town pariah. People are already talking about me. What if they start avoiding my antique shop?" Clementine stood so she was looking down at the chief. "Go out there and act like a policeman and find a way to arrest him." She walked toward the door.

Chief Tubbs followed her. "Let me say, Mrs. Loftis, that if you want to keep public awareness of the incident down, you ought to stop accusing Gary Wiggins. People like him, and nothing makes a story more interesting than accusing an unlikely suspect."

"Don't be afraid of the truth, Chief Tubbs," Clementine said. "You do your job, and everything will be taken care of."

On the way back to her car, Clementine cursed the demons in this nightmare that had become her life. First, Gary, of course, but then Chief Tubbs for not finding a way to arrest him, and even herself, for being so sure the DNA would solve everything. What were the chances that anybody saw Gary go into her shop that night? Pete already said he saw Gary get in his car and drive away. All the cursing made her head hurt. She'd have to tell David about the DNA. And Erlene. And Jackson and Elizabeth. It was going to be a long night.

After Clementine's phone call, Erlene thought about the DNA results with the curiosity raised by her everyday involvement with blood and saliva at the dentist's office. "How on earth did that man have sex with Clementine and not leave one trace of himself behind?" she asked Alfred, who was resting his swollen feet on their overstuffed ottoman after his shift at the hospital. "You know how messy people are. I mean, you can't hardly touch another person without getting sweat or something from them on you."

Alfred rubbed one of his ankles and groaned. "Nobody knows better than me how wet and sticky people can be, what with me handling all those patients, but I'm guessing Gary was mostly dressed, so there wasn't a lot of skin contact, except where it mattered, and I agree there should have been something there." He scratched his upper lip with his lower teeth. "I'm betting Clementine was so addled she didn't remember he put on a rubber, and that's understandable. She just wasn't thinking straight."

Erlene tweaked his ear. "You don't know Clementine like I do, or you wouldn't say that." Alfred brushed her hand away. "She remembers everything that happened that night. Every detail. She doesn't get addled. There's something fishy going on here."

"Well, if there's something going on, it's not your place to figure out what it is. Leave that to Charles and the other cops. If there's something to figure out, Charles'll do it."

"Not if that snooty Chief Tubbs won't let him." Erlene settled her buttocks on the arm of Alfred's easy chair. "Aren't you buddy enough with some of the guys in the lab at the hospital to ask them what might be going on?"

Alfred shook his head. "Sweet Jesus, Erlene. I'm not sticking my nose in where it don't belong. And besides, these aren't local tests." He rubbed his ankle again.

Erlene stretched her arm around his shoulders. "But you can at least ask."

"I'm telling you it won't do any good," Alfred said with a shrug.

At the end of April, Clementine's daughter, Elizabeth, flew to North Carolina and spent Easter weekend with her mother. Her solution to the stalled investigation was for Clementine to hire a lawyer. Get a good lawyer, file suit against Gary—civil charges if nothing else—to bring the bastard to justice. "There's no evidence," Clementine reminded her. "It's my word against his. What good would a lawyer do?"

"Then how about a private investigator?" Elizabeth pressed on as she sat with her mother in Clementine's backyard. Clementine didn't have money for a PI. Everything she could spare was sunk into the antique shop. Plus, Gary's threat of a slander suit made hiring an investigator a risky choice, but she didn't want to tell Elizabeth about the threat. Knowing about the rape was enough.

"I can't afford a private investigator," she said. "So, unless I can come up with an idea to prove what Gary did without spending a lot of money, I'll have to rely on the police to find something. And that doesn't look very promising."

Elizabeth tilted her head to one side and smiled. "Don't be so pessimistic. The laws of the universe are on your side."

"Yeah, well, the laws of the universe don't seem to know that. Nothing's holding Gary accountable. I don't think I can rely on karma for this."

"Maybe karma just needs a little push. Let's work on that while I'm here."

But when Elizabeth went back to California on Monday, they had no new ideas for stirring up the universe.

As twilight began to push its way past dinnertime, Clementine was ready to launch her series of evening events at Back in the Day. She scheduled the first gathering for a Thursday in the middle of May. The featured speaker was a community college design instructor whose specialty was nineteenth-century pottery. David still didn't like the idea of Clementine's being at the shop after dark, so he insisted on attending the event and taking her home afterward. Erlene said she'd be there too, whether out of interest in pottery or friendship, Clementine didn't know. But she was glad both of them were coming. Her biggest fear was that nobody would show up. With at least two people in the audience, the event would look respectable enough to encourage any passersby on the street to stop in.

At six forty-five, fifteen minutes before the talk was scheduled to begin, David and Erlene were the only people there. Together, they had helped Clementine arrange the chairs and benches in the shop the best they could to make a comfortable seating arrangement for the presentation. The speaker had spread a cloth across a stretcher table in front of the jewelry counter and set out pitchers, bowls, and plates to illustrate her presentation. Now she sat behind the table, clicking a pencil against her folder of notes. Clementine's stomach bounced from one side of her abdomen to the other. So many of the seats were empty. Did the people in Tanner not care about nineteenth-century pottery, or did they not like to go out at night, or were they avoiding her?

At six fifty, Ona Jones hobbled in with her cane, followed by Suzanne Jessop, whose husband was Frank, the manager at Shimlock's Winery. Clementine's joint promotion with Shimlock's in April had gone so well that Frank had given her a discount price on several bottles of merlot to serve at the gathering. Suzanne was a buxom, gregarious woman, whom Clementine had liked the first time she met her. The fact that Suzanne had bought a craftsman stool at the shop made Clementine like her even more. Suzanne waved enthusiastically before she sat down.

At seven o'clock, the speaker looked at Clementine, her eyebrows raised in a question. Clementine nodded, and the presentation began. A few minutes after seven, a man and a woman whom Clementine didn't recognize slipped quietly into the shop and quickly found seats. Then Marcie Davis from the yoga studio down the street came in, letting the door slam behind her. The loud noise turned every head in the shop, but the speaker was undaunted. Clementine waved at Marcie, although she blamed the yoga teacher for getting Francisco Coutino dragged down to the police station.

Marcie raised the total attendance to seven, which wasn't bad for a first event. But Clementine's stomach still bounced. She hovered near the front door to welcome any more stragglers and prevent any more slams. Outside, the sidewalk was mostly empty. A few people went in and out of the drug store next door, and one stopped to read the large poster in the antique-shop window advertising the speaker inside, but he moved quickly away after reading.

Eventually the street was deserted, and Clementine turned her attention to the speaker. Around seven thirty, as the sky grew dusky, she thought she heard footsteps outside. As she turned to look at the sidewalk again, a man spun away from the poster in the window and hurried down the street. Clementine drew in a quick breath. She hadn't gotten a good look at his face, but in the glare of light from the shop, she couldn't mistake the huge forehead and combed-back hair, or the broad shoulders and thick middle. The man was Gary Wiggins, no doubt about it. He was gone in a flash, but Clementine's breath kept coming in short gasps.

Concentrating on steadying her breathing, Clementine walked over to David and tapped him on the shoulder. She motioned for him to follow her before heading to the front of the shop, as far away from the speaker as she could get. Erlene followed David, until the three of them huddled next to the window. "Gary was here," Clementine whispered.

"Where? When?" David's voice was loud enough to cause a few people to look in his direction, but they turned their attention back to the speaker when they didn't see much going on.

"Outside. In front of the window." Clementine's voice trembled. David darted out the door. He walked a short way down the sidewalk in both directions, then stood in front of the shop and shook his head.

Erlene took Clementine's hand and led her outside to David. "So we can talk better," she whispered on the way out. If the speaker thought their actions were strange, she didn't show it. On the sidewalk, Erlene asked, "Are you sure it was Gary?"

"Absolutely." Clementine's heart pounded in rhythm with her quick breathing.

"What was he doing?" David still scanned Main Street in all directions.

"Reading the poster, I think. Or hiding behind it while he looked in the window. When I turned to him, he ran away."

"I hate to say it, but it's not a crime for him to be standing in front of your shop." Erlene squeezed Clementine's hand.

"It could be if he's doing it to harass her." David's lips pressed together in a grim line.

"Do you want me to call Charles Yarboro?" Erlene asked. "Maybe you should report it."

Clementine took a deep breath. Her chest was slowly settling back to normal. "No. Gary'll have some excuse to prove that he wasn't here, so it'll just be my word against his again, even if I can construe what he was doing as harassment. Y'all didn't see him. Nobody saw him but me." Inside the shop, the speaker was taking questions from the audience, a sign that she was winding down. "Right now I have work to do for my antique shop." Clementine went back into the shop, willing her mouth into a smile.

The speaker held up a dark red bowl in response to a question from Suzanne. "Like I said before, this is a piece of American antique redware, made between 1850 and 1880. The red color comes from iron deposits in the clay."

"Was it made in North Carolina?" Suzanne asked.

The speaker shook her head. "No. North Carolina pottery from the early part of the nineteenth century often had a glossy greenish glaze. I don't have any of those pieces with me tonight, but there are some samples at the college if you'd care to stop by sometime. Or drive down to the Seagrove area. The potters who're still working there today often have some of the older pieces for sale."

Erlene had followed Clementine back into the shop and stood with her close to the front door. "I didn't know people in North Carolina made pottery," she whispered.

"Sure they do," Clementine whispered back. "People come from all over to see it and buy it."

Erlene nodded and turned her face back to the speaker, who was answering another question. Clementine was pleased that the people who came to the event were interested enough in the topic to ask questions. She'd planned to ask some questions herself to get the conversation started if she needed to, but thank goodness she didn't have to. Seeing Gary had chased her questions right out of her mind. As Marcie raised a question about a jug, Clementine looked behind her at the sidewalk outside her window. David had stayed outside to make sure Gary didn't come back or at least to ask him what he was doing there if he did, but Clementine couldn't see David from where she was standing. He must have walked farther down the street looking for Gary. Clementine hoped he wouldn't start a fight.

"Well, if there're no more questions, thank you for coming." The speaker smiled as the small group applauded.

Clementine snapped out of her thoughts about David and walked toward the display table. "Yes, thank you all for coming," she said, "and feel free to look around the shop before you leave. Also, please sign our guestbook." Erlene lifted the book from a table next to the door, and Clementine pointed to it. Then she walked to the couple she didn't know and introduced herself. Slowly, the visitors glanced around the shop and then left. The speaker packed up her display pieces, and Clementine thanked her for coming.

By nine o'clock, only Clementine, Erlene, and David were in the shop. David had wandered back inside a few minutes after the speaker finished her presentation. "I didn't see Gary anywhere," he said when the three of them were alone. "I even went inside the drug store, but he wasn't there. All the other stores are closed. He must have had his car parked close by."

Clementine studied his face. "You believe me when I say I saw him, don't you?" She turned to Erlene. "And you too?"

"Of course we do," Erlene said. "He just got into his car, like David said, before anyone else saw him."

Clementine was glad they believed her because she was beginning to doubt herself. Sometimes she thought she saw Gary when he couldn't possibly have been there. At those times, she thought she might be losing her mind. Tonight, however, she was sure the man was Gary, but she had to expect that. They both lived in this little town, and they were bound to see each other occasionally. "I have to get used to seeing him," she said, "because it's going to happen."

David put his arm around her shoulders. "Have faith, Clementine. Something's going to break. This won't go on forever."

"Why not? The police can't find any evidence. And he's sure as hell not going to confess. I'm afraid he'll be walking these streets for as long as I live." Clementine slid out from under David's arm. "Let's talk about something else. How do you think the meeting went tonight?"

"Attendance was good," Erlene said. "They all seemed interested."

"I thought the speaker was good—at least the part I heard." David settled on a three-legged tavern stool.

"Me too." Erlene's voice perked up. "Especially when she mentioned North Carolina pottery. I can't believe I've lived here my whole life and never heard about North Carolina pottery." Clementine wondered if Erlene was really that interested in pottery or if she just wanted to take Clementine's mind off Gary.

David chuckled. "To be honest, Erlene, I never had either. But then I'm not the type to hang out in pottery shops."

"I'd like to see some of it," Erlene said. "I guess I could go over to the college or down to Seagrove."

"You could do that." Clementine began gathering up the used wine glasses scattered about the shop. "Or you could go with me to the auction I'm going to in Asheboro next week. Asheboro's close to Seagrove and that whole pottery-making part of the state, so some of it will probably show up there."

"Are you sure?" Erlene's face was bright.

"If not, I promise we'll go on down to Seagrove from there."

"It's a deal." Erlene moved the chair she'd been sitting in back to its usual spot. David slid off his stool and put it where it belonged. When all the furniture was back in order and Clementine had the glasses ready to take home for washing, she checked to make sure the back door was locked and led the way out the front. She no longer parked the van in the alley behind the shop, but left it instead in a lot a block away. She felt safer on the lighted street than in the alley alone. Tonight, however, the van was already back at her house, and she walked with David to his car parked at the insurance agency. Erlene left them when they reached her car parked on the street. Clementine had scoffed at David's wanting to take her home, but now she was glad for his caution. Shadows filled every doorway they passed. Behind any of those shadows, Gary could be lurking.

10

Lucky for Erlene, the auction was on Wednesday, so she already had the day off, but she would have taken a day of vacation if she had to. Clementine's passion for antiques had dropped a little of its fairy dust on her. She was excited as the women jostled along the highway in Clementine's van. She'd never been to an auction before. "Is this like an estate sale where everything belongs to one family?" she asked when they crossed the Randolph County line.

Clementine pulled the van into the left lane to pass a tractor-trailer. "No, this is a consignment sale, so anybody—like dealers, owners, or estate trustees—can submit something for sale. If the auction company accepts it, then it's in."

Erlene watched the pastures and fields roll by as she envisioned the various items she might see. "So what are you going to buy?" she asked after a while.

"Depends on what's there. But I do have my eye on some lamps I saw in the online catalog." Clementine steered the van off the highway and onto a six-lane boulevard teeming with car dealerships, fast-food restaurants, and small office buildings. After a sharp right turn at a traffic light, she whipped the van into a winding parking lot surrounding a three-story brick building. "This is it," she said. Among the rows of cars and trucks, she found an empty space far off to the side. "The building used to be a hotel when the road beside it was the main state highway. I remember driving past it with my parents when we went to visit our relatives in Asheboro. It looked so elegant surrounded by trees and green lawns. I don't know if the hotel was supposed to be a country oasis or if they thought the city would grow out to meet it, but the interstate—and the motels that came with it—put the hotel out of business."

Clementine pulled the straps of the quilted bag that doubled as her purse over her shoulder and climbed out of the van. Instead of entering through the large double doors at the center of the building, she led Erlene through a door on the far right. "The room that used to be the lobby is the auction room now," she explained, "so they use another room as the entry area." Inside, a group of mostly middle-aged men and women gathered before a long desk staffed by smartly dressed young women working with laptop computers. The ceiling in the room was high, at least ten feet, Erlene guessed. She wondered how the room was used in the original hotel.

When Clementine's turn at the desk came, she registered herself and then asked Erlene if she wanted to register. "What for?" Erlene asked. "I don't plan to buy anything."

"You never know. Just show them your driver's license and a credit card and you can get a bid number." Clementine nudged Erlene toward the desk. Reluctantly, Erlene produced the necessary cards. She really just wanted to watch.

Armed with their bid cards, Clementine and Erlene walked into the auction room. If the ceiling in the first room was ten feet high, this one was at least twenty, maybe more. And the room was ten times bigger. What a magnificent hotel lobby it must have been. Today it held rows of benches filled with people in all manner of dress: a few men in business suits, women in dresses and scarves, others in casual clothes, even a few in overalls and cut-off jeans.

Erlene started to take a place on one of the benches, but Clementine motioned for her to come into another side room. Before she followed, Erlene couldn't help staring for a few minutes at the auctioneer and the giant screen beside him. On the screen was a huge photograph of a nightstand. As the auctioneer began his chanting, bid cards rose and fell, and then wham! The auctioneer lowered his hammer, pronounced "Sold!", and the next picture came up on the screen. It happened so fast.

Clementine leaned toward Erlene and whispered, "This auctioneer sells about a hundred and fifty items an hour. Come on. I want you to see this pottery before it goes up for auction." She scurried toward a side room filled with furniture and cabinets holding pottery, silver, jewelry, and other small items. "There." Clementine pointed to a green vase with loop handles. "That's North Carolina pottery, I'm sure."

The cabinet was locked, so Clementine motioned to a thin boy wearing a lanyard with a clump of keys hooked to it. At Erlene's request, he unlocked the cabinet and handed the vase to her. She ran her fingers over the vase's slick, cold surface, smooth except for four raised rings around the neck. "Those are finger circles," Clementine said. "The potter made them from the inside."

"It's beautiful." Erlene caressed the vase one more time before handing it back to the boy with the keys. "It would look great in my living room."

"So keep an eye out for when it comes up," Clementine said. "You have to be quick with your card." She threaded her way through the aisles of the preview room, sometimes pausing to look at an item or two.

Erlene looked at most things with only mild interest until she saw a pair of brass candlesticks. She was rubbing her fingers along their polished edges when she noticed a plastic bag filled with wooden implements lying beside them. "Why are these things in a bag?" she asked Clementine.

"It's what they call a *lot*. They sell things by lots, and you can put as many things as you want to in a lot, but you only get one price for it." Clementine studied the bag. "That looks like a bunch of carved miniatures. See? That's a canoe. Look at the details in the seats. And those are paddles, and those look like snowshoes." Clementine leaned closer to the bag. "Wonder what that is." She pointed at a wooden block about five inches tall and five inches wide. "It's too big to be a child's toy, and if it were, there should be more of them."

Erlene was more interested in the candlesticks, which she was still holding, but she glanced at the block. "Looks like a doorstop to me."

"It's not a doorstop. It's not heavy enough." Clementine lifted the block within the plastic bag. "It's got some kind of markings on each of its sides." Carefully, she opened the bag and slid the block out. The markings were raised, carved out of the sleek polished surface of the wood. Clementine turned the block over in her hands and ran a finger along the raised lines. "Wonder what these mean. I bet they were special to somebody. See what you think." She offered the block to Erlene.

Erlene set the candlesticks down and took the block. It was heavier than it looked, but not heavy enough to be a doorstop. She tilted it slightly, allowing the light from the closest window to brighten the lustrous wood and illuminate the carvings. The lines were simple: triangles, s-shaped squiggles, clusters of short lines suggesting snowflakes, and curved lines that dipped like exaggerated smiles.

Erlene's heart rate quickened as she turned the block to see another drawing. This one had two long curvy lines resembling identical snakes stretched out vertically with their bodies curled in a loop at the bottom of the block. Erlene knew exactly what the block was, even though she hadn't seen one in many years. "It's just a block, maybe a paperweight," she said as she hastily stuffed it back into the bag.

Clementine wrinkled her nose. "No, it's not. You know something about it. I can tell. Your expression changed when you examined it."

"And who are you—some psychic that can read people's expressions?"

"No. But I saw something in your face. Tell me what you know about it." Clementine reached for the block again, but Erlene hurried down the aisle away from her. Clementine hustled after her. "What is it, Erlene? Tell me."

Erlene stopped next to an array of lamps. "It's nothing. Don't you want to look at some lamps? Are these the ones? Isn't this why we came?" She pointed at the lamps next to her. Clementine's lips curled, but she kept silent.

The bronze lamps were soon located on a nearby table. Clementine's fingers crept around them carefully as she held them up to the bright windows. "They're good," she murmured with a slow nod. Replacing them on the table, she asked Erlene if she wanted to see anything else. Erlene shook her head, so the two women walked back to the auction room and settled on a bench about eight rows from the auctioneer. Erlene focused on the photos flashing on the jumbo screen, glad to have something to think about besides the wooden block. Although she hadn't seen one in years, she could still feel the pain that objects like that had caused her family.

Suddenly Clementine poked her elbow into Erlene's ribs. "There it is. Your vase. Quick. Bid."

Erlene watched as the bidding went from two hundred to four hundred dollars in seconds. Clementine tugged at the bidding card clutched tightly in Erlene's lap, but Erlene snatched it away. "I don't want it that much," she hissed as the bidding rose to six hundred dollars. "If *you* want it, you buy it."

Clementine rolled her eyes. "I want you to have it. If I buy it, I'll have to put it in the shop."

Erlene glared at her as the vase was sold and new pictures popped up on the screen. China, pottery, silverware, and then the miniatures with the wooden block appeared. "Fifty dollars," the auctioneer said. "Who'll give me fifty?" Clementine raised her bid card.

"What the hell are you doing?" Erlene croaked.

"I want this lot," Clementine said, raising her card again after a card went up a few rows ahead.

"No, you don't. You're just trying to irritate me." Erlene reached for Clementine's card just as Clementine had done to her. Clementine's eyebrows pushed the wrinkle between them deeper into her forehead. "Please don't," Erlene whispered fiercely.

"Okay." Clementine's face relaxed, but it was too late.

"Sold," the auctioneer called out, "to the lady in the eighth row." He pointed at Clementine. "Hold up your bid card, please." Erlene's stomach clenched. She wished she'd never come to this auction.

"I'm sorry," Clementine said as she raised her card, "but whatever that block is, it can't be all that bad."

Erlene sighed. No, it wasn't all that bad, but she could easily have gone the rest of her life without seeing one or any of the other objects her grandmother had kept in a trunk under her bed. She hoped the auction would be over soon, even though she dreaded the ride home. Clementine was sure to bring the subject up again.

Item by item, lot by lot, photos slid across the screen. Around two o'clock the first lamp Clementine wanted came up for bid. Clementine raised her card repeatedly as the price rose and finally won it for six hundred dollars. Erlene shook her head. Who in Tanner did Clementine think was going to buy that? She was glad to see Clementine dropped out of the bidding when the second lamp's price rose to eight hundred. At least the woman had *some* sense. And maybe now they could go home.

As bidding commenced for the next item on the screen, Clementine touched Erlene's arm. "Let's go," she said. She led Erlene back to the entrance room and waited her turn to pay for her purchases. When the cashier handed Clementine the bag with the wooden miniatures, Erlene looked away. She was glad when Clementine stored the bag along with the lamp in the back of the van.

On the road leading to the highway, neither woman spoke. Erlene watched the restaurants, car dealerships, and office buildings glide by, thinking she should talk about anything to keep Clementine from asking about the block, but she couldn't come up with a single subject. She was too preoccupied with the block. As the highway signs came into view, Clementine finally ended the silence. "I'm sorry I bought that lot. If I'd known it would upset you so much, I wouldn't have done it." She waited for Erlene to respond, but there was nothing for her to say. "If you don't want to talk about it, okay, but I can't make it up to you if I don't understand why you're so upset." Clementine looked away from the road long enough to glance at Erlene. Her eyes were soft.

Erlene slouched in her seat. If she expected to be friends with Clementine, she should be willing to share things about herself and her family, even if they weren't pretty. Clementine had certainly been open with her about the rape, or at least she seemed to be. Erlene turned her head toward Clementine. "The block is a talisman for root medicine, a particular kind of root medicine that my grandmother practiced."

Clementine slowed the van down as she drove onto the highway and stole another quick look at Erlene. "That doesn't sound so bad. Root medicine can be worked for good as well as evil, can't it? What exactly did your grandmother do?"

"I'm not sure. I didn't see her after I was about twelve years old. She died the year Alfred and I got married." Visions of her grandmother's tiny blue house and the dirt yard around it swirled in Erlene's mind, along with memories of the short, pudgy woman, so much cuddlier than Erlene's sharp angled mother. "I remember her talking about a few spells. Most of them involved powders made from herbs and other plants. She'd put them in people's food, or they'd wear them in a poultice bag hung on a string around their neck." Erlene leaned her head back and closed her eyes. She hadn't thought about this in so long.

"So what does the block have to do with it?" Clementine asked. She'd settled the van behind a pickup truck and made no move to pass it.

Erlene kept her eyes closed. She didn't want to look at her friend, even though Clementine was facing the road. "The drawings on the block are symbols of spirits that intervene between human beings and the universe. To call a spirit, Nana would spread flour on the ground and draw the symbol in it, or sometimes she'd bake a flat little doughy thing and press the symbol into it. That's probably how that block was used."

Clementine continued to drive behind the pickup truck. "What were the spells for?"

With her eyes still closed, Erlene thought back to days spent in Nana's blue house. Once, when Erlene was playing with her dolls on Nana's living room floor, a young woman came to beg Nana to make sure her next baby was a boy. She had four daughters, and her husband threatened to leave her if she didn't have a boy next. Nana threw flour no more than six inches from Erlene on the floor, drew a symbol in the flour, said something Erlene didn't understand, and gave the young woman a poultice bag to wear. Whether she had the baby boy, Erlene never knew.

Then there was the time an old man came by Nana's house shivering like a mound of Jell-O. Sweat was pouring off him, and he was sure somebody had conjured something against him, but Nana told him more likely he'd been poisoned. She mixed black chunks of something Erlene thought looked like asphalt with boiling water and told him to drink it when it cooled.

"They weren't always spells." Erlene opened her eyes and turned toward Clementine. "Sometimes they were, but sometimes they were more like real medicine."

"So she helped people."

"Most of the time."

"Then I don't understand why you're so upset about it."

Erlene drew a deep breath. She had started weaving this tale, and there was no unraveling it now. "The last time I remember going to my grandmother's house, it was winter, and the house was closed up tight. We were huddled around the gas heater in the living room, saying prayers before we children went to bed, when a man burst open the front door without knocking or ringing the bell. He had big red sores on his face, and his eyes were red-rimmed and puffy.

"He grabbed Nana and shook her, screaming, 'You did this to me. You did this.' Mama herded us into the bedroom, but I could still hear what the man and Nana were saying. 'What makes you think I did anything to you?' Nana asked, and the man yelled, 'My wife told me so. She told me she gave you my dirty drawers so you could put a hex on me. Look at me. I got these damn sores all over my body.' Nana's voice was calm. 'Isn't it possible you got a sickness from that tramp you been fornicating with?' I had to ask Mama what fornicating meant.

"Then the man made a grumbling noise, sort of like a growl, and I looked at Mama to see if she wasn't worried about Nana. Daddy wasn't with us that night, so there was nobody to protect us. Mama looked more mad than scared, like she wanted to beat up that man herself. But it wasn't the man she was mad at. When Nana spoke again, she sounded mad. She told him to stay away from that tramp and he wouldn't get any more sores. The next thing I heard was the door slamming.

"Mama told my sister and me to go to bed, so we did, but I could hear Mama and Nana talking back in the living room. Mama asked Nana if she put a hex on the man, and Nana said if she did, he deserved it. Mama said, 'I told you I can't bring the girls around here long as you keep messing in that stuff.' The next morning we left, and we never went back."

The truck in front of the van sped up suddenly. A mattress resting precariously on top of tables and boxes in the truck bed slid to one side. "This doesn't look good," Clementine muttered, cutting the steering wheel to the left. When the van was safely in the left lane, she mused, "So Miss Myrtle didn't like her mother working root medicine."

"It's worse than that," Erlene said wearily. "She didn't just not like it—she hated it. I think it embarrassed her that her mother was doing something so primitive. Mama doesn't have much education, but she's proud of what she has. And she insisted that my sister and I finish high school and get as much training beyond that as we could." A knot caught in her throat. "She wanted to make sure we didn't grow up to be maids."

Clementine nodded solemnly.

"It was her idea for me to become a dental hygienist. Maybe because she hates root medicine so much, she thinks anything to do with modern medicine is wonderful. She wanted me to be a nurse, but we didn't have the money for nursing school."

Clementine drove in silence for a while. Traffic began to build as rush hour approached. When the cars and trucks settled to a steady stream, she said, "So the block reminds you of the rift between Miss Myrtle and your grandmother." Her forehead wrinkled slightly.

"I loved Nana." Erlene surprised herself with the force behind the pronouncement. "Not being able to see her left a hole in my childhood. And because Mama abandoned Nana, my Aunt Lanita abandoned us, which meant I didn't get to see my cousins, either. So much anger and grief. That's why I don't want that block around." Now the tale was told. Erlene hoped they could move on to something else and maybe Clementine would get rid of the block. How much farther did they have to go before they were home?

"Erlene," Clementine said gently, "do you think your grandmother really caused those boils on that man?"

"Of course not. He had syphilis or something like that."

"But your grandmother implied she might have caused them, and Miss Myrtle must have had some fear or faith in what your grandmother was doing to keep y'all away."

"She didn't want us thinking there was any truth to it. Those were the old ways. She wanted us firmly planted in the twentieth century, smart and modern as the next person."

"But sometimes old ways can be good too."

"Not those old ways."

Clementine nodded, but she didn't look convinced. Erlene thought about asking her to throw the block away, but that wouldn't necessarily end her curiosity. She just hoped Clementine would put it where she never had to look at it again.

Later that afternoon, after leaving Erlene at her house and un-
loading the packages from the auction at home, Clementine set
the mysterious block on the dining room table. It looked so innocent, but maybe it did have power. Her rose-quartz pendant,
warm against her chest, reminded her she trusted it to help
calm the chaos inside her and make sense of the madness swirl-
ing around her. Who could say whether root medicine might
change or direct those same energies? Maybe Erlene's grandmother should have used root medicine to give Miss Myrtle a
change of heart and bring her back into the family.

Clementine turned the block to look at it from a different
angle. The wavy lines carved out of the wood resembled heat-
bent light rays above a hot surface. Heat could be good or evil.
She extended her finger to trace the lines, but the crash of a
door slamming shut made her jerk her hand back. Immediately
she thought of Gary. Instead of stalking her at the shop, had
he decided to come after her at home? She rushed toward the
front door, then paused with her hand on the knob. The house
was quiet. No sound of footsteps in the kitchen. She waited,
but still the house was silent. She crept back to the dining room
and looked into the kitchen. No one was there. The back door
was closed, and so was the door leading into the hallway. The
door to the hallway was never closed. A breeze from the open
kitchen window must have slammed it shut.

Clementine dropped into one of the dining room chairs and
lowered her head. Every day she was tortured while Gary ran
around free. With the DNA results offering no help, he would
probably run around free and happy forever. She clenched her
fists and let out a guttural cry. Something had to be done. She

raised her chin slightly, putting the mysterious block directly in her line of sight. If Miss Myrtle could heave punishment on wayward husbands, surely root medicine could do the same for Gary. She patted the block as she went to find her phone.

Erlene thought it was odd that Clementine asked her to come by Back in the Day after work the next night since they'd spent nearly a whole day together at the auction, but the urgency in Clementine's voice let her know she'd better go.

When she arrived, Clementine ushered her to a cushy wing chair and pulled up a side chair for herself. "What's going on?" Erlene asked. "Has Gary done something else?"

"Only in my mind," Clementine said before she related the fright of the slamming door the night before. "But before that happened, I was thinking about root medicine. Does anybody in your family still practice root medicine?"

"Why?" Erlene squirmed on the chair's soft seat.

Clementine's eyes showed hope. "Because I think root medicine might help me. I want to put a hex on Gary."

Erlene's breath jumped in her chest. "Why in God's name would you want to do that? It most likely won't do you any good. My grandmother may have helped a few people with herb medicines, but I don't think she ever really conjured anything. Put your energy in finding some evidence against Gary. That's what you need to do."

"But there is no evidence. DNA was my only hope, and now that's gone." Clementine's eyes dimmed. "The police are looking for people who may have been in the alley that night, but even if they find somebody, it won't prove anything. With no

DNA and no evidence, there's no case." Her voice cracked with the last words.

"Oh, Clementine. I wish I could do something for you." Erlene was startled by the emotion in Clementine's voice. The poor woman had no idea how to cope with adversity. She was grasping at straws. "But this is not the answer. Even if we get somebody to put a hex on Gary, there's no assurance that it'll do any good."

"There's no assurance that the police are going to find anything, either. At this point I have as much faith in root medicine as I do in them. There has to be something to root medicine, or people wouldn't believe in it. Maybe your grandmother really did cause those sores. If she did, I want to know how she did it."

"Clementine, I want to help you—I really do—but this isn't the way. Even if we knew it worked, it's not a game you can dabble around in. My mother tore my family apart to keep me away from this, and now you want me to go back there?" The air in the shop grew warmer, stuffier.

"Please, Erlene. I wouldn't ask you if I weren't so frustrated." Clementine leaned forward, her hands pushing against her knees. "There's no DNA, and the only person who saw Gary in the alley that night has pretty much given him an alibi. I don't know what to do. Maybe your family can give me some hope that Gary will at least be punished a little."

"No, I won't go back there." Erlene turned her head and stared at a painting on the wall. She didn't like having to choose between her family and her friend.

"Then give me a name and I'll go by myself."

Erlene focused on a tiny red flower in the corner of the painting, reluctant to show her anguish to Clementine. Even if she wanted to help her, she couldn't. She didn't know if anybody in her family practiced root medicine or not. The day they left Nana's house for the last time, Miss Myrtle vowed that they would never mention root medicine or root doctors or conjuring again. "I don't know a name."

"What about your Aunt Lanita? Would she know?"

"I haven't talked to her in years."

"Then I bet she'd like to hear from you. She can't blame you for what your mother did."

"Yes, she can." Despite her resolve, Erlene couldn't stop her mind from wandering back to Christmases spent at Nana's with Lanita and her children, all the cousins turning the little house upside down looking for presents while Lanita made banana pudding. She had missed Aunt Lanita almost as much as she missed Nana. "And even if Aunt Lanita would talk to me, Mama would kill me if she found out."

"You don't have to get in touch with her. Just tell me how to do it."

Erlene closed her eyes. The whole idea was ridiculous. Clementine couldn't put a hex on Gary. Probably Lanita would tell her the same thing. Moments passed as neither Erlene nor Clementine spoke. When Erlene opened her eyes, Clementine was chewing on her lower lip. In the months since the rape, Erlene had admired Clementine's courage and her determination not to let this crime get swept aside. Right now, though, she looked so vulnerable. If she meant what she said about Nana's medicine being her only hope, maybe Erlene should help her. At least let her find out for herself that there was no hope there. Miss Myrtle would understand that. "I'll see what I can find out. I don't even know where Aunt Lanita lives anymore. So I'm not promising anything."

Clementine's chewed-on lip stretched into a smile. "Thank you, Erlene. You're a good friend."

Erlene looked at the naked gratitude in Clementine's expression and hoped both of them wouldn't end up regretting all of this.

11

David hated being kept waiting, especially when he was waiting for a person who had asked for his help. He'd arrived at the mayor's office on time at four o'clock, and his Swiss Army watch now said four twenty. If the mayor didn't show up in ten minutes, he was leaving. Almost as if the mayor had heard what David was thinking, he came bustling through the door. Dressed in a dapper navy-blue suit with his gray hair neatly trimmed, he looked vigorous for his age, which David guessed was at least late sixties and maybe early seventies. Dr. Jeff Colton had been a primary care physician in Tanner since David was a teenager. He was well respected for his ability as a doctor and for his love of the town, which some people said had caused problems between him and his wife a few years after he brought her here. David didn't know the details of the story—he'd been so young at the time—but whatever happened, maybe Tanner was better for it.

The doctor had served multiple terms on city council, and this was his third time as mayor. During his tenures, the Tanner library had been expanded and connected to the statewide network of libraries, the high school had added new chemistry and biology labs, plus a new gymnasium, and new customers were found for Tanner's water treatment plant. And probably there were a lot more improvements that David was unaware of. Dr. Colton was that kind of leader. But when it came to managing local unemployment, David found him totally lacking. If the town had been doing what it should, in David's opinion, there'd be no need for David's volunteer counseling service. Now, in the last year of what Dr. Colton said was his final term as mayor, he was finally tackling Tanner's unemployment problem. Initiating vocational training classes at local venues was the first forward-thinking thing he'd done on that front.

"Sorry to keep you waiting," Dr. Colton said in a breathless voice. "My last patient appointment ran late." So he was still seeing patients. Maybe he wasn't as old as David thought. The doctor dropped into the chair behind his desk. "I gather from your emails that you have instructors lined up for our classes next fall."

David pulled an envelope stuffed with contracts from his inside coat pocket. Starting in September, five courses would be offered in Tanner—two occupational training, two GED preparation, and one basic skills. The instructors from the community college had been glad to oblige as soon as they found out a grant from a nonprofit organization ensured they would be paid. "Everything's set," David said. "I have their signed contracts right here." He took the contracts from the envelope and held them out toward the mayor.

Dr. Colton flipped through the papers and smiled. "Good job, David. But then I knew you'd find the right people when I asked you to take this on."

"Helping folks go back to school's been my favorite part of the counseling service," David replied. "But one of the problems we've faced is the inconvenience and expense of driving twenty miles to the college." David tried to hide his resentment that it had taken the mayor so long to lend a hand. "I've already got twelve people registered for the local classes, and most want to know why they can't start sooner."

"You assure them that God willing and the Creek don't rise"—the mayor smiled at the old familiar phrase—"they'll be in class in the fall."

"How about classrooms? Do we have a definite space where these classes can be held?" David didn't trust the mayor to have carried through on this part of the plan.

"We're going to use the high school. The school board signed off on a few rooms as long as I have a police patrol car drive by every half hour to scare off any vandals. Doesn't seem likely to me, but if that's what it takes, I'll do it." Dr. Colton shrugged, creating wrinkles in his perfectly pressed suit.

"Okay." David was pleasantly surprised. "So next we have to spread the word. Put some announcements in the *Observer*, put up posters, and hand out flyers at the unemployment office." Filling the classes wouldn't be hard. Limiting the enrollment would be. "Do you want me to work on that?"

Dr. Colton's eyebrows rose along with the corners of his mouth. "Why, David, my man. You are a Godsend. I couldn't ask for a better point person on this effort." He leaned forward across his desk, resting on his elbows. "If you ever need anything from me, you let me know."

David assured the mayor that he would.

As he left the stained limestone building that housed the mayor's office, David passed the police station in the brick building next door. For a moment, he stood outside the door pondering the people within. Charles Yarboro meant well, but beyond him, David wasn't sure. Chief Tubbs seemed to have doubted Clementine's story from the beginning, and that Vincent McQuarrie dragging poor Francisco Coutino down to the station just for being in the alley that night. David shook his head. He'd like to go inside and shake all of them.

Then an idea rippled through his mind. Maybe he could use his newfound buddy-ism with the mayor to put a little pressure on the police. Dr. Colton *had* said, "If you ever need anything from me." David wasn't exactly sure what the mayor could do, but he decided to make a start by seeing if the police would tell him anything new about the case. He also wanted to tell them about Gary's hanging around outside Back in the Day during the presentation on pottery. Still miffed that Charles had said they couldn't do anything to Gary for threatening Clementine with a lawsuit, David hoped this latest appearance would at least make the police consider a stalking or harassment charge.

After taking a deep breath, David opened the heavy wooden door. Behind the glass barrier that separated the squad room from the entry area, four uniformed policemen exchanged heated remarks. David recognized McQuarrie, but not the other three officers. The barrier muffled the sound so that he couldn't tell what they were talking about. Since no one was sitting at the stool behind the slits in the glass, David rapped on the window. All four men looked up. McQuarrie nodded slightly but didn't move. A shorter officer with curly black hair left the group and approached David. "Can I help you, sir?" he asked through the slits.

"I was just next door talking with the mayor," David began, hoping to establish some clout early on and make the visit seem more than an opportunity to complain about Gary. "We were discussing the job training courses offered at the high school next fall, and Dr. Colton said y'all would patrol the area while the classes were in session." If the officer knew what David was talking about, he didn't show it. "Anyway, it occurred to me that you might like to have the names of the instructors who'll be teaching the courses in case you need to question them about anything suspicious that you see."

"Okay," the officer said. "I'll pass the names on to Chief Tubbs." He held out his hand, expecting David to give him a list.

David reached for the empty envelope, which he had stuck back in his pocket. Using a pen lying in the barrier's pass-through trough, he wrote down the instructors' names. He knew he was being unprofessional, but at least he had established a reason for being there, and he could casually move on to his real agenda. As he passed the envelope through the trough, he said, "As long as I'm here, I'd like to have a few words with Officer McQuarrie." He'd hoped for Charles Yarboro, but he didn't see him anywhere, and at least McQuarrie was familiar with Clementine's case.

The curly-haired officer gave David a perplexed look, but he turned to the group of policemen, who continued their conversation in a calmer fashion. "McQuarrie, he wants to talk to you."

Vincent approached the counter, freeing the other officer to return to the group. "Can we speak somewhere private?" David asked.

"Sure." Vincent motioned for him to come through the door and buzzed him in. Then he led David to a far corner of the squad room while the curly-haired officer watched them suspiciously. "What's up?" Vincent asked.

David turned his back to the other officers and spoke in a hushed tone. "Gary Wiggins has been harassing Clementine Loftis again." Vincent's lips tightened into a deep slit. "She won't tell the police," David went on, "but I think you need to know."

"What do you mean, he harassed her?"

"Last Thursday, Clementine—Mrs. Loftis—hosted a meeting at her antique shop down on Main Street. It was a presentation, actually, for her customers about antique pottery. During the presentation, Gary stood outside on the sidewalk and stared into the shop. He didn't try to join the meeting, like a normal person, he just stood outside and stared. When we went outside to speak to him, he disappeared."

"Disappeared how? Like vanished into thin air?" The passion drained from Vincent's face.

"No. Not into thin air. He must have gone into another store or had his car close by. The point is he wasn't there for the event. He was there to scare Clementine. He's already threatened her once. He shouldn't be allowed to stalk her like that."

"Wait a minute," Vincent said. "There's a lot more to stalking than standing on a public street outside somebody's public store."

"It wasn't *what* he was doing. It was the *way* he was doing it."

"All right. We appreciate you letting the police know about this. Does Mrs. Loftis want to file a formal complaint?"

"If that's what it takes to get you to do something about it."

"Then tell her to come down and file the complaint."

David hated the tone the conversation had taken on. He'd hoped to keep things on a friendly level, chummy enough to have them build a case against Gary without so much formality, and chummy enough to extract a little information about what they were doing on the case now. To try to smooth things over, he put on a weak smile. "I'll have her do that," he said. "I'd also like to be able to tell her if you've uncovered anything new in the case. Have you?"

Vincent pursed his lips. "I can't talk to you about an ongoing case. It's police policy."

"Then it is ongoing? Because y'all haven't reported one thing to the victim since you dragged poor Francisco Coutino in for questioning months ago." David regretted his harshness as soon as the words came out of his mouth. Again, this wasn't what he wanted. He should have known better than to talk with McQuarrie. Maybe Charles Yarboro would be more forthcoming. "Never mind," he said. "I mainly wanted you to know what Gary's up to. Clementine is the victim here, and yet she has to put up with his threats and menacing appearances."

"She needs to file a complaint." Vincent paused, looking over at the officers still clustered on the other side of the room. "Is there anything else?"

"No, thank you." David walked toward the door, and Vincent buzzed him out.

As the heavy outer door banged shut behind him, David swore at himself. He had handled the conversation all wrong. He'd meant to take some pressure off Clementine and to stir up the police force a little bit, but he'd accomplished neither. He was going to need the mayor's help to get anything done, but God help him, he'd have to do a better job approaching the mayor than he had just done with the police.

Having mentioned Francisco Coutino to McQuarrie reminded David he hadn't talked to Francisco since the night at the police station. He'd meant to make sure the man was all right after the frightening night with the police, but time had gotten away from him. He should swing by the doughnut shop on the way to his car.

He arrived at the shop just as the manager was locking the front door. "Sorry, we got to close. We open at six tomorrow," the man said with a faint Hispanic accent.

"Is Francisco Coutino here?" David asked quickly as the door was closing again.

The manager sighed. "I think he just left out the back. Come on in. He's probably still out there."

"Thanks." David slipped through the half-opened door and dashed toward the kitchen, in the direction the man's extended arm and forefinger indicated. As he ran, David's nose twitched at the odor of disinfectant instead of the fresh doughnut aroma he expected. Funny how people expect places to always be the same.

Francisco was sitting on the back stoop of the shop, probably just like he was the night of the rape. David glanced at his watch. Yeah, it was about the same time of day. Hardly bigger than a child, Francisco rested his elbows on his knees and his chin in his hands. His shoulders curved around his neck like a half-moon. "Waiting for your ride home, Francisco?" David asked.

Francisco jerked his head around, his eyes wide. "Hola, Mr. Adams." The muscles in his face relaxed only a little when he saw David. "Sí. I'm waiting for Emilia. She will come get me after her work at Walmart." Francisco hunched his shoulders closer together, making him appear even smaller. "Is something wrong?"

"No. I just haven't talked with you since I saw you at the police station, and I wanted to make sure everything's all right. Are you all right?" As Francisco nodded, all alone on the Dunkin' Donuts stoop, David looked past him to Back in the Day's back door. He knew today was one of Clementine's auction days, so she wasn't in the shop, but he was struck by the proximity of the door to the stoop where Francisco sat. "Francisco," he said, "that night when you were sitting out here—just like this—back in February when Mrs. Loftis was assaulted, did you see anybody around her back door?"

Francisco's face paled in the late afternoon light, his eyes again growing wide. He shook his head wildly. "I didn't see nothing."

"You don't have to be afraid. I'm not the police. I'm just me. Your friend. I just realized that if you were sitting here, like Marcie said you were, you could have seen anybody who went in or out of the antique shop."

Francisco continued to shake his head. "I don't even know which door is the antique shop."

"Right there." David pointed at the shop. "The one next to you. If somebody went in or out of there, you're bound to have seen it."

"That was a long time ago. And it was dark. I sit here every night waiting for Emilia. They're all the same. I don't remember seeing nothing." Francisco stared down the alley, obviously hoping to see Emilia.

"What about cars? Did you see any cars behind the antique shop?"

"If that's the antique shop, there used to be a white van parked there a lot. It was probably there that night."

"What about cars? You didn't happen to see a red Honda Accord, did you?" If they were in court, the opposing attorney would have accused David of leading the witness, but on the stoop, he could say anything he wanted, and David knew Gary drove a red Honda Accord.

"I don't know. Maybe I saw a car. I told you it was dark. The car could have been red. I think it was driving away when I got here." Francisco's hands covered his face.

David was badgering the little man as much as the police had. "Okay, Francisco. Thanks for trying to remember. If you think of anything else, please call me. Okay?" He started to walk away when he remembered something odd from the night Francisco was at the police station. "Let me ask you one more thing. Your boss said you left work early that day. Why were you sitting out here so late in the afternoon?"

Francisco opened his hands and looked at David with a puzzled expression. "I went to the clinic to get medicine for my cough. Then I came here to wait for Emilia."

David smiled and patted him on the back. "But you're doing all right now? And Emilia and the kids are good?"

Francisco nodded.

"By the way, the mayor's offering some GED classes and some job skills training classes over at the high school in September. If anybody in your family or any of your neighbors are interested, tell them to call me."

Francisco nodded again.

"And stay in touch. I'm here if you need me."

"Thank you," Francisco whispered.

David assumed the Dunkin' Donuts back door was locked by now and started walking down the alley. A light breeze rattled garbage cans and sent odors of used food containers and snacks that had outlasted their shelf life floating through the air. All was quiet behind Back in the Day, but David checked the door just to be sure it was locked. As he walked past Pete's hardware store, he stopped and looked back at the antique shop, just to see how far it was. Pete said Gary drove straight out of the alley without stopping. But Francisco said maybe a red car was leaving just as he came outside. Leaving from where? And what time was that? There were so many pieces, but the truth was that even if they could be matched up, they didn't amount to much. David shoved his hands into his pockets and made his way to the end of the alley.

Clementine was waiting in David's living room when he got home. He'd given her a key soon after the rape, but she'd never used it without calling first. She hoped her being there didn't startle him too much.

"Hey, you," he said as he leaned over and kissed her forehead. She had settled on the couch with his dog snuggled next to her. "You're nice to come home to."

"Hey, yourself." She nudged the dog over to make room for him to sit on her other side.

"How was the auction yesterday?" he asked. "Any bargains?"

"It was good. I bought a bronze lamp to sell in the shop, but I'm more excited about something I bought for me." She reached into the bag at her feet and lifted the wooden block to her lap. "This is it," she said. "Doesn't look too threatening, does it? But let me tell you what it can do." She handed the block to him after he sat down, and as he ran his fingers over its designs and put his nose close to get a whiff of its musty odor, she told him Erlene's stories of root medicine and the role the block played in it.

"If I'd known buying this thing would upset Erlene so much," she said, "I wouldn't have bought it, but now that I have it, I'm going to use it. I'm going to put a hex on Gary. Erlene remembers times when her grandmother caused sores and sicknesses to plague men who'd mistreated their wives. I want to give Gary Wiggins the worst kind of sickness there could ever be."

The edges of David's mouth quivered for a second, before dropping into a frown. "Clementine, honey, there's no such thing as spells. Does Erlene really believe her grandmother caused those sores?"

"She doesn't know for sure. Nobody does. But what's wrong with believing in things you can't prove? What about angels and ghosts? Voodoo and zombies? And good karma? What's that all about? This is no different from that. And Erlene's seen root medicine get results."

"I thought you said she wasn't sure."

"Well, she remembers some spells that she thought her grandmother caused, but her mother didn't let her stick around long enough to be sure. About the time Erlene was twelve, Miss Myrtle stopped letting her visit her grandmother."

"So how's Erlene going to help you with this?"

"She's going to put me in touch with her aunt, who maybe knows something about root medicine."

David glanced at the ceiling for a second, then back into Clementine's eyes. "You're smart and you're brave, and I've admired your dignity throughout this horrible thing that happened to you. But root medicine doesn't make any sense, and I don't want you to get your hopes up for nothing."

Clementine's spirits sank. "So what do you think I should do? I deserve justice, David, any way I can get it. I want Gary Wiggins to pay for what he did to me. If I can't have him put in jail, then I want him to wish he were dead."

"You don't wish him dead?"

"Oh, no. That's too easy. I want him to suffer like I have. Like I still am."

David slid closer on the couch and stroked Clementine's cheek. "I know you're suffering. I see it in your eyes and in your anger and in the way you've pulled into yourself. I see your hurt, and I want to help. Erlene wants to help. Jackson and Elizabeth want to help. We're trying."

"But there's nothing you can do. Can't you understand that?"

David shook his head. "Listen, I went by the police station today to tell them about Gary hanging around outside the shop the other night. If you'll file a complaint, maybe they can do something."

Clementine slid away from David's hand on her face. He still didn't get it. "If the police were going to do anything, they would have done it by now. I have to find another way."

"But like this?"

"Do you have a better suggestion? You want me to shoot him or something? Then *I'd* just wind up in jail. I have to be more subtle than that. And a hex is done almost anonymously. Nobody except you and Erlene and her family will know I did it. If it works, great. If it doesn't work, I haven't risked anything. And right now this is the only idea I have. I have to try it, David."

David reached for her hand. Clementine hoped his touch was a gesture of support and didn't pull away. "Maybe there is another way," he said. "I talked to the mayor today. He's really happy about the work I've done on the job training courses. He implied that he might be willing to show his gratitude for that work by helping me out in some way. I don't know how he can help us yet, but there has to be a way. Put pressure on the police, maybe."

Clementine pulled her hand away. How could David be so naïve? "Forget the police, David. You know, I'm not even sure I blame them anymore for doing nothing." The icy realization crept through her brain. It had been so easy to be angry with the police for not getting her the justice she wanted. Blame them because she felt so abused.

"I know Gary's guilty," she said. "I told them Gary's guilty. But they have to have proof. I can't give them that. Maybe there is no proof. So it's up to me. I have to be stronger than I've been before. And smarter." She seized David's shoulders and turned him so that he was looking squarely into her eyes. "Will you help me or not?"

A blood vessel at David's temple pulsed. He leaned closer to her face. "You honestly think this root medicine can give you peace?"

"It's all I've got right now. I have to try."

"Then tell me how I can help."

Clementine smiled into his deep-set blue eyes. For the first time since the rape, she felt the magnetism of his angular jaw and solid shoulders. "Thank you," she said before touching her lips to his.

David slid his arms behind her, drawing her toward him as he leaned against the back of the couch. "You are a remarkable woman," he whispered against her mouth. Was she remarkable? She wondered. Or was she just desperate? David increased the pressure of his mouth against hers. This man had been so good to her, giving her what she needed when she needed it. Was this what she needed now? Could she do this now? Keeping her eyes alert, she studied the smooth texture of David's skin as he kissed her. The corn-silk color of his eyelashes. He was gentle, his hands exploring with an easygoing manner that teased fire into her nerves.

She wanted to be close to him, feel his warmth press into her. He slipped the buttons of her blouse from the buttonholes. Was she really ready for this? She wasn't sure. She relaxed into his embrace and waited to let her body act for itself. She felt no stabs of fear or revulsion as David slid off his shirt and his skin met hers. She was ready when the time came. Safely ensconced in his bed, she let herself be swept into the waves of their lovemaking, lovemaking the way she remembered, missed, and thought she might never experience again.

She wasn't going to let Gary take that away from her too.

12

Summer rolled lazily into Tanner as Independence Day approached. With the rising heat, customers at Back in the Day seemed to linger a little longer, the urgency evaporated from their lives. Clementine appreciated the extra business the slow days brought her. And she really couldn't blame the heat or the customers for the sensation she had that time was barely moving. Five weeks had passed since the trip to the auction, and Erlene still hadn't arranged a visit to see her Aunt Lanita.

During those weeks, Clementine and Erlene had spoken several times, but neither had mentioned Lanita. Clementine wanted to ask but knew arranging the trip was hard for Erlene, so she waited. She kept the talisman block next to her bed so it was the last thing she saw before she went to sleep at night. Knowing what it represented gave her hope and helped her battle the insomnia that plagued her every night. But during the day, her eagerness to use the block was eating her up.

Finally, Erlene called about the trip. "Aunt Lanita lives with my cousin Brianne now," she said, "but they're still in Murfreesboro. Brianne uses her maiden name, so I was able to track her down."

Clementine listened for any hint of resentment in Erlene's voice and was relieved not to hear one. "They were happy to hear from you, weren't they?" she ventured, hoping she was reading Erlene's mood correctly.

"I don't know. I think maybe Brianne was. We were close as little girls. I didn't talk to Aunt Lanita because she was sleeping when I called. Brianne said her mother is pretty stove up with arthritis and stays in bed a lot."

"Did you ask her if I could come visit?" Clementine's fingers were starting to tingle. She gripped the phone harder.

"I've been thinking about that." Erlene took a deep breath. "It'd probably be better if I went with you. They don't know you, and if I'm lucky, they'll be glad to see me. I told her we'd come next Tuesday. I figured you'd close the shop after the long Fourth of July weekend, and you're always closed on Tuesdays and Wednesdays, anyway. Is that okay?"

Okay? Clementine was nearly jumping up and down. "If you were standing next to me, I'd kiss you!" she shouted into the phone.

"You realize Murfreesboro is a five-hour drive from here. It'll have to be a two-day trip."

"I can do that. I'll pay for both of us to stay in a motel."

"Brianne said she has room for us at her house, since her kids moved out."

"Are you sure that'll be all right? I don't want to impose on her."

"You'll hurt her feelings if you don't."

"All right, then. I don't know how I can ever repay you for this." Clementine flopped down on her bed.

Erlene chuckled. "Don't be so eager for payback yet. I'm not sure you're going to like the way this turns out. Like I said, I don't think they can help you, but we'll see. I told Brianne we'd get there about four o'clock on Tuesday. That's when she gets off work."

Clementine agreed to pick up Erlene at ten o'clock Tuesday morning, then clicked off her phone. She seized the block from her bedside table and turned it slowly. She knew almost nothing about the strange carved cube of wood and even less about what she might be getting herself into, but she was willing to take the chance. Tracing her finger around one of the raised symbols, she pondered what kind of curse she wanted for Gary. Maybe she should go straight to the source of the problem and have his penis fall off. Were there hexes for that? Probably not. If things went as Clementine hoped, Lanita would be able to suggest the appropriate hex. But if Lanita was practicing root medicine, would Erlene be upset? In that case, maybe Lanita would know someone who could put a hex on Gary. In the best scenario, Lanita would introduce that person to Clementine while she was in Murfreesboro. But Clementine would be happy with just the name of someone who could help her. Whatever happened, the trip to Murfreesboro was going to be an adventure.

Erlene tried to wait by the front window for Clementine to pick her up, but she couldn't sit still. She'd spent a lot of time selecting the dress she was wearing and the linen dinner napkins she was taking as a hostess gift, but nothing about her felt right. How do you present yourself to relatives you haven't seen in decades and who may not be glad to see you now? Brianne had been cordial on the phone, maybe even pleased that she'd called, but Erlene hadn't told her they wanted to know about root medicine. If she'd told her that, they might not be going.

She also didn't want Brianne to think that was the only reason for the visit. Surely someday she would've gone on her own without Clementine to push her. She hoped she would have. As she went out the door to meet the car, she said a quick prayer that they'd accept her.

Five hours on the road went by much too fast. Clementine drove until they stopped at noon for lunch, but after they ate, she asked Erlene to take a turn. "I didn't sleep much last night," she said before she dozed off.

Erlene thought about taking a side trip to delay their arrival, but she knew how silly that was. They had to get there eventually. About an hour out of Murfreesboro, she pulled into a service station to use the restroom, and Clementine slid under the steering wheel to finish the trip.

Inside the city limits, Erlene opened her purse and took out a printed email with directions from Brianne. Pointing out every turn, she led Clementine down quiet residential streets of modest one- and two-story houses, mostly covered in white clapboard or siding. Even with a few school buses dropping off kids, traffic was light. "Not much going on here," Clementine said.

"It's a tiny town," Erlene replied. "There's a historic district and a small college, but we're not going to drive past those. We need to get on over to Brianne's. Maybe tomorrow if we have time we can take in the sights." She laughed. "It'll take us about fifteen minutes."

In less time than that, the house with Brianne's address appeared. Erlene's stomach jumped. "That's it," she said. "That's Brianne's house."

Clementine parked the van next to the curb, climbed out of the driver's seat, and opened the back of the van to retrieve Erlene's linen napkins and the basket of fruit she brought for Brianne, but Erlene couldn't move. What were they going to say when she asked them about root medicine? Did she have the right to ask for their help with this power her mother had so viciously scorned? How could she expect them not to be angry after her part of the family had severed all ties with them? She shook her head to try to clear her thoughts. She'd been over all these questions before she made the decision to call Brianne. It was too late to back out now.

When Erlene didn't leave the van, Clementine waited patiently on the sidewalk as if she knew how worried her friend was. Erlene looked at the house's front windows to see if anyone was watching. No faces appeared. With a shrug of resolve, she opened the door and went to join Clementine, who patted her back on their way along the cracked sidewalk to the house.

At the door, Erlene took a deep breath and knocked. Within seconds, the door opened to reveal a tall, dark woman, swirls of gray in her close-cut hair, a welcoming smile on her face. "Erlene," she said softly. "I'm Brianne."

Her smile widened as she slipped her arms around Erlene and pressed her cousin to her slender frame. Tears washed across Erlene's eyes before Brianne released her, exclaiming, "I'm so happy y'all are here. Do come in."

Please, God, let her go on being happy to see me no matter what happens, Erlene thought. "I'm glad to see you too," she said. Then she introduced Clementine as Brianne ushered the two of them into the living room.

"Clementine. That's a nice name," Brianne said as Clementine gave her the fruit basket. "Thank you so much. We love fruit." She set the basket on a table and gestured for them to sit on the black leather couch behind a glass-topped coffee table.

When Erlene gave her the linen napkins, she fingered their delicate texture and murmured, "So fine, Erlene. Just like I remember you. Thank you." Still holding them in her lap, she said, "Now tell me everything. I want to know about your husband and your children—you are married, aren't you?—and your job. Did you grow up to be a nurse? You always said you wanted to be a nurse."

"Well, not exactly," Erlene said as Brianne settled into a chair next to the couch. "I'm a dental hygienist."

"Imagine that," Brianne said. "Tell me more."

Not sure what to include and what to leave out, Erlene gave an abbreviated account of her life since she was twelve, just hitting the highlights like how she met Alfred when they were both working in the weave room at the mill. And of course she had to mention that her daughter was valedictorian of her high school class.

"I wish I could've come to your wedding," Brianne said. "Remember when we used to pretend like we were brides?"

"Of course," Erlene said with a giggle. "We'd drag the sheets off the bed and wrap them around us. What about your wedding? Who did you marry?"

"I married a sorry-ass loafer from over in Virginia. We tried to make a go of it for about ten years and then I couldn't take it anymore. We split up in 1989 and I've been living single and loving it ever since." Brianne sassed her shoulders back and forth and tilted her head.

"Oh, my goodness," Erlene said. "What's that like?"

Brianne launched into tales about trips to Wrightsville Beach and pig pickin's with hundred-pound young pigs that had Erlene and Clementine both laughing and shaking their heads. "Of course, most of that's stopped since Mama came to live with me," Brianne concluded. "When I'm not at work, I have to be here looking after her. But I owe her that." She shrugged. "Oh my. I haven't even offered y'all anything to drink. How about some ice tea? Or I reckon it's late enough for a real drink if you're so inclined. Dinner's in the slow cooker, so we can eat whenever we're ready. Mama likes to eat no later than six, so sometimes I feel like I've barely digested lunch when I'm shoving dinner in right after it."

"How is Aunt Lanita?" Erlene really wanted to see her aunt, no matter what happened later.

"She's fine. Just feeling her years. Can I get y'all some bourbon? Or I think we have some wine." Brianne walked toward the kitchen.

"I'll take a little bourbon," Erlene said.

"Me too, thank you," Clementine added.

Erlene and Clementine sat in silence as the sound of ice clinking into glasses drifted from the kitchen. Then softly from the hall came the sound of slippers padding against the hardwood floor. A gnome of a woman with shoulders hunched and tiny eyes peering out of a face like a walnut shell shuffled into the living room. In front of the couch, she stopped and stared. "Do I know you?" she asked.

Erlene wanted to cry. "I'm Erlene, Aunt Lanita. Myrtle's girl."

The tiny eyes blinked several times. "Mercy me. You're all growed up. But I can see it's you. Come give me some sugar."

Erlene rose from the couch and bent over to kiss Lanita's cheek while tears dampened her eyes again. She couldn't believe how slight and frail the old woman looked. In Erlene's memory, she was solid and strong.

Lanita's pencil-thin lips turned up at the edges. "And who's that?" She pointed at Clementine.

"She's my friend Clementine."

Lanita shuffled to a straight-backed chair and sat down. "Why's she here?"

A prickle of fear ran through Erlene. She hadn't expected to get to the purpose of the visit this quickly, but apparently Lanita's direct approach to life hadn't changed with age. Erlene had to try to hold her off so they could enjoy seeing each other a little longer after so many years. "She came along to keep me company," she said.

"Why are you here?"

"To see you and Brianne. It's been a long time." Erlene's voice had a slight quake.

"Too long. How's Myrtle? Does she know you're here?" Lanita's mouth continued to move after she spoke, making soft sucking sounds.

"Mama's doing okay. She broke her ankle last year and that's slowed her down a lot. But she's okay."

"I wish she'd come with you." Lanita wiggled farther back in the chair, her feet barely touching the floor.

"Well, she's eighty-four now, you know, and her ankle and all. I'm afraid the trip would be too much for her. Maybe next time."

"Well, hey, Mama," Brianne came from the kitchen, clutching two short drinks. "I didn't know you were in here. I thought you were back in your room watching your shows. Would you like a little nip before dinner?"

"Shows are over. How come you didn't tell me we have company?"

Lanita reached for one of the glasses in Brianne's hand.

Brianne handed her the drink with an apologetic smile at Erlene and Clementine. "I was gonna tell you after your shows. Do you know who this is?"

"Course I know who it is. Though it's a wonder after all these years." Lanita turned to Erlene. "You didn't tell me whether Myrtle knows you're here. My guess is she don't."

Erlene licked her lips. "I thought I'd wait and tell her after the visit."

Lanita grunted. "Probably a good idea. Myrtle never wanted to be the first to try anything."

After dinner, the four women settled back in the living room. Erlene was glad to see Lanita take her seat in the straight-backed chair. She had feared the old woman would go back to watching television or maybe go straight to bed, and she wanted to squeeze out every moment she could with her aunt during their short visit. She tried to continue the dinner conversation, which had included some surprising, some shocking, and some heartwarming bits of news about family members, but Clementine was giving her meaningful looks. Erlene knew what she wanted. And she was right that this was the time to do it, with everyone feeling mellow after cocktails and dinner.

Erlene pulled up all the courage she could. "Aunt Lanita," she said. "Does anybody around here still practice root medicine?"

Lanita's sparse eyebrows darted upward. "Who wants to know? Not you, I'm guessing."

A nervous shadow swept across Clementine's face.

Erlene swallowed hard. "No, ma'am. It's not me. It's Clementine."

"Uh-huh." Lanita nodded. "I would've figured that." Her tiny eyes fixated on Clementine. "What you be needing the medicine for?"

Erlene ached for her friend in having to tell the story again, but Clementine never flinched. "I was raped," she said, "and I know who did it, but I don't have any proof, so the police won't arrest him. Getting justice is up to me."

Lanita continued to nod, her forehead more wrinkled than before. Brianne's posture stiffened, erasing the casual openness she'd exuded since Clementine and Erlene arrived. "So that's why you came. I thought you didn't approve of root medicine," she said to Erlene.

This was the moment Erlene had feared, and it hit her like a hot poker. Now their real feelings toward her would come out.

"That's Mama," she said as confidently as she could, "not me. I don't disapprove of root medicine. In fact, I don't know much about it. But I will say that I hate as much as I hate anything what root medicine's done to our family." She made a gesture to indicate the three family members in the room. "I hate that I missed growing up with you, Brianne. And that I haven't seen you, Aunt Lanita, in thirty years. I hate that my mother abandoned her own sister like she has. I hate that there've been these voids in my life. The one thing I do know about root medicine is that it sure didn't do our family any good." Erlene lowered her eyes, awaiting their rebuff.

"She's doing this for me," Clementine spoke up quickly. "I asked her to. Don't blame her. It's all for me. And I never realized how hard it is for her until now."

In the silence that followed, Erlene felt Lanita and Brianne staring at her. When she looked up, she held their gaze for several minutes, not knowing what else she could say. Then the words came to her. "Nana always said root medicine could be used for good or evil. It did so much evil to our family. Maybe it can do some good for Clementine. Will you help her?"

Lanita twisted her mouth from one side to the other. "Ain't no guarantee with the medicine," she said. "It's backfired on a few folks. What you wanna do to this man?"

Clementine raised her chin and said in an even voice, "I want him to feel as violated as I do. I want to trample something he values, and I want him to be afraid that what happens to him will happen again." Erlene watched for changes in Lanita's expression, but nothing about the walnut face moved.

Then, quietly, Lanita asked, "Are you thinking about harming some part of this man's body? Or do you want to make him miserable in his head?"

"I don't know," Clementine said. "I don't know what's possible. I just know I want him to go on hurting, just like I do."

"Is there a hex that acts like that, Aunt Lanita?" Erlene asked.

Lanita turned slowly to look at her daughter. "I'm not the one you should be asking. Unlike my mama, I don't have the gift." She waited for her words to sink in. "Ask Brianne," she said at last. "She's got the gift."

Brianne shook her head. "No. I don't do that."

"But you can," Lanita said, her tiny eyes glowing.

Erlene spoke up. "If you don't want to do it, can you tell us somebody else who can?" Nothing would please her more than moving the medicine outside the family.

"No need for that." Lanita's thin voice swelled. "Brianne can do it."

Brianne pursed her lips in resignation. "I'll have to study up on it. Look at Nana's notes and journals. I can't tell you anything now. Maybe tomorrow."

Lanita pushed herself out of the straight-back chair. "Tomorrow," she said and walked down the hall. The shushing sound of her slippers hung in the air behind her.

"You'll have to excuse me too," Brianne said. "I have work to do. Good thing I'm taking the morning off. We'll look at anything I find then. Come on. I'll show you where your bedroom is."

Erlene followed her cousin down the hall, not certain now if she was welcome or resented.

Lying in the frilly twin bed across from the matching bed where Erlene lay, Clementine watched a breeze move moon-shadow leaves on the bedroom wall. She was too keyed up to sleep. Maybe Brianne really could help her even the score with Gary. If someone had told her six months ago that she'd be drawn into hexes and root medicine, she'd have laughed. But when the accepted channels are closed, who knows where you'll turn. She tried to imagine what kind of hex Brianne would come up with.

As her thoughts moved on to the huge debt she owed Erlene, Erlene's voice drifted through the darkness. "Clementine, are you awake?"

"I'm here," she answered. "Are you all right? You were so brave tonight."

"I'm just wondering something. You don't have to tell me if you don't want to, but it's been on my mind a while." Sheets rustled as Erlene rolled onto her side to face Clementine. "Why do you think Gary raped you?"

Clementine clasped her hands behind her head on the pillow. "At first I thought he was still carrying a grudge for something that he says happened in high school. But adults write nasty letters about things like that or they embarrass you at a high school reunion. They don't rape you. There's something deeper going on inside Gary. That high school thing was an excuse, I think. He's probably been needing a target for a long time, and then I came along."

"Do you wish you hadn't moved back to Tanner?"

Clementine sighed. "Yes. But there's nothing I can do about that now. I'm not the same person I was before the rape." The air conditioning came on with a whooshing sound, like a spirit entering the room. Clementine shivered. "Before the rape," she murmured, feeling a fluttering in her chest, "I knew where my life was going. I was back in Tanner, the place I've always thought of as home, no matter how many other places I've lived. I was home, and I was building the business I've dreamed of for years. With the antique shop and David, I felt like I was really moving forward for the first time since Gordon died." She stared at the ceiling.

"And now how do you feel?" Erlene's voice was as soft as Clementine's.

"Like somebody threw me into a hole. And that good life I had before is still up there, but I can't get back to it unless I can dig my way out of the hole and wash off the dirt. And I don't know if I can ever do that."

"I think you can."

"Maybe. But it's not going to happen until Gary pays for what he's done. You'll never know how much I appreciate your bringing me here and getting your family to help me. I hope it doesn't cause problems with Miss Myrtle."

"We'll just have to see," Erlene said with a muffled edge to her voice.

Clementine had no answer for that. She lay silent in the shadowy room until she finally fell asleep.

Sunlight illuminated faded papers and a few tattered notebooks spread across the kitchen table the next morning. A cup of coffee in one hand and a pencil in the other, Brianne was perusing the papers when Clementine came into the room. Erlene stood by the stove stirring a pot of grits while Lanita, perched on a stool, flipped bacon in a crusty black skillet. Clementine had heard Erlene moving around their room at least an hour earlier, but lack of sleep made it hard for Clementine to drag herself out of bed. Now she was relieved to see Erlene and her relatives apparently getting along fine.

"Morning," Brianne mumbled, looking up from the papers. "I may have something for you." Erlene and Lanita went on cooking and exchanging soft remarks. "You said last night you wanted to destroy or take away something this man values," Brianne said. "Here's a hex to make a man impotent. Seems appropriate to me."

Thrilled that Brianne was reading about root medicine, Clementine peeked over her shoulder, eager to see what a hex looked like on paper. The instructions appeared squeezed together in tight, cramped handwriting. The ink had faded from black to gray but was still readable. "Take the underwear the man sheds to have sexual relations and tie it into seven knots. Weight it with a rock and throw it into a river while saying: 'Moon of darkness, visit upon this man. Take his manhood, gnarl it like this cloth. Hold him powerless, weak and twisted as a rag.' The man will be able to have relations again only when the underwear is retrieved and the knots are untied."

"You know," Clementine said, "that may be too obvious. Is there something more subtle? And something that will make him worry about whether it's going to happen again."

Brianne shuffled the papers around and flipped through some of the journals. "Here's one that has to do with money," she said, pointing to a page in a notebook. "It says you can make money disappear from someone's wallet or purse, but it's kind of complicated. Let's see." She began to read aloud. "In dark of night or other time of secret, take a paper bill from the person's wallet or purse. Light a black candle and burn the bill while saying, 'Power of darkness, descend this plume of smoke.

Occupy these ashes with your will to disappear.' When the ash-es have cooled, mix them with flour. Take the mixture to the person's home and spread it on their threshold. Every time the person crosses the threshold, whatever bills are in their wallet or purse will disappear."

"Why do you have to use flour?" Clementine asked.

"Because flour is the root of our most basic food and there-fore a sustainer of life. You know, staff of life and all that. So the power of flour ensures the hex will continue to live." Brianne handed the notebook to Clementine. "What do you think?"

"I think y'all need to eat some breakfast," Erlene said. "Don't make any big decisions on an empty stomach." She pushed aside a pile of papers and set a platter of scrambled eggs and bacon on the table.

"We got grits and biscuits coming up," Lanita called from her perch on the stool. "Brianne, get the molasses out of the cupboard, and get some butter too."

"Yes, ma'am," Brianne said. "What about the hex, Clemen-tine?"

"I'm afraid it's not enough. Gary may not carry much cash at a time. And I don't know how I'd get money out of his wallet. But I like that it keeps happening. Maybe something involving money is a good idea. It just has to be more money."

The four women gathered around the table and read more of Nana's notes as they ate. When Brianne began to carry empty plates to the sink, Erlene pointed to a scrap of paper in front of her. "If you want something scary involving money, how about the IRS? Look at this." She passed the paper to Clementine.

Called "IRS Revenge Spell," the instructions were long and detailed. First, the person casting the spell should write the intended victim's name on a blank 1040 form. The form must be an official form printed by the IRS, not a copy. Next, write the amount of tax the person wants the target to have to pay.

Then, bake the form in an oven until it's brittle, but not ashes. Pulverize the form into powder and mix it with dirt from the target's footprints or a place where he frequently walks.

Bag the mixture in a tightly sealed bottle or bag. Then create a confusion powder from lodestone sachet, graveyard dirt, valerian root, poppy seeds, and black mustard seeds.

Clementine looked up from reading the spell. "I don't know about this," she said. "There's a lot to it, and in between steps, you have to change your clothes and wash yourself with lemon and bitterroot water."

"If you want a strong result you gotta make a strong effort," Lanita chided as she finished the last strip of bacon. "Root medicine ain't easy, girl. What else is there to it?"

Clementine read on. Once she had the IRS form mixture and the confusion powder, she'd need van van oil. She stopped reading again. "What's van van oil?" she asked.

"It's like a multi-purpose conjuring oil," Brianne said. "Used to be you could only get it in New Orleans, but nowadays you can order it right off the Internet. You won't have any trouble getting it." Brianne's voice was light as if she were dispensing everyday knowledge.

Clementine turned back to the instructions. The next step was to combine the form mixture and the confusion powder with the van van oil, but not enough to make it clumpy. It still needed to be powdery. Then go to a wind-free place off the hex maker's property. While taking nine steps backward, sprinkle the combined mixture along a path where the target will walk. Turn around and walk or run away without looking back.

A giggle started rising in Clementine's throat. This couldn't be real. Even if the powder had some power, who's to say Gary would be the first person to walk on it. Or maybe he would walk on some of it, but somebody else could come along and step in it too. She stifled the giggle. "What if somebody else steps in the powder?" she asked as seriously as she could.

Lanita glared at her as if she were a dull, stubborn child. "It don't matter if somebody else steps in it. It's got the man's name on it, so it won't bother nobody else."

"Oh, yeah," Clementine murmured, feeling chastised.

"So is this the type of thing you're looking for?" Brianne asked.

"I'd go for the impotency one if I were you," Erlene said. "Let him wonder if he's ever gonna get his manhood back."

"Ain't no reason you can't do both." Lanita's grin shot more wrinkles through her tiny dark face. "Mama used to offer back-up charms just to make sure."

Clementine smiled as she reached for the papers with the two hexes written on them. Holding the papers made her fingers tingle. She still couldn't believe she was doing this, but if it had worked for generations of Erlene's family, who was she to doubt it?

"I'd like to do both, but how on earth am I going to get the underwear Gary takes off to have sex?" The obvious answer made her shudder. She dropped the paper with the impotency hex on the table. "No, I'll stick with the IRS one. If I do it right, he'll end up in jail just like Al Capone, and that's where I want him, for a long, long, long, long time."

Brianne gathered the papers together and tucked them into one of the notebooks. "You know I can't make any promises about this."

"You got to believe, child, just like Mama did, if you want it to work." Lanita's words were almost a hiss.

Brianne sighed. "Is it okay if I copy these instructions with the copier, or does Clementine have to write them all down herself?"

"You got to write 'em down and bless 'em before you give 'em to her. That's where the gift comes in." Lanita handed a scrap of paper to Brianne, who got up from the table and took the paper into her bedroom. Erlene and Clementine finished clearing the dishes as Lanita shuffled to her chair in the living room.

A few hours later they were on their way back to Tanner with the hex instructions stowed securely in Clementine's purse. For the first time since the rape, Clementine felt a sense of power. An IRS audit wasn't the worst thing that could happen to Gary, but at least it was a start.

13

Erlene kept the visit to Murfreesboro a secret from Miss Myrtle for three days. She hadn't planned to tell her ever, but seeing Aunt Lanita and Brianne after all those years stirred up such a strong yearning for family that she had to share her feelings with her mother.

Finding the right time to tell her was crucial. She had to find a time when Myrtle's ankle wasn't hurting and she was in a good mood. Usually those two things coincided, but not always. Erlene decided her best bet was their Saturday afternoon outing, which in the summer involved a trip to the Tanner municipal park riverside to watch the canoes and kayaks drift by and sometimes throw a line in the water in case a misguided bass or catfish swam by.

The Saturday after the Murfreesboro trip was sticky hot, but Erlene found a spot by the river in the shade of a mimosa and set up Myrtle's canvas director's chair with a pillow in the back. She left Myrtle in the air-conditioned car while she carted the fishing rods and the tackle box from the trunk and placed them next to the director's chair along with a plastic folding chair for herself. After pausing just long enough to pat the sweat from her forehead, she went back for her mother.

"I don't know about this," Myrtle muttered as Erlene helped her from the car to the fishing site. "It's probably too hot for them fish to bite. They're smart enough to stay on the river bottom when the weather gets like this."

"As long as we're here, we might as well give it a try," Erlene said. She settled Miss Myrtle into her chair and handed her a rod. As the old woman squinched her tiny eyes to stare at the river, Erlene was amazed at how much she looked like Lanita. Anyone would know they were sisters. Myrtle grunted, then lifted the rod behind her shoulder with both hands and flung the soft plastic lizard on the end of the line into the water. Once the lure was settled, Erlene slid a three-legged stool under Miss Myrtle's bad ankle. Satisfied that her mother was comfortable, she tossed her own line into the water and sat down in the plastic chair.

Before long, a canoe with two teenage girls swept by, clinging to the far side of the river to give the fishing lines a wide berth. The girls waved, and the fisherwomen waved back. Soon a kayak followed the same path, its occupants waving also. Then the river was empty. Its ripples and gurgles rolled on endlessly in their own undisturbed rhythm. At one point, Myrtle tilted her chin down toward her chest and closed her eyes. Erlene would have sworn she was asleep except she never dropped the fishing rod and sat up suddenly when her line went taut. The line went slack again just as quickly. "Nothing but a nibble," Myrtle mumbled and closed her eyes again.

A lazy breeze made the afternoon heat bearable. Erlene pushed up her sleeves to catch as much of the breeze as she could. She couldn't keep Miss Myrtle out here too much longer, so she had to get the conversation going. "Mama, I want to tell you something."

Myrtle raised heavy eyelids and looked around her fishing rod.

Erlene laid her rod on the chair seat. "I did something this week that you may not like, but I'm glad I did it." Myrtle's eyebrows rose slightly, and her lips curled as she waited for the news. "I went to see Aunt Lanita and Cousin Brianne." Erlene quickly blurted out the words, figuring that was the best way to get it done.

At that moment, a man in a canoe shouted, "Catching anything?" but when no one answered him, he floated on by.

Myrtle's eyes were bright and her lips twitched. "You know we don't have nothing to do with them no more."

"Well, we should. And that's why I went to see them." Erlene reached for her mother's hand, but Miss Myrtle snatched it away. "Lanita said she misses you. She wished you'd come with me. Mama, Nana is dead. You can't hold what Nana did against Lanita forever."

Myrtle tugged on her fishing rod. "I heard Lanita is into the medicine just like Mama was."

"She's not. I promise you she's not," Erlene said, praying that Miss Myrtle wouldn't think to ask about Brianne.

"I don't believe you." Myrtle reeled in the plastic lizard with ferocious turns of the spindle. "Take me home."

"But, Mama. I want to talk about Lanita."

"Take me home."

Just then a strong jerk almost pulled Erlene's rod out of the chair. Erlene grabbed the rod with the reflex of a cat. "I have a fish!" she shouted.

"Then pull it in." A great sigh escaped from Miss Myrtle.

Erlene yanked the line to set the hook in the fish's mouth. Then she slowly reeled it in. Out of the water, the fish flipped its tail in every direction, trying to get free. With the grace of an experienced fisherwoman, Erlene grabbed the fish's middle and gently worked the hook out of its mouth. From nose to tail, the fish was only about eight inches long. "Should I keep it?" Erlene asked, but Miss Myrtle was busy taking the lizard off her line and storing it in the tackle box. She didn't answer. Erlene threw the fish back into the water.

With the lure put away and her line fully reeled in, Miss Myrtle sat with her arms folded across her chest, staring at the river. If she'd had her purse in her lap, she'd have looked exactly as she looked every Sunday morning of Erlene's childhood waiting for the rest of the family to get ready to go to church. Her expression showed the same impatience and annoyance.

"But Mama, we need to talk about this," Erlene said once the fish was gone.

"Take me home."

Erlene waited, undecided about what to do. "All right, then. I'll take some of our stuff to the car and turn the air conditioning on. Then I'll come back for you."

Miss Myrtle didn't answer.

Erlene gathered up everything except Miss Myrtle's chair and started for the car. She had no idea what to do next. Her mother and aunt didn't have many years left. If they didn't make up now, they might never have the chance. But Erlene was sure after this conversation that she could never tell Miss Myrtle the reason for the trip to Murfreesboro. And if Lanita let it slip out, Miss Myrtle might never forgive Erlene.

Erlene thought about Clementine and the fledgling friendship they'd formed in the past year. Was she sacrificing her relationship with her mother for her relationship with Clementine? Was any friendship worth that? Erlene stuffed the fishing gear into the trunk of her Camry. Clementine was the reason she had gotten to see Lanita and Brianne again. The reunion meant a lot to her, regardless of what Miss Myrtle thought. She slammed the trunk lid down with a resounding thud. She knew she would have to open it again for Myrtle's chair, but slamming it gave her so much satisfaction that she opened and slammed it again. All these women—Myrtle, Lanita, Brianne, and Clementine—were important to her, and by God, she was going to make them get along. She trudged back to the riverbank with a half-smile on her face.

Clementine's van van oil and lodestone sachet powder arrived via UPS one week after the trip to Murfreesboro. Getting the IRS to send her a 1040 form took longer. While she waited for the form, she gathered the other ingredients she needed for the hex. To her delight, she found several sources for the poppy seeds and black mustard seeds. Most health food stores sold them, or if she was afraid of running into somebody she knew at GNC, she could order them from Amazon.com. She chose Amazon. Getting valerian root was a little trickier, but she found it in an organic health food store in Charlotte. The store proprietor, a wizened little man with bright green eyes, agreed to order bitterroot from a store in Montana. He assured her she'd never find it on the East Coast.

To dig up graveyard dirt, Clementine ventured into the Tanner cemetery early one morning, when she hoped nobody would be there. Explaining what she was doing could be difficult. The hex instructions didn't say if the dirt had to come specifically from a grave or if it could be dirt surrounding the graves. To be on the safe side, she took it from one of the oldest graves at the edge of the cemetery, hidden from the main roads and paths by a pair of towering oak trees. She knew the spot well because it had been a favorite hiding place of hers when her father used to bring her to the cemetery to play hide-and-seek decades ago.

When she had the dirt safe in the bag she'd brought for that purpose, she paused for a while, gazing out across the lichen-covered headstones. Some of the graves were more than a hundred years old. The tallest ones in the center of the area marked the final resting places for several of Tanner's founders. Her father used to tell her stories about these men and their brave exploits in getting the town started. A few were farmers, and some were merchants. One was a manufacturer who started the cotton mill that grew to employ most of the townspeople before its demise threw Tanner into the economic slump it was in today. Maybe Clementine should use dirt from one of their graves to hex Gary. What would their ghosts think about that? Or their descendants, for that matter? No, she decided, she would stick with the dirt she had from the old familiar grave she knew as a child. Once she had tried to learn something about the person whose name was on the headstone, but she'd had no luck. "Getting justice for me will be your claim to fame," she whispered over the grave just before she left.

Collecting the final ingredient was the most challenging. Somehow she had to get dirt from an area where Gary frequently walked, which she figured had to be either his house or the restaurant where he worked. The restaurant was pretty much surrounded by concrete, so her best choice was the house.

When she told David she was going to get dirt from Gary's yard, he yelled like he thought she'd suddenly gone deaf, causing her to almost drop the phone. "You are not going anywhere near his house." The words hung in the air between Clementine's ear and the phone she instantly held at a distance.

"I have to," she said when she returned the phone to her ear. "I don't know anywhere else to get dirt he walks on. Do you?"

Silence told her David didn't know any more about Gary's walking habits than she did. "I'll get the dirt," he volunteered at last.

Now Clementine was in a quandary. Did she trust that David would actually go to Gary's house, or would he give her any old dirt and tell her it came from Gary's? "David Adams, do you solemnly swear that you will get dirt from Gary's house that you are reasonably certain he walked on?"

"Jesus, you sound like a lawyer," David said. "Yes, I swear on my beloved Mini Cooper that I will get you genuine dirt from Gary's yard."

"This is serious, David."

"Okay. I promise I'll get you some of Gary's dirt. If you'll promise me you won't go over to his house alone."

"I promise."

As fortune would have it, the IRS form arrived the day before David showed up with the dirt. Clean and crisp, the form gave off the vinegar smell of fresh ink. "Never thought I'd be glad to see one of these," Clementine said aloud as she placed the form on the slender desk in her bedroom with the other ingredients. Now all she needed was the dirt.

David rang her doorbell at five o'clock the next afternoon, a paper bag clutched in his hand. Although it was Saturday, one of the busiest days at the antique shop, Clementine had closed a little early when David called to say he had the dirt. "Let me see it," she said as soon as he was in her living room.

"It's just dirt," David said. "It looks like dirt."

"Let me see it anyway." Clementine grabbed the bag and stared inside. "How'd you get it?"

"I waited till I saw him leave for work this afternoon. Then I walked over to his back steps and used a whisk broom to brush the dirt from the steps he'd just come down. And in case that wasn't enough, I dug up a little dirt from the patch of ground between the steps and his driveway."

"How'd you know what time he left for work?"

"I guessed. I finished talking with a fellow at the counseling center about two o'clock—he was a sad case. Just lost the second job he's had since he was laid off from the mill." David shook his head as a mournful punctuation. "Anyway, I decided to go on over to Gary's and see if he was home. His car was in the driveway, so I waited in my car down the street till he left. By the way, Gary came to a Kiwanis Club meeting last week. He wants to join."

Clementine tamped down a swell of anger. "Look at him. The stellar citizen."

"I just thought you'd want to know."

"All the more reason to do the hex. Thanks for the dirt." Clementine carried the bag to the kitchen with David trailing behind her. Clustered in a corner of the kitchen counter was an array of bottles and plastic bags.

David studied the containers with their powders and pills. "What's this?" He picked up a bag holding a reddish forked object that looked a little like a radish.

"Bitterroot. I have to boil it with lemon and wash with the water between steps of the hex."

David's nose wrinkled in distaste. "How much of you do you have to wash with that stuff?"

"All of me, I guess."

David shook his head. "This seems so pointless. I mean, really, at best it's a waste of time. But I know you believe it might work."

Clementine took the bag of bitterroot away from him. "I've said all along if you don't want to be part of this, you don't have to. But I'll tell you this—there are more energies and powers in the universe than anyone understands, so who are we to discount any of them? Now I'm going to get started. Do you want to help or not?" She raised her eyebrows and waited, her hands planted firmly on her hips.

"What about Erlene? She got you into this. Doesn't she want to help? Shouldn't we call her to come over?"

"Nope. She wants as little to do with this as possible. Miss Myrtle would kill her if she found out Erlene was messing with root medicine. I don't think Erlene's even told her we went to see Lanita."

David sighed. "I swear this is going to cause more trouble for you and Erlene than it's worth. But we've been over that before, haven't we?" He leaned against the refrigerator. "So what do we do first?"

"We boil the bitterroot so we have bitterroot water." After running water into a large pasta pot, Clementine plunked in the bitterroot and turned on the burner. "Now we have to fill out the form and bake it in the oven. Let me see." She turned to the refrigerator—shoving David aside—and consulted a paper held to its door with magnets. On the paper, Brianne's neatly printed words appeared organized and regimented, the exact opposite of the mayhem they were supposed to cause. "Yep. That's right."

Clementine took a pen from the container next to the telephone and sat down at the old battered worktable she had salvaged from another antique dealer's barn to make her kitchen eat-in. She printed Gary's name on the first line, then flipped the form over to the back page. "How much tax should I have him owe?" She looked toward David and waited. Her first inclination was to write some exorbitant amount, but even the IRS might find that odd and figure a mistake had been made. "It has to be so much that he can't possibly pay it and he'll end up in jail," Clementine said, "but not so much that nobody would believe he really owes it."

The blank expression on David's face showed he didn't think it mattered one way or the other what she wrote on the form. "Thanks for nothing," she muttered as she pressed the pen against the "amount you owe" line and carefully wrote a figure she thought was probably about twice his annual salary. That should do the job.

On the stove, the bitterroot water was boiling, sending clouds of steam into the air. "Wonder how long I should let it boil?" Clementine asked, not so much of David, since he probably had no opinion about that either, but more of the universe in general. "I'll give it thirty minutes, and then it has to cool so I can wash with it between steps."

Clementine set the timer on the microwave and fixed martinis for David and her. When she handed one of the drinks to David, she said, "We can only have one because we have serious work to do tonight, so make it last."

By the time the buzzer sounded, the martinis were gone, and Clementine had a nice warm feeling. This hex was going to be the answer she was looking for. She squeezed the juice of five lemons into the water—again relying on intuition since the hex instructions didn't specify how much juice was needed.

"Time to move on," she announced to David, who was twirling his empty martini glass and smiling slightly. She dropped the tax form onto a cookie sheet and shoved it into the preheated oven.

"How hot do you have that set for?" David asked. "You know paper burns at four hundred fifty-one degrees, don't you?"

"Yes, I know that. I read Ray Bradbury. I've got it set at four twenty-five. And I'm watching it." Clementine closed the oven door. Soon the paper turned brown and curled at the corners. Clementine removed the brittle form, tore it into pieces, and dropped them into a large porcelain mortar that she used with a matching pestle to mush up garlic. Working with the pestle created a harsh scraping sound.

David grimaced. "Can I help?" he asked.

"Put the dirt you brought into that plastic bag," Clementine said, pointing to a ziplock bag on the counter. Keeping a stern supervising eye on David, she continued to crush the paper until all she had left was a coarse brown powder. Then she poured the powder in with the dirt in the ziplock bag and closed it tight. "Now I have to wash with the bitterroot and lemon water. Maybe you better wash too."

"Oh, come on." David backed away a few steps.

"If you want to help, you have to go all the way. I hope you brought a change of clothes."

"Hell, no, I didn't bring a change of clothes. Why would I do that?"

"Then you can't help anymore. We have to follow the instructions to the letter." Clementine let her loose dress fall from her shoulders and drop to the floor.

"All right by me." David grinned. "I'll just watch."

Tenuously, Clementine dipped a clean dishcloth into the bitterroot water, hoping it had cooled enough. Satisfied she wasn't going to get burned, she saturated the dishcloth and wiped it over her arms, legs, and face. "I don't know if I have to change my underwear, but the instructions don't say anything about underwear, so I'm going to assume not. It was covered up by my clothes."

"Oh, I think you definitely need to change your underwear," David said, grinning wider.

"Shut up. I'll be back in a minute." Clementine fled into the bedroom and came back dressed in shorts and a T-shirt. "You can carry my dress to the clothes basket in my closet," she said. "We'll be like the wet hand, dry hand system in breading okra for frying. You can take care of anything I shouldn't touch after I've bathed with the bitterroot and lemon."

David swept up the dress and headed for the bedroom.

Clementine consulted the instructions on the refrigerator door, then assembled the lodestone sachet, graveyard dirt, valerian root, poppy seeds, and black mustard seeds. Back in the kitchen, David sat at the worktable and watched her combine the ingredients in a large yellow mixing bowl.

"You see this bowl?" she asked. "It's perfect for what we're doing. It's the sole survivor of a set of Pyrex bowls my mother had from the 1940s. It's full of memories and spirits from Mother's cooking. Makes me feel like she's here with us. I hope she'd approve."

David gave her a winsome smile but said nothing until she separated a capsule and dumped the contents into the bowl. "That looks like a sleeping pill," he ventured.

"You're close. It's valerian root. It helps you sleep, and it's also good for anxiety. I think it's where Valium comes from." Clementine added the seeds and reached for the bag of graveyard dirt. As she poured in the dirt, David frowned.

"That's an awful lot of dirt you're using. How's that dirt different from what I brought you?"

"This is graveyard dirt, rich with the remains of long-departed souls."

David's eyes widened. "Jesus Christ," he whispered.

"This mixture is important, I think," Clementine said. "It's a confusion powder. The hex instructions don't say this, but I bet it's to confuse the universe and make things happen that weren't supposed to happen, like Gary owing money to the IRS."

David shrugged. "If you say so."

Clementine mixed the powders and seeds in the bowl until they looked as blended as they were going to get. Then she stripped off the shorts and shirt and wiped herself down with the bitterroot and lemon water again.

"Why don't you take off all your clothes and brew this up in the nude? Then you could just wash yourself after every step and save the time it takes to change clothes."

Clementine laughed at David's mixture of lasciviousness and practicality. "Because I have to follow the directions exactly, and the directions say to change clothes between every step." She went into the bedroom and came back in another pair of shorts and a T-shirt.

"How many more times do you have to change?" David dutifully gathered up the first pair of shorts and shirt.

"We're almost done." Clementine opened a little bottle of yellow liquid. "This is van van oil," she said. "It brings everything together." She dumped the tax form mixture into the confusion powder and added a few drops of van van oil. "But you can't use too much. The mixture still needs to be powdery." She stirred all the ingredients in the bowl until she was satisfied the mixture felt right. "Okay." She turned to David. "Now's the big moment. We have to take it over to Gary's house."

David gave a skeptical look at the powder in the bowl. "But I was just there digging in his yard a few hours ago. I don't want any of his neighbors to see me back there doing something peculiar in his yard again."

"Then you stay here. I'll take the powder over there. What do you think I should carry it in?" Clementine rifled through paper bags tucked away in one of her cabinets.

"No, you will not go over there alone. I'll go, but let's wait until dark. A little extra time couldn't possibly screw up the hex."

Clementine didn't want to wait, but doing it in the dark made sense. "All right. Let's eat some supper and then we'll go." Then, as if they were an old married couple who agreed on their summer vacation, they ate.

Finally, the sun went down and the sky blackened enough to suit David. Clementine was afraid transferring the powder to another container would spoil the hex, so she covered the mixing bowl with plastic wrap. The duo set off in David's car with Clementine holding the bowl in her lap. Neither of them said a word as they rode—the possible consequences of their mission were too heavy. A few children ran through neighborhood yards, playing hide-and-seek in the summer evening, but most people were inside in the air conditioning. Lightning bugs winked on and off as the car slid by. Gary's street was particularly quiet, which Clementine took to be a sign that forces were aligned in her favor.

David drove by Gary's house looking for Gary's car in the driveway. The house was dark and the driveway empty, so he turned back and parked out front. He offered to do whatever had to be done with the powder, but Clementine refused. She was sure she had to do this part herself. She had tucked the instructions into her purse, and she read them one more time, even though she had the final step memorized.

"This won't take long," she said. "I'll be back before you know it." As quietly as she could, she slipped out of the car and made her way down the driveway. The asphalt was still warm from the afternoon sun, oozing heat through her sandals' thin soles. She surveyed the house next door, pleased at the lack of any signs of life. Only a single light gleamed in an upstairs window.

When Clementine reached Gary's back steps, she stopped, still as a statue, focusing on the air. The slightest breeze would destroy the hex. Her skin waited, ready to detect any flicker. Nothing. *Take nine steps backward, sprinkling the powder as you go along a path where the target will walk* she recited to herself. She scooped a handful of powder and took a backward step. Careful not to drop all the powder in one spot, she scattered it on the path from the stairs to the driveway, counting her steps as she went. On step nine, she emptied the bowl and turned around to run without looking back like the instructions said.

As soon as she turned, a screech from David's car horn sliced through the still night. Clementine recoiled at the noise, barely managing to hang on to the bowl. In the next second she realized why David was pounding on the horn. Gary's car was creeping up the driveway, its headlights illuminating the yard at the side of the house. Clementine fled into the shadows, hoping he hadn't seen her, but it was a futile wish. In the next second, he stopped the car and flung open the door.

Hey!" he yelled. "What are you doing in my yard?" Clementine kept moving toward the street, but Gary was following her now. "Stop!" he yelled. Aware that she was carrying the evidence of what she'd done, Clementine flung the bowl into a bush. The soft thud distracted Gary for a second, but he soon grabbed her arm. "Fuck," he said. "It's you. What the hell are you doing at my house?"

Clementine had managed to get close enough to the street for a streetlight to shine onto Gary's face. Narrowed eyes and tightened lips rose above the shadows around his nose. "Let go of me!" Clementine shrieked. She tried to pull away from his grasp, but he was too strong. Even a clobbering kick in the shins didn't move him.

"You bitch. What are you doing to my house? You're trespassing, you know. I could shoot you and nobody would blame me."

"Let her go, Gary." David had reached the two of them and locked his fingers around Gary's wrist.

With a sudden jerk, Gary released Clementine's arm. "Now I have two trespassers. And if both of you don't get off my property right now, I will call the police."

Clementine rubbed her arm where Gary's fingers had dug into her flesh. The sight of him, smell of him, horror of his hand on her again made her feel faint. "Don't worry. I can't stand being anywhere near you," she barked as she turned to walk toward David's car.

"Then get out of town. I don't know why you came back in the first place. We don't want you here." Gary's voice rang out over her retreating body. David walked beside her, and she could sense the tension in every step he took. He wanted to yell back at Gary, but he didn't.

David didn't speak again until they were in the car and moving down the street. "He was right, you know. We were trespassing."

"I don't give a shit. How does trespassing compare with rape?" Clementine clasped her hands between her thighs to stop their shaking. "I put the powder where he's sure to walk on it, and that's all that matters." She drew in two quick breaths. "And if he thinks I'm going to leave town, he's got another think coming. This is my town as much as anybody's, and there are people who want me here."

David patted her leg. His hand was cool despite the warm summer night. He drove her home and stayed with her until she left to open the shop on Sunday morning.

～

By Monday Clementine lost the edginess the trip to Gary's house had caused. Although she still saw his hate-filled face whenever she closed her eyes, her skin no longer crawled at the horror of his hand touching her again. Time spent at the shop on Sunday had a calming effect. She loved being with her antiques, and because business was brisk, she'd had to keep her mind focused on her work.

Today she planned to strip paint off a desk she bought at an auction the week before. She didn't do much refinishing, but the desk had been priced way below what it was worth. She could tell from peeling a bit of paint off the top that it was solid walnut and worth a little elbow grease. David had stopped by on his way to work to help her carry the desk out to her backyard where she wouldn't have to worry about ventilation for the stripper fumes. Around mid-morning, she was making good progress, scrubbing away in her rubber gloves, when someone called her name. Charles Yarboro, in his short-sleeved summer policeman's shirt but no hat, stood at the corner of the house. His somber expression told her this was not a social call.

"What can I do for you, Charles?" Clementine asked as she pulled off her gloves and extended her hand.

Charles shook her hand but offered no smile. "I hope you don't mind that I came around the house," he said. "I rang your doorbell, but when you didn't answer, I heard some noise in the back, so I thought you might be here." Clementine shrugged, so he continued. "This is not an official police visit. Chief Tubbs didn't send me. I guess I'm here more as a friend." He looked around the yard as if to see if anybody else could hear what he was about to say. "Gary Wiggins came down to the station yesterday to file a trespassing complaint against you. He said he came home from work Saturday night and found you sneaking around his yard. He said he wants to file a complaint and get an injunction against you."

"So what did you tell him?" Clementine wiped sweat from her face with a rag she pulled from her pocket.

"We gave him the form to file the complaint. We had to." Charles's forehead compressed into deep grooves. "Were you really in his yard? He'll have to have proof that you were there for anybody to take the complaint seriously." He paused and stared at her. "Why would you go there?"

Clementine put the rag back into her pocket and folded her arms. "I'm not a lawyer, but I watch enough TV crime shows to know I shouldn't comment one way or the other about Gary's accusations."

Charles's lips turned up slightly. "Okay. But this could get serious. It's not a joke, and if Gary wants to press it, things could get unpleasant for you. If you want my opinion, though, I'd be surprised if he follows through, especially if he doesn't have photos or videos of the trespasser, whoever it was."

"Well, I guess we'll just have to wait and see what happens. But I appreciate your letting me know, Charles. If Gary's saying things about me to the police, I need to know it." Clementine studied Charles's face. He was so open and earnest. "I don't suppose this new evidence of Gary's anger against me might cause you all to believe me when I tell you he raped me?"

The somber expression Charles wore when he came into the yard slid right back onto his face. "Well, I guess I can't comment on that, so we're tit for tat, aren't we? But I will give you a piece of advice—stay away from him. Don't make this any worse for you than it already is."

"I assure you I don't want to be anywhere near him." Clementine permitted a soft smile. "And I really do thank you for coming over here, Charles. You're the one policeman in this town I trust."

Charles nodded and walked back around to the front of the house. Clementine waited until she was sure he couldn't see her before she hurled her rubber gloves against the desk. That bastard! Filing a complaint against her for being in his yard! She should've filed a complaint when he threatened her with slander or when he was loitering outside Back in the Day. Or any of the dozens of other times she thought she saw him following her or watching her. Without bothering to put the gloves back on, she poured a puddle of paint stripper on the desk and rubbed it into the wood with so much fury the threads of her rag separated, creating holes in the thin material.

At least Gary couldn't prove anything against her any more than she'd been able to prove anything against him. She smiled ruefully at this bitter twist of fate. Then she remembered the mixing bowl. If Gary had seen her throw it into the bushes, he could pull it out as evidence that someone had been there, and if there were fingerprints on it—she grimaced at the thought. She had to get the bowl back.

Johnny's Restaurant was closed on Mondays, so Gary could be home at any time, and the last thing Clementine needed was to get caught again. She decided not to involve David this go-around. The fewer people, the better. On Tuesday night, she drove up Gary's street, pleased that once again not many people were out. The only visible person was a woman walking a large black dog headed toward Gary's house. Clementine circled the block, waiting for the woman to move on up the street. When Clementine returned, all was quiet. She parked her van in front of the house next to Gary's and slipped into the corner of Gary's yard.

She thought she remembered exactly where she threw the bowl, but now, in the dark, the bushes all looked alike. And she had been so startled by Gary's appearance, she might not have even looked where she was throwing. Quietly, she reached under the first bush that seemed familiar. Hoping she wouldn't encounter any snakes or slugs, she felt around in the grass, but no bowl. Her heart beat faster. Maybe he had seen her toss the bowl and had already retrieved it.

She moved to the next bush, squatted, and extended her hand. This time a stray branch scraped her wrist, almost causing her to speak, but she stifled the sound soon enough. The grass was still damp from a shower earlier in the day. She moved her hand through the wetness until her fingers bumped against something hard and cold. If it wasn't her bowl, she didn't want to know what it was. Trusting that the object was the bowl (her knees wouldn't let her squat low enough to see under the bush's low limbs), she inched her fingers upward and felt a rim. Hallelujah! It was the bowl! The round shape was lodged so far under the bush that Gary might not have been able to see it.

Clementine snatched the bowl from under the bush and, resisting the urge to run, crept silently back through the yard, glancing over her shoulder to be sure there was no action inside Gary's house. When she reached the sidewalk, she stopped. The woman with the dog was quickly approaching. *Good lord. How long can a person walk a dog?*

"Good evening," Clementine said as the woman passed her. The woman nodded, her eyes drifting to the bowl. Acting as if holding a wet, empty bowl on the sidewalk after dark was nothing unusual, Clementine walked to her car and got in. She was safe. Now all she had to do was wait for the hex to work. And what if it didn't? She shivered. If the hex didn't work, she would find another way.

14

Sun brightened the brick walls of the old American Tobacco Company building. Although cigarettes hadn't been manufactured there in decades, Erlene still imagined the clack of machines and the sharp smell of tobacco drifting through the windows, just as she remembered the first time she came to Durham when she was a child.

"Remember when we all drove up here from Murfreesboro to see a baseball game?" she asked Brianne. The two women weaved their way among the patio tables crowding the walkway outside the row of restaurants in the old brick building. Transformation of the factory and warehouses into restaurants and event space was Durham's current pride and joy.

"Of course I do. Daddy made us come over here to see where his precious Lucky Strikes were made. We kept saying it stunk and we wanted to leave, but he made us get as close as the guard at the gate would let us. Then we went to the ballgame, and after about three innings, all us kids were ready to go home. Not a great day, all in all, but I still remember the giant Cokes and peanuts." Brianne stopped in front of a restaurant with a large green awning. "This is the place. My girlfriend says they have great pizzas."

"At last." Erlene fanned her face with a map of the restaurant area she'd found at the entrance. "Why'd we pick the hottest day in the history of North Carolina to come here?"

"Because the last time we did this it rained, and you didn't like that either. Besides, every day in August is nearly this hot, so if you don't like the heat, we'll have to wait until October."

Brianne and Erlene had met for lunch one other time since Erlene's trip to Murfreesboro. Both times Erlene felt at least ten tons of guilt pressing down on her as she drove out of Tanner. Ever since Miss Myrtle found out about Erlene's secret family reunion, she'd refused to talk about the trip and about her sister and niece. Her only comment had been delivered in the car on the way back from the river: "Don't you never go down there again. You hear me?"

Erlene had kept silent then, but she knew that wasn't the end. She called Brianne a week later to arrange the meeting in Durham, which was about halfway between their two towns.

Today they were visiting the American Tobacco Historic District, mostly out of curiosity. "Amazing what they've done with these old buildings, isn't it?" Erlene said when they were seated in the cool recesses of the restaurant, a welcome relief from the heat-radiating brick walks and walls outside. "I suppose anything can be restored if you have enough money and time."

"Do you suppose we'll ever restore any sisterly love between our mothers?"

Erlene shrugged. "What does Aunt Lanita think we ought to do to bring my mother around? Is she as eager to get the family back together as we are? The way I remember it, Lanita quit talking to Mama because Mama didn't want anything to do with Nana."

"Oh, my lord, let's not worry about who started this." Brianne rubbed her fingers across her forehead and into her short salt-and-pepper hair.

"I'm not trying to blame Aunt Lanita. I just wondered if she's willing to talk to Mama."

"She said she wished Myrtle had come with you to Murfreesboro." Brianne glanced at the menu as a server approached the table. "Give us a minute," she said to the young woman dressed in jeans and a T-shirt. "But if you can bring us some ice tea now, that'd be nice." The server sauntered off to another table. "I think Mama's afraid she's going to die without ever talking to her sister again. Doesn't that worry Aunt Myrtle at all?"

"I don't know. She won't talk about it." Erlene focused on the menu, a little ashamed of her mother's stubbornness.

Brianne was quiet, her attention focused on the menu too. "Let's get a House Special pizza and split it. It's the best thing they make here."

Erlene didn't care what they ate. She hadn't come to eat. "Fine."

Brianne laid the menu aside. "What if we tell Myrtle that Mama is terrible sick and maybe not going to live much longer? Would she fall for that?"

Erlene pictured her cantankerous little mother. "Not likely. And she'd be madder'n ever at us for lying to her. What if we got Lanita to tell Mama she understands why Mama hates root medicine, and since Lanita's not working the medicine, they can get along now?"

"Lanita would never do that. You know how strongly she believes in the medicine, and how she says I have the gift, and how she keeps pushing me to work some spells." Brianne tapped her fingernails against the table. The nails were long and expertly manicured with creamy pink polish. "Speaking of which, did your friend try that IRS hex I gave her?"

"She did. And she wants me to ask you how long she has to wait before it takes effect." Erlene had been so concerned about her mother she forgot Clementine's request. Good thing Brianne brought it up.

"How long's it been since she did it?"

"About three weeks, I think. Should something have happened by now?"

"Maybe. Does she know anybody who can ask the guy if he's having tax problems?"

Erlene doubted if Clementine knew any of Gary's friends, assuming Gary had any friends. The only person she could think of who might be able to ask Gary a question like that was David. "She might."

"Tell her to give it a try. Otherwise, she'll just have to hope for the best." The server returned, and Brianne ordered the pizza. "We don't seem to be solving anybody's problems today, do we?"

"Don't give up yet."

"Then what's our next idea? I still say we need to get 'em together. Let's do it. See what happens."

Erlene laughed. "Can you imagine? Those two little old ladies slugging it out? Because that's probably what'll happen. We ought to do it in a public place so maybe they'll be too embarrassed to hit each other."

"You never know," Brianne said.

By the time the pizza arrived, the idea of a reunion was starting to sound pretty good, and Erlene was hungry after all. The pizza was delicious.

Back in Tanner, Erlene called Clementine to tell her what Brianne said about the hex. "I guess there's no real time frame for these things," she said. "They happen when they happen. Can David ask Gary if he's having any tax problems?"

Clementine felt drained. She had fairly jumped from customer to customer at the shop all day because she was so excited about Erlene's meeting with Brianne, and now this was all Erlene had learned. Waiting for magic to work was more nerve-racking than waiting on the police. "I suppose David can find out. I'll ask him," she told Erlene, but she didn't like the idea. She'd been asking a lot of David, and prying was not his style.

She rehearsed how she would broach the subject to him while she dressed for their date that night. The Tanner Community Theater was performing *Oklahoma!* in its open-air amphitheater during August. As she and David rode in his car toward the theater just outside the city limits, she told him what Brianne had said about the hex. "So do you know any way I can find out if the hex is working?" she asked.

"No." David focused on his driving, his eyes pointed straight ahead. "You probably should have thought about this before you went to all the trouble of following those crazy directions."

Clementine gave him a nasty look, which he couldn't see because he was driving. "I just need a little reassurance that it's working. I want to know if he's at least gotten the notice about what he owes."

The car rolled on past some of the oldest homes in Tanner. David stopped at the last traffic light at the edge of town. "I have a feeling you're going to ask me to find out if anything's going on with Gary," he said. "Is that it?"

"Can you?" Clementine was relieved he mentioned her idea first.

"Probably not." The light changed and David drove on.

"Then what about one of the other guys at the counseling center? One of them worked with him, didn't they? You could ask that guy how Gary's doing. If Gary's having any financial troubles, he might mention it, counselor to counselor."

David shook his head. "We don't talk about people we counsel like that. Unless we think it'll help somebody else. This isn't going to help anybody else."

"It'll help me." Clementine felt the edge in her voice.

"I mean help somebody else looking for work."

Okay, so asking David to do her dirty work was a bad idea. Clementine would have to figure out a way to see if the hex was working by herself. She and David drove on in silence. Just as they pulled into a space in the theater parking lot, David said, "I did hear something this week that could affect Gary, but it didn't have anything to do with taxes."

Clementine jolted out of her self-pity reverie. "What?"

"It's kind of complicated, and we need to get to our seats before the play starts. I'll tell you about it later."

Later? Clementine wanted to pinch him. He was teasing her to get even with her for asking him to pry into Gary's life. How long was he going to make her wait? Face fixed in a scowl, she followed him to the theater and sat next to him without saying a word. She was still frowning when the first actor came on stage.

About halfway through act one, Clementine relaxed enough to enjoy the music. The play's familiar story wasn't intriguing, but the characters were entertaining and the music had held up through the years.

Finally the stage lights darkened, signaling intermission. Clementine put her hand on David's arm. "Now tell me," she said.

"Not here." David took her hand and led her out of the row and up the steps toward the theater's entrance. When they had made their way through the crowd filling the plaza around the refreshment area, he walked away from the theater to a wooden bench in a small grove of trees. "It's not something I want anybody else to hear," he said. "It's not good. At least, not for Johnny and Johnny's Restaurant."

Clementine sat on the bench with her back to the theater entrance. "Go on," she said.

David planted his foot on the bench next to her. "I meant it when I said we don't usually talk about the people we counsel down at the center, but you probably need to know this. One of the men I counsel, who happens to be Mexican, told me he applied for a job washing dishes at Johnny's but got turned down even though he knew they were looking for a dishwasher. He asked his buddies about it, and they said Johnny wasn't hiring undocumented Mexicans anymore because he got caught."

"Got caught? What do you mean?"

"Johnny's always hired undocumented immigrants. But he's always managed to keep it under the radar. Nobody says anything about it because he needs the help and the Mexicans need jobs. Johnny's cook Luis is documented, but a lot of the others aren't. Johnny's a good-hearted man, and he knows the Mexicans are hard workers. He means well. But what he's doing is still illegal."

"And somebody turned him in?"

Another couple passed by the bench. David smiled and said, "Hello." When they were gone, he gestured to Clementine to get up. "Let's walk." He headed across the grass of a previous cow pasture, and Clementine followed. "It's usually not that big a deal. I would never report him because he provides steady jobs in this town, and we need every job we can get. Other people feel the same way. But obviously somebody didn't. Or else immigration enforcement agents found it on their own when they audited Johnny's employment eligibility forms. They're called I-9 forms, and lying on them is fraud."

Clementine was stunned. "So what happens now?" The sky was growing dark away from the lights of the theater.

"It's already happened. It'll be in the newspaper soon. Johnny's been fined ten thousand dollars."

"Oh my." The words tasted sour. "But if he pays the fine, nothing will happen to him, right? As long as he doesn't hire any more illegal Mexicans." She didn't want Johnny to be in trouble. He was a good friend to everybody in town. Then she thought of something else. "How will this affect Gary?" she asked.

Lights at the theater began to flicker. Intermission was ending. David stopped walking. "It could affect everybody at the restaurant. I heard that Johnny doesn't have the money to pay the fine. I don't know what that means for him, but I suspect he could do some jail time if he can't pay. And then what happens to the restaurant? This could ruin the business. Johnny doesn't have a partner to take over for him or to come up with the money." David was hurrying Clementine toward the theater now. The lights flickered again.

Clementine paid little attention to the rest of the play. She couldn't stop thinking about Johnny's dilemma. *Ruin the business* kept echoing in her head. She didn't want Johnny to lose the restaurant. But if the business was ruined, could Gary be ruined too? Most likely not. He was only the chef. Even if the restaurant closed, he'd move on to another restaurant. Maybe to a restaurant in another town, which would be a nice way to get him out of Tanner, but would be no big problem for him. Maybe there was a way to turn the situation against Gary. Make Johnny's problem destroy Gary. Clementine turned the facts around and around, trying to put them together like a Rubik's cube in a way that would do what she wanted. Unless Johnny would blame Gary for hiring the undocumented workers, which he wouldn't do—there was no reason to—and even that wasn't all that bad. But the thought started Clementine thinking about the power Johnny had over Gary because he was his boss. She liked the idea of power over Gary. She'd like some of that power herself.

And then it came to her—a plan that could help her and help Johnny. What if she paid Johnny's fine in exchange for selling her an interest in the restaurant and making her a silent partner? She smiled to herself. What a great position to be in. She still had faith that the hex could work, but three weeks had passed, and nothing had happened. She needed to come at Gary from more than one angle.

She didn't know how yet, but if she were a partner in the restaurant, she would find a way to obliterate Gary's career as a chef. His precious career that he was so proud of. She remembered his face as he told her about losing his job at the mill and then saving his wrecked life by studying at the community college and becoming a cook. That job made him whole again. Clementine was filled with a raging urge to take that job away from him forever. Not just the job at Johnny's, but any cooking job. Throw him back into the depths where he'd been when the mill laid him off. Throw him into even deeper misery if she could. Fix it so he'd never feel whole again, like she would never feel whole again.

As the cast belted out the final reprise of "Oklahoma!", Clementine knew what she needed to do. She thought she wanted prison time for Gary, but she liked this idea better. She could control this herself, but she'd have to get in touch with Johnny soon before he did something drastic, like sell the restaurant to pay the fine.

Clementine almost told David her plan during the ride home, but she decided to wait until she had more details. She wasn't sure what his reaction would be. He was totally skeptical about the root medicine, but he had helped her anyway.

Remembering that gesture, she patted his thigh as he drove. The sky was dark now, and only the porch lights of the old homes blazed. David covered her hand with his. The heat between his hand and thigh was comforting. He was so good to her and seemed to care a great deal about her. Maybe he even loved her. She hadn't been this close to a man since Gordon died, and she liked David a lot. He was smoothing over the sharp ridges of loneliness that had filled her life for the past two years. Maybe she loved him. She watched his profile in the dim light. She didn't want to press him to get involved with her plan, but she didn't think she could do it without him.

Sunday morning Clementine called Johnny as early as she dared. She had to catch him before he went to the restaurant to get ready for Sunday brunch, but she didn't want to annoy him by calling too early. Her sweaty fingers left tracks on the phone. She hoped her voice wouldn't shake.

"I know Sundays are busy for you," she said when he answered, "but could you spare a little time this morning to have coffee with me? I have an idea for a business plan that I think could be good for both you and me."

When Johnny asked for details, she explained she needed to present it to him face to face. "Can you come by Back in the Day? Or I can come to the restaurant. Either place is fine as long as the meeting is completely private. I don't want anyone to see us together. And please don't tell anyone I called."

Johnny sounded doubtful, but he agreed to meet her at the antique shop, which was a small victory for Clementine. She could be sure of privacy there, and meeting on her home turf meant she'd have more confidence and control.

To give the two of them a place to talk, Clementine cleared a round oak table near the back of the shop. She'd always liked the table and considered taking it home for herself, but it had a high price tag that could do a lot for her bottom line if it sold. After dusting it carefully, she arranged herself in a chair next to it and reviewed her pitch for Johnny. She was somewhere between reviewing and praying with her head resting in her hands and her elbows on the table when Johnny knocked on the back door as she'd told him to do. Her stomach lurched as it always did when she opened that door, but she couldn't risk having him come in the front.

Obviously on his way to work, Johnny was spruced up for the Sunday crowd. A single button held his chocolate brown sports coat stretched across his belly while a tightly knotted necktie caused excess skin to spill out over his collar. His expression was apprehensive as Clementine ushered him through the tight pathway leading to the table and poured coffee from the Mr. Coffee she kept on top of the small refrigerator.

"I don't want you to think I'm a town busybody," Clementine began after they were both seated, "because I'm not. I don't care what anybody in this town does most of the time. And I don't listen when people try to tell me gossip. Ask my customers. They'll tell you I don't want to hear that stuff." She took a deep breath. "But before I could stop them, a close friend mentioned that you have some trouble with the immigration enforcement people."

Johnny folded his arms across his protruding middle. His lips dipped downward into his heavy cheeks.

"The information would have stopped there." Clementine leaned back in her chair. "I never repeat hearsay. But I've been looking for another business venture to add to the antique shop, and I thought I might be able to help you as well as make a good investment for myself." This was a thundering lie since Clementine had yet to earn back her initial investment in the antique shop and was barely breaking even on monthly expenses.

"How can you help me?" Johnny's narrowed eyes were those of an experienced businessman who would protect his family's business with his life.

Clementine cleared her throat. "I'm willing to pay your fine if you will sell me a partial interest in the restaurant and make me a silent partner. A very silent partner. I don't want anyone to know I'm involved. In fact, if you tell anyone about my proposal, the deal is off."

Johnny shifted in his chair, causing the old wooden frame to creak. For a second, Clementine feared for the antique's safety. "How big a piece of the restaurant do you wanna buy?" Johnny asked. "And are you planning to get involved with managing the place?"

"The size of my investment is up to you. How much are you willing to sell and how much money do you want for it, including the ten thousand dollars to pay the fine? As for management, I'll leave that to you. You have experience, and I don't. Since I don't want anybody to know I'm involved, I likely won't come anywhere near the restaurant except as a customer."

"What's in this for you? I don't get it."

"Purely an investment. I'll expect a percentage of the profits, of course. We can work out the exact percentage when we draw up the contract. Oh, and about the contract. You can have your lawyer write it so you're comfortable with it, but you can't tell him who it's for. Leave the name blank and we'll fill my name in later. Tell him it's a hypothetical contract in case you decide to take on a partner later."

"What if I don't want a partner?" The chair creaked again.

"That's up to you. I just thought it would help with the fine. And give you some new cash." Clementine's heart rate quickened. She hadn't imagined he would turn her down. "Think about it," she said. "Just don't tell anybody, and I hope you won't do anything drastic to get the money."

"Why can't I tell anybody?"

"Because I have my own creditors to worry about, and I don't want them to know I'm taking on any risky investments. Not that I think the restaurant is risky, but you never know. And I don't want the people of Tanner to think I've come home to take over the town. I want them to think of me as the hometown girl who's now the friendly antique dealer." Would he buy that? The creditor part was partially true. She owed a lot of money on her house.

"So you'll give me the money, and all you want in exchange is a percentage of the profits?"

"A percentage of the profits and your promise to keep my involvement secret."

Johnny nodded. "Let me think it over."

When he had gone, Clementine returned lamps and china to the tabletop. The shop would open soon. As she worked, her brain spun reams of calculations. Depending on how much money Johnny wanted, she would draw down her cash savings and sell some stock in her retirement portfolio. The restaurant would provide her with income (how much she didn't know yet), and surely the antique shop would turn a profit soon. She could pull it off. She had to.

15

Johnny took his time deciding about Clementine's offer. A week passed, and still no answer. Clementine worried that his delay meant he was going to turn her down. She toyed with the idea of contacting him again, but decided to be patient. If she seemed over-eager, she might scare him away.

Late in the afternoon on the following Sunday, she was re-arranging her miniature portraits and waiting for the last customers to leave Back in the Day when Charles Yarboro came into the shop. He pretended to look at a collection of silver flatware until Clementine noticed him and approached him. She was grateful to him for his discretion. If he had rushed up to her as soon as he entered the shop, the customers would have suspected something was up. Instead, Clementine's regulars who had seen him in the shop a few times just thought he was another antique collector. "Anything new?" Clementine asked quietly.

"Gary never filed the trespassing complaint. If he hasn't done it by now, I don't think he will. I was going to call you, but I happened to be down here this afternoon, so I thought I'd come in to make sure you're all right. Have you heard from Gary? Or seen him? I was afraid since he hasn't filed the complaint that he was harassing you instead. But don't tell anybody I said that."

"No harassing." Clementine glanced over at the customers, who were walking toward the door. "Thanks for stopping in," she called to them. "Come again."

"It's good he's not bothering you," Charles said. "Stay away from him. I'm keeping an eye on him for you."

Clementine smiled her appreciation. At least somebody on the police force was following up on her case. "Is anybody trying to find new evidence linking him to the rape?"

Charles shook his head. "Yours is pretty much a cold case now. Chief Tubbs thinks the new stuff popping up every day is more important. It's not like TV where they have a bunch of detectives for every case. We only have one official detective, and he's doing everyday police work too. Unless something happens to turn up, we're not likely to make much more progress on your case. I'm sorry. I know that's not what you want to hear, but that's the truth. Even if you tried to put pressure on Chief Tubbs, I don't think it would do any good. We just don't have the manpower."

Clementine remembered David had said something about calling in a favor from the mayor. Apparently, even that wouldn't help. "I'll tell you if Gary causes me any more trouble," she said to Charles.

"And I'll let you know if anything develops down at the department." And then he was gone. Clementine tallied her receipts and bundled the money to take home for deposit the next day.

~

When Johnny finally called on Monday, Clementine had been to the bank and was in the van headed for an estate sale in

Lenoir. She pulled into a McDonald's parking lot to take the call.

"I'm interested in your offer," Johnny said. "Meet me at the restaurant around noon and let's talk about it." Clementine balked at meeting at the restaurant, but Johnny assured her they'd be alone. "The place is closed today. Nobody'll be there. Most of the men who work for me are strong family guys. If they have a day off, they'll be with their kids. Or working around their houses." Clementine wondered if Gary fell into that description. He lived alone, as far as she knew.

After ditching the estate sale, Clementine arrived at the restaurant a few minutes early. In the empty parking lot, the van stood out like a giant white mushroom. Nobody else in Tanner drove a Mercedes van, especially not one with "Back in the Day" in Old English lettering painted on the side. She left the parking lot and drove a few short blocks to a small strip mall that had marked Tanner retail's earliest expansion out of the downtown area. A variety of stores had moved in and out of the mall in the past thirty-five years. Now the main tenant was a Big Lots store that regularly drew a crowd. Parking the van next to Big Lots would not seem out of place at all. She waited until five minutes after noon to be sure Johnny was waiting for her. Then she walked to the restaurant.

Johnny sat at the table nearest the door when she arrived. He invited her in and ushered her to a small room off the kitchen with "Staff Only" printed on the door. Inside was a desk covered with papers, two chairs, and two tall filing cabinets. "This is where I hide when the place gets too crowded," he said with a smile.

Clementine was glad he left the door to the office open, even though rhythmic strains of Latin music drifted in from the kitchen. She could sense the claustrophobia that would have settled around her otherwise. Johnny must have noticed her looking at the door. "Do you want me to turn off the music?" he asked. "It's the Spanish-speaking radio station coming in from Charlotte. It's always on when the guys are here, and I get used to it. Seems lonesome when it's not on." Clementine shook her head.

"Like I told you on the phone, I've been thinking about your offer," Johnny said when Clementine was seated and he had settled into an old office chair behind the desk. His forehead glistened despite the air conditioning. In fact, the room was uncomfortably warm. Maybe he had raised the temperature since the restaurant was closed. "I studied the figures, looked at the restaurant's profit and loss for the past year, tried to guess what our cash flow will be in the coming years, and kicked around what it would mean to have a partner."

He rose a little from the chair to pull a handkerchief from his hip pocket. He wiped his face, stuffed the handkerchief back into his pocket, and dropped into the chair with a thud. "I've never been much of a businessman. I'd rather be behind the stove like I used to be, to tell you the truth, but I seem to be pretty good at running this place. And from what I can tell, some new money would be good for us. So, if you're serious about being a silent partner, you're on." The sweat was back on his forehead. Clementine wondered if it was caused by the heat or nerves.

"So how much money do you want, and how much of the restaurant will I own?" she asked.

"Oh, yeah. The details." Johnny smiled. "See what you think about this." He took several papers from his desk drawer and pushed them toward her. Then he leaned back in the old chair and scratched his neck behind the necktie.

Clementine studied the first page. She was determined not to flinch, even though the price was higher than she expected. Should she negotiate with him? Offer him less? How desperate was he to pay the fine? "That sounds high for only thirty percent," she ventured.

"Not really. Flip over a few pages and look at the figures."

Based on what Clementine had learned about business in running the antique shop, Johnny's calculations looked solid. The restaurant had a steady earnings record, which she didn't doubt. It had been a favorite in Tanner for many years, going back to the time when Johnny's father owned it. Even the franchises that had sprung up all over town in the past twenty years hadn't slowed its business. But recently, nicer restaurants had moved into a few of the vacant retail spaces downtown, and nobody knew how they would affect an old restaurant like Johnny's. Clementine shuffled the papers. *You aren't in this for the money,* she reminded herself. But she couldn't afford to lose a lot of money. Spending this much would make a huge hole in her savings. She had used a lot of what she and Gordon had accumulated to buy inventory for the antique shop because it had been easier to get a house loan than a business loan. Now she had a mortgage and a lot of antiques she hoped she could sell. "With a thirty percent interest, that means I get thirty percent of the profit, right?" she said.

"That's right." Johnny put his elbows on the desk. "I didn't use to do this, but I'll start paying myself a salary for managing the restaurant, and then we'll have a clean profit statement so we can figure your thirty percent. Also, I retain full ownership of the building. We're just talking about the business and equipment here."

"What's your salary?"

Johnny leaned over the papers and put his pudgy finger on one. "Line ten," he said.

The mention of salary reminded Clementine of another question she wanted to ask him. "What about the employees' salaries? Are they unionized? Do you have to pay union scale?"

Johnny scoffed. "They don't have a union. There aren't enough of them. Look here." He pointed to another item in the papers. "I pay them well so they don't have to think about a union."

"So they're happy with their salaries? None of them complaining about financial problems?" She held her breath. If Gary had heard from the IRS about a big amount due, he might have asked for a raise or an advance.

"God, no. The Mexicans are happy to have jobs." His voice trailed off. Obviously his immigrant workers were still weighing heavy on his mind.

Clementine looked over the papers again. "All right, Johnny. We have a deal. Get the contract drawn up, but leave my name out of it." She handed the papers to him with a steady gaze and extended her hand. He shook it, enclosing her palm in a strong, fleshy grip.

As Johnny escorted her through the front dining room, Clementine looked up at the wall behind the space where the counter used to be, expecting to see the regulator clock that had been there as long as she could remember. When she came there on dates as a teenager, she always relied on that clock to tell her it was time to leave for home to make curfew. But today the wall was bare. "What happened to your dad's clock?" she asked. "I didn't notice it was missing when I came in."

"Had to get rid of it months ago," Johnny said. "It wouldn't work right. It kept losing time. Not much, but enough to make a difference by the end of the day. A couple of servers complained it caused them to work overtime last winter." He laughed. "And we wouldn't want that, would we?"

As summer crawled into autumn, Clementine kept her secret smothered inside her. Johnny had written the contract just the way she asked. To buy her partnership, she had to sell most of the stock portfolio that was her safety net, even though the market hadn't fully recovered from the 2008 recession. She still went to estate sales and auctions, but she bought less, only small items with meager price tags. On several occasions, she'd rearranged the furniture in the shop to cover up the empty spaces left by large pieces she sold. That was good and bad. She needed the income, but she was afraid to buy replacement pieces because her available cash was so low. Her first month's check from Johnny was less than she expected, based on the figures he had shown her, but he explained business was down because people were on vacation. She reduced withdrawals from her savings to the absolute minimum she needed to pay her bills. And she waited. She couldn't make a move against Gary yet. If anything out of the ordinary happened too soon after she became a partner, Johnny would make the obvious connection. The only risky action she took was asking Johnny to send her monthly financial reports, which she studied to see if Gary had been given a raise or cash advance. She also combed through the real estate listings on local realtors' websites and in *The Tanner Observer* to see if Gary's house was for sale. Nothing. No changes.

If David and Erlene noticed anything different about Clementine, they didn't mention it. In fact, she'd hardly heard from Erlene since July. The one time they had lunch at the tearoom, she'd gotten the feeling that Erlene was spending a lot of weekends meeting Brianne in various cities.

"Aren't you ever going to invite her to Tanner?" Clementine asked, but Erlene shrugged off the question. Clementine would have loved the chance to talk with Brianne again, so she could ask her more about the hex they put on Gary, especially when she could expect it to work, but she didn't feel right calling her on the phone, and Erlene was obviously disinclined to set up another meeting. She seemed disinclined to do much of anything with Clementine, a development that worried Clementine. She missed her friend and worried that her involvement with Gary and the root medicine had alienated Erlene.

David, on the other hand, was as attentive as ever. During one of his many evenings at her house, he told her Johnny paid his fine for employing undocumented immigrants. "I don't know where he got the money," he said, "but I'm glad he did. We need that restaurant. I just hope he doesn't get in trouble again." Clementine was tempted to tell him about her partnership, but she wasn't ready yet. She wasn't sure what her next move would be.

On the evenings she was without David's company, Clementine went to the library and used its computers to research ways to destroy a chef's career. She still hoped the hex would work, but her new plan could be even better. She considered doing the research on her laptop at home, but she didn't want to take a chance on having her search results traced back to her computer if she were ever suspected of being involved. And besides, she liked the library. When she was a teenager, she'd spent many nights there researching term papers and gossiping with friends. It had been a cozy, safe place for young people to gather. Today, it served as a meeting space for many groups in town, from Girl Scouts to the Kiwanis Club, so most nights it offered a pleasant buzz of people with a purpose. Also, the building stood next to a waterfall, one of the loveliest spots in Tanner, along with the mountain views and tree-lined streets.

On the nights Clementine had to wait to get a computer, she strolled beside the waterfall and wondered what was going to happen to her. She'd had such high hopes for her life in Tanner, but almost nothing had turned out the way she planned.

When Gary was taken care of, she could be the person she'd hoped to be.

After weeks at the library computer, she concluded that food poisoning was her best bet for ruining Gary's career. Everything she read pointed to the damage sick customers would do to a restaurant and to a chef. An actual food poisoning case had happened in a town not far from Tanner. Kitchen workers preparing for a community festival had brought a goat into the restaurant kitchen when the owners weren't there. They planned to use the restaurant equipment to butcher the goat and prepare it to cook at the festival. Everything went off without a hitch, and the festival was a big success. Back at the restaurant, however, juices from the raw goat must have contaminated stored food because there was an outbreak of E. coli. More than twenty people got sick. The article about the outbreak explained that any contamination that occurs at a restaurant is ultimately the chef's fault. *Ultimately the chef's fault.* Clementine loved that idea. Anything that happened in Johnny's kitchen would ultimately be Gary's fault. The more she read, the more plausible the idea seemed. And she knew exactly how she would do it.

Toward the end of October, David invited Clementine to take a ride up the Blue Ridge Mountains to view the fall foliage. Year after year, a young Clementine had made this trek, first with her parents and then with teenage friends. The dazzling colors of the leaves never ceased to amaze her, so she was delighted when David suggested the trip. On the appointed day, she waited by her front door like a child expecting Santa Claus. The morning was clear and crisp with an azure sky. David was in an especially good mood because his trade classes had attracted and retained ("That's what really matters," he said, "whether they stay or not.") more students than expected. The timing for the trip was perfect. Around each bend in the twisting road, the leaves seemed brighter and more deeply hued than the ones before.

Close to eleven o'clock, they set up their picnic supplies in a park just off the Parkway. When they'd finished eating the chicken fingers and potato salad that David brought from the grocery-store deli, they set off on a short hike among the trees that covered the hills and valleys of the park. Because it was the middle of the week, they had the entire park to themselves. For the first half mile or so, they didn't speak. Clementine was content to breathe in the pungent odor of the dying leaves on the ground and marvel at the kaleidoscope of color overhead. David held her hand gently, just enough to keep them together, but not an attempt to lead or propel her.

The footing was rough, but not dangerous, and Clementine maneuvered through it easily until a mockingbird's screech seized her attention and she stumbled over a pile of rocks along the path. She reached for her foot as pain shot up from her ankle, so her face was only a couple of feet above a rolling rock when a dark snake bedecked with white circles like bracelets around its belly slithered from the original pile. Clementine froze with her foot in her hand. David wrapped his arms around her.

"It's a king snake," he said. "It's not poisonous, and it doesn't want to bite you. You startled it, that's all." He held her still as the snake slid around the dislodged rock, which had stopped rolling, and disappeared into a dense thicket. Clementine released her foot but didn't move from David's embrace. After a few minutes, he lowered his arms and slid his hand into hers. "Come on," he said. "We'll go in a different direction."

The sun hadn't moved, and the leaves were still bright, but Clementine felt a darkness in the air. She had thought that being alone in the park was a gift to be savored, but now she realized that being alone also meant she and David were vulnerable. Wild animals abounded in the mountains. Most were harmless, but poisonous snakes were common, and sightings had been reported of bear and coyote. Even more frightening than the slithering reptiles and four-legged animals were the two-legged kind. If she and David stumbled upon someone who wanted to harm them, just like she had stumbled on the snake, there was little they could do to defend themselves out here, miles away from the Parkway with no markers to give police any idea where they were, assuming they could get any cell phone coverage.

"Let's go back," she said and turned to face the way they had come. In the shadows beneath the trees, a hazy figure with Gary's combed-back hair and clunky build seemed to peer out. Fear swelled through Clementine like it did every time she thought of Gary. She shuddered and grabbed her upper arms to try to stop their trembling. Her eyes snapped shut. When she opened them, the figure was gone. She pressed her arm and shoulder against David as he began to walk beside her.

"What's wrong?" he asked.

"I thought I saw Gary," Clementine said. "Why does this keep happening to me? I want it to stop."

David put his arms around her and pulled her close. "Sweetheart, I really think you need to talk to a doctor about this."

Clementine shook her head. "I really need to take care of Gary."

They walked in silence with David still holding her close. Should she tell him her new plan? She wanted to reassure him she was dealing with her problems in her own way. And she didn't like keeping secrets from him. "I need to tell you something," she said. "And I hope you won't get upset."

David gave her a puzzled look. "Go on."

Clementine squeezed his hand. "I'm going to tell you this, but you have to promise you will never tell anyone. One other person knows part of it, but he's signed a contract saying he won't reveal what he knows."

"Wait a minute." David stopped walking. "Are you making this up?"

"I swear it's true. Please listen."

"Can we at least stop walking while we talk?"

"When we get back to the picnic site. I need to be closer to the car and the Parkway."

David started walking again, faster this time, his broad shoulders hunched forward, eyes focused on the ground. "Tell me what you're talking about."

Clementine hastened her pace to stay next to him. She stared at the ground too, wary of any rocks or roots—or snakes—in her path. "I own a third of Johnny's Restaurant," she said. "I bought into the business two months ago."

David turned to stare at her, questions hovering in every crevice of his face, but he didn't speak or stop. He moved forward like a man on a mission. As he walked, Clementine told him the details of her contract with Johnny. She finished by saying, "I did it because it gives me power over Gary Wiggins."

"My God, Clementine." David's voice was husky. "I thought you were counting on that hex to work. What about that? Why in the hell are you doing this other thing?"

"To get justice for myself. You know I'm going to do that, whatever it takes. I've waited three months for that hex to work. I need a backup plan." Clementine's breath came in gasps caused by the exertion of keeping up with David as well as her anxiety.

"So how is owning part of the restaurant going to help?" David walked faster. "I think you may be losing touch here."

Offended by the suggestion she might be nuts, Clementine opened her mouth to lash out at him, but she was breathing so hard the words stuck to her tongue. Saying nothing, she jogged by his side. The trees were sparser now, the picnic area in sight. Soon their cooler and blanket were visible on the wood and stone picnic table where they left them. Clementine dropped down on the stone bench beside the table and pulled a half-empty water bottle from the cooler. David leaned against the table, staring at her, waiting.

After a few swallows of water, she was ready to tell him the rest of her plan. When he heard the details, he'd know she wasn't crazy. "Owning part of the restaurant gives me access to the kitchen, the dining room, the books, and anything else I want to get my hands on."

"Didn't Johnny question why you wanted to buy in? Does he know the history between you and Gary?" David took another bottle of water from the cooler and opened it.

"I don't know if he knows or not. But he didn't say a word. He was too eager to get the money to pay his fine." Clementine took another swallow of water. "Now that I have access to Gary's life at work, I'm going to ruin it." David's eyes widened. "When I'm through with him," Clementine continued, "he'll never be a chef again. He'll never be a cook again. He'll never work in any restaurant anywhere. And here's how I'm going to do it." David slid onto the bench across the table from Clementine, his face as cold and hard as the stone beneath him.

"The restaurant has a business luncheon scheduled for managers at Duke Energy right before Thanksgiving," Clementine said. "Twenty or thirty people coming, I expect. The night before the luncheon, I'll use my key to get into the kitchen after everybody's gone. All I have to do is get some chicken out of the refrigerator and rub chicken juices on the salad mix they'll have ready for the next day. With a crowd like that, they always do as much as they can in advance. Then the next day, they'll serve the salad to the folks from Duke Energy."

"You're talking about food poisoning." David's voice scaled up in disbelief. "Clementine. People get really sick from food poisoning."

"The only people who get really sick from food poisoning are old people and little children. This is a business meeting. There won't be any children there. And these managers are healthy and strong. They won't get very sick. I've done a lot of research on this. Of the people who get foodborne illnesses in the United States, less than half of one percent go to the hospital." She took another swallow of water. "But they'll tell their friends where they ate before they got sick, and they'll put it on Facebook and Twitter, and pretty soon nobody will go there. And if I don't miss my guess, some of those big shots from Duke Energy will complain to the county health department, which will probably spark an investigation."

David glowered at her. "That is downright vicious. How can you harm innocent people like that? Some of those guys from Duke Energy are pretty old. Or they might have some underlying condition that you don't know about. You have no idea what you're doing. And what if you get caught? Doesn't Johnny have security cameras?"

"No, Johnny doesn't have security cameras. I checked that. And I have researched this and researched this. I know what I'm doing. With chicken, the most likely food poisoning is salmonella. And hardly anybody stays sick longer than a week with salmonella. Most people are sick only a couple of days. So nobody suffers for long, but—and this is the important part—no matter what really happened, the chef is almost always blamed."

David moved his head slowly from side to side. "*Almost* always blamed. You have no idea what's going to happen with any of this. And think about it this way—if people stop coming to Johnny's because of your food poisoning, the restaurant will go out of business, and you'll lose the money you put into it and any income you might get in the future. That's cutting off your nose to spite your face. So why?"

"It won't happen like that. I'll convince Johnny to let Gary take the fall to save the restaurant. That's another advantage of being a partner now. I have a say in the matter. I'll get Johnny to make a big deal of firing Gary and, you know, I hope the health department does get involved, so we can tell them this happened on Gary's watch. Maybe they have some kind of blacklist of chefs with records of food poisoning that they share with other health departments in the state or maybe the state health department."

Clementine leaned away from the table and considered this new idea. Yes, she would have to be sure the health department got involved. An anonymous letter should do the trick, in case those Duke Energy managers didn't have the guts.

"What's happened to you?" David's blue eyes focused intensely as if he could bore right into her soul. "I think it's great that you're not backing down from making Gary pay for what he did to you. I respect you for that, and I'll go with you as far as you want to go as long as it's legal, even crazy hexes. But this is different."

"So you respect me. Well, I'm a woman who respects herself too much to let Gary Wiggins go unpunished for what he did. He's going to suffer for the rest of his life, just like I am."

"If you want to be vicious, figure out a way to cut off one of his fingers. Hurt him if you have to, but don't get innocent people involved." Color rose in David's face.

"Ruining his career will hurt him more than losing a finger. Lots of people lose fingers and toes and go right on with their lives like nothing happened. For me to have true justice, he has to suffer for life."

David balled his hands into fists and banged them against each other. "You're not talking about justice, Clementine. You're talking about revenge. Revenge is a weapon. It's used to hurt people. Justice is supposed to restore balance. Make things right."

"But they're the same thing. My life can't be made right unless Gary suffers the way I'm suffering." Clementine sat up straighter, prepared to defend her plan no matter what it took. But David's comment disturbed her. Was there anything she could do that would truly make things right? The only way her life would be the same as it was before was if somehow the assault had never happened. And that was impossible. Maybe there could never be justice for victims like her. Maybe revenge was all she could hope for.

David turned his gaze to the trees behind Clementine. "I need to take you home now," he said. He stood and began folding the blanket they had spread across the table. He handed the folded blanket to Clementine, picked up the cooler, and walked toward the parking lot without saying another word. Clementine followed silently behind him. In the car, he turned on the radio and adjusted the volume to a level that would make talking difficult. Moving faster than was prudent, the car wound its way down the mountain.

"Call me," Clementine said when he let her out at her house. "We can talk about this some more."

"Maybe," he said before he drove away.

16

Weeks passed, and David didn't call. Leaves on the maples and oaks around town matched the brilliant colors on the mountain, covering some of the streets with red and yellow canopies. Thanksgiving was coming up fast, which meant it was almost time for Clementine to put her plan in motion. Nearly every evening, she rehearsed the plan in her mind. One night she sneaked over to the restaurant to make sure her key worked and to review the locations where the meat and produce were stored. She was ready, but David's absence made her uneasy. She expected him to at least phone to see if she'd changed her mind, but no call came. She could have called him, but she wanted to give him all the time he needed to think through what she had told him.

In her free time at the shop, she watched to see if he passed by. Maybe he was keeping an eye on her, but he never appeared. She hadn't heard from Erlene either, which made her feel very alone. She needed the comfort of a friend to keep her calm before she made her move. On a chilly Saturday night in November, Clementine asked Erlene if she could stop by her house for a visit.

Erlene and Alfred had just finished washing the supper dishes when Clementine arrived. The little house felt cozy and warm after the brisk autumn evening. Clementine had always admired the house's inviting lived-in look with its comfortable corduroy furniture and deep green walls. She wanted to pull it all around her and hold it close, but settled for a quick hug with Erlene, who exclaimed, "Where you been keeping yourself, girl? I haven't seen you in ages. You look thinner."

"How about you? Where've you been? Is that dentist making you work overtime?" The depth of Clementine's sudden joy at being with her friend surprised her, just like the boost the kitchen's cheery curtains and flowered tablecloth gave to her spirits.

Alfred chuckled. "That man don't have the nerve to ask Erlene to work overtime. He knows better."

"He's not gonna work overtime himself," Erlene said with a smile. She let the water out of the sink and dried her hands on the dishtowel Alfred was using to dry the last pot. "I don't know what I've been doing lately. I just seem to stay busy all the time. Mostly I'm spending too much time cooking for him." She poked Alfred in the ribs, causing him to let out an exaggerated "oof." Erlene grinned. "That reminds me. I bet we have some of that chocolate cake left. You want some?" Clementine nodded, and the three gathered around the kitchen table while Erlene sliced up thick wedges of cake. "So how's David?"

Clementine flinched. "To be honest, I haven't seen him much lately." Erlene cocked her head and raised her eyebrows. Clementine hesitantly poked at her cake, causing Alfred to lift his plate and announce he would finish his dessert in front of the TV.

"What's going on between you two?" Erlene asked when he had gone.

"I don't know. But whatever it is, it'll work itself out." Clementine had no intention of telling Erlene the real reason David was avoiding her. After much deliberation, she'd decided to share her plan for Gary with Erlene, and the last thing she needed was for David's reaction to turn Erlene against her too. "What's new with you?" she asked, hoping to change the direction of the conversation for now.

Erlene took a bite of cake, still frowning as if she wasn't satisfied with Clementine's answer about David. "Okay," she said after she swallowed. "I won't pry into your business about David, but you know if you wanna talk, I'm the world's best at keeping secrets. As for me, same old, same old. Work, cook, sleep, get up, repeat. Altho-o-ough . . ." She dragged out the word with a twinkle in her eye. "I'm planning a Thanksgiving surprise for Mama. You won't believe what it is."

"Then tell me." Clementine was glad to see Erlene excited about something.

"You know I've been meeting with Brianne off and on ever since we went to see her in Murfreesboro. It's been so much fun, Clementine. I can't tell you how good it is to feel close to my cousin again. I missed her without even realizing I was missing her. And I've learned so much about my grandmother from her. Like I never knew Nana was the first black woman in Murfreesboro to drive a car. Brianne said Nana had an old Ford Model T that she drove all around, delivering potions and medicines to sick people."

At the mention of potions, Clementine couldn't help perking up.

"Yes, I asked about your hex the last time I saw her, but I'll get to that in a minute. Let me tell you about my big plans first."

Clementine nodded and waited for Erlene to continue.

"So every time I meet with Brianne, she tells me Aunt Lanita wants to know when Mama is going to come see her. Or when she can go see Mama. Well, you know how Mama feels about that, so I've been reluctant to do anything, but Brianne keeps bringing it up and wanting us to do something, so finally I gave in. Brianne and Aunt Lanita are coming to my house for Thanksgiving." Erlene clapped her hands with glee. "Isn't that a hoot? I hope Mama doesn't kill us all."

"Or drop dead herself. How's her heart? Seriously. That kind of surprise might be more than she can handle."

"Oh, she's stronger than she looks. Her ankle's pretty much healed, and she's getting around okay now. I took her fishing all summer, and she baked a blackberry cobbler a few weeks ago. She can stand the shock of seeing Aunt Lanita. In fact, I'm betting she's gonna like it once she realizes there's nothing she can do about it and she settles down to talk to her sister. And to give Brianne and me moral support, I'm having my daughter and granddaughter come too. Surely Mama won't cause a big scene in front of her great-granddaughter."

Clementine patted Erlene's hand. "You're a brave woman, my friend. I hope this all goes off without a hitch. Reuniting your family after all these years would be something, all right. I'd like to think maybe I had a tiny little part in it by getting you to take me to see your aunt."

"Of course you did. And oh, yes, the last time I saw Brianne, I asked her again about the hex and why it hadn't worked yet. She said she had no idea how long it took a curse to work, since she wasn't in the habit of casting them. Aunt Lanita was with her for lunch this time, and boy, did Aunt Lanita scoff at that idea. She said her mother could get results in weeks and sometimes days, but she'd heard of a few spells that took months to work. Then she said Brianne needed to practice more so she could get faster results. In a nutshell, they don't know what you should expect."

Now, Clementine thought, *this is where I need to tell her about Gary,* but she didn't feel ready. She needed to be relaxed and comfortable in the conversation, and she wasn't there yet. Although she wanted to share with Erlene, the plan was a hard subject to talk about. It had seemed simple at first. And not really all that risky, considering who was going to be at the luncheon. But David's reaction had unnerved her. Maybe it was riskier than she thought. But she really wanted to do it. She needed Erlene's opinion.

"Well, I can be a little patient," she said, laying her fork beside her half-eaten cake. "I've put myself in a position to keep a closer eye on Gary, so I'll know if we get any results."

Erlene's lip curled. "Oh my God. What have you gone and done now, girl?"

"It's a business investment as well as a way to gain more control over Gary." Erlene's eyes flashed. Clementine folded her hands in front of her plate. "I'm now a secret partner in Johnny's Restaurant. I own a third of the business and have owner privileges."

"Oh my God," Erlene said again. "I don't believe it."

"It makes perfect sense, don't you think? I'm a business-woman in town. I should invest in more businesses."

"I don't believe it. You have more nerve than anybody I ever met."

Clementine shrugged. "So now I'm likely to know if anything bad happens to Gary. He's my employee." She smiled.

"Does he know you're his boss?"

"Lord, no. I'm a secret partner."

"How in the world did all this come about?"

Clementine explained that she heard from David about Johnny's needing money, being careful to leave out the part about the undocumented immigrants out of respect for Johnny, although Erlene could easily have read about it in the newspaper. She described the details of the contract, and concluded by telling Erlene she couldn't tell anybody about the arrangement, not even Alfred. "I really am a secret partner," she said. "It's in the contract that Johnny can't tell anybody about me. But as you said, you're the world's best secret keeper, and I trust you."

Erlene shook her head. "If you don't beat all. Miss business owner and big investor. As if casting spells wasn't enough for you, you go buy part of a restaurant. I still can't believe it. But you promise you'll tell me if anything screwy happens with Gary?"

"Of course I will." Clementine nodded and turned the conversation to the new Dollar General store moving into one of the empty storefronts downtown.

When Erlene finished eating her piece of cake, she brewed a pot of decaf coffee, took a cup to Alfred in the living room, and settled back at the kitchen table with Clementine while they sipped from their own cups. Their voices rose and fell as their comments moved from the new store to other local news and on to national news and back to complaining that all the movies at the only theater in Tanner were animated or filled with car chases and gunfights. Eventually their conversation was punctuated with the soft buzz of Alfred's snoring as he slept in front of the TV. Clementine leaned back in her chair and savored the friendship she felt with Erlene. Erlene would understand why she had to do what she had to do. Now was the time to tell her.

"Since I've been part-owner at Johnny's, I've come up with a way to make sure Gary gets what he deserves," she began when there was a lull in the conversation. Erlene leaned closer, elbows folded on the table, obviously aware Clementine was about to say something big. "Gary took a piece of my life that I can never get back, and now I'm going to take a piece of his. I'm going to fix it so he'll probably never work as a chef again." As matter-of-factly as she could, Clementine laid out the parts of the plan, ending with an explanation of how salmonella usually lasts less than a week. Still smarting from David's harsh reaction, she braced herself for what Erlene might say.

For a few seconds, Erlene said nothing. She sat with her chin resting on her hands and studied her friend. "That's a very dangerous plan," she said finally. "Not so much because of what you know will happen, but because of what you don't know. There're too many uncontrollable parts. What if, for some reason, they don't serve that salad to the men at the luncheon? What if they decide to save it for the dinner crowd? What if one of the dishwashers or the servers helps himself to a little of the luncheon food to take home to his wife and kids? What if you accidentally get some of the chicken juices on something other than the salad? What if Gary calls in sick that day?" Erlene's forefinger drew circles on her other hand. "If you wanted to serve some of that contaminated salad directly to Gary, I'd say, 'Fine. You go, girl.' But the way you're setting this up, you don't know what might happen. Think about it."

Clementine slumped in the hard-backed kitchen chair. Now there were two people who opposed her plan and could expose her. She shouldn't have told anybody. "You think about it, Erlene," she said. "Imagine Gary unable to get a job at any restaurant. I can't say it makes me happy to think about him in that kind of a fix, but it's what he deserves."

"Sure, he deserves it. He deserves that and more. But not like this." Erlene's mouth twisted. "And what about Johnny? He's a good man. He doesn't deserve to have people think they can get poisoned at his restaurant. What if everybody quits going, and they never come back? The restaurant will go out of business."

"That restaurant's an institution in this town. It won't go out of business. Johnny will get rid of Gary, hire a new chef, advertise about the new chef, and people will come back." Somehow, Clementine promised herself, she would make them come back.

Erlene shook her head. "You did a good thing getting yourself in at Johnny's, and you'll find a way to use it to get what you want, but not like this. Come up with a different plan."

The warmth Clementine had basked in for most of the evening dissipated like a spritz of perfume. She was alone. Ever since the rape, she'd relied on David and Erlene. They were there for her, even in the darkest times, even more than her children were, but no longer.

"All right," she said flatly. She stood and asked for her coat, and even though Erlene begged her to stay and promised to help her come up with a new idea, she left, moving quietly past the sleeping Alfred and out into the November night, which was much colder than it had been before.

Alfred's sleeping lasted only until the door closed behind Clementine. "Wake up, you old goat," Erlene announced, wildly shaking his feet, which were propped on the little round ottoman. Alfred snorted and slid one foot to the floor with a thud, barely missing the cake plate he'd set near his chair. "Wake up," Erlene said again. "I've got something real important to tell you."

Alfred cleared his throat and slowly opened his crinkled eyelids. "What's so damned important you have to ruin a perfectly good dream?" he asked. "It was me and Beyoncé at a Panthers game, and the Panthers was winning."

"What I have to tell you is more like a nightmare." Erlene shook his foot again. "Are you good and awake?"

"I don't know how good I am, but I'm as awake as I'm gonna be. If this is gonna be some deep conversation, have you got any more of that coffee?"

Erlene brought him another cup of coffee and then told him about Clementine's plan.

"Holy Jesus!" Alfred exclaimed. "What's gotten into that woman?"

"I don't know, but it scares the hell out of me," Erlene said. "I'm not sure she's in her right mind anymore. I told her not to do it, to come up with another plan, but unless she finds something else to latch onto, I'm afraid she's gonna go through with it. You have to help her."

"Me? Whatcha want me to do? I don't even hardly know her."

"Well, I was thinking about this before, but I wasn't sure whether to do it or not. Now we have to. We have to dig up some dirt about Gary. Something she can use in her case against him."

"What in the sam hill do you think we're going to dig up? And how are we supposed to do it?"

"You can start at the hospital. You've got buddies there, don't you? Didn't you tell me about some girl in medical records? Gary's lived here all his life. Maybe's there's something there Clementine can use."

"Don't you know anything about HIPAA? Medical records are practically sacred. Looking at one of them's worse'n peeking in some naked woman's window. Nobody's going to do that for me."

"How do you know if you don't ask? You might be surprised. Especially if they didn't think they'd get caught. And maybe there's nothing there, but we have to start somewhere."

"So what are you gonna be doing while I'm getting arrested for sticking my nose where it don't belong? Not that I'm saying I'll do it."

"I don't know. I'm not as well-connected as you are." Erlene smiled and tugged on Alfred's ear. "But I'll figure out something. If I don't, all hell's going to break loose in this town, and Clementine's going to be smack dab in the middle of it."

Alfred ran his hands over the rough skin on top of his head. "Oh, Erlene, baby." He reached for her hands and pulled her onto his lap. "Don't you have enough to worry about with your mama and your Aunt Lanita? You can't solve all the world's problems. And I can't help thinking you're getting in over your head with Clementine. What's that boyfriend of hers think? Can't he help her? Why does it have to be you? To be us?"

"Something funny's going on between her and David, and I don't know what it is." Erlene slid from Alfred's lap to the arm of his easy chair.

"I bet I know. She told him about this crazy scheme of hers and he backed away as fast as he could, just like I'm trying to do."

"Do it for me, Alfred. Not for Clementine. Do it for me."

"The best thing you can do for her is tell Johnny what she's planning. He'll put a stop to it real fast."

"I can't do that," Erlene said, horrified at the idea of letting anybody else know what Clementine was planning. But if she had told David, maybe that's what the rift between them was about.

"I think I'll talk to David," she said. "I bet she told him, and he might have some ideas about how we can stop it. But while I'm doing that, you promise me you'll see what you can find out about Gary at the hospital. We need some new information to steer Clementine in another direction."

Alfred slurped coffee from his cup, his eyes avoiding Erlene's. "Thank you, sweet man," she said and kissed his forehead. She was pretty sure she could count on him to do what she asked.

Erlene knew better than to nag Alfred about the information. He would do it, but he would do it in his own time. The problem was she had less than three weeks before Thanksgiving, which meant even less time before the Duke Energy luncheon. She assumed the luncheon was on the Tuesday or Wednesday before Thanksgiving, and she prayed it wasn't any sooner. When she called David to see if he had any ideas about stopping Clementine, he said telling Johnny should be a last resort. "I don't believe she'll go through with it," he said. "Not the Clementine I know. If we tell Johnny, her life in Tanner is over."

"Then help me," Erlene pleaded. "Help me stop her. She said you haven't spoken to her in weeks. How is that helping?"

David sighed. "It's not. But I was so damn mad at her for even considering this I couldn't stand to be in the same room with her. Or even hear her voice. I'll make myself call her. Maybe I can talk some sense into her, although I didn't have any luck doing that the first time. I'll let you know what she says."

Worrying about Clementine, waiting to hear back from David, waiting to see what Alfred might find out, and worrying about the Thanksgiving reunion between Myrtle and Lanita all pressed on Erlene until she thought she might explode. At work, she dropped dental instruments, something she'd never done before. At home, she couldn't sit still long enough to read a magazine or watch a TV show. She called Clementine a couple of times, and while she could tell Clementine was struggling with the plan and maybe wavering in her resolve, she wasn't sure what her friend was going to do. The poor woman needed help. Erlene prayed for her every day.

Brianne kept calling about the reunion until Erlene almost snapped at her, which was the last thing she wanted to do to her cousin. They needed to be on the same side if they were going to pull off this reunion.

Finally the pressure cooker inside her let out some steam. Little more than a week before Thanksgiving, Alfred came home from work with news. Erlene was futzing around in the kitchen, sort of preparing dinner and sort of just rearranging pots and pans, as had become her custom recently, when Alfred slid in behind her unnoticed and wrapped his arms around her waist. "I got something for you," he whispered.

"Not now, you dirty old man. I'm fixing dinner." Erlene didn't even turn to look at him.

"Not that," he said. "I got something about Gary Wiggins. You better sit down."

Erlene dropped the potato she was washing into the sink and immediately situated herself in a kitchen chair. "What is it?" she asked. Her heart pounded against her chest.

"I ain't gonna tell you who told me this, and I ain't gonna tell you how they know it, but I will say it came from medical records, so it's true. And I don't know if it's gonna do Clementine any good, but it's the only peculiar thing my buddy could find."

Erlene's heart slowed down a bit. "So what is it?"

"And you better be glad Gary's wife's doctor uses the new medical network because that's where it was."

"You mean his ex-wife. He's not married anymore."

Alfred sat down across from Erlene. "Well, about fifteen or twenty years ago, Gary had a wife, and she was trying to get pregnant, but she couldn't, so she and Gary had a bunch of tests. Turns out the wife was fine, but Gary had something wrong with him so that he might have been shooting, but nothing was coming out. You get what I mean?"

"Yeah, I think so."

"It's got a name. Here. My buddy wrote it down." He took a crumpled piece of paper from his pants pocket and thrust it at Erlene.

Erlene unfolded the paper. Printed on it was the word *anejaculation*.

"I've never seen this before. I'm going to look it up." She turned off the stove and went into the bedroom where they kept their computer. A search for the word brought back several links, and by the time she had read through some of them, Alfred was standing behind her, staring at the screen over her shoulder. "It says," she explained, "that anejaculation means a man can get hard and even come, but no semen comes out."

"Holy crap. That must be awful. What causes it?"

"A lot of things, according to this. Some psychological and some physical. Here, it says diabetes can cause it. I wonder if Gary has diabetes."

"Damned if I know. And don't ask me to get somebody to go back into the records to find out. That's it. It was a one-time deal, and this is all they found."

Erlene nodded as Alfred's words drifted over her head, barely penetrating her brain, which was busy trying to think of a way this information might help Clementine. "At least this explains why they couldn't find any semen on her. He didn't leave any," she murmured.

While supper sat cold on the stove, Erlene phoned Clementine. She still had no idea how the information could help, but she wanted Clementine to know. A few minutes later, she told Alfred, "I'm going over to Clementine's. Be back as soon as I can."

"What about my dinner?" Alfred looked longingly toward the kitchen.

"Have a beer and some crackers. I won't be gone long."

Erlene barely touched the doorbell before Clementine flung open the door. "Get in here," she said, her face bright with excitement. "Why wouldn't you tell me what you know on the phone? I've been going crazy waiting for you."

"It's not the kind of thing you discuss over the phone," Erlene said. She took off her coat and threw it on a chair. "Now sit down. Here's what Alfred learned."

Erlene explained Gary's condition as best she could. When she finished, Clementine was quiet for several minutes, the elation gone from her face. "Well," she said finally, "so that son of a bitch has a built-in protection system. No wonder he didn't worry about wearing a condom. He knew he wasn't going to leave any traces that way."

"Maybe this gives you some new evidence against him," Erlene suggested.

"How?" Clementine asked, her voice heavy with resignation. "It doesn't prove he did anything. It just tells us why he didn't leave any DNA. And even if the information would do us any good, Alfred and his friend can't say where they got it, because when that guy told Alfred what he found, he broke the law."

"So maybe this doesn't help." Erlene hated facing what she knew was true all along. "But there must be something that does. Let's give ourselves some time. We can still get Gary without hurting anybody else. You have to believe that." Erlene slid closer to Clementine on the couch. "We'll figure out a way. You don't have to do that thing at the restaurant."

Clementine leaned her head against the back of the couch. "I don't know, Erlene. I just don't know. I don't know what to do." She lifted her head and looked at her friend. "Tell Alfred I said thank you for doing this. I know it took some nerve on his part. And Erlene, it's good to see you."

Erlene left for home soon after, not knowing any more about Clementine's state of mind than she did when she arrived. The pressure inside her was building again.

Clementine closed the front door and returned to the bowl of warmed-over beef stew she'd been nursing for supper. She had no appetite. Truth be told, she'd had no appetite for weeks. She pushed the bowl aside, folded her arms on the table, and rested her head against them. Beginning as gentle ripples in her belly, sobs rose up through her chest, scraped her throat, and exploded in her head.

Before the rape, she'd thought she was moving through the excruciating loneliness of losing Gordon, the loneliness that left her hollow, sleepwalking through the days, afraid she couldn't make it on her own. Tanner and the antique store had given her something to look forward to. With David and Erlene, she thought she might actually be happy again. But Gary had destroyed that. He'd made her feel abused, violated, and afraid again. How could she look forward to anything, knowing she'd always be looking over her shoulder? Erlene's news didn't help. It didn't prove anything. Now she was back to planning a crime. And it was a crime, no matter how much she tried to rationalize it. David and Erlene were right. What she was planning to do was despicable. But, God help her, she had to do something. Her sanity was at stake. David said she'd lost her mind, and maybe she had.

I am insane, she thought. *A person would have to be insane to deliberately make innocent people sick. Along with everything else Gary's stolen from me, he's taken away my sanity and my humanity. Who am I? I've turned into some heartless wretch of a person. That bastard has dragged me down into the gutter with him. And I don't know if I'll ever get out.* The sobs continued to wash over her in waves.

A few hours later, she dried her eyes, found her phone, and called David. "I'm not going to do it," she said. Then she called Erlene and told her.

17

Thanksgiving Day dawned clear and cool with a soft breeze stirring the few leaves that remained on the trees. Erlene woke as the sun came up, certain that she'd hardly slept at all. She remembered checking the clock at one and again at three and again at five. At seven, she gave up and left Alfred snoring in the bed. She imagined Brianne and Lanita loading the pies they were bringing into the car so they could leave home at seven thirty. Brianne had promised to be at Erlene's no later than one. The other relatives were arriving at noon, so there'd be a big buffer for the fireworks Erlene expected when the Murfreesboro women walked through the door. Alfred had threatened to volunteer for work at the hospital on Thanksgiving, but when Erlene said she would send all the leftovers home with their daughter and Brianne, he promised to be present for the showdown.

The day before Thanksgiving, Erlene had been sure she was going to have a nervous breakdown. Thank God Clementine had abandoned the food poisoning plan because she couldn't have handled the stress of that along with what she was facing at home. She'd rushed around the house all day, cooking cranberries, peeling sweet potatoes, dusting already spotless tabletops, and doing anything she could think of to keep her mind busy. She'd even cooked a big pot of vegetable soup for supper that night despite Alfred's protests that she was subconsciously trying to run herself into the ground so she could take to her bed and tell all these folks not to come. Nothing could be further from the truth. She and Brianne had been looking forward to this day for months, although she was terrified Miss Myrtle would never forgive her for doing it.

Now the gathering was only hours away. Erlene showered and stared with regret at the cashmere sweater and long tweed skirt she planned to wear. She wasn't particularly fond of the skirt—it lay like a wool rug against her thighs—but Myrtle loved it and was always telling Erlene to wear it more often. Wearing it today was a small sacrifice she could make. She threw on a pair of jeans and a sweatshirt for the morning. At eight o'clock, she put the turkey in the oven. As Alfred stumbled out of bed and fixed cereal for breakfast, she set the table and carefully planned where everyone would sit. Alfred would be at the head of the table, and she would sit around the corner to his left in the seat nearest the kitchen. Miss Myrtle would sit next to her, where she could keep an eye on her. Aunt Lanita would sit across from Myrtle—Erlene wanted them close enough to talk to each other, but not so close that Myrtle could whisper spiteful things to her sister. Erlene's daughter, LuAnn, would sit at the foot of the table with Brianne next to Lanita and Erlene's granddaughter, Aliyah, next to Myrtle. Of course, all this planning assumed every guest would stay long enough for dinner, not a certainty that day.

When the doorbell rang a little after noon, Erlene was as ready as she'd ever be. Aliyah stood at the front door, a pink ribbon in her hair and a vase filled with colorful dahlias in her hands. LuAnn followed her with three bottles of wine.

"What beautiful flowers," Erlene said to her granddaughter, "and how lovely you look." After hugging both her and her mother, Erlene told LuAnn, "Open that wine and pour us a glass. We're gonna need it." Alfred had gone to pick up Miss Myrtle and arrived with her a few minutes later. "Have a glass of wine and join the party," Erlene said to her mother. Miss Myrtle had a strict one-glass-only rule regarding wine, and Erlene wanted to get it into her before Lanita arrived.

The three women retired to the kitchen to tend the vegetables on the stove and catch up on family news. While she stirred the green beans, Erlene exchanged worried glances with LuAnn, who knew Brianne and Lanita were on their way. Over the refrigerator, the wall clock ticked away the minutes.

And then it happened. A light tapping on the front door followed by muted voices suddenly interrupted by an exclamation. "My heavens, Aliyah. You is the spitting image of your grandma when she was a little girl." Alfred's deep voice jumped in, trying to cover up Lanita's remark, but the surprise was sprung. Miss Myrtle had been letting the conversation in the kitchen float around her, but now her head jerked up. Her eyes were like two tiny drops of oil. Her bantam body stiffened on the stool where she was perched.

"Erlene Hubner Duncan," she said. "Who is that in the living room? Tell me you haven't defiled this good Baptist holiday with that believer in the black arts."

"Now, Mama, Aunt Lanita is as good a Baptist as you are. And you haven't seen her in forty years." Erlene struggled to keep the anger and fear out of her voice. "She doesn't practice root medicine, and even if she did, couldn't you overlook it for one day? It's Thanksgiving. Be grateful that you have a sister and she's still alive so you can make up with her before it's too late." If Erlene expected backup support from her daughter, she wasn't getting it. Silence swamped the room. Miss Myrtle's wrinkled cheeks drooped along with the corners of her mouth.

"Take me home," she said, squirming to inch her narrow hips off the stool.

"Now, Mama," Erlene began again, but she was interrupted by the tight gaggle of people who crowded through the kitchen door, led by the diminutive form of Aunt Lanita. Alfred had his hand on Lanita's arm, but she obviously wasn't paying any attention to him. Brianne squeezed in behind them, pressing on Aliyah, who was peeking around Alfred's hip with eyes as big as doughnuts.

"Myrtle, my dear, dear Myrtle," Lanita said. "It's been way too long." She reached to hug her sister, who had managed to slide off the stool and drop to the floor. Myrtle's expression and body were stiff as a poker, but she let Lanita embrace her. As the two old faces grew close to each other, Erlene was astonished at how alike they looked. She tried to remember which one was older, but she couldn't. For all she knew at that moment, they could have been twins.

"I'm mighty tickled to see you," Lanita said, taking a step back to stare at Myrtle. "And we have our darling daughters to thank for bringing us together. Praise the Lord, we have so much to be thankful for today."

Erlene wasn't sure she wanted the credit for this meeting yet. Myrtle looked like she was about to either slug somebody or make a run for the door, despite her still fragile ankle. "Let's all go back in the living room," Erlene said. "We have a lot of catching up to do. Get Aunt Lanita and Brianne some wine, Alfred." She needed to stay with the vegetables, but she was afraid to leave Miss Myrtle's side. Feeling like a shepherd, she tried to shoo everyone out of the kitchen except Alfred, who looked deeply grateful to be given a job away from the battlefield as he took wine glasses from the cabinet and set them next to the wine.

The crowd followed Erlene's directions, all except Myrtle, who refused to move until Erlene put an arm around her shoulders and gently forced her to walk. In the living room, Erlene led her mother to Alfred's easy chair, which the others had left conspicuously vacant, but Myrtle froze in front of it, and Erlene had no idea how to make her sit.

"Make yourself comfortable, Myrtle," Lanita suggested. "I want to hear all about your life and this beautiful granddaughter and great-granddaughter you got." Aliyah had settled quietly on the floor at her mother's feet, her face still telegraphing amazement.

"Tell Aunt Lanita how you like to fish, Mama," Erlene said, but Myrtle didn't budge. "I bet Aunt Lanita still makes that great banana pudding," Erlene tried again.

Miss Myrtle folded her arms across her skinny bosom. "I don't care about no banana pudding. I just wanna know if you's still a root doctor."

Lanita huffed loudly. "I never did do the medicine. That was Mama. And she did a lot of good. Remember that baby that was drowning in its own spit? Mama fixed it right up. And she scared that grubby kid Willie Hendricks so bad inflicting warts on his hands that he never stole from anybody again. Remember? I wished I could do the medicine, but I can't. I don't have the gift." Erlene held her breath, praying that Lanita wouldn't mention that Brianne had the gift. And surely she wouldn't say anything about the hex for Clementine.

"Believing it's just as bad as doing it," Myrtle said. "And you believed it enough to choose Mama over me when the time came."

"Don't forget you turned your back on us first. You can't imagine how much you hurt Mama, refusing to talk to her like you did." The warmness had leaked out of Lanita's voice. Her tightened face resembled her sister's even more. "I was mad at you for that, real mad, but I got over it. You's the one that never got over it."

Myrtle turned her head slightly. Alfred had slipped into the room, glasses of wine in his hands. Myrtle locked her eyes on his. "Alfred, take me home now or I'll walk." Alfred looked at Erlene, his face full of alarm and pleading. What was he supposed to do?

"Alfred's not going to take you home, Mama," Erlene said. "This is Thanksgiving, and we're a family that's been separated way too long. Nana's dead and buried. It's time we made up and started appreciating each other. Now I need somebody to come in the kitchen and give me a hand or our Thanksgiving dinner is gonna be ruined." She took the glasses of wine from Alfred and handed them to Lanita and Brianne. Then she steered him to the front door, figuring he would know why he was there. When she passed Myrtle, the little woman took a few steps behind her. Erlene was relieved, thinking her mother was following her to the kitchen, but Myrtle made a sharp turn and walked straight to the guest bedroom. She disappeared behind the door, and with a loud click let them know the door was locked.

"Oh shit," Erlene said, low enough that she hoped Aunt Lanita and Aliyah wouldn't hear. The others in the living room didn't move, except Aliyah, who squeezed next to her mother on the couch. "Well, come on, somebody. I said I need a little help." Erlene let her annoyance color her voice. "She'll come out when dinner's ready. She loves turkey and cranberry sauce."

Miss Myrtle didn't come out, even though Erlene knocked on the door when the others gathered around the table. No sound came from the room. Alfred offered to take the lock apart if Erlene was worried about her mother, but Erlene was more peeved than worried. Most likely, Miss Myrtle had fallen asleep, and if she was still sitting in there stewing, she could stay there as far as Erlene was concerned. She had other company to entertain, and she was going to make damned sure they had a good time.

Everyone complimented Erlene on the food. The conversation at the table moved briskly, led mainly by Erlene, with Brianne jumping in from time to time. Lanita was mostly quiet and brought food to her mouth like an actress in a slow-motion movie. Her tired eyes suggested her efforts with Myrtle had worn her out. Erlene hurt for her aunt, knowing how disappointed she was, but there was nothing Erlene could do. She'd honestly thought Miss Myrtle would come around with the whole family gathered together like you're supposed to do on Thanksgiving. Erlene had wanted to take a photograph of everyone seated at the table, but Myrtle's empty chair was too obvious.

After dinner, Alfred found a football game on TV, and the women went to the kitchen to clean up, all except Lanita, who asked if she could lie down on Erlene and Alfred's bed. Aliyah sat in a corner of the living room playing games on her iPod Touch. As they cleaned, the women worried about the matriarchs hidden away in separate bedrooms. "I could make Mama come out," Erlene said, "take the lock off and march in there and drag her out, but it wouldn't do any good."

"We tried," Brianne said. "My heart aches for my mother, but sometimes you can't escape the transgressions of the past." She looked around the room at each sad face. "We should take a lesson here. Aunt Myrtle should never have disowned Nana, and Mama should never have disowned her. Some things can't be fixed."

A sly look crept across LuAnn's face, sending a warning chill up Erlene's spine. There was no telling what her daughter might say. "Maybe, Aunt Brianne," LuAnn drawled, "you could cast a spell and make everything all right."

Erlene didn't know whether to slap her or laugh. She chose the latter. "Whatever happens between those two old women, we got one good thing out of this," she said. "We got each other. Me and Brianne will always be close, and I'm counting on LuAnn and Aliyah getting to know you too. And Aunt Lanita. We'll come see y'all, and y'all can come see us, no matter what Mama thinks."

As the afternoon wore on, Erlene heard Miss Myrtle come out of the bedroom and go into the bathroom twice. Both times the bedroom door locked behind her when she returned. Once Erlene saw her peeking into the living room, but before anyone could catch her, she'd disappeared into the bedroom again. Around five o'clock, Brianne said that they had better get on the road. "I wish y'all could stay here tonight," Erlene said, "but with Mama holed up in our only guest room, I don't know what to expect."

Brianne assured her they weren't driving all the way home. "We're gonna stop in Greensboro and spend the night with Cousin Marvin. Do you remember him? He's Uncle Otis's oldest son. Mama always liked Marvin, even when he was a nasty little boy always playing with worms. He works at the zoo now. Wouldn't you know it?" She laughed and hugged Erlene. "Y'all have a merry Christmas, now," she said. And then she and Lanita were gone.

Erlene knocked on the bedroom door. "You can come out now, Mama," she said. "Your sister left."

Clementine's Thanksgiving Day started earlier than Erlene's, but not because she planned it that way. Her daughter, Elizabeth, had said she could afford to fly to North Carolina only one more time that year and she'd rather come for Christmas, so Clementine wasn't expecting her. Jackson promised to drive down from Pennsylvania Thanksgiving morning, and that's where the rub came. Clementine was sleeping soundly when the text message alarm blared from her cell phone at six thirty. Through a sleepy fog, she read that Jackson was on I-81, and if the traffic didn't start backing up, he'd be there by one thirty or two. *You could have waited till later to tell me* ran through Clementine's hazy mind as she looked for signs of daylight outside the window. She'd been awake until at least three o'clock as usual. A few streaks of light behind the pine trees suggested the sun wasn't far away.

Her body lay limp and heavy on the bed. She'd felt that way ever since she gave up her idea of poisoning the food. She knew she'd made the right decision, but having no plan made her feel helpless. The hex might still work, but it was awfully slow. For weeks, the food plan had given her the tingling sensation of imagining Gary's fall from grace. Now she pictured him happily enjoying Thanksgiving, although with whom she didn't know. She tried to imagine him all alone eating leftovers from the restaurant, which, according to Johnny, he did a lot.

The last time she'd seen him was at the restaurant a few days earlier. She'd started dining there every so often to keep an eye on her investment and to make Gary think he was off her radar. He seldom came out of the kitchen at Johnny's, but when he did, she studied him for signs of stress. He didn't show any. And the customers all acted happy to see him. Did they not know he was a rapist? What did they think of her now? David had been her gauge for town gossip, but he was no longer around to keep her apprised. Even after she told him she was not going through with the plan, he stayed away. She missed him sorely.

When she began planning Thanksgiving dinner for Jackson, she called David and invited him to join them. He answered the phone, which she feared he might not do, but he coolly said he had other plans. What other plans, she wondered. He'd told her last summer that his college-aged daughter was spending Thanksgiving with her mother and Christmas with him this year. It was possible that a friend or one of his coworkers at the insurance agency had invited him for dinner, but Clementine had a gnawing suspicion that he was spending the day with his old flame, Amanda Byrd. Amanda was a frequent customer at Back in the Day, so Clementine had gotten to know her fairly well. For the past few weeks, however, Amanda had been a no-show at the shop. Now Clementine understood.

After Jackson's ill-timed text message, Clementine got up and made a pot of coffee. As the coffee brewed, she caught herself humming holiday songs. Even robbing her of sleep couldn't spoil her eager anticipation of Jackson's arrival. For the past week, she'd thrown herself into planning food for Jackson's visit, glad to have something to divert her attention from her miseries. Looking at her menus, anyone would have thought she expected a houseful of company, but Jackson ate as much as two or three normal people. Now it was time to pull it all together.

Jackson drove into the driveway just as the turkey came out of the oven. He swore he could smell it all the way from I-40. Nestled around the drop-leaf table in the cozy dining room, mother and son ate and talked and reminisced. Clementine felt the most relaxed she'd felt in months. When Jackson took a breather from inhaling mounds of turkey, she seized the opportunity for a little motherly interrogation. "So how's work going?"

"Nothing new," Jackson declared and reached for another roll, but when Clementine gave him her strongest look of parental dissatisfaction to let him know he wasn't going to get off that easily, he tried again. "I guess the most exciting thing that's happened in the past few months was the stolen computers. You remember those robberies I told you about several months ago? Well, the thieves got bolder and started taking computers, plus the monitors and keyboards. They didn't get mine, but some of the writers had to wait days for a new computer before they could get back to work."

"That's terrible. Did they catch who did it this time?"

"Still don't know who did it, but the building manager blames our security service. So he fired them. They obviously weren't doing their job, and one of them might even be the thief. They have people watching the building all night long, and they all have keys."

Jackson reached for the potatoes, as Clementine pondered the fate of the security guards. He who has the responsibility takes the fall, she figured. That was the way of the world.

The conversation soon turned to movies and TV shows and the upcoming presidential election. Clementine could argue politics with the best of them, but her mind was stuck on the security guards. If they were fired because they couldn't stop robberies from happening where they worked, what chance did they have of ever getting another job as a security guard? Hire me and get your stuff stolen wasn't much of a recommendation. For them, a robbery was as bad as spoiled food was for a chef. The comparison started Clementine's brain rolling. Maybe instead of food poisoning, she could use robbery against Gary.

If expensive equipment started disappearing from the kitchen, Johnny might blame the problem on Gary. Gary was in charge of the kitchen. She could subtly suggest to Johnny that Gary should be held responsible for the loss. Maybe Johnny would fire Gary and make it damn hard for him to get another job.

As Thanksgiving Day wound down, Clementine had a lot to be thankful for. The heavy feeling that had plagued her in the morning had lifted. She had her son for a short visit, and she had a new plan for sealing Gary's fate.

A week passed before Clementine could put her new plan into action. The timing couldn't have been better. Christmas season was one of the busiest times at the restaurant, a time when any disruption would be magnified many times over. Also, Clementine realized, during the Christmas season, the restaurant ordered more lobster and steak and other expensive food for seasonal parties and to give the restaurant a more festive flair. If that food started disappearing, Johnny would definitely feel the loss. She waited until the first order of crabmeat came in to make her move.

When she went back to the restaurant late at night, Clementine felt strangely at home. The sound of Latin music in the kitchen startled her at first, but she remembered what Johnny said about the guys keeping the radio on all the time. They must have forgotten to turn it off when they left. Ignoring the music, she retraced the steps from her previous rehearsal, only this time she removed the target food from the refrigerator and slipped it into the largest cooking pots she could find. She had positioned the van in the parking lot's one unlighted spot, which allowed her to slip into the shadows to load the pots. Someone could possibly see her coming out the back door, but that wasn't likely. The late hour meant the surrounding businesses were closed and few cars traveled the street in front. When the first round of pots and food were securely in the van, she went back to take some frying pans. She thought about taking the computer from Johnny's always unlocked office, but decided to save it for later.

Driving through the deserted streets, her secret booty riding behind her, she felt giddy as a teenager. Putting the hex on Gary had taken nerve, but this was more dangerous. Technically, it wasn't stealing. Since she was part-owner of the restaurant, she could argue the food and equipment belonged to her if she was ever found out, but her late-night shenanigans would be hard to explain, and her reputation in Tanner would be destroyed. She shivered as she turned the van onto the street where she lived.

With the van backed into her dark driveway (she had left the porch lights off on purpose), she unloaded the pots and carried them to the basement. The old coal bin had sat empty since she moved into the house, but now she had a purpose for it. The outside coal chute had been sealed up long ago, and the iron door that separated it from the rest of the basement was just the right size to shove a large pot through. The steak, shrimp, and crabmeat she hid at the bottom of the extra freezer she kept in the basement. Eventually she would eat it in small portions. No need to waste something that good.

18

Johnny called Clementine the next day to tell her about the missing items. "Now, don't you worry a lot about this," he said. "It's probably just some kids looking for a little fancy food and some stuff they can pawn for drug money. Although for the life of me, I can't figure out how they got in. The doors and windows were locked just as good as they were when we left. I told Arnold Tubbs about it, and he sent a couple of guys out to investigate." Clementine's heart skipped a beat when he mentioned police, even though she was sure she left no fingerprints. "I doubt they'll catch who did it," Johnny continued, "and the insurance will cover most of it, but the last thing we need is for our premiums to go up. You know that."

Clementine knew that very well. The restaurant's profits were still slim, so much so that Clementine was a little worried about her own financial stability. Like most retailers, she was counting on Christmas to put the antique shop in the black. She was able to pay her monthly bills, including her mortgage and rent for the shop, but not much money was left over. And buying into the restaurant had taken a big chunk of her savings. What little she had left she'd lowered even more by splurging at the past two estate sales to increase her inventory for Christmas shoppers. She assured herself, however, that a few more trips to the restaurant with the van would be enough to force Johnny to fire Gary, and the restaurant would be back on safer ground.

The Tanner Observer's Friday edition printed news about the robbery on the front page. Clementine checked the restaurant's Facebook page, and sure enough, people were posting all kinds of comments about who they thought was at fault. Mostly they shared Johnny's belief that the culprits were teenagers, even though there was no sign of forced entry. None of the comments mentioned Gary or any of the servers, but that didn't matter to Clementine. Casting blame wasn't the kind of rumor she wanted to see started. She wanted the people in town to speculate about the quality of the food or the service. Probably it was too soon for that. She had more work to do.

On her next midnight trip to Johnny's, Clementine hit upon a true serendipity. She was rummaging through one of the drawers, gathering up the most expensive cooking tools she could find, when she discovered a thick three-ring binder. Inside, each page was filled with recipes, some handwritten, others neatly typed or cut from books and magazines. All had handwritten notes in the margins describing variations in ingredients or amounts. On the first page someone had written, "Property of Gary Wiggins. Do not touch."

Clementine's first inclination was to take the book along with her other loot. What better way to sabotage the quality of Gary's cooking? And thank goodness he hadn't transferred all his recipes to digital records. But then it occurred to her that taking the recipe book would free Gary from blame. Why would he steal his own recipe book? There had to be another way. She flipped through the pages and noticed that a lot of the margin notes were made in pencil. And even some of the hand-written recipes were in pencil. She flew into Johnny's office and returned with a stubby yellow Ticonderoga. She changed a few ingredients, but mimicking Gary's handwriting wasn't easy. Changing numbers was easier and safer. At first, her hand trembled as she wrote. Then, as she got into what she was do-ing, imagining the effects of her changes made her chuckle. She could see the confusion and bewilderment on Gary's face when his favorite recipes betrayed him. Finally, she tucked the book back where she found it and dropped the tools she had gathered into a shopping bag. With the bag handle over one arm, she lifted a brand-new double Panini grill press that had to have been expensive.

This time Quentin Harper buried the story of the robbery on the third page of the *Observer*. A repeat robbery was appar-ently old news. Johnny didn't see it as old, however. Clementine got exactly the response she wanted from him.

"Enough is enough!" Johnny yelled into the telephone at Clementine. "I told Arnold Tubbs he better put a stop to this. That's his job, for God's sake. But you know what that son of a bitch said to me? He said it had to be an inside job to have happened twice like this with no forced entry. And fingerprints are a lost cause with so many people touching things all over the restaurant. Tubbs said I better look at my staff and figure out which one was the thief. Can you believe that?"

Clementine kept her tone calm, wanting Johnny to see her as the voice of reason. "Well, Johnny, he may have a point. I mean, how would anybody else get in?"

"But who? Who could it be?"

"Keep an eye on everybody. See who acts suspicious." Clem-entine was betting that Gary would be agitated about the dis-ruption in his cooking routine. She needed to make Johnny suspect him.

"You're right." Johnny's voice brightened. "You know what I'm gonna do? I'm gonna put in that surveillance camera I keep talking about and never buy. God knows I can't afford to spend the money right now, but crap, I don't have a choice. I can't let this go on any longer, and the camera will make the insurance company happy."

A streak of panic slithered up Clementine's back. She wasn't finished with her late-night pilfering at the restaurant. She could learn to turn the camera off, but she didn't like this kink in her plans. "You don't need to go to that extreme," she said. "Just watch the employees."

"Nope. I can't watch 'em all every minute. And this way I'll see for sure who's up to no good after closing. I'll find one today and get it installed now. Those companies say they have service on demand. Well, let 'em prove it."

Clementine sat for a long time after the call ended. She'd planned to wait until the week before Christmas before making another run to the restaurant, but now she couldn't afford to wait. She would have to go tonight.

A light freezing rain started to fall as Clementine pulled the van behind the restaurant at around one that morning. Sneaking into the restaurant again so soon made her nervous. Surely Tubbs had a patrol car cruising the area. She checked for headlights in the darkness before turning into the lot, and she extinguished the headlights on the van as soon as possible.

Originally, she'd intended to take more small pieces of equipment and some food, but now she had to step up the plan and go for the big stuff—the computers. Standing in the doorway, she didn't see any cameras. She searched for cameras again from the entry to the kitchen before she felt safe. Her first move was to grab the three-shelf cart from the corner, since her targets this time were more than she could carry. Before long she had the cart filled with items, including the countertop electric fryer, the drawer warmer, and the rice cooker. Hunched over her plunder, she rolled the cart carefully across the slick asphalt between the door and the van. Icy rain pinged against the van roof and stung her face when she looked up to move her goods. She pulled her sock cap down to her jaws. Her fingers tingled inside thin leather gloves.

Back inside the restaurant, she pushed the cart to Johnny's office, intending to take his computer, but at the last minute she left it. Better to confine the missing items to the kitchen where Gary was in sole control. If she remembered correctly, there was a laptop computer stashed in one of the kitchen drawers. Gary used it, but she was certain it didn't belong to him. The restaurant owned it, so it was fair game for her plan. Quickly she hunted through the drawers, conscious of how much time she had already spent inside. The longer the van stayed in the parking lot, the greater the chances of its being seen. The laptop finally appeared under a stack of menus. She seized it and ran out the door, wondering if she would find anything interesting on it when she got home.

Snow mixed with the freezing rain as Clementine made her way along a different route to her house. Straining to see through the slushy mix the wipers swept across the windshield, she had a vision of herself, a thief lost somewhere in the darkness. If anybody had suggested a year ago that she would be sneaking around in the middle of the night, taking items that technically may have been hers but that others depended on, and lying to a good man like Johnny, she would have said they were crazy. She was a good woman who had lived a half century always trying to do the right thing, never intentionally breaking any rules, and never deliberately hurting another person. She had been a good role model for her children. What would they think of her now? She shuddered at the thought of

Jackson and Elizabeth watching her creep through the kitchen, shoving loot into a bag like a common criminal.

You never know what you're capable of until something pushes you to the edge, she thought. She hated that she was causing problems for Johnny, but once Gary was gone, she would do everything she could to make things right for him. The insurance would pay for the food and equipment, and she would go on a personal crusade to keep customers coming to the restaurant. Maybe the garden club she'd joined last year could meet there. And she'd find every reason she could to encourage the antique-shop customers to eat there.

This time Johnny didn't call. Instead he sent Clementine an email that said, "We got hit again last night. Surveillance cameras going in today. We'll get that bastard, whoever he is." Clementine sighed as she read the email. Had she done enough? Asking Johnny to show her how to operate the cameras could raise suspicion. And for Johnny's sake, she didn't want to take more than she had to. She decided to bide her time and see what happened.

As the days went by, she kept an eye on the restaurant's Facebook page to see what kind of comments popped up. Nothing much was said about the third robbery, even though Quentin moved the story back to the front page of the *Observer*. One person noted, however, that she had taken relatives to Johnny's for Sunday brunch and been disappointed in the quality of the food. She asked if anybody else had had a similar experience. Clementine smiled as she remembered the fun she'd had with Gary's recipes. Maybe her changes had nothing to do with the food problems—after all, Gary was having to manage with fewer pots and appliances unless the insurance payments had come through already, which she doubted—but she was grateful that her efforts were having an effect.

A week before Christmas, Johnny called her to say the restaurant was having its worst holiday season ever. Dining traffic was way down, which in some ways was maybe a blessing because they hadn't replaced all the stolen equipment, a handicap that slowed their service significantly. Still, fewer customers meant lower revenue and a decreasing, almost disappearing, profit. "I'm gonna have to let some of the staff go if things don't pick up soon," Johnny said, "and I hate like hell to do that at Christmas." He paused. "I won't do that at Christmas, but come January, I may not have a choice."

Clementine spent several agonizing evenings trying to figure out what her next move should be. Her days at the antique shop were blessedly busy with Christmas shoppers—at the last auction she'd wisely bought a large supply of small items that would fit most gift budgets—but her mind kept drifting to the restaurant. Johnny was on the right track talking about letting staff go, but she had to make sure he got rid of Gary and not one of the innocent others. Also, she didn't want to drag out her restaurant sabotage any longer than absolutely necessary. She had to make it painful enough for Johnny that he'd fire Gary, but she didn't want to destroy the restaurant or Johnny, and her own finances were suffering. If her income from the restaurant didn't turn around soon, she might have to choose between her house payment and the shop rent, a choice she wasn't sure she could make.

As her evening worries stretched on past midnight, she always found herself asking if getting revenge was worth sacrificing her beloved antique shop. It was a question she could not have imagined facing when she arrived in Tanner, full of hope and anticipation. She wished she had somebody she could talk to, somebody she could spill her guts to, tell them how violated she still felt ten months after the rape, ten months and six days, to be exact. Violated, and now wrenched in a terrible decision. But nobody other than Clementine knew the whole story. After upsetting David and Erlene so much with the food poisoning plot, she vowed to keep to herself any other plan she devised. It was the kind of self-incriminating secret she could have told Gordon, but Gordon wasn't there.

Finally, she decided to do nothing until after Christmas. Problems at Johnny's Restaurant were rolling with their own momentum now, and she didn't want to make any more trouble during the busy Christmas season. After the holiday, she would figure out those surveillance cameras on her own and make one more strike before suggesting to Johnny that he had to let Gary go.

In the meantime, she wanted to do something nice for Erlene. When they'd met for lunch soon after Thanksgiving, Erlene told her about the debacle of the Miss Myrtle and Aunt Lanita reunion. Despite Erlene's protests that at least she and Brianne had gotten close during all their plotting, she still wasn't herself. More like a gloomy version of herself. Clementine wanted to do something nice for her, something that would cheer her up.

And David. She didn't know what to do about David. Or even what she wanted to do about David. She missed him fiercely. For a while she had thought their relationship was headed toward something serious, a possibility that both frightened and pleased her. She and David seemed to understand each other. At least they did until she told him about her plans to punish Gary.

As Christmas drew close, Clementine decided to reach out to David again. Maybe the holiday season would soften his feelings toward her. If she included Erlene in her plan, she could make the meeting less awkward for David, and if things went well, maybe raise Erlene's spirits a little. If David refused to come, she could focus on Erlene. Inviting them both for dinner was worth a try.

Erlene and Alfred accepted the invitation immediately. "December twenty-sixth?" Erlene said. "Sounds good to me. The day after Christmas is always dull at our house. Just me exhausted after all that shopping and cooking and Alfred complaining about spending too much money. What can I bring to help with dinner?"

David was less enthusiastic. "I may have to meet with clients from the counseling center that night. Christmas is a hard time for folks with no jobs."

Clementine sighed. "I know this is short notice, so let's just leave it open. Come if you can, and if you can't, that's all right." At least he hadn't outright refused.

Christmas Day passed quietly for Clementine. Elizabeth flew in from San Francisco on December twenty-third and immediately took over.

"Now, Mother," she said when she arrived, "you don't have to worry about a thing. There's no reason for you to drag yourself home from the shop at nine o'clock at night and then start cooking and wrapping presents. Have you done all your shopping? If not, don't worry about it. I'll get something for you to give Jackson."

Jackson drove home on the twenty-fourth, and the three of them celebrated Christmas Eve with mulled wine, ginger cookies, and Christmas movies on TV. On Christmas Day, they attended the Sunday morning service at the First United Methodist Church. Clementine hadn't attended church regularly for years, but she had such fond memories of the

Christmas service at this church that she couldn't resist. The sanctuary still looked the same with holly wreaths in every window, while the traditional carols ringing through the familiar setting took her right back to her days in junior choir, back to when she won a gold star for perfect Sunday school attendance. After the service, the family came home to open presents and watch another movie. For Christmas dinner, Clementine surprised her children with shrimp and crab cakes.

"I know we usually have turkey," she said, "but I'm a businesswoman now, so I can afford to serve something more elegant for the holidays." She smiled to herself, knowing the food came from Johnny's, but Elizabeth and Jackson would never suspect anything was amiss. They knew nothing about the disappearances at the restaurant. At least Clementine hoped they didn't. She certainly hadn't told them anything. She was too afraid Jackson might see the similarities between those robberies and the robberies at his company. But if they had any suspicions about the change in the dinner menu, they didn't let on. They were too busy gobbling down the shellfish.

Brother and sister both left Tanner the day after Christmas. Clementine was sad to see them go, as always, but she was excited about her dinner party that evening. Since December twenty-sixth fell on a Monday, Back in the Day was closed. Clementine had kept the shop open every day for the first weeks in December, but she refused to make a special opening after Christmas "just so folks can come looking for post-holiday sales," she told Elizabeth, and Elizabeth agreed.

The first thing Clementine did after her children left was make a chocolate cheesecake, David's favorite dessert. For Erlene, she planned to cook twice-baked potatoes, the menu item Erlene always talked about when she had lunch with Clementine but never ordered because she said she'd be wearing it on her hips forever. Clementine didn't know what Alfred's favorite food was, but Erlene said he liked everything, so Clementine figured he'd be happy no matter what. The centerpiece of the meal was going to be four superb filet mignons that had been waiting in Clementine's basement freezer for just such an occasion. "Thank you, Johnny," she whispered as she poked one to make sure it was adequately thawed.

Erlene and Alfred arrived on time and were well into their second cocktails with no sign of David. "If he doesn't show up in fifteen minutes, I'm putting the steaks on the grill anyway," Clementine said. Using the gas grill was a skill she'd become proficient at since Gordon died. She didn't even mind venturing onto the chilly patio in winter. Particularly not for steaks as fine as these.

Ten minutes later, she began seasoning the meat. She pretended to listen to Erlene and Alfred chit-chatting at her kitchen table, but her mind was focused on David. She wished he had refused the invitation outright instead of leaving her hanging. She needed to accept that their relationship was over, yet he kept giving her glimmers of hope. She shouldn't care about him at all. He obviously disapproved of her. Yet she clung to him like the schoolgirl she used to be, the one who fervently sought approval.

The doorbell rang. Clementine was so deep in thought that the sudden noise startled her. "Easy, girl. I'll get it," Erlene said.

"No, I'll get it." Clementine wiped her hands on a dishtowel and ran her fingers through her hair. David didn't use to ring the doorbell. What had he done with her key?

David stood on the front porch, hands thrust into his pockets, his blue eyes seeming to be set even deeper than usual. Clementine couldn't read his expression, somewhere between determined and sad. Certainly not filled with holiday joy. "I apologize for being late," he said. "My meeting at the counseling center took a long time. I hope I haven't screwed up dinner. If y'all are already eating, I can go on home."

"Don't be silly. Come in. I was just about to put the steaks on the grill." She led him to the kitchen and fixed him a martini. Erlene pulled out a chair at the table and motioned for him to sit down. Alfred was telling a convoluted tale about Christmas ghosts on the farm where his father had worked many years ago, and soon David was smiling. Clementine watched the threesome as she tossed the salad and ran back and forth to the patio to tend to the steaks. Maybe David had forgiven her for the food poisoning plan.

Soon the four of them moved to the dining room. Clementine put the food on the table and asked David to pour the wine. Everyone seemed happy. Clementine sipped her wine and felt a warm glow, whether from the alcohol or the fellowship, she wasn't sure. Having the dinner party was a good idea. She loved being with her friends. As the steak and potatoes (Erlene said a soft "oooh" when she saw the potatoes) were consumed and the candles burned down, conversation flitted about the table, light as a bird. Even David joined in, almost like his old self.

They all talked, but Alfred talked the most. Clementine didn't mind—Alfred could be very entertaining. When Clementine served coffee and dessert, Alfred took one bite of his cheesecake and exclaimed, "Mercy, Clementine, I had no idea you knew your way around a kitchen this good. Biting into this is like sinking your teeth into a dream. Hope you got enough for seconds."

Clementine cringed as "knew your way around a kitchen" brought memory flashes of herself in Johnny's kitchen. Erlene poked Alfred in the ribs and made a shushing sound, but Alfred just laughed. "It's a compliment, Erlene. Clementine knows that. I bet she appreciates a man who appreciates good food. And believe me, I am that man. I can sure tell you the best restaurants to eat at in this town."

Erlene gave him a stern look. "Old man, you don't know anything about restaurants in this town. You never eat in any."

"You don't know everywhere I eat." Alfred displayed a mischievous grin. "And I'll give you a tip about one not to eat in too. Folks say the food at Johnny's Restaurant's been going downhill lately." He paused and took another bite of cheesecake. Heat began to creep up Clementine's cheeks. Erlene's and David's faces froze.

"Hush, Alfred. You shouldn't be repeating gossip." Erlene shot her husband a stern look.

"No, it's okay," David said. "Let's talk about what's been going on at Johnny's Restaurant. That's one of the reasons I came over here tonight. All those robberies and the stories about the food. I want to talk about it." Clementine's heart began to pound.

"I don't think there's much to say," Erlene ventured. "What was in the newspaper is most likely all there is to it."

"You don't believe that," David said. "Nobody at this table believes that."

"I do," Alfred said. "Sorry I brought it up."

David frowned. "What do you think about it, Clementine? It's your restaurant, and don't pretend like Erlene and Alfred don't know that. I'm sure they do."

"I can't tell you any more than was in the newspaper." Clementine tried to steady her breathing. With a deliberate motion, she laid her fork beside her half-eaten piece of cheesecake and raised her face to meet David's gaze.

"What does Johnny think about it?"

"I'm not going to talk about it." Clementine pressed her hands against her chest to try to calm her nerves. "That's unprofessional. What's going on at the restaurant is nobody's business except Johnny's and mine. Now, would anybody like more coffee?"

"I would!" Erlene exclaimed, even though her cup was half full. Alfred stared at his lap, his bushy eyebrows nearly hiding his eyes.

"I heard Johnny thinks one of his employees is doing the stealing. Some of my clients at the center say the Mexicans think Johnny's blaming them. Is that right?" David kept a firm grasp on his untasted cup of coffee.

"I said I'm not going to talk about it." Clementine took Erlene's cup and started for the kitchen.

"But it would be a true tragedy if one of those minimum-wage earning dishwashers lost their job for something they didn't do," David called after her. When Clementine didn't answer, he went on. "Because most likely, they didn't do it, did they, Clementine?"

Alfred picked up his cup and followed Clementine into the kitchen. "I b'lieve I'll have some more coffee, after all." Inside the kitchen, he whispered to Clementine, "Do you want me to tell him to shut up, you know, man to man? Or I could tell him to leave. He's being a real asshole, pardon my French, and it's all my fault."

Clementine was touched by Alfred's concern. "It's okay, Alfred. You didn't do anything wrong. I can handle David." The few minutes in the kitchen had given her a chance to muster her composure. She marched back into the dining room, thrusting Erlene's coffee cup ahead of her like a sword. "Johnny's counting on the police to find out who stole from him," she said. She plopped Erlene's cup on the table so firmly that coffee sloshed onto the tablecloth.

David stared at Clementine. "All I can say is I hope that if one of those innocent people who are so grateful for that job that they would never do anything to jeopardize it, if one of them gets blamed for this, I hope the real thief will tell the truth about what happened." He paused. "Because if that doesn't happen, I may be forced to tell Johnny and the police some things I know about that restaurant and its silent partner."

Alfred had just settled into his chair, but he rose to his feet. "That's enough, David. You come here for this nice lady's hospitality and then you attack her with nasty threats. You better change your attitude or get out of this house."

"I think David's made his point." Clementine spoke up quickly. "Nobody has to leave. Let's go into the living room. A change of scenery will do us good."

Alfred continued to watch David as the four moved to the living room. Clementine turned on Pandora, but the luster had left the party. Only the women were talking. The men sat across the room from each other and glowered.

At ten o'clock, David said he had an early appointment the next morning, so he'd have to leave. Clementine got his coat and walked him to the door, but the two of them exchanged very few words. When Clementine returned to the living room, Erlene said maybe they'd better leave too. "Unless you want to talk."

Alfred's eyes widened at the suggestion that they might have to discuss David's behavior with Clementine. Fortunately for him, Clementine declined. "There's nothing to say. I want to apologize to you all, though, for letting the evening turn into such a downer. I wanted to cheer you up." She hugged Erlene. "I know things have been tough for you since Thanksgiving. I shouldn't have invited David, but I . . . " Her voice trailed off. She couldn't explain all the mixed-up feelings she had for David. Erlene kissed her cheek, then went silently to the coat closet. A few minutes later, Erlene and Alfred left, and Clementine watched them walk to their car. She closed the door softly and went to the kitchen to clean up.

The next morning Clementine was up at five o'clock. She'd hardly slept all night, but now she knew what she had to do. With David watching everything that happened at the restaurant, she couldn't wait around for Johnny to blame Gary. She had to point him in that direction to make sure he didn't even consider blaming anybody else.

She also had to try to convince David she wasn't a terrible person. The look on his face as he threatened to tell the police about her secret partnership with Johnny and the food poisoning plan burned in her memory.

At seven, she called Johnny. "I hope I didn't wake you. I need to talk with you as soon as possible, and I don't want to do it over the phone. Can you meet me at the restaurant before the crew comes to work? I'll be there whenever you say."

Johnny's voice was thick with sleep. "You'll have to make it not much later than eight. Some of the boys come in around nine to start cutting up vegetables for lunch. Okay?" He yawned.

"Okay."

At seven thirty, Clementine called David and caught him just before he left for work. She knew he'd want to get to the insurance office early since he'd been out for several days during Christmas. "I can't stand the way we left things last night," she said. "Please let me come talk to you. We need to talk."

David agreed to meet her at his office that afternoon.

When Clementine walked into the restaurant at eight, Johnny was eating scrambled eggs and toast at his desk. He offered to cook some eggs for her, but her stomach was too nervous for her to eat. "So what's up?" Johnny asked. His dark hair was still wet from the shower, and for a second, Clementine's maternal instinct made her worry that the cold ride from his house could have made him sick.

"Remember what you said last week about having to fire some of the staff if things here don't get better soon? I've been thinking about that all during Christmas." Clementine couldn't keep her hands still. She touched her chin, then her elbow, then the arm of her chair. Johnny watched her closely. "First of all," she said, "are you firing them because you think you know who stole our stuff, or are you firing them because we can't afford to pay them anymore?"

Johnny swallowed his last bite of eggs. "If I knew who did it, of course I'd fire the bastard. But since I don't, I'm gonna have to lay somebody off to make ends meet."

"Too bad nothing's shown up on the surveillance video." Clementine was fishing for information, and when Johnny didn't contradict her, she assumed she was right. "Here's what I think. The Mexicans are too glad to have a job to do anything to screw it up." She could hear David talking in her head. "The servers aren't ever here by themselves, so they don't have any opportunity. That leaves you and Gary, and I know you didn't do it."

"What about Jones and Luis?"

Clementine shook her head at the mention of the line cooks. "Just like the servers," she said. "They're rarely here alone. If one's here, the other one's usually here, so unless they're in it together, which I doubt, they don't have any opportunity. If we rule out everybody else, that leaves Gary. It's his kitchen. He's responsible."

"But he's my chef. He does a good job."

"Really?" Clementine pushed the sarcasm out of her voice. Her question sounded genuine.

"He did until recently. Just lately something's been wrong with the food. I told him to figure out what it is, but we're still getting complaints. And where am I going to find another chef?"

"The same place you found him. At the community college. And probably for a lot less money. You pay Gary a pretty hefty salary."

Johnny shoved his empty plate away. His shoulders sagged as he rested his elbows on the desk. "Gary's been acting strange lately. I thought he was just upset about the complaints and the missing stuff, but maybe it's more."

"What did he say about the missing stuff?" Clementine leaned forward in her chair.

"He did a lot of yelling. Ranting is probably a more accurate description."

"What did he say? Does he think one of his coworkers is to blame?"

"No." Johnny shook his head emphatically. "No, he's loyal—almost protective—about the guys in the kitchen. He was yelling about how he didn't deserve this and the world is out to get him. I've seen him get worked up before, but this was a real doozy. He never said who he thought did it. Just that he didn't deserve to have this happen to him. When I asked him about the food, he muttered that he was cooking the same way he always had, so I told him to be more careful and to taste the food he was sending out to the dining room. He didn't like that. I could see the anger in his face, but he nodded and said he'd be more careful. Now he mostly avoids me."

"So even he doesn't think it's one of the other people at the restaurant. Unless he's protecting them. But then he's still responsible."

"Something's sure wrong in that kitchen." Johnny rubbed his temples. "Let me think about it."

"Who else could it be? Gary's in the kitchen all the time. If anybody was stealing or screwing with the food, he'd know."

Clementine could see from Johnny's face that her point had sunk home.

"Then why would he get so angry about it?"

"To make it look like he didn't do it." Clementine drew a deep breath. "It has to be him."

Johnny sighed. Clementine didn't need to say any more. But there was one other thing she needed to do.

She glanced at her watch. "I should get going. The crew's going to show up soon. I'm curious about the surveillance cameras, though. Can you give me a quick tour?"

Johnny pointed at a black box on the corner of his desk. "That's the heart of it, right there," he said. "There are eight cameras set up in various places, and whatever they pick up is recorded in the DVR." He continued pointing at the box. "Then I can see the recordings on my computer. Come around here, and I'll show you." He gestured for her to come around the desk.

When she was where he wanted her, he made a few clicks on his computer screen, and a view of Clementine standing behind him popped up. "See. There you are."

Clementine looked up to find the camera mounted on the wall in front of her.

"It even has sound. Listen." Johnny increased the volume on the computer and ran the video back a little way. His voice came through, explaining the system.

"What if it accidentally gets turned off?" Clementine asked.

"That's not likely to happen. Somebody would have to get into my office, and I've started locking it when I'm not here."

Clementine nodded. "Too bad we didn't have cameras before the last robbery. They might have caught Gary in the act. Thanks for showing me the system." She walked back to her chair and grabbed her coat. "I need to go. I don't want to be seen here." Then she hurried out the front door. As she drove the van out of the parking lot, Luis turned his pickup truck into the lot's other entrance. She hoped he didn't notice the van.

In the hours before her meeting with David, Clementine took down a few Christmas decorations and dusted the areas where they'd been. She usually left them up until New Year's Day, but she couldn't sit still, so she had to find something to do. Finally it was time to meet David. He was waiting in his office and quietly closed the door after she arrived. Always the gentleman, he helped her take off her coat and asked her to sit on the leather loveseat under the window while he returned to the chair behind the desk.

"I've missed you," Clementine said. "I hoped last night we could work on at least being friends, but you don't want to do that, do you?"

David pushed away from the desk and stretched out his legs. The wheels of his chair squeaked on the laminate floor. "I don't trust you," he said. "I don't know what you might do next. And frankly, you scare me."

"You don't have to be afraid of me." Clementine drew a deep breath. "The food poisoning plan was wrong. I know that. I didn't do it, David. Can't you forgive me for thinking about it?" Her throat began to tighten, but she was determined not to cry.

"What about the robberies at the restaurant?"

"I promise you Johnny isn't blaming it on the dishwashers or the serving staff or the cooks. He isn't blaming it on anybody. He just wants to find out who did it. I talked to him this morning. He's put in surveillance cameras so hopefully he can see who's doing it."

David pulled his chair up to the desk, a wan expression on his face. "I used to think I loved you, Clementine. But I don't know anymore. There's a side to you I never would've expected."

"I didn't know that side of me either. I'm finding a lot in me I didn't know was there, some good and some bad." The words trailed off as Clementine realized she'd never articulated that thought before.

"So who are you, really?"

"I guess I'm a lot of people." She took another deep breath. "Right now, though, I'm a woman who wants her rapist to suffer for what he did to her. And I'm learning it's going to take everything in me to make that happen."

"I hope your better angels win." David sighed softly.

"Can we be friends again?"

"I don't know. I suppose that depends on the angels inside of me."

Clementine had nothing else with which to make her case. She stood and took her coat from the coat rack by the door.

19

The week after Christmas, shopping traffic at Back in the Day was light. Buyers weren't inclined to return antiques or exchange them the way they did sweaters and picture frames. Clementine had time to browse around the shop, rearranging items, fondling the ones she liked best. The miniature portraits of ladies with their tiny hair ribbons and shadowed cheekbones especially made her smile. She loved being an antiques dealer. The thought of maybe having to give all this up if the restaurant didn't become more lucrative was like a punch in her gut. Thinking about what the loss of revenue was doing to Johnny was just as bad. He needed to get rid of Gary soon.

Now that she'd seen the surveillance cameras, she was less frightened by them. Since Johnny had given her a key to his office, she could easily access the DVR and turn it off. But she'd rather that Johnny fire Gary without her having to make another late-night run. She decided to wait a few more days.

On Saturday, New Year's Eve, she was locking up the shop for the night when Charles Yarboro came to the door. Clementine slipped the key into her pocket and invited him in. She hadn't seen him in months. "So how've you been, Charles?" she asked.

Charles removed his police hat. The tops of his ears were pink from the cold outside. Or maybe he was embarrassed because he hadn't talked to her about the rape case in so long. "I'm fine," he said. "I hope business is going well for you." He looked around the shop as if he could tell whether merchandise was moving or not.

"I've had a good holiday season," Clementine said. "Are you looking for anything in particular today, or is there something else on your mind?"

Charles cleared his throat. "I've been meaning to come by here for days. I think I ought to tell you that Chief Tubbs has officially taken your case off the active list. We haven't had any new leads or any new information at all about the case in over four months."

Clementine nodded. "Uh-huh. And it messes up Tubbs's reports to the mayor to have an active case with no activity." She folded her arms and frowned. "Is the mayor okay with taking the case off the active list?" Clementine remembered David's promise to get the mayor to pressure Chief Tubbs about her case. Obviously he hadn't done it, or the chief hadn't listened.

"I guess so. The chief just told me he was moving it to inactive. I'm sorry. I wish we could have done more." Charles's face showed real anguish. If only he were chief, Clementine thought. Then maybe she could have gotten justice—or revenge, if that's what it was—the way she was supposed to. She still couldn't think about that night without seizing up physically and emotionally. And she'd never been able to bring the camelback sofa out of the basement.

She stared at Charles for a few seconds of awkward silence. There was nothing she could say to change what he had told her. She knew this day was coming. "Well, thanks for stopping by. I appreciate your telling me what's going on with my case, even if I think Chief Tubbs is a total jerk who never had any intention of proving Gary raped me."

Charles drew a deep breath. "Clementine, we really tried to find out who did it, but there's just no evidence."

"Thanks, again, Charles, for stopping by." Clementine opened the shop door. Charles put on his hat and left. When he was gone, Clementine paced around the shop. She told herself she was only turning off lamps, but she was really trying to get control of the anger that was welling up inside her. Outside on the street, Christmas lights still blinked merrily as more cars than usual moved along on their way to New Year's Eve festivities. It would be a big evening for the few nightspots in town, including Johnny's Restaurant. If she had made another strike the night before, Johnny's place would be facing a real dilemma. Maybe that would have pushed Johnny over the edge about Gary. But what a blow it would have been to the restaurant's bottom line. She should just shoot Gary, if she had a gun. That would be less confusing.

She paced until she felt more in control. All the lamps in the shop were off. Clementine put the overheads on night beam and went out the front door. She never went out the back door at night, and she kept it locked unless another person was with her in the shop.

When fireworks started popping around Tanner at midnight, Clementine was home alone. She poured herself a single glass of champagne and watched the Times Square ball drop on TV. She couldn't help wondering where David was and who was with him. In September, she and David had talked about spending New Year's Eve at a ski resort in the mountains. Was he there with Amanda?

By morning she had put David out of her mind. She spent New Year's Day gathering her courage to tackle the surveillance cameras and relieve the restaurant of enough food and equipment to force Johnny to act. No more pussyfooting around. Gary's life as a chef needed to end now.

Around one o'clock the next morning, Clementine crept into the restaurant for what she hoped was the last time. She didn't enjoy being a thief. She wore an old black raincoat she kept in the back of her closet for carrying in firewood and a thin black scarf over her head and face. She could probably avoid the camera near the door by sticking close to the wall it was mounted on and crawling to Johnny's office, but she had to be careful. She kept her head down as she inched on hands and knees to the office door, which she unlocked without looking up. Inside the office, head still down, she hunched behind Johnny's desk. She had planned to simply cut the power to the recorder, but it occurred to her that she could probably erase any footage that showed her coming through the front door. She'd just have to check to see if her crawling had spared her or not.

Still on her knees, she slid around the edge of the room and stood up under the extended bracket that held the camera. By stretching up on her toes, she was able to bat at the camera and push it so that it pointed away from the desk. Certain she was out of its range, she walked back behind the desk and woke up the computer. She had watched Johnny call up the surveillance video before. Now she strained to remember exactly what he did. Click, click. She was confident she was headed in the right direction. Sure enough, the surveillance logo came across the screen. Now she had to find the right cameras. Beneath the raincoat, her arms and chest were clammy.

A few more clicks and she had a picture of the office. She clicked to run it back, but the reverse went faster than she expected. When she stopped it, she could see two people in the office. The time stamp in the corner said five p.m. on New Year's Day, about eight hours earlier. That would have been around the time the restaurant was closing. The only meal they served that day was a lavish New Year's brunch. The picture wasn't distinct, but Clementine was sure she was looking at Johnny and Gary. Johnny's hands were planted firmly on the desktop, his arms supporting his shoulders as he leaned toward Gary. Gary sat in a chair opposite him, shoulders hunched forward. The camera didn't show his face, but Clementine recognized the brushed-back hair and broad back. She increased the volume so she could hear what they were saying.

"Look at it from my point of view," Johnny said. "The restaurant's losing money. Our insurance premiums are going up. You're in charge of the kitchen, and that's where all the trouble's been. I have to hold you responsible." He folded his arms. "Plus you're the highest-paid employee I have." His voice was softer as if he hated to add this last piece of information. Clementine's mouth opened in awe as she realized what she was watching.

"Goddamn it, Johnny. This is not my fault." Gary's voice was rough. "Why in the hell would I steal the most important stuff I need to do my job? It doesn't make any sense."

"It doesn't make any sense that things keep disappearing right under your nose. How can it be happening without you knowing what's going on? If you're not a thief, and I'm not sure that you're not, then you're a mighty poor manager, and I have to let you go. Here's your last paycheck." Johnny lifted a check from the desk and handed it to Gary. "Now let's go into the kitchen and you can collect your personal things before you leave."

Gary rose slowly from the chair. His face still wasn't visible on the video, but Clementine shuddered at the sight of his bulky form. He was so massive. "I am not a thief. I did not take anything from this crummy restaurant."

His hand shot across the desk and seized Johnny's shirtfront. He grabbed Johnny's arm with his other hand and dragged Johnny around from behind the desk. Clementine's arms trembled with the memory of Gary's grasp. Johnny tried to shove him away, but Gary held on tight. "I am the best fucking chef you will ever have. I earn every penny you pay me and more, and you can't get rid of me just 'cause you're having problems. You wanna see problems?"

He let go of Johnny's shirtfront and punched him on the left side of his nose and cheek. Blood streamed from Johnny's nose as he managed to pull away from Gary's grip on his arm. Johnny tried to land a blow to Gary's shoulder, but Gary clobbered him in the stomach almost simultaneously, and Johnny doubled over in pain. "Now you got problems," Gary said. He picked up the chair he'd been sitting in, raised it over his head and brought it down across Johnny's back. Johnny collapsed onto the floor. He tried to rise to his knees but quickly sank to the floor again. This time he didn't get up.

Clementine shrieked and grabbed the phone. She was starting to call the police when she remembered where she was and what time it was. She couldn't call anybody from there. She stood frozen, torn between wanting to rush home and get on the phone to find out where Johnny was and if he was all right and wanting to see the video to the end. On the computer screen, Gary left the office while Johnny lay motionless. She hit fast forward and watched video rush by, but Johnny didn't move and nobody came into the office. At last Luis knocked on the closed office door, then opened it, and seeing Johnny on the floor, called the paramedics, who showed up some time later. They lifted Johnny to a gurney and left.

Clementine, trembling but talking to herself to keep calm, fast-forwarded the video again until she reached the latest time stamp. If she was lucky, no one would notice the gap she created while she was watching the recording. Her slinking around on the floor had worked because she didn't see herself in the final minutes. Before she started the recorder again, she returned the camera to its original position. Then she started the recorder and crept out the way she had come in.

Safe at home, she puttered with one project after another as she tried to make the time pass until morning came and she could call Johnny. At eight o'clock, she called his cell phone. Ring after ring sounded in the empty distance until finally an unfamiliar female voice answered. "Johnny Johnson's phone. He can't talk now. Can I take a message?"

Clementine stumbled over her reply as she wondered who could be on the other phone. When she finally spit out her name and identified herself only as a friend of Johnny's, the mystery woman repeated the information away from the phone before she spoke again to Clementine. "Johnny says it's okay to tell you he's in the hospital. He was injured last night, but he's all right." Another voice murmured away from the phone. Despite being muffled and a little distorted, the voice sounded like Johnny's. Then the woman spoke again. "He says to ask you if you can come by the hospital this afternoon. I can tell you he's a little groggy from the painkillers, but I guess he wants to talk to you. Oh, by the way, I'm his sister Melba. I came over from Winston this morning."

Clementine promised to be there at one o'clock. Surely Johnny wasn't hurt too badly if he was able to talk to her. Still, the video of the chair coming down on his back kept playing in her mind. She had never intended for him to get hurt. Only

Gary was supposed to suffer. She was horrified that her scheme had caused so much pain for Johnny. She had to find a way to make it up to him.

Johnny was alone in the hospital room when Clementine arrived. The bed next to his was empty, and Melba was nowhere to be seen. A large white bandage covered his nose and part of his cheekbones, just below the blue and black splotches under his eyes. His usually round face looked even more rounded and bloated. His eyes were closed, and she wondered if he were sleeping.

"Johnny," Clementine said softly. His eyelids rose, and he looked at her through red-streaked orbs. "I'm so sorry this happened to you," she said, her own eyes growing moist. "I had no idea," she began, but then remembered she wasn't supposed to know what actually happened. "How did you get hurt?" she asked instead.

Johnny swallowed and blinked a few times. "Gary," he said. "When I told him to leave."

"He did this to you?" Clementine didn't have to fake outrage at this explanation. Her anger and revulsion had only increased since she saw the video.

"Said he wasn't a thief. Hit me with a chair." The words seemed difficult for Johnny to get out.

The covers on the hospital bed were pulled up to Johnny's shoulders, but one arm lay outside. Clementine couldn't resist taking the exposed hand in hers. "I am so sorry, Johnny," she said.

Footsteps sounded in the door behind Clementine. She immediately released Johnny's hand and turned to see a stout middle-aged woman carrying a large bouquet of roses. "Hey," the woman said. "You must be Clementine. I'm Melba. I just went to pick up these flowers from the information desk. Aren't they beautiful? Look, Johnny. They're from the guys at the restaurant." She held the flowers near the bed for Johnny to see.

"They're lovely," Clementine said, suddenly ashamed about coming empty-handed. "And so soon after your injury."

"Luis found me," Johnny said. "Called the paramedics."

"And we called Jones this morning to tell him he'll have to be in charge because Johnny's going to be out for a while," Melba said. "He already knew what happened, so I'm sure the word spread quickly."

Clementine flinched when Melba mentioned Johnny's being away from the restaurant. "How bad is he hurt?"

"Besides the broken nose, he's got two broken ribs and three cracked ones." Melba cleared a place on the table to set the flowers next to Johnny's bed. "They ran a lot of tests last night to see if he had any organ damage, but everything looks good."

"Won't let me go home," Johnny mumbled.

Melba leaned toward her brother so she was looking straight into his face. "They're gonna keep you at least one more day to keep an eye on your lungs and spleen, make sure there's no bleeding. Don't be so impatient." Johnny closed his eyes and sighed.

Clementine could hardly look at him. He seemed so vulnerable lying there, and she felt so guilty. She turned to Melba instead. "Please let me know if I can do anything to help." Melba assured her she would stay in touch. Johnny appeared to be no longer interested in company, so Clementine said her goodbyes and left.

The rest of the afternoon and into the evening, Clementine cooked casseroles to take to Johnny's house the next day. Since her cooking skills were limited, she was self-conscious preparing food for a former chef, and probably the men at the restaurant could keep Johnny well supplied with meals, but she felt like she had to do something. At least Johnny would know she meant it when she said she was sorry, even though he had no idea how much she had to be sorry for. After seeing the seriousness of Johnny's injuries, she realized Gary could have killed him. Thank God he wasn't hurt any worse than he was. But she would have to spend the rest of her life knowing she could have caused his death. And no casserole would ever make up for that.

Melba was true to her word and called to let Clementine know when Johnny got home on Wednesday. A light snow had fallen Tuesday night, and although the roads were clear, yards, houses, and trees were covered in a clean, still sheet of white. The dazzling brightness of the reflected sun made Clementine think of a pristine world. Now if only Johnny would heal and she could start her life in Tanner all over again.

Although he looked less puffy and more alert lying on the couch in his living room, Johnny was obviously not healed. Skin on the upper part of his face ranged from black and blue to green and purple. A row of blue sutures stretched across his eyebrow. "I told him to go to bed where he'd be more comfortable, but he insisted on staying up to see you," Melba said as she took Clementine's bags of food. "I never knew him to be so vain before." She dropped a quick wink.

Clementine settled into a chair next to the couch. "You're looking better. How're you feeling?"

"Like a Mack truck smashed into me. I can't hardly breathe without hurting. And don't expect me to move at all. One twitch and it's like a knife in my side. But other than that, I'm fine." Johnny smiled. "It's either that or stay groggy all the time. Which I may go for soon."

"I'm so sorry," Clementine said for what seemed to her like the hundredth time, she had repeated it so often in her head. "I guess I'm stupid, but I never thought Gary would hurt you. What's going to happen to him now?" Even though she'd been exhausted after all her baking the night before, she'd still had trouble falling asleep. She couldn't stop thinking about what she'd done to Johnny, and she feared Gary might come after her next. She didn't see how he could link her to his getting fired, but maybe he could.

"He'll be arrested," Johnny said. "In fact, he probably already has been. Vince McQuarrie came to the hospital the night it happened, and I told him Gary did it." Johnny's face contorted. "Damn it. Moved something by mistake."

"I hope the police believe you." Clementine lowered her eyes.

Johnny frowned. "They will. I have proof. Remember the surveillance cameras? Jones said the attack is there, in the recorder. He met Vince at the restaurant this morning and gave him the recorder as evidence."

Clementine held her breath, afraid that maybe she had shown up on the video after all. When Johnny didn't mention her, she exhaled. "What happens after he's arrested?"

"Vince said he'd likely be charged with assault and battery. He could do a few months' prison time. Just because my injuries are as bad as they are. Could face a fine too. Depends on the judge."

"And then what?" Clementine was glad Gary might end up in prison, even for such a short period of time, but she really wanted him out of town. And out of work.

"I don't know. Quentin Harper's got the story on the front page of the *Observer* today. Melba showed me. I can't believe Gary'll stay in Tanner after this. And between the thefts and the assault, he'll never get another job as a chef."

Melba came into the room and handed Johnny a pill. He stared at the white disk for a moment before he swallowed it quickly with the water she brought. "You need to get some rest," she said.

"I should be going." Clementine reached for her purse on the floor.

"Wait a minute." Johnny lifted his head from the pillow and immediately let it drop back down with a grimace. "I have something else I want to tell you. I know you're feeling guilty because you think you pushed me into firing Gary, and that it's your fault I got beat up like this. But it's not. The more I think about it, the more I think Gary might actually be the thief. I just didn't want to admit it because he was a good chef. At least he was until all the trouble started and his food wasn't as good anymore. That was probably because he was so stressed out that he might get caught taking stuff, and he had some other problems."

"Other problems?"

"That's why I think he started stealing. He had money problems. He was counting on getting a big tax refund this year, but when he filed last April, the IRS told him they'd already processed his return and sent him his refund. When he told them he never got a refund, they started nosing around and decided somebody stole his identity and his refund. Last I heard, they still haven't found out who did it, and they still haven't given Gary any money. I think he was going to use the refund to pay off some debts, which have probably just gotten bigger." Johnny sighed. "I might've helped him if I could, but he never asked, and the restaurant hasn't been doing that great all year. Even before the robberies started."

As she listened to Johnny, Clementine had to suppress a gasp. Johnny thought Gary was the thief. Gary had tax troubles. She smiled at the bandaged face with the eyes that were beginning to close. "If Gary was the thief, then you did the right thing in getting rid of him. We'll be fine, Johnny. The restaurant will be fine. You just get well." She patted his arm. He nodded weakly.

During the drive home, Clementine tried to sort out what would happen next.

If Gary was arrested, which Johnny seemed certain he was, could he be out on bail by now? She'd stay home with the doors locked until she had to open the antique shop on Thursday. She didn't want to risk going anywhere near him. If only the police would keep him behind bars for a long time, maybe she could stop constantly looking over her shoulder.

The information about Gary's tax troubles was perplexing. The hex was supposed to make him owe money to the IRS, not the other way around. And the identity fraud had happened before she put the hex on Gary. Still, the fraud hadn't been resolved yet, and maybe the hex had something to do with that. She would find out what Erlene thought about it as soon as she could.

With Johnny confined at home, Jones and Luis would have to manage the restaurant until he was well enough to work. Business would probably be at an all-time high as news about the incident spread around town. People were ghoulish that way. They'd want to go to the place where the trouble happened.

So much had gone so terribly wrong, and yet Gary was getting at least part of what he deserved. Clementine should be glad about that, but Johnny's bandaged face haunted her as she drove.

20

Luis and Jones were able to keep the restaurant running well enough until Johnny returned near the end of January, an event they celebrated with a festive dinner, including roast pork, sweet potatoes, and broccoli rabe.

"I was so touched and impressed with what they did, I thought maybe I don't need to hire a new chef," Johnny said with a shrug as he and Clementine ate an early breakfast at the restaurant several days later. Bright against a clear winter sky, the sun lit up the dining room windows and added a luster to the silverware and glasses. These early breakfasts before the crew came in had become a regular date for the two of them during the months leading up to Christmas. Johnny called the breakfasts the partners' meetings.

"But I could see that just two weeks of all that responsibility was taking a toll on Jones, so I jumped right in, and you know what? I'm really enjoying it." Johnny smiled as he added more syrup to his Belgian waffle. The waffles had surprised Clementine. Usually their breakfast fare was simpler. This time Johnny presented her with a waffle that was at least an inch thick, topped with a mountain of strawberries and a cupful of whipped cream. Pure maple syrup in a warmed pot stood next to a platter of tiny sausage links.

Clementine was elated to see Johnny looking so well and happy. She could tell by the way he moved that his ribs were still tender, but he could obviously make his way around the kitchen with enthusiasm. The waffle was the best she'd ever tasted. How badly she wanted everything to be good for him again. "So what's your plan going forward?" she asked. "You can't continue to manage the kitchen and the business end of the restaurant, can you?"

"Oh, God, no," Johnny said, "which is why I've prepared this scrumptious breakfast for you. I'm softening you up for a business proposition."

The role reversal of his making a business proposition to her made Clementine smile. "Yes?"

"I've decided I want to go on being chef. I didn't realize how much I've missed it. But I'm going to need a business manager." He paused. "And I think you're the best person for the job. You obviously have a good head for business. Look at what you've done with the antique shop. I know you can learn about restaurants. I'll share the responsibilities with you, but you can do all the routine work I don't have time for. You and I seem to work pretty well together, or at least I think so. Wouldn't you like to give it a try?"

He couldn't have surprised Clementine more if he'd asked her to be chef. She would never have seen this coming. She had her shop and maybe her life back, and she wanted to try to focus on those. "I'm flattered, Johnny, that you would ask me. I appreciate your faith in me, but I don't know if it's the right thing to do. I love my antique shop. I had a really good holiday season, and the shop is finally in the black. I don't see how I can abandon it now. And I don't know anything about the restaurant business."

Johnny's round cheeks sagged as the joy drained from his face. "I can teach you the restaurant business. Between the two of us, I'm sure we can make the restaurant the most popular place in town. It'll be like all this trouble with Gary never happened."

There is no way all this trouble with Gary will ever seem like it never happened, Clementine thought. In fact, working with Johnny could make matters worse. She still worried that Johnny or others might realize her true motivation for buying into the restaurant. And seeing Johnny every day would be a constant reminder that although the plan had worked, in some ways it had gone terribly wrong and could have been worse.

"I want the restaurant to succeed, Johnny. Truly I do." The words came hard, but she did the best she could. "Even though Back in the Day is doing better, I could use the extra money. I promise I'll do everything I can as the secret partner, but I can't leave the antique shop, and I still don't want anyone to know I own part of the business." She forced herself to take another bite of waffle, although her appetite was gone.

"Nobody has to know about our partnership." Johnny's eyes regained some of the light they'd had at the beginning of breakfast. "We'll just say you're the new business manager. That's all anybody has to know."

Clementine believed he meant what he said. Trusting people came hard for her now, but she thought she could trust Johnny. Plus, keeping the secret was one of the conditions of their partnership. Erlene was a true-blue friend, so Clementine didn't have to worry about her causing problems. The only other person who knew about the partnership was David. He was obviously bitter and disappointed that she wasn't the person he wanted her to be, but since none of Johnny's employees or customers had been hurt, he wouldn't go after her. David was principled and protective, but not vengeful. Maybe she didn't have to worry about the secret getting out. But there were so many other reasons not to do this.

"And we can work out a salary for you, so you'll have a regular income," Johnny continued. "Come on, Clementine. At least say you'll think about it."

She didn't want to think about it. If she thought about it, her debt to Johnny would weigh heavy in her decision. The man's business had suffered, and he had taken a beating for her. He needed her now, but he was asking a lot. The price for getting her revenge against Gary was growing higher.

"Look, don't give me your final answer right away," Johnny pushed his empty plate aside. "Take some time."

"I can do that." Clementine didn't think she'd change her mind, but a lot of voices were arguing in her head. She hoped the subject was closed for now and tried to find lighter conversation topics for the rest of the meal, but the sparkle had left the morning.

The next day was Saturday, another clear, cold day that brought out shoppers eager to enjoy the sunshine. Clementine was glad to keep her mind occupied with customers and antiques. Most of the night before, she'd worried about Johnny's offer. She knew what she wanted to do and what she should do, and she could find no middle ground. As long as she was busy, she could push the dilemma to one side of her brain, but as afternoon wore on and the shop became quieter, the agony returned.

At six o'clock, she checked the back door to make sure it was locked, although she rarely unlocked it. She also never went into the alley behind the shop unless she absolutely had to. Satisfied that everything was secure for the night, she went home to fight the battle of her thoughts for another long night.

On Monday, Johnny began sending Clementine emails that provided reasons for her to accept his offer, a different reason each day. Monday's email was about money—more of it, Johnny hoped. Tuesday's appealed to her ego—nobody could do it better. Wednesday's was emotional—he needed her. That was the one she found hardest to ignore. It ate at her like a carnivorous worm that wouldn't leave her alone. If there was going to be an email on Thursday, she couldn't imagine it would offer a more persuasive argument.

But there was no email on Thursday. Instead, Johnny came to Back in the Day in person. Around the middle of the afternoon, Clementine was rearranging a collection of vintage music boxes near the front window when Johnny pushed open the door and came to face her across the elaborately carved instruments. It was only the second time she could remember seeing him in the shop. He'd been there once when she invited him to discuss buying into the restaurant, but he hadn't been back. His expression showed he wasn't used to being around delicate objects squeezed into a tight space.

"You're not answering my emails," he said, "so I've come to make my case again in person." As he spoke, his belly bumped against the table between him and Clementine, causing one of the music boxes to play a few notes. He looked down at the box and then raised his gaze to take in other parts of the shop. "You have quite a business here," he said.

"I've worked hard on it," Clementine answered. "I have a lot of nice things."

Johnny looked from the Queen Anne table to the Windsor chairs to the porcelain, pottery, and other collectibles. When he spoke again, his voice was lowered in deference to two customers examining a pie safe.

"I have an idea," he said. "What if you brought your antiques with you to the restaurant? We could take out a few tables and show some antiques in the dining room for now. Then someday maybe we could open up part of the storage room to create a separate area for the antiques. You can manage my books *and* sell antiques."

His face got more animated as he fought to keep his voice down. "Eventually, the folks who come in to eat might buy an antique, and the folks who come in to look at antiques might want lunch. What do they call that? Cross-pollination? You know, it'll be either a restaurant with antiques or an antique shop you can eat in, depending on your point of view." He was silent for a minute. "I've even got an idea for a name. We can call it Johnny's Back in the Day. What do you think?"

Clementine had no response. The idea was so far-fetched she couldn't imagine it. Displaying her precious antiques at the restaurant? "I don't know," she said. "This space means a lot to me." As she finished speaking, both customers waved goodbye and left the shop.

When the door closed behind them, Johnny said, "We've never talked about this, but I know this shop is the place where you were attacked. At the restaurant, you could start fresh, and you'll be safer because you'll never be alone."

Clementine didn't accept Johnny's offer that day, but she couldn't forget the look on his face as he told her she'd never be alone at the restaurant. She'd used him to punish Gary, and now he was concerned about keeping her safe. The truth was she needed to do this for him—and for herself. And she found the strength to do it.

When she told Erlene about the move, she said it was because he offered to let her continue selling antiques and the new arrangement would put her on better footing financially. But those weren't the real reasons. She'd asked herself many times if, knowing what she knew now, she would still have framed Gary for the robberies. The question was impossible to answer because she didn't know then that Johnny would get hurt, and even if she wanted to, she couldn't go back and change things any more than she could change the fact that Gary raped her. She could only move forward. She would always be indebted to Johnny. She would do whatever she could for him, and she would never, ever tell him about the food poisoning plan or her role in the disappearance of the equipment. It would be like telling a spouse about an affair that was long ended. Coming clean might make her feel better, but the knowledge would be terrible for Johnny.

21

Clementine held the flaps of the cardboard box together while Erlene sealed them with a long strip of packaging tape. "That's enough for tonight," Clementine said. "Let's go eat." Erlene nodded and set the box on top of a stack of others pushed against the wall in the basement below Back in the Day. Dim lights on the basement ceiling put out just enough illumination to make the boxes visible and prevent the women from walking into furniture gathered in the center of the floor. The Victorian camelback sofa was missing from its usual place by the stairs. Otherwise, Clementine would never have been able to do the work that needed to be done there. Johnny had sent two men from the restaurant to take it away, and as payment, Clementine gave them the antique sofa. She didn't know what they did with it, and she didn't care. She could never erase the memories of being pinned to its rough surface during the attack.

In a few weeks, the same men would help her move the boxes and furniture from the basement to the storeroom of Johnny's Restaurant—unless she sold enough furniture during the Valentine's Day Festival to warrant moving some of the basement inventory upstairs. The holiday event had been so successful the year before that the town council voted unanimously to do it again, this time on an even larger scale. Instead of one huge welcoming banner, they had two—one at each end of Main Street. Not exactly a New York ad campaign, but a good start for Tanner. More kiosks were perched on the sidewalks, ready to be moved to the center of the street when the festivities started the next morning. At Clementine's suggestion, Johnny had ordered a small wooden structure with signs advertising the restaurant to set outside the antique shop. Clementine and Erlene had spent most of the previous evening decorating the shop and front window with frilly valentines from the late 1800s. Clementine loved Victorian valentines—the more cupids, lace, and cut-outs, the better. Last year she had saved the frilliest one for David, but this year they all went in the shop. She hoped Johnny would give her a free hand decorating the restaurant for Valentine's Day next year.

"Come on," she said to Erlene as she started up the stairs. Erlene wiped her dusty hands on her jeans and followed. Lights in the shop created a warm ambiance compared with the dimness in the basement. Standing at the head of the basement stairs, Clementine took a nostalgic look around the shop. She loved this space. She loved the way the morning light made the glass lamps sparkle. She loved the small area's warm aroma of old wood and varnish. She loved the deep gold walls. She had worked so hard to restore them, and memories of the day she knocked a hole in the plaster still made her smile. But she wasn't the same woman who made that hole. Sometimes a darkness crept under the morning light. It was time to move on.

"So where shall we eat?" Erlene's voice turned Clementine's attention away from staring at the shop.

"Let's go to the tearoom." Clementine would miss being so close to the quaint stores and restaurants of downtown Tanner.

Since Back in the Day opened, she hadn't been able to frequent the other shops as much as before, but she liked the ease of meeting David or Erlene there for dinner on nights she didn't want to cook. But she wouldn't be meeting David there again anyway.

The tearoom was nearly empty when Clementine and Erlene arrived. "Not much of a crowd for a Friday night," Clementine muttered. "Guess everybody is home resting up for the big Valentine's kick-off tomorrow." She weaved through the mismatched tables and chairs to a small oval table partially hidden next to a bookcase and cushy furniture that formed a reading area on one side of the room. A server immediately appeared with menus and glasses of water.

"Are you okay?" Erlene asked when the server left. "You look a little peaked. I know the move's gonna be hard for you."

"If I could make it through this past year, I can make it through anything that's ahead of me." Clementine tried to smile a reassuring smile.

"Still, you seem less enthusiastic than you should be. Actually, you've been this way ever since Gary showed his true colors and lost his chef job. He may even be on his way to prison. Seems like you'd be thrilled, but you don't act like you are. What's wrong?" Erlene pushed her menu aside and clasped her hands on the table.

Clementine was hesitant to answer. She wasn't sure she could explain everything happening inside her head. "There's just so much going on. Johnny getting hurt, and now this move. And no matter how hard I try, I can't stop being scared. I'm thrilled Gary's going to suffer. It's what I've wanted since the night he raped me. But knowing he's going to suffer doesn't make everything all right. Not the way I thought it would. I'm still looking over my shoulder, Erlene. I mean, I think I'm okay, but then all of a sudden, I'm afraid. And the worst part is, I have no idea how long I'm going to feel this way."

Erlene reached for Clementine's hand that was clutching the menu and squeezed it. "It can't last forever. Taking care of Gary was one step. Maybe now you can take the next one."

"I think maybe it can last forever." Clementine slid her hand away from Erlene's. "Loss is a terrible thing, Erlene. Loss of somebody you love, or loss of innocence, or loss of trust. I learned about loss when Gordon died. It doesn't go away. You just struggle every day to live with it. And I'm afraid this is going to be the same."

"One step at a time, Clementine. It's all you can do." Erlene smiled gently. "Or I know somebody who could mix you up a powerful potion if you want it. Just might not turn out exactly like you think."

Clementine shook her head. "No, thanks. Dealing with these feelings is up to me." Erlene's mention of the unpredictability of potions made her think of something else. "I still can't figure out if I caused Gary's problems with the IRS or not," she said in a hushed voice even though the tables near them were empty.

"I told you Brianne said you never know which way a hex is gonna go. Especially when you got an amateur like you mixing it up. Or it could be that you did such a bad job that nothing happened and you just got lucky." Erlene smiled again. "Or it could be that the real hex hasn't worked yet. These things don't have an expiration date, you know."

"So is Brianne going to be doing any more root medicine?"

"Probably not. But if you need something." Erlene's voice scaled up and her eyebrows rose inquisitively.

"No. Like I said, I'm out of that business."

The server appeared again and took their orders. After she left, they sat in silence. Clementine realized she was exhausted. No wonder Erlene thought she looked peaked.

"You know," Erlene said, her voice as perky as she seemed to want Clementine to feel, "I'm impressed with you for agreeing to help Johnny with the restaurant. I mean, I know you've been helping him out financially for a while, but now you're gonna work for him too, and that's gonna take time away from your antique business, not to mention it's something entirely new you've gotta learn." She paused. "But you're a capable woman. I realized that the day you marched into Chief Tubbs's office and gave him what for about not arresting Gary."

Clementine lifted her head from her hand, where she'd been resting it. "I'll tell you one thing I've learned this year. I've learned I'm capable of doing things I never thought I'd do."

"Well, that's good."

"Some good and some bad."

"But you didn't do anything wrong. I told you another opportunity would come along, and it did. Gary caused his own downfall." Erlene's eyebrows rose slightly. "Didn't he? I mean, he stole the stuff from the restaurant and then he beat up Johnny."

"Yeah, he brought it on himself. He's got real anger issues, along with about a zillion other personality disorders." Clementine lowered her eyes to stare at the table in hopes Erlene would get the idea she didn't want to talk about Gary anymore.

After a few minutes, the server brought their food. Erlene must have sensed Clementine was lost in her own thoughts because she kept her attempts at conversation light and sparse. As soon as they finished eating, they hugged and separated for home.

To start the first day of the festival off with a bang, Johnny promised Clementine another special breakfast at the partners' meeting. "This time I'll make you one of my famous Mexican omelets," he said. "Famous for all of two weeks. I learned everything I know about it from Luis."

The sun was bright and the temperature climbing when Clementine arrived at eight o'clock. This year the Valentine's Day Festival would not have to contend with bone-chilling weather. The forecast called for pleasant February temperatures in the fifties. Clementine remembered the coffee urns and kerosene camp stove in the outdoor kiosks last year. Most likely the coffee urns would be back but probably not the camp stove. Too bad. She liked the cozy atmosphere the heat from the stove created. But then she didn't have to stand out there all day.

Johnny had bacon fried and grits simmering on the stove. "The biscuits'll be done in about ten minutes," he said. "They'll stay warm in the oven while I prepare my masterpiece." He whipped a wire whisk through a pond of yellow eggs in a red bowl. Clementine dragged a wooden chair from the end of the stainless steel counter where he was working and settled in close to him. She enjoyed watching him flash ingredients around. He had a real flair for cooking. Putting himself behind a desk had been a mistake.

Satisfied that the eggs were well mixed, Johnny reached for a pan hanging with several others above the counter. "You see this pan?" he asked. "This is an omelet pan. Not a frying pan. Not a skillet. I never could convince Gary of that. He always wanted to use a straight-sided frying pan to make omelets." Johnny placed the pan on the stovetop and dropped in a pat of butter. "But I guess he won't have to worry about that anymore." His tone turned solemn.

"You really don't think he'll ever work as a chef again?" Clementine twisted in the hard chair.

"I don't know. Maybe in some grade C diner way out in the boondocks. No reputable restaurant will hire him without a recommendation. I guess he could start his own restaurant if he can get the money, but like I told you, I'm pretty sure he's struggling financially as it is. And the lawyer I talked to said the judge will probably give him a hefty fine, since he pleaded guilty at arraignment." The eggs made a sizzling sound when Johnny poured them into the pan.

"Were you surprised he pleaded guilty?"

Johnny didn't look up from tending the eggs. "I was there, you know. At the arraignment. I watched his face when he came into the courtroom and before he got up to speak. The lines around his mouth were set in resignation. No fire in his eyes at all. He knew there was no way out. I mean, all the evidence we needed was right there on the video."

"What about all the missing stuff? Are you going to press charges on that too?"

"I'd like to, but I don't have any way to prove it. I'm afraid that crime's a lost cause." As he talked, Johnny spooned a greenish-red mixture onto half of the cooking eggs.

Clementine looked into the pan. "What's that?"

"A little avocado, a few little chilies, onion, lemon juice, and a few secret ingredients." Johnny smiled, a tiny twinkle in his eye, and then pinched a smidgen of grated cheese between his fingers to sprinkle over the filling.

"When's Gary's sentencing?"

"In a few weeks. The judge wanted to get him evaluated by an anger-management counselor before sentencing him. That'll take a while." A bell sounded on the stove's timer. "That's the biscuits," Johnny said. He maintained his grip on the omelet pan with his right hand while he turned off the oven with his left.

Clementine couldn't get her mind off Gary. "I hope the judge gives him more than a fine," she whispered. "I hope he has to go to prison, even if it's only for a month."

Johnny expertly folded the empty side of the eggs over the filling on the other side. "Well, I know he'll have to pay restitution to cover my medical costs. And he'll probably have to go through an anger-management course, and there'll be a restraining order to keep him away from me. Beyond that, I don't know. Prison's a possibility, and so is community service. Depends on the judge." He slid the omelet over the pan's sloping side onto a plate.

"Oh lord, I hope it's not community service," Clementine said. "I really want him gone from this town."

Johnny looked a little perplexed at the passion in her voice, but he didn't question it. "I doubt the judge will go that easy on him. The fact that he hit me with a chair will make a difference."

He cut the omelet in half and added bacon to the plate. "Breakfast is ready," he said. "You carry this, and I'll follow you with the biscuits and grits. The table near the window in the dining room is set for us."

Johnny had already put a dish of butter and three containers of jam on the table. After he set down the basket of biscuits and bowl of grits, he brought two steaming cups of coffee. Clementine served herself from the omelet and bacon. The food was hot and delicious. She had a good feeling about the days ahead. While she ate, her eyes wandered around the dining room, finding spaces to show her antiques to their best advantage. She was especially enamored with the windowed alcove where she and Johnny sat. It was perfect for her cases of antique jewelry. The light would make each piece gleam.

When all the food was consumed, mostly by Johnny, Clementine apologized for having to leave so quickly. "I had an idea last night about working more valentines around the interior of the shop to make it more festive. You should have seen me rushing into Walmart just minutes before it closed and grabbing anything I could find to use. I need to get on downtown and do my decorating before I open at ten."

"Run on," Johnny said. "I'll excuse you from KP duty today. Call me later and let me know how things are going. And sometime you need to let me know when you want to start moving antiques up here."

"Will do," Clementine said. She returned his warm smile before she slipped on her coat and closed the door behind her.

On Main Street, the roadblocks were in place with banners flying brightly above them. The kiosks had been moved from the sidewalks to various spots in the street. Merchants buzzed around them like bees while they put merchandise on display and posted advertising signs. Not far from Back in the Day's front door, employees from the six-screen Cineplex out on the highway popped popcorn in their kiosk. The familiar smell wafted around the signs and the people milling about. Clementine had come out on the sidewalk to check her front window display one more time. Before she went back inside, she couldn't resist watching all the bustling activity and inhaling the popcorn aroma mixed with a sense of excitement. She loved her hometown, despite all that had happened.

As she started to go back inside, Pete from the hardware store called her name. "Just a minute," he said, "if you don't mind." Clementine waited for him to reach her, his legs swinging freely with their characteristic long strides. "I know we both gotta get our stores open soon, but I wanted to tell you something." He took a few deep breaths as he stood beside her. "I just wanna say that I think your antique store's been a great addition to Tanner and to Main Street this year, and I'm sorry to hear that you're closing." He nodded with the finality of a man who had said his piece and was done.

"Thank you, Pete," Clementine said. "And this coming from a man who didn't think I'd last a week."

Pete smiled sheepishly. "I think I gave you a month. And like I said, now I hate to see you go. I've heard some mighty nice things about your store."

"I'm not going far." Clementine pointed to a sign in the shop's window. Beneath a cluster of cupids and bows, large red lettering spelled out MOVING SALE—Get the antiques you want at reduced prices. After March 31, come see us at Johnny's Back in the Day, located in Johnny's Restaurant at 221 Mountain Street.

"You're going to Johnny's?" Pete looked puzzled. "And the Lord hath wrought more wonders than we can behold."

Clementine laughed at the garbled Bible verse. "I'm going to miss you, Pete. But the move is for the best. Since Johnny's working as chef now, he's hired me to do some of the paperwork and business managing. It'll work better if we combine our businesses in one location. I'll still be selling antiques, just from a different place."

Pete stroked his chin with his long, thin fingers. "You'll still be Tanner's antique lady, no matter where you go." He studied the sign in the window. "How come you're leaving so soon?"

"The landlord's got a bookstore dealer who wants to move in as soon as possible. I tell you, Tanner's reputation as an arts center is growing."

Pete shrugged. "Maybe I oughta hang a few paintings in the hardware store. Make it a package deal. Buy the art and everything you need to hang it with in one place." He smiled. "I gotta go, and so do you. Hope you have a mighty profitable festival weekend. Maybe the folks on the street can give you a proper send-off before you leave." He turned and loped down the street toward the hardware store.

Clementine went back into the shop and waited for customers to arrive. She remembered how worried she had once been that they would look at her with pity or disgust. She couldn't bear to have them think less of her. They didn't really know who she was. How could they when she didn't know who she was? She knew herself now, for better or worse. If she had come home to Tanner to find herself, she had done it, though not in the way she expected. And Tanner had found her too. Pete had given her a nickname: the antique lady. And didn't that mean she was accepted here in this small town of her birth? The customers would follow her to Johnny's, and maybe that was where she belonged. She scooped up her favorite miniature portrait, a tiny likeness of a solemn woman with upswept black hair, and slipped it into her pocket. With a quick pat of the smooth oval frame, she stepped forward to meet the first customer who walked through the door.

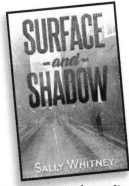

ACKNOWLEDGMENTS

When Enemies Offend Thee came into being because many people were willing to help. They offered their talents and their time in numerous ways, and I am sincerely grateful to each of them.

Thank you to Janey Boyer and Sonia Linebaugh, who first piqued my interest in root medicine. Thanks to Karen S. Bennett, who read each chapter as it was written and offered immediate feedback. Thanks also to Mark Willen, Patricia Schultheis, Martha Newland, Eliza Whitney, Sonia Linebaugh, and Harrison Demchick of The Writer's Ally, all of whom read various drafts and provided valuable criticisms and suggestions. Sadly, Sonia passed away not long after the novel was completed. I will miss her insightful guidance on my next novel and her friendship.

When I needed specialized knowledge for aspects of *When Enemies Offend Thee,* I turned to a great team of advisers: Tracy Tomson, executive director, and the Restaurant Facility Management Association; former chef Darin Linebaugh; Dan Swaim, owner of Cimarron Steakhouse in Winston-Salem, N.C.; John French with the Baltimore Police Department

Crime Scene Unit; and Mary Heininger, RN, BSN. They generously gave me the facts, which I used as accurately as I could. Any errors are strictly my own.

Thank you to the Virginia Center for the Creative Arts for awarding me a fellowship that provided time and space to complete much of the novel's revision.

Thank you to Duke and Kimberly Pennell of Pen-L Publishing for once again leading me through the canyons of the publishing world and helping me emerge with a book I can be proud of. Their editor Lori Draft saved me from embarrassing mistakes that I still cannot believe I made. Thank you to Eliza Whitney and Kelsey Rice for the cover and interior design.

And many special thanks to my wonderful family. Although my husband, Greg Whitney, passed away before the novel was completed, he did everything he could to support the early writing of it, including building a door to my study so I wouldn't be disturbed. His unfailing encouragement stays with me still. My sister, Martha Newland, was always there when I needed her. My sons, Nathan Whitney and Andrew Whitney, to whom I dedicate this book, gave me the love and emotional support I've needed to stay strong through the past four years. I hope I've made them proud.

READING GROUP GUIDE

At what point in *When Enemies Offend Thee* do you think Clementine changes from victim to avenger? What causes the change?

When Erlene asks Clementine in Chapter 12 why she thinks Gary raped her, Clementine says, "At first I thought he was still carrying a grudge for something that he says happened in high school. But adults write nasty letters about things like that or they embarrass you at a high school reunion. They don't rape you. There's something deeper going on inside Gary. That high school thing was an excuse, I think. He's probably been needing a target for a long time and then I came along." Do you agree?

What role does the loss of jobs in Tanner play in what happened to Clementine, if any?

In Chapter 13, Erlene wonders if she risks ruining her relationship with her mother by helping Clementine with the hex and whether the new friendship is worth that risk. Do you think it is? Would you help Clementine? Is it possible Erlene has another motive for helping Clementine with the hex?

Why do you think Erlene remains faithful to Clementine throughout the novel?

What do you think of Clementine's plan to cause food poisoning? Does her purpose justify her means?

What or who ultimately leads her to abandon the plan? Why do you think she ignored other calls for her to abandon it before that point?

What do you think of Clementine's efforts to ruin Gary's career as a chef by changing his recipes and making him appear to be a thief?

Does Gary deserve what happened to him? What do you think of Gary?

The novel is written from three points of view: Clementine's, David's, and Erlene's. Would the story be improved by hearing what other characters are thinking? If so, which ones?

Does David love Clementine? Does he do enough to help her try to get the justice she thinks she deserves?

Does David do the right thing by ending his relationship with Clementine? If you were David, would you end the relationship?

Do you think the relationship between Clementine and Johnny will become more than friendship? Whether it does or not, can it survive if Clementine never tells Johnny about her plans to poison the salad or her involvement in the thefts? Can it survive if she does?

Why do you think Clementine chooses not to tell him? She believes that her relationship with David won't survive if she doesn't tell him about her plan. Is she right to have a different attitude about her relationship with Johnny?

Should she have told Erlene about her involvement in the thefts?

Do you think it's all right to keep secrets from the people you love?

Clementine moves the antique shop to Johnny's Restaurant largely because Johnny needs her and she feel indebted to him. Does she do enough to redeem herself for what she has done to him? Does she need to redeem herself?

Is Johnny totally innocent in the beating Gary gives him or is he at least partly to blame for starting the series of events at the restaurant by hiring undocumented immigrants?

In Chapter 15, Clementine thinks "maybe there could never be justice for victims like her. Maybe revenge was all she could hope for." What do you think? What should justice be for her? Is justice different from revenge? If so, how?

What long-range effects does Clementine's obsession with getting justice for herself have on her? Are they good or bad? How has Clementine changed?

Where do you see Clementine, Johnny, David, and Erlene five years from now?

ABOUT THE AUTHOR

Although Sally Whitney has spent most of her adult life in other parts of the United States, her imagination lives in the South, the homeland of her childhood. "Whenever I dream of a story," she says, "I feel the magic of red clay hills, soft voices, sudden thunder storms, and rich emotions. The South is a wonderland of mysteries, legends, and jokes handed down through generations of family storytellers, people like me."

Sally is a fan of stories in almost any medium, including literature, theater, and film. She'd rather spend an afternoon in the audience across from the footlights than anywhere else, and she thinks DVDs and streaming movies are the greatest inventions since the automobile. She loves libraries and gets antsy if she has to drive very far without an audio book to listen to.

The short stories she writes have been published in literary magazines and anthologies, including *Best Short Stories from The Saturday Evening Post Great American Fiction Contest 2017* and *Grow Old Along With Me—The Best Is Yet To Be,* the audio version of which was a Grammy Award finalist in the Spoken Word or Nonmusical Album category. Her first novel, *Surface and Shadow,* published by Pen-L Publishing in 2016, tells the story of a woman who risks her marriage and her husband's career to find out what really happened in the suspicious death of a cotton baron in Tanner, North Carolina in 1972.

In nonfiction, Sally's worked as a public relations writer, freelance journalist, and editor of *Best's Review* magazine. Her articles have appeared in magazines and newspapers, including *St. Anthony Messenger, The Kansas City Star, AntiqueWeek,* and *Our State: Down Home in North Carolina.*

Sally is a member of The Authors Guild and has been a fellow at the Virginia Center for the Creative Arts.

She currently lives in Pennsylvania. When she isn't writing, reading, watching movies, or attending plays, she likes to poke around in antique shops looking for treasures. "The best things in life are the ones that have been loved, whether by you or somebody else," she says.

FIND SALLY AT

SallyWhitney.com

FACEBOOK: SallyMWhitney

TWITTER: @1SallyWhitney

Dear Readers,
If you enjoyed this book enough to review it for Goodreads, B&N, or Amazon.com, I'd appreciate it!

Thanks, Sally

Find more great reads at
Pen-L.com

Made in the USA
Middletown, DE
19 January 2021

31950615R00194